CASH

OUT

CASH OUT

GREG BARDSLEY • *a novel*

HARPER PERENNIAL

NEW YORK • LONDON • TORONTO • SYDNEY • NEW DELHI • AUCKLAND

HARPER PERENNIAL

This book is a work of fiction. The characters, incidents, and dialogue are drawn from the author's imagination and are not to be construed as real. Any resemblance to actual events or persons, living or dead, is entirely coincidental.

P.S.™ is a trademark of HarperCollins Publishers.

HarperCollins books may be purchased for educational, business, or sales promotional use. For information please write: Special Markets Department, HarperCollins Publishers, 10 East 53rd Street, New York, NY 10022.

FIRST EDITION

Designed by William Ruoto

Library of Congress Cataloging-in-Publication Data is available upon request.

ISBN 978-0-06-212771-6

12 13 14 15 16   OV/RRD   10 9 8 7 6 5 4 3 2

For Nancy

One

Palo Alto, California

· · · · · · · ·

2008

Rod Stone scrunches his face as he thinks about it.

"So this guy's gonna handle your testicles?"

I stare back into Rod's gray eyes and glance down at the stubble on his square chin, refusing to crack a smile, knowing he certainly won't. He gives me this look, like I'm chewing a grasshopper, and squints. Juts his jaw. "This man will need to soap you up, won't he?"

I wave him off and look away. "Okay, okay."

"He'll shave you."

I nod, conceding.

"His hands soft and gentle"—he shudders in mock disgust—"as they drip warm, soapy water over your balls."

We look at each other.

"Your legs spread wide open for him."

I have to look away, unable to keep my straight face a minute longer. Then I take my pint glass and lift it toward him.

It is noon on a Tuesday, and I'm sitting in a dark lounge.

By Friday, I'll have $1.1 million deposited into my bank account. I'll be like a bird uncaged, ready to fly away with my family, ready to start a new life. All I need to do is last another three days. Oh, and brave my way through a vasectomy.

"To my testes," I say.

Rod Stone squints and juts his jaw out again, looking away. "That doc's gonna rip out your plumbing like a—"

"Okay, that's enough."

Fifty minutes later, my teeth are gritted, my back is arched, and my fists are clenched.

"So what's FlowBid stock at now? One-twenty?"

The doctor has my legs in stirrups. I've got a surgical clamp hanging out of my privates. I am not in my *safe place*.

"I should've bought when it was at ten."

I nod and gasp. "Ten."

"I bet you got in low, huh? What, you started there in oh-five, right?"

I grimace. "Oh-five."

"You hang on a little longer, and you'll be sitting pretty the rest of your life."

My jaws clench. "Sitting pretty."

God, my wife would love seeing this. After birthing two ten-pounders and enduring decades of OB-GYN visits, she's been more than a little amused by the prospect of Vasectomy Day—by knowing that finally I'd be the one in stirrups, exposed and uncomfortable, the one whose crotch was absorbing wave after wave of throbbing pain. Of course, I don't think any of her OBs were ever as rough as my jock-swaggering urologist. You see, guys aren't gentle with each other—even when it comes to vasectomies. When Doc gave me his presurgery scrotal wash down, it felt like he was scrubbing a pot.

Then, as I lay on the table, I am suddenly struck by it all. The statement I'm making with this surgery, this de facto announcement that I'm done fathering babies, hits me like a ton of unexpected emotional bricks, and I'm transported back to two of the most amazing moments in my life.

Six years ago.

Three years ago.

Six Years Ago

I am a new daddy. Forty-eight hours after Harry's birth, and I am still overcome with joy. When my wife and son sleep, I can't stop crying. My new family is safe, my son Harry is here, and my life will never be the same. It's instant love, and it's the most beautiful thing on Earth. What did I ever do to deserve this?

Sometimes it blows me away to think that six years have passed since then. When I drive Harry to school, I watch as he bolts from the car to join his buddies, smiling and joking, fully independent there on the playground, complete and well-adjusted and on his way, and think back on everything: all the times I slept beside his bassinet with my fingertips on his chest, worried he'd stop breathing; all the times I changed his diapers; all the times he needed to be rocked; all the times I had to put a favorite toy in "Daddy Jail"; all the times he cried out in the night and I'd come padding down the hallway;

all the times he needed Mommy and no one else would do. I think back on all the firsts: the first steps, the first words, the first day in big-boy underwear, the first haircut, the first rush to the hospital, the first time he saw something that truly ignited his imagination, the first time he insisted that his mysterious and elusive imaginary friend, "Abey Dabey Cabey," was real and much too complex for us to understand.

Would be nice to go back to that time, for a moment.

Three Years Ago

It is less than an hour after Ben's birth. I am a new daddy again, and I am overcome with joy. I look down at him, and he is beautiful. I'm still staring at him when a newly minted doctor slips into our room, refusing to look me in the eye. She announces that our son has a massive tumor in his abdominal cavity.

In an instant, our world darkens and tilts. This can't be happening. But I know all too well that the worst does happen to people—every day. The doc leads me to another room and shows me an X-ray of Ben's little tummy. On one side, all you see is solid white.

I stand there and nod. I can't speak.

That night, I cry on the phone with Rod Stone. I hold Kate's hand until she falls asleep. I pace the hospital floors until the wee hours. I stare at the walls. I stare at Ben—he is so beautiful.

The next morning, a platoon of doctors parades in with news: It was all an awful misdiagnosis. The white mass in that X-ray was nothing more than an air pocket. A trip to radiology confirms it. I am numb. My family is safe, Ben is actually healthy—in fact, uncommonly strong.

It takes a long time—months and months—before I really believe the doctors. After all, I know the darkness always looms, is always right around the corner—waiting for its moment, waiting to toss lives upside down, waiting to make anyone wilt in its iron grip. It has hit before, and we know it will return someday, as it does for us all.

Someday.

My urologist is cutting and pulling and snipping. It doesn't hurt anymore, not exactly, but it *is* screwing with my head.

"I'm conservative, Dan. A belt-and-suspenders guy."

I grimace. "Suspenders."

He throws something at the trash can. A wet slap against the plastic liner.

"So"—*yank*—"I'm thorough."

Smoke. I smell smoke. *What the hell?* I lift my head just enough to see a stream of thin white smoke meandering out of my crotch. I close my eyes and lower my head.

"What I do is, snip, double-tie, double-tie, cauterize. That's what you're smelling."

I have to change the subject. "I was gonna say—you didn't buy any FlowBid early on?"

"No." He sighs, irritated. "I was stupid. My adviser told me to buy eight hundred shares, and I passed. I was a nonbeliever, Dan. I mean, who could've predicted this?" Another snip, another wet slap against the trash can. "But what do you think? You think there's still some upside there?"

People always ask me that. They always want to know how much higher the FlowBid share price can skyrocket, how much more money it can make them, whether there's still decent coin to be made if they get in now—because, hell, *someone's* buying more and more of FlowBid, given its ever-skyward share price.

Such a dilemma.

The FlowBid story is just one of many that have played out in the last decade, across Silicon Valley and all the way up the peninsula to San Francisco. Google. Facebook. NetApp. The reborn Apple. Along with hundreds of smaller companies, they're fueling this second Internet boom—along with skyrocketing property values and easy loans, that is. That dotcom crash eight years ago? These new economists warning about a storm brewing off-coast? The chance that it all could come crashing down? *Meh*—that's all just noise. Moderation? Caution? That's for losers. So more and more fortune seekers come pouring into the area every year, from across the country and around the world, sending rent and home prices into the stratosphere, clogging the freeways with an endless procession of BMWs and Audis and Porsches, flooding posh restaurants and spas, overcrowding the Whole Foods aisles and espresso shop lines. And with them they're bringing an entirely new kind of lifestyle to the Bay Area: Out go the values of balance, tolerance, and diversity, *in* come fast and easy wealth, unquenchable greed, insane work hours, outsider arrogance, and supreme indifference to anything that's more than five years old.

My world is tilted.

The place where I grew up is gone.

I want out.

Just a few years ago, I felt like I was making a difference. I was working as a reporter, calling out people hurting other people, people taking things that didn't belong to them, while shining a light on people who were doing amazing things, people who wanted more from their government. I covered issues that mattered to real people, issues that dwarfed the IT babble that now dominates my life.

Now I find myself with the suits, dealing with people like Janice from Finance.

Take yesterday. Janice pops into my cube, her face worked up into a knot.

"Waddlington needs the PMO master doc for the P5s by EOB. And if you can't get the Q1 POD results sooner, then we'll need to put the P6s into the FOD, and that includes the L2s and L6s."

"Um . . ." I squint at her, confused. "I write speeches. I think you've got the wrong guy."

Her face tightens. "No, I don't."

"Huh?"

"Beth Gavin sent me. She's Stephen Fitzroy's—"

"Executive assistant. Yeah, I know."

Beth Gavin loves this kind of thing: throwing shit assignments my way, assignments that have nothing to do with my job, that throw me off my game. This is what Beth Gavin does.

Janice adds, "And don't forget the SWAT reports for the L10s and L16s in the FOD."

My throat is so dry, I feel like it'll crack. *How did I get here?* Not that anyone else around here ever indulges in second thoughts. They're too busy talking about *the new guy.*

"Fitzroy loves the new guy," Barbara from Procurement keeps telling me.

"Oh, yeah?"

"Out-of-the-box thinker," she says. "That's what they're saying. 'Out-of-the-box thinker, out-of-the-box thinker.' On and on and on."

The new guy doesn't look like us. He has this whole I-don't-give-a-shit vibe going. Long, dark beard that comes to a point near his sternum. Big head of black wavy hair. Big, thick tribal tattoos on his long, muscular arms. Dark sunglasses, worn indoors. Heavy, charcoal-gray jeans, worn-in T-shirts, and big black boots. Yeah, he's a pretty jarring sight around FlowBid.

I wish I could dress like the new guy. Then I realize, *In a few days, I can.*

Back on the vasectomy table, the doc asks, "So what do you think, Dan? That stock of yours have more gas in the tank?"

And, like an idiot, I say what I always say: "We still see a lot of upside."

Because, hell, FlowBid ain't never gonna crash.

I realize I'm still arching my back, still gritting my teeth, my fists still balled up at my sides. I pull in a deep breath and force myself to relax. Then the doc swaggers around the table, takes my hand, and squeezes it hard.

"All done," he says. "Now, remember what I said—ice on,

ice off, every twenty minutes, for the next twenty-four hours. Use a bag of frozen peas. No strenuous activity of any kind." He squints at me. "You screw up my work, I'll kill you."

In a minute, my tighty-whities are stuffed with a mound of gauze and the doc is leading me out. "You're still packing heat the next ten times, so be careful where you point that thing."

The nurses are mute as I pad through the waiting area and head for the elevator. I know what they're thinking, and they know what *I'm* thinking—that we're all thinking about my nuts and scrotum, which I have to admit is kind of funny. When my cell phone breaks the silence, I know who it is without looking.

Kate.

She's giving me her you-poor-baby voice, slightly amused. "How they hanging?"

"Not hanging. Hurting."

"Poor little Danny had a little procedure."

The elevator doors open, and I shuffle in. "I get the couch tonight? Doc's orders."

"I know, I know. You sure you can still do this appointment?"

Appointment? Mind scrambles. *Oh shit. . . . Fuck.*

That would be our weekly meeting with our sex counselor, the professional who's supposed to help us get our groove back, help me prove to Kate once and for all that I really do love her. Like a macho idiot, earlier this week I insisted that we keep the appointment on the books. A little snip wouldn't put this man out of order.

I grit my teeth. "Oh, I'm fine."

"You sure? I can just go solo."

Solo? Not with our counselor. "No, no. I'll be there."

"You sure?"

"Just grab me a bag of frozen peas, if you can."

"What?" Pause. "Oh, right, you're packin' peas now. Assume the boys don't care what brand?"

"Good one."

"You gonna let me take a look?" It's like she's about to laugh. "I'm kind of curious."

"You're crazy," I say.

"Oh, that reminds me. Calhoun came over again."

Calhoun. In our house? "Tell me you're kidding."

"I'm not."

"You let him in?"

"Don't worry. I just stood in the doorway, didn't budge. But he wants to talk to you."

Calhoun is our freak neighbor. We try to cope with him, but after five years we've learned it's better to avoid him. It's a shame, and we feel like dicks, but we've learned one thing: If you *do* look at him, or wave to him or engage with him in any way, you *will* lose about ninety minutes of your life—ninety minutes lost in Calhoun's strange, gelatinous world.

"He said he'll come back."

"Great."

"Says it's urgent."

"Sure it is."

"The kids are screaming. Gotta run in a sec."

"Okay."

"Oh, and someone from FlowBid called."

"Yeah?"

"Janice from Finance. I think. That sound right?"

I sigh. "Yeah."

"She wants an FOD in the P6, or something. I wrote it down."

"Okay."

"Someone's crying. Gotta go."

Pushing through the doors and into the San Mateo sunshine, I keep telling myself, *Three days.* In three days, not only will my wounds be healed, but my first round of stock options will vest, at which point I'll cash them out. Result: more than a million bucks in profit. I had never imagined the possibility of amassing so much wealth in one small moment; two years ago, *no one* would have guessed that FlowBid stock would increase like it has. But now here I am, just three days away from a whole new life.

In three days, my first block of options will vest—5,300 in all. It's the first of two installments from my original 2005 grant of 10,600 options, but I'm not going to stick around another two years to pocket the full grant. Hell, I won't even stick around another week.

As soon as the options vest, I'll call Smith Barney to place a same-day sale—purchasing my options at the grant price of $8, and selling them immediately at the current market price of $216. The funds will be wired to my FlowBid-issued account at Smith Barney, which will arrange to have the check printed two days later at its Menlo Park office near Sand Hill Road, the epicenter of the venture capital world. I'll show up in my Corolla, pick up the check, and proceed directly to nearby Mountain View to deposit it into our checking account.

The next day, I'll give FlowBid my two weeks' notice. I'm sure it will shock the hell out of them. Conventional wisdom around here is that only a numskull would walk away with $1.1 million when he can stick around two more years for another million—or much more, assuming the stock keeps climbing, assuming the bottom doesn't fall out. But that's the difference between the conventionally wise and me.

I want out.

We'll call our real estate agent to put our little peninsula cottage up for sale, for what's sure to be an insane profit. Seven years ago, we bought that little 1,200-square-foot, two-bedroom place for $589,000; today, there's guaranteed to be a bidding war, and it's bound to go for at least a million. Par for the course on the peninsula.

That night we'll go out for Mexican food, to a worn-in, hole-in-the-wall place we love, peopled by longtime locals and phenomenal margaritas. The next day, we'll get up, pack the car, and head over the hill and south along the shoreline, straight for the coastal communities between Santa Cruz and Monterey, where we'll start the search for the perfect "beach shack." Kate will say, "You're really gonna go barefoot the whole day?" And I'll glance back at her, a big grin spreading across my face, and nod.

Within a month, after all the dust settles, we'll have bought a waterfront property with great views and beach access. It won't be luxurious, just functional and well made. We'll either have a tiny mortgage or none at all, and the profit from our cottage sale will be sitting in savings.

Out will go the twelve-hour workdays, the endless chatter about the need for more server capacity, the continual asides about stock options and growing fortunes, the late-night slide-deck drills with a jittery VP three years out of college, the sheer exhaustion that makes you want to avoid eye contact with the world just so you can get home already. Out will go all those San Francisco dinner parties, those thinly disguised boasting contests where guests compete for top bragging rights on everything from whose house has the newest amenity, to who has the most "nanny help," to whose kid is succeeding the most without trying. Out will go the Range Rovers and Mercedeses and BMW utility vehicles. Out will go Janice from Finance.

Out. All of it.

In will come Hondas and sandals and Fords and old VW buses with longboards tied to the roof. In will come locals riding on old beach cruisers, smiling back at us.

In will come our new life.

I want to do the things we'd stopped doing on the other side: making meals from scratch, enjoying lazy visits with friends, spending real time on the phone with loved ones, smiling at strangers, getting caught up in a good book. I want to work in the front yard and get my hands dirty, my body scraped up, my sweat mixed with dirt. Sure, it'll stink, that mixture of sweat and dirt—until I run across the beach and dive into the ocean.

We'll leave our TV in a box, in the garage.

Wi-Fi? We'll never even unpack the router.

I'll spend real time with my wife and children, the kind of

time I never quite manage to spend in my current life, that life on *the other side* where I just can't stop to count my blessings.

We'll spend the whole summer on the beach. In the morning, Kate will run her three miles on the hard, wet sand as the boys and I prepare breakfast: melons, toast, and Raisin Bran, a coffee for Daddy. In the afternoon, I'll sit on our old canvas beach chair, a kid on each side of my lap, my father's forty-year-old Coleman sunk into the sand, icing apple juice, water, and a few cans of Tecate, as I read them another installment of *Robinson Crusoe*. When evening approaches, I'll take a siesta in the sand, the pulsing of the waves sedating me, the Pacific breeze washing over me, as Kate brings the boys home and sparks up the barbecue. At night, the boys and I will build castles and car garages out of blocks, the sound of crashing waves easing through the windows and mixing with the saxophone-heavy ska echoing throughout the house.

When the house is quiet, Kate and I will sit on the couch and hold hands and talk. We'll actually hang out and talk. We need that, Kate and I. We've needed it for a long time.

This is all doable, I think as I hobble to my Corolla. *It's not a dream. It's a plan.*

My reverie is interrupted by the sound of footsteps.

Then a bizarre sight: two little geeks, coming at me like a pair of bats out of hell, running awkwardly, each of them holding one end of a rope.

"Hey!"

Before I know what's hit me, they've got the rope wrapped around me, circling me in opposite directions, pinning my wrists to my hips. In seconds I'm wrapped up, immobilized, toppling over. The asphalt comes in and out of view, gets closer and closer, until I twist just enough to land on my shoulder. Shards of pain shoot through my shoulder, my back, my privates. Especially my privates. I screw my eyes shut, tense my muscles, and fight the pain.

And then, a high-pitched voice. "Stay cool, stud machine."

What is this? My mind is scrambling. *A prank?*

I open my eyes. From my upside-down view, I see an unmarked white van skid to a stop. The side door rolls open, and I'm pulled off the ground and made to hop toward the van. When I try to resist, they poke me in the spine with something hard and threatening.

My head floats. "What the hell is this?"

"Wouldn't you like to know," one voice says, shoving the barrel of something deeper into my back.

"What do you guys want with me? I have a wife and kids at home."

"I'm sure they're darling." They push me. "Sit down."

What choice do I have? Grimacing, I hop to one of the bench seats.

"Hit it." The van peels out of the parking lot.

I give my kidnappers a quick glance; they look dimly familiar. The tiny driver is a rail-thin, pasty-skinned nerd in his thirties; I swear he's wearing a Star Trek shirt. The guy seated beside me is tiny, too, with jeans pulled up to his ribs—not floods, but high-riders. I can't help but give them a very long double take.

The third guy is small but muscular, with a giant head of wavy, flaming-red hair—he may be the alpha male in this pack of tinies. He sits on the bench seat ahead of me, turns, and squeaks, "You realize what you were about to do back at that doctor's office?"

I squirm in the rope. It's getting looser.

Little Red squints at me. "You were about to emasculate yourself."

And then I realize where I know them from: work. Maybe not Little Red, but the others. Nevertheless, the realization that they're FlowBid guys comforts me a little. *Maybe this is some kind of FlowBid prank*, I think, *a bizarre "abduction" for a wacky corporate offsite.* But I know I'm fooling myself.

"If this is about my vasectomy, you're too late." I shift my weight, trying to find relief from the hot pain shooting through my crotch. "I just had it."

The van skids to a halt, and I'm launched off my seat. Shots of agony surge up to my rib cage and down to my knees. I lower my lids and hiss.

Star Trek says, "The Enterprise has landed." Little Red snarls.

High Rider says, "His Treo said noon. I have it printed right here."

He's right. My vasectomy *was* scheduled for noon, but the doc's office had called and asked me to come an hour earlier. I just hadn't changed the time on my Treo.

Star Trek asks, "Should we dock?"

High Rider closes his eyes, takes a deep breath. "Proceed."

Star Trek hollers, "Prepare for warp speed."

We jerk forward.

High Rider stares at me a moment. "We need to discuss Fitzroy."

Crap.

Stephen Fitzroy is my CEO. That's my job: I write his speeches. I travel on the company jet with him; I go to his compound to work on speaker notes and slide decks; I put words in his mouth. Stephen Fitzroy is worth nearly a billion dollars; he's one of those visionaries who's always in the right business at the right time.

A lot of people don't like Stephen Fitzroy.

I look around the van for guns. Nothing.

High Rider squints at me. "You may recognize us. Of course, hotshot pretty boys like yourself usually looked right through us at FlowBid. We were expendable, weren't we, Dan? IT guys like us."

IT guys? Aw, man.

I try to stay calm. "No, I remember you."

"Good, because we remembered *you*. Sure, we got outsourced. And him over here"—he nods to Little Red—"his job got offshored to Bangalore. But we remember you." He glances at Star Trek, who snickers. "How could we forget the tall and charming speechwriter to the great Silicon Valley icon Stephen Fitzroy?"

I shake my head. "I'm not like that, guys."

"You may not have known our names, but we knew yours. How could we not, Dan? All that interesting IT activity of yours? All that inappropriate use of FlowBid IT resources?"

Wait, what?

"You know, the kinds of activities I don't think you want your CEO knowing about."

My heart sinks and my skin cools. *IT guys.* When it comes

to the network, those guys can go anywhere and see anything. Like the calendar on my Treo, for instance.

The van makes a hard left. High Rider pulls out some kind of printout. "Here I have a high-level summary of the IT activity of one Dan Jordan at FlowBid. It's quite interesting." He glances at me. "So, in no particular order: approximately one hundred and fifty-six hours spent on personal e-mail accounts. Ninety-eight hours spent working on your personal Web pages. The photocopying of some twelve hundred pages of fliers for your son's preschool, at a cost of six hundred dollars to the company. And the laser-printing of some three thousand Yahtzee score sheets for some stupid prank, at a company cost of nearly fifteen hundred dollars."

"Oh, come on. Find me one FlowBid staffer who doesn't use the goddamn Xerox machine."

"All right, then." High Rider takes a thick red folder from Little Red, and glances at me as he pulls out a page. "From one of the many personal e-mail accounts of Dan Jordan, employee number 452 at FlowBid, I read you correspondence from said employee's private Yahoo! Mail account to Dave Hatch, reporter at *BusinessWeek*."

Shit.

"'Hi, Dave,'" he squeaks in a mocking tone. "'This e-mail is not for attribution, but you are free to use it for your profile of Stephen Fitzroy. I am his speechwriter (you and I met after Evan's keynote at CES last month), and now that I have spent nearly two and half years with him, I think it is only fair to FlowBid shareholders (and the public) that your story be as comprehensive as possible. Again, this is not for attribution; as a former journalist myself, I am trusting you will respect my wish to remain anonymous. My livelihood relies on it. So, with that, here are a few things you may want to look into.'"

High Rider pauses, exchanges glances with Little Red. "'Stephen Fitzroy has, shall we say, a pretty bad reputation around the office. He's often reduced lower-level female employees to tears by making fun of their weight and questioning their intelligence. . . . He has three sexual-harassment claims and one paternity suit pending against himself and FlowBid; the company's trying to settle them out of court. . . . Fitzroy had the company jet fly him and his wife to a Palm Springs vacation (on FlowBid's dime) the same day FlowBid laid off sixty people in favor of less expensive employees in India. . . . Fitzroy believes in the value of 'strategically sabotaging' office rivals; he considers it one of the factors behind his early success in business. . . . Some of the brightest and most successful people at FlowBid have left the company because they refuse to work with him. . . . Oh, and did I mention he has hair plugs?'"

My face is burning. How the hell did they get into that personal e-mail? Not *once* have I accessed that account from work.

High Rider is smiling. "I'd hate to see your CEO read that one."

I stare at him.

"Okay, shall I go on? All right, then. What about . . . sixty hours spent at MILFs in Heat dot-com? Forty-three hours spent at an assortment of websites specializing in the female posterior? Or . . ." He turns over to look me in the eye. ". . . seventeen minutes exchanging erotica with a married coworker?"

I'm about to pass out.

"Mr. Jordan," he squeaks. "Would you like us to share this information, including transcripts of said erotica, with the entire workforce at FlowBid?"

I can see where this is headed. I feel like I'm about to vomit. "No."

"Good." He pauses. "Would you like us to send your correspondence with *BusinessWeek* to Stephen Fitzroy? Or, for that matter, to everyone in the company?"

My head feels like it's floating. "No."

"And would you like us to send details of your improper use of FlowBid IT resources to the business conduct office? Surely, any of these offenses would suffice to have your employment summarily terminated, making you ineligible for scheduled disbursement of noncash compensation and benefits?"

In my line of work, leaking damaging rumors to the press is a capital offense. If the company found out, I'd lose everything: my job, my options, my ability to get rehired. I think of that $1.1 million in options, of these final three days before they vest, and I see stars.

"I don't believe you'd want us to do that."

A jolt of pain ripples through my crotch. Twenty minutes ago, a clamp hung out of it. Suddenly, it's the least of my problems. I shake my head, hoping for clarity. "You guys are IT?"

"No, we *were* IT. Now we're just outsourced, offshored, and unemployed. We just had the foresight to back up some very interesting data before we packed our bags."

I try to steady myself. "So now you want something."

He leans forward and snaps, "We want your cooperation, pretty boy."

Little Red releases a noise, adds, "Pretty boy."

High Rider pauses, examines my reaction. "We want you to do as we say, when we're ready." Another pause. "Otherwise . . ."

Little Red finishes, " . . . no more fat hookers for you."

High Rider glares at Little Red. "Keep your fantasies out of this." Then, to me: "Otherwise, we'll release your information."

I look away and shake my head. Of course there is the $1.1 million, but I'm thinking about Kate and the boys. What will happen to our family if the other stuff gets out—the stuff where I tell another woman I'd like to burrow my face into her hindquarters? With my long hours, Kate's already feeling abandoned at home—hence the couples counseling sessions. She jokes about the notion of me cheating—"You're always getting home too late for dinner. You have some hot admin there willing to take your order?"—but lately the joke part has sounded a little halfhearted. I just roll my eyes, wave her off, because in truth I've never been tempted—well, almost never.

The van skids to a stop, and I realize we're back in the parking lot, in front of my car. "Would you like some good news, Dan?" says High Rider.

I stare at him.

"The good news is, we don't want any of your precious stock-option money."

"Your fat-hooker money," Little Red adds.

High Rider turns to him. "That's your thing, and you know it."

Little Red snaps, "Maybe he likes big girls, too."

"Stop it."

I keep staring at High Rider.

"But we *do* want your collusion. We're going after that bowl of loose stool you call a CEO. When we come calling—and it will be soon—you *will* assist us. Shouldn't be hard for a sellout like you."

Sellout? Damn. These guys did their homework.

"Otherwise, you will lose everything: the chance to cash out your options, the comfy little life with your hard-body wife, the ability to support your sweet little family."

I look at High Rider's left hand. No ring.

"Get out, Dan. Get out of the van."

Still tied up, I hop out of the van, stumble, and crash to the asphalt. I roll and groan.

"And one more thing."

I glance up at him.

His eyes twinkle. "Have fun with the sex counselor." He rolls the door shut, and a loud burst of laughter erupts inside the minivan.

Damn, my crotch hurts.

Sellout.

Yeah, that's me. Fucking sellout.

Twelve years ago, back when I was a reporter, it was the last thing I thought I'd become. Then life got harder and I got tired. I got tired of driving around in a '92 Dodge. I got tired of barely having enough money to buy new 501s or pay rent. I got tired of watching the suits sucking dollars out of the newsroom, forcing us all to do more with less and fail badly, destroying editorial quality, leaving us all to crank at a frenzied pace each day, eliminating the chance for any kind of enterprising investigative work. I got tired of watching my beloved newspaper industry lose more and more readers to the Internet.

When Harry was born, things got more tense, and I knew we couldn't live in an apartment forever. I was a daddy now, and I was gonna do whatever it took to make my family safe.

So I sold out.

The way I tell it to my newspaper friends, at least I sold out well. I landed a ghostwriter's job at a promising start-up. While I sometimes felt like a rare bird, being one of the few folks there with any Mexican blood, the work was good, and soon I was promoted to speechwriter to the CEO. As luck would have it, FlowBid's e-commerce software was the right solution at the right time, and when we went public on NAS-DAQ in '06, we raised $1.7 billion in a day. Fitzroy made it to the cover of *BusinessWeek* that year. And just like that my options were worth something.

That was 362 days ago.

The closer I get to 365, the more I find myself spending time with my old-time California friends, the natives—people like Rod Stone.

Rod and I have been friends since we were eighth graders in the East Bay. The older we get, the more our lives head in opposite directions. But we still share a connection, this bond that won't break. Maybe it's because we've both dealt with some nasty moments and got through them together. But more than anything I think it's because we can cross over into each other's very different worlds without breaking stride.

I love my family, and he gets it.

He fights in a cage, and I get it.

Rod is shaven nearly bald, with just a rind of stubble on his scalp. His body is rock-hard, but not giant. No fat under those loose cotton, solid-gray fatigues and flimsy, worn-in T-shirts. He's got a natural squint and a thuglike underbite that gives people pause.

Rod thinks I was wrong to sell out. A few weeks back, over a few pints, he told me, "Elgin says it best. I think it was in *The Triumph*: 'Those who chase riches lose before the chase even begins.'"

I rolled my eyes. "Elgin never had a mortgage in the Bay Area."

I'm parked in front of the Safeway in Menlo Park, surrounded by a fleet of $60,000 imports. I gaze into space, failing to devise any kind of plan. Maybe the pain meds are making me stupid. Maybe I'm still in shock from what just happened. Was I really roped up by a band of IT geeks? Were they really setting me up for some kind of extortion? Did that guy really call his van the Enterprise?

My cell rings, gives me a jolt. I'm so out of sorts, I don't even look to see who it is.

"Yeah?"

"Dan, this is Janice from Finance."

My chest tightens. "Yeah, listen, Janice—I'm out today and—"

"Dan, you need to put the P6s into the FOD, and then next week we can worry about the L26s in the PLT."

"Janice," I snap, and catch myself, "I'm out today. I had a medical thing, and I'm on meds right now. And I don't even know what you're—"

"Dan . . ." I can hear the irritation in her voice. "I need those P6s in the FOD by EOB."

"Janice . . . Janice, listen." Long pause. "Janice, I need you to understand—"

"Can you at least give me the P6s?"

"Janice, you've got the wrong guy."

"No, I don't."

"Janice, I'm a speechwriter. I don't know the first thing about P6s, or this FOD."

Long pause. "Beth Gavin says you're supposed to take care of this."

"Janice." I close my eyes and count to seven. "Janice, we'll have to talk about this tomorrow. I'm out of action today and—"

"I sent you eight e-mails with the relevant attachments."

"Janice, I'm going to have to let you go now."

"But I—"

I end the call.

Three more days.

I reach for my cell and call home. Kate picks up, sounding harried—the boys are yelling in the background.

"You okay?" she says.

I stumble on my words.

"Dan?"

"You won't believe what just happened."

One of the boys lets out a bone-rattling scream. Kate puts the phone down and snaps, "Harry, leave him alone. C'mere, Ben." A second later, she says to me, "Okay, I'm back."

"I just had these geeks throw me into a van."

Another scream. Sounds like Ben.

"Geeks? What kind of geeks? What van?"

"I had to ask this guy in the parking lot to untie me."

There's a loud crash, then screams. I can barely hear her over the racket. "Hold on. Harry, get over here this instant." And then, "Okay. Now, *what*?"

"Let's talk later."

The boys return to screaming. "Might be better." Her voice tightens. "And if you have time to get those peas yourself, that would be great. I still have to make their lunches."

"No problem."

"Okay. Bye," she says, the line going dead right as she hollers, "Harry, leave him—"

Standing bowlegged in front of the frozen-food doors, I'm thinking about everything *but* peas. I'm thinking about covering my ass, about calling the cops, about getting a lawyer, about contacting my boss, about notifying FlowBid's corporate security. I'm thinking about trying to stop this thing before it gets out of hand. Only problem is, if I call any one of those people, my career will be over, and my family will lose all that money—all that *future* I've been working toward the past two years, money for which I've given up my one true career passion.

Maybe all they want is some easy favor . . .

I open a door and grab a long bag of Jolly Green Giant peas.

Maybe they want some harmless scrap of information . . .

I back up and close the door, weighing the bag in my hand.

Maybe they don't want me to do anything illegal? Maybe . . .

I turn around—and slam smack into a pit bull of a man. Or, rather, he smacks right into me.

He is white, bald, and compact, his enormous upper body nearly too big for his blue blazer. When I look into his dark eyes, I know I'm in trouble: These aren't the eyes of someone who is surprised or worried. These eyes are like Rod's—calm and in control. Then he grabs hold of me and sends me across the aisle and through a freezer door.

It happens so fast—it's so effortless—that I have no time to feel surprised. Glass goes everywhere, yellow Eggo boxes tumble over my head, a woman shrieks, and I'm getting pulled out of the freezer and pushed across the aisle.

He slams me against the metal frame of a glass door and eases his jaw toward mine, completely calm, reeking of some oaky cologne. "You need to watch yourself, Gomer."

I try to pull free, but he's too strong. Scary strong.

"I didn't—"

He pulls me closer, bites his lip and drives a knee into me—right between the legs.

He does it again.

"'Member what I said," he whispers as he lowers me to the ground. "Watch yourself."

The pain envelops me. It sucks my breath away, paralyzes my limbs, and overtakes my senses. Iron rods of agony slowly spread to my stomach and down my legs, worse than anything I've ever felt. Slowly, I slide to the ground and ball up on my side, battling the urge to vomit as I watch this guy stride toward the front, people scrambling to get out of his way, everyone parting for the pit bull in a blazer.

I hobble through the Palo Alto medical office, twenty-five minutes late for our "appointment." I know this will be ugly, so I don't even look at the blond receptionist; I just keep hobbling down the narrow hallway toward that solid-oak door with the black nameplate and white lettering: Dr. Heidi M. Douglas. I stop and take a few deep breaths, preparing myself. I know they're in there expanding on the list of things I must do if I ever want to have sex with my wife as frequently, and as passionately, as we used to.

I open the door and poke my head in.

A cold, wet bag nails me in the face.

"There's your fucking peas."

I look up, and Kate is standing in front of the couch, her cheeks flushed with anger. Heidi the counselor, is seated on the other side of the room, grabbing the arms of her leather chair, bracing for something close to a category 4 hurricane.

Kate turns to sit down, folding her arms in a huff. "Knew you'd be late."

Kate has fixed herself up, and holy shit, does she look good. Silky blond hair falling to her shoulders, a few strands dropping over her giant blue eyes. Form-fitting T-shirt highlighting her narrow torso. Tight, dark blue jeans that she knows drive me crazy. Black leather boots with square tips and thick heels, just the way I love them.

Heidi says, "Tell him how you're feeling right now."

Kate is staring at me, her nostrils flaring. "Like I wanna hit him."

Heidi soothes, "Dan?"

"You guys, I was attacked at a Safeway. Some guy threw me into the Eggos."

Kate looks confused. "What?"

I lower myself onto the couch. "He kneed me, Kate. This bald guy kneed me, right in the groin. Right after the vasectomy. The police held me for like an hour to give my statement." I look at them both, my chest rising. "I got here as fast as I could."

Kate looks skeptical. "Was this bald guy one of the geeks in the van?"

"That was earlier," I blurt. "The Eggos came later."

Kate and Heidi glance at each other. I use the moment to slide the frozen peas under my loose sweatpants, closing my eyes and hissing as I arrange the bag between my legs.

"Are you serious?" Kate asks. "Two attacks in two hours. I'm supposed to believe that?"

"I have the detective's card, honey—"

Heidi stops me with a wave. "Dan, are you acting like a man?"

This startles me. "What?"

"Are you being a man right now?"

What the . . .

"I've been attacked, Heidi. I had a vasectomy less than three hours ago, and now I've been *kicked in the nuts.* Do you understand?"

Heidi says, "A man keeps his word, Dan. He does what he says he'll do, and he'll be where he's supposed to be, *when* he's supposed to be there." She pauses. "That's what a man does."

"Dr. Douglas, don't tell *me* about—"

Heidi waves me off. "You knew today was an important commitment, Dan, but you dropped the ball. How do you think that makes her feel? You know being there for Kate is a big issue with you two."

I sit back and look away.

"We've been over this before, Dan."

I turn and stare at her.

"Right now, who's the one who decides if you will have sex?"

I look away again. "Kate."

"Do you want to have sex with Kate more often?"

"Yes," I mumble.

"But she decides."

I roll my eyes and nod.

"So what do you think, Dan? Should you try a little harder to do things to help put Kate in the right frame of mind? The right kind of relaxed and rested physiological state? You know, reduce her stress levels around the house? Give her time to rest?" She looks at me, concerned. "Are you getting the texts?"

Part of the Heidi Douglas program is that the husband agrees to receive automated text messages from the good doctor. They're reminders for hubbies who'd otherwise fall off the wagon. In my case, I'm reminded to make a family dinner each week—and it can't be "a giant platter of meat," as Kate adds, meaning I need to include vegetables, a salad, stuff like that. To say the texts annoy me is an understatement, but I keep telling myself, *Obey the text, get more sex.*

"Yes, I'm getting the texts."

"And you must follow them, because we need to prove to her that you won't let her down. That last one's a biggie, isn't it, Dan? Kate might put on a good face in front of the kids, but you can see how scared she is that you'll let her down, can't you? These kinds of fears are common for people who were hurt at an early age, aren't they?"

She's right. "They are."

"And for Kate, the most natural reaction is to shut you out, to avoid any kind of intimacy, because when she felt that wonderful closeness as a child—when it counted most—it was always taken away."

Kate's eyes have welled up, but somehow she also seems happy—glad that someone is finally putting her feelings into words. And it's like a sock in the gut, seeing her there, so vulnerable, when I realize what she may soon learn about her husband.

Heidi pierces me. "What do you say to Kate right now, Dan?"

I look at Kate again, at those enormous, experienced eyes that have bewitched me for so long, at her lower lip easing out in that vulnerable way, and I melt.

"Kate, honey." I pause. "I'm never gonna leave you."

She nods and wipes away a tear. "But you don't love me."

"That's not true, honey."

She sniffs. "Not like before."

I wince. *How do I do this?* "Kate, I know what you're going through. And I'm sorry I was late. But I've just been attacked twice in the span of two hours. A gang of nitwits kidnapped me and threw me into a van. And then some beefy little bald guy threw me through a freezer door. Look—I have the detective's card." I show it to her, then catch Heidi giving me the stinkeye. "But—yeah, I should've called."

Kate looks off into the distance. "I had my cell the whole time, Dan."

I take her hand. "I guess I was in shock."

Heidi says, "Dan, do real men make excuses?"

Twenty minutes later, after doing everything I could to placate Kate—or Dr. Heidi, I'm not sure which—I convince my wife to walk with me to our usual post-therapy date spot—the small bar in Cafe Fino in downtown Palo Alto. I'm sure we're quite the sight, with Kate looking so ultrafine, and me looking like I've been neutered, abducted, and thrown through a freezer door.

I try to take her hand, but she eases away.

"I'm really sorry about being late, Kate. I've been having kind of a tough day."

"So some kids from work really threw you into a van? What was it, some kind of prank?"

"I wish." Call me a coward, but I don't want to say too much.

"And this bald guy at the store—he was with the guys in the van?"

"Don't think so." I reach into my sweats and rearrange the peas. An older woman walking toward us gives me a stern look. "The bald guy—God knows what the hell that was." I sigh. "You think I should see the doc again? You know, after getting kneed?"

"No idea, dude. I don't have a scrotum."

The gin martini at Cafe Fino feels good going down. Really good.

"Wish I'd been there," Kate says, staring straight ahead. "Bald little fuck would have a big gash in his scalp right now."

Kate likes to fight. Or, I should say, she used to. When I met her, Kate was a competitive kickboxer. (As you probably can tell, I have an affinity for fighters.) But that was then, and now Kate is all about being a good mom, and her kickboxing days are a distant memory.

Back then, in our single days, when we were really just kids, things were so much simpler. You didn't have to whittle away on long self-improvement lists for the chance to screw around with your wife, the gorgeous creature who used to wake you at 3 A.M. every other night, her naked body pressed against you. Back then, you had no children for whom you'd sacrifice everything. Back then, you had no gigantic sum of stock to lose just days before it vested.

Kate crosses her legs on the stool. "All right, walk me through your bad day."

As we sip our martinis, I give Kate the blow-by-blow: the

IT ambush, the extortion scheme, the frozen-food knock-down. When I tell her about the IT nerds' scheme, I leave out the sexual subplot—but I admit that I did leak damaging tidbits to *BusinessWeek*.

Kate covers her eyes. "I can't fucking believe you."

I sink my head. "I know."

Eyes still closed. "With everything we've been working for, Dan. You jeopardized it all."

"I know. I just . . ."

She opens her eyes and looks around, raises her hands as if to say, *What the fuck?* "I mean, this affects everything we've talked about for the past five years."

I reach down and rearrange my peas. "I know."

"Why, Dan?"

"I've told you why, Kate. Fitzroy's a prick. The man destroys careers for sport. *BusinessWeek* reached out to me, and he had it coming."

Kate puts her martini down and turns to me, those giant eyes searching my face. "Who gives a shit about Stephen Fitzroy?" she whispers. "All you had to do was hang on for a little longer—just a *few days longer*—for the options to vest."

I look at her.

"A month from now, you could've leaked stuff to *Business-Week* every day."

"I'm sorry, Kate."

"Makes me wonder what else you've done."

I squint at her. "What?"

"You heard me. Makes me wonder what else they have on you. Something you don't want me to know about."

Like a flash, I am reminded of "the erotica."

Not erotica, exactly. But a handful of stupid instant messages I had with a married woman who works down the hall,
which the nerds have intercepted. The thought of Kate reading a transcript of my dirty online chat with Anne Browne, a
hot public-relations coordinator, makes me sick. My skin goes
cold, and I'm overcome by a wave of guilt that twists my gut
into a knot.

*I'm such a fucking idiot, such a fucking horny scumbag, such a
fucking animal.*

The thing with Anne was, it came out of nowhere—kind
of. Sure, I liked the way she paid attention to me—smiling at
me a little longer, giggling flirtatiously at my lame jokes, letting her eyes settle on me and stay there. But I never wanted
it to go beyond that. Then one day we were exchanging some
banter on IM, pretty harmless, talking about preferences and
turnoffs and crap like that, and the next thing I knew we were
trading sex secrets. We never did touch—not that Kate would
care. Nor that she would even necessarily believe me.

I hate myself.

After a long pause, Kate says, "Are you sure you can't go
to FlowBid security?"

"First thing they'd do is scour my activity on the network,
and we'd be fucked."

She sighs and looks away. "We need to find a lawyer."

"Kate?" I rearrange the peas again. They're starting to
thaw. "What do you say we call it a day?"

Kate turns to me, crestfallen again.

"I'm sorry, honey. My crotch is soaked."

•   •   •

Kate calls our sitter, Stacey, to say we're coming home early. *Dan's testicles are throbbing*, she explains, *and he needs to lie down*. Through the cell, I can hear Stacey laughing. Stacey says she and the boys have walked to Burton Park, where they're playing in the sand lot.

At the parking lot, standing between our cars, Kate says, "Why don't I go pick them up at the park? That way they don't have to walk back, and we can send Stacey home, and you can go frost your testes on the couch?"

"That's okay," I say, trying to be conciliatory. "I can go get them."

Kate frowns. "I thought you were supposed to be in pain?"

"I'll manage. You go home and get their bath ready and set the couch up for me with a bunch of pillows." I reach into my sweats, pull out the wet bag of thawed peas, and toss it to her. "Just throw these in the freezer."

The April sun is still pretty strong, and the interior of my old Corolla feels like a vinyl oven set for 120. The AC crapped out three years ago, but right now I have the windows rolled up. A few minutes later, Kate calls my cell. I'm still glad to hear her voice.

"Calling for a nuts update?"

"I wanna reiterate, Dan. We have a plan for this matter with the nerds."

"We do?"

"Yeah," Kate says, "the plan is, you're going to find an employment lawyer ASAP."

Lawyer? Who, some greasy guy in a wood-paneled office

above a pawnshop? I don't want to deal with a lawyer. Who does? But as I head north on El Camino, I realize she's right: I *do* need one of these people—pronto. Any other option— contacting FlowBid security, HR, even the FBI—will lead to immediate devastation. Who but an employment lawyer can give me an accurate reading on the how-fucked-am-I scale?

Kate says, "You know anybody who knows a good lawyer?"

"Isn't Larry a lawyer?"

Kate laughs. "Crazy Larry? Across-the-street Larry?"

"They say he's brilliant."

"They? Who's they?"

Good question. "They just say—"

"Dan, the man was disbarred. Like, ten years ago. He walks around in a skin-colored Speedo and heaves buck knives at his garage door." She's almost yelling. "You want go to Crazy Larry for legal advice?"

"No, no, no. I'm thinking he can refer us to someone who's practicing. They say he's brilliant, and we all know brilliant people know other brilliant people." I pause. "Plus, you know he's sweet on you."

Kate says, "Well, I'm not asking him."

"Fine, all I'm saying is it's better than Googling 'Peninsula employment lawyer.'" I pause. "Plus, he'll want to help. His eyes twinkle when I mention you."

She moans. "What is it with you and freaks?"

"They're not freaks. They're just interesting people."

"All right, fine. You can check with Larry when you go see Calhoun."

Calhoun rents a granny unit in Larry's backyard.

"Calhoun? I don't want to deal with him right now."

"Well, you have to."

"No, I don't."

"Yes, you do. He came by again, just as I was pulling out of the driveway. I just rolled down the window and said you'd come see him, and just kept backing out."

I cuss.

"Hey, you're the one who said you like 'interesting' people."

I shake my head. "When I get home with the boys, I'll go see Crazy Larry, then check in on Calhoun."

"See what Larry says. But we need to get other references before we pick one, okay?"

"Fine."

"In fact, why don't you do that now? This whole thing with the geeks is freaking me out. I'll call Stacey at the park and have her walk the boys home."

"Fine."

Kate says, "I'll pick up something for dinner. Meet you at home."

"Fine."

"Just don't mention me to Larry, okay?"

"You think that'll stop Crazy Larry?"

"Yeechh," she shudders, and hangs up.

Crazy Larry lives directly across from us. And Kate is right; on most days, he does saunter around his yard in a skin-colored Speedo.

And flip-flops.

And cocoa butter—lots of cocoa butter.

Back in the 1980s, Larry traveled the world designing power plants—until, according to Larry, "they made me stop." At which point he went to law school, passed the bar, and eventually practiced corporate law at several software companies—until, according to Larry, "they made me stop."

That was then. Now, Larry turns off the lights at night and sits on his covered porch facing our house, smoking and drinking, listening to Alvin and the Chipmunks on an ancient tape player. We can't see him, just the glowing red ember of his tobacco pipe.

I'd like to make him stop.

When I pull up to the front of my house, Larry is sitting on his porch, staring at me, his face stoic as always, his dark brown eyes peering into me, it seems, observing me the way a lab researcher might study a confused mouse. For a man pushing sixty, he looks pretty damn good in the Speedo—deeply tanned, fit and trim, and spry.

I can feel him watching my legs as I approach.

"Hi, Larry."

Larry is silent. He glances at me and gazes into space.

"Kate and I were wond—"

"Kate?" He cocks his head, like he's picked up a radio signal.

"Yeah, Kate. We were think—"

"You *will* tell Kate I said hi."

"Of course, Larry. My pleasure. It's just that—"

"Dan?" His eyes twinkle. "Tell her I said hi."

"I will, I—" I stop myself, count to five. "I mean, sure, Larry, I'll definitely tell her you said hi. For sure."

He loosens, turns his head, and smiles into space. "There we go."

"Good," I say. "So we were wondering if you could recommend a good lawyer."

Larry turns his head, looks at my feet. "I don't practice law anymore." He looks up, gazes into space. "They made me stop."

"Yeah, I know, Larry. We just thought you might know of a good employment lawyer we could contact. You know, a reference."

Larry turns and examines my mouth. "Try the Internet."

And suddenly I recognize the idiocy of going to Crazy Larry for a legal reference. I can string sentences together okay, but at times I have the judgment skills of a squirrel monkey.

"Okay, Larry. Thanks anyway."

"Yeah." Larry picks up the hardcover book beside him: *The Paradigm Shift of Radical Granularity.* "Bye-bye," he snaps.

"Oh," I say, and wince. "Is Calhoun back there?"

Larry looks up, stares at me in silence for a real long time.

"Okay, well, I'll just go see if he's in."

Larry squints into his book, snaps, "Yeah, bye-bye."

I take the narrow path leading to Calhoun's granny unit.

Larry's backyard is packed with cactus. Tall cacti. Short cacti. Skinny cacti. Plump cacti. Covering the rest of the yard is a thick layer of jagged gravel. Larry likes his cacti and his rocks.

In the far corner of the yard is a little structure, painted yellow with white trim. Two large wood-frame windows with panes. A solid-oak door in the middle. All of it under a generous overhang. It's tiny, but nearly cute—which always surprises me, considering what lurks inside.

I tap on the door, and it moves a little.

Then comes a singsong voice, stretching each word extra long, making it obnoxious. "Come ih-nnnnnnnn."

With the back of my hand, I push the door open. I step in, trying not to breathe through my nose, trying not to pick up his trademark scent of baby powder and boiled-egg-gone-bad. There sits Calhoun, in his ripped-up recliner, wearing his red threadbare sweatpants and the same old brown sweatshirt, decorated with smears and hardened crumbs across the chest. I stand there looking at Calhoun, eyeballing the belly hanging over his crotch, glancing at his light brown Bozo-the-Clown hair, looking at his enormous tits. We're probably talking three hundred pounds—three hundred pounds of jelly.

His voice is delicate and precious. "This is a nice surprise." When he snickers, his tits jiggle. "Mr. Wonderful coming to see little ol' me."

I force a straight face. One must never encourage Calhoun.

"You have something urgent to tell me."

Calhoun's eyes have turned to slits, and his entire body is shaking and jiggling from silent laughter. He sighs, long and happy, examines his overgrown fingernails.

"Mr. Danny, Mr. Danny, Mr. Danny." Another exaggerated sigh, still enjoying his fingernails. "What are we gonna do with you . . . you little . . ."

I look at him, wait for more.

". . . rascal?"

He wheeze-laughs.

"Yeah?"

"Well . . ." Long pause. "Well, little ol' me saw something kinda weird on your property this morning."

Suddenly, my mind races.

Shit—the geeks? I try to stay calm. "Oh yeah?"

"But first . . ." He looks away. "We need to talk about what I do."

My brow crinkles. I've never seen Calhoun do anything. "What you do?"

"Yes." His face reddens, and his mouth puckers. "What I do to antisocials?"

I stiffen. "Just tell me what you saw."

He closes his eyes, nearly smiles. "I need to tell you what I do to antisocials, Danny."

"Antisocials."

"Yes." He says it like an angry five-year-old. "Antisocials who fail to invite their sweet neighbor to their backyard barbecue party."

"What?" I squint, grit my teeth. "You're talking about last Saturday?"

He folds his arms, puckers his lips, and nods.

"Calhoun, that was Harry's birthday party. You know? For six-year-olds."

He's not listening. "What I do is . . . Someday, I'll be visiting with my big mug of creamy coffee, and at some point, silly ol' me will need to use the lavatory. And silly ol' me—well, I will have chowed down on lots of carnitas and beans, and I'll just have to visit your upper deck."

"Upper deck?"

"You see, Mr. Danny." Closes his eyes, sticks his chin into the air. "I like to teach antisocials a lesson. So I visit their upper decks."

Freaking loony tunes.

"You see . . ." He returns to his fingernails. "I just gently remove the lid to the upper water basin of the toilee, and I pull my sweats down and I just work it until my little rump is practically falling into your exposed water basin, my feet planted firmly on the toilee-seat lid, my hands reaching out for stabilization, and then—oh, Mr. Danny, the exquisite exaltation—I release a nasty little guy into your upper deck . . ."

He studies my face, waiting for a reaction.

". . . where it will do one of two things."

I try not to grin.

"It will either wreak immediate havoc on your flushing system, or it will simply reside unnoticed for months on end."

"Dude, it was a party for six-year-olds."

"I don't care." Folds his arms, looks away. "I like balloons and party favors."

I'm laughing now. "Calhoun, c'mon."

"Before I tell you what I saw, I want a promise from Mr. Danny Wonderful."

"Okay, okay."

He folds his arms. "No more antisocial behavior."

"Okay, okay."

"You promise?"

"Yes, yes. I promise."

He sits back and closes his eyes again. "Okay, then." He pauses as he fails to fully suppress a burp. "Now I can tell you about the beefy little bald gentleman I saw prowling around your house this morning . . ."

He examines my stoic reaction.

". . . when your wife and children frolicked inside."

A jolt of pain goes straight to my crotch.

I turn left onto Brittain.

Kate again. "Where are you?"

"I'm at Lunardi's. I'm just gonna get one of those chickens."

I'm nearly breathless. "I'm going to get Stacey and the boys."

"What? . . . Dan, I just called and told her to—"

"I don't care."

"Is everything okay?"

"Don't think so."

I stop at an intersection, and Calhoun whizzes past me on his little moped scooter, his body dripping over the seat, his Bozo hair dancing in the wind.

What the . . .

"What's going on, honey?"

I pull a left onto Cedar and slow down, approaching the park. Calhoun motors past the park, pulls a right, out of sight.

"I talked to Calhoun."

"And?"

"And he saw a guy."

"What?"

I'm scanning the park, the sidewalks.

"Dan, how many pills have you taken?"

I look for familiar faces. My breathing is still shallow. "Calhoun saw a guy outside our house."

"What? Who?"

I peer over to the fire-truck play structure. No one.

"Sounded like the guy who kneed me over at Safeway."

Kate drops the phone.

"Kate?"

When she comes back, her voice is high. "Danny, what's going on?"

"Okay, I'm here."

I look toward the giant sandbox and see Stacey standing with the boys—and a guy. A short and beefy bald guy—playing with Ben, squatting beside him, showing him how to dump sand out of a giant Tonka truck, a big smile on his face. I hit the brakes, lower my head, and squint for a better look.

"Dan?"

That's him. The Safeway guy. "I gotta go."

I'm at least fifty yards away, and his blazer is gone, but I know it's him. The compact little body. The giant shoulders and the calm, confident look on his face, that face with the strong jaw and the little eyes too close together.

This guy, with my kids?

Blood races to my face. Rage shoots through my body.

I slip into autopilot. I dash out of the car, stopping traffic on Cedar, striding toward the giant sandbox of Burton Park, cell phone in hand, staring at the back of this guy's bald head as he plays with my kids.

What the hell is he doing with my kids?

God help him.

•   •   •

I call Stacey on her cell.

She giggles as she picks it up. "Little tender today?"

"Stacey, don't say a word. I need you to grab Ben and Harry and walk away from that man."

"What? . . . Dan? Where are you?"

Thirty yards away. Closing in.

"Stacey, get my kids away from that man. Get them out of here. Now."

Then, from the opposite end, I see Calhoun.

Crap.

He's doing an exaggerated tiptoe routine as he approaches the bald guy and the kids, pressing an index finger to his pursed lips.

"Stacey," I whisper into the phone. "Take them. *Now.*"

Stacey gets it. She slips her cell into her back pocket, says something to the man, and snatches my sons with a half twirl, tugging them away. Ben protests; Harry drags, twisting for one final look at this unusual new friend.

Calhoun closes in from his side. I quicken my pace.

Stacey sees me and I wave her away, sending her in the opposite direction. She obeys and pulls the boys so their backs are to him, just the way I want it.

This guy. This fucking maggot, screwing with my life, handling my kids. This violent psycho with his back to me as he makes one final comment to Stacey, something light and friendly. This guy standing there as Stacey, her face drawn and cold, turns back to force a smile but can't resist glancing at the movement behind him, at the crazed daddy preparing for impact, this daddy coming at him, jaw clenched, elbow out.

When Calhoun announces, "Surprise, surprise!"

The bald guy looks up at Calhoun, turns, and sees me. He smiles, reaches behind his back, and pulls out a switchblade.

Flips it open, starts toward me.

I'm frothing. "My kids."

Calhoun darts from behind, whacks the knife out of his hand, and falls on him. Baldy groans and squirms. Calhoun wheezes, looks up at me. "Maybe he's a relative, Mr. Danny. Maybe he's a long-lost uncle to your kids and he wants to say hi."

Baldy struggles under Calhoun, who starts to laugh, wheezing. "No tickling."

People yell for their kids.

Finally, Baldy pushes Calhoun off, rolls and jumps to a stance, facing. I come straight at him and somehow land a roundhouse to the side of his head.

We go down.

Calhoun is on his back, trying to get up, yelling, "Stop it, you little rascal."

Baldy's reaching for me as I get to my knees and grab hold of the Tonka, this giant metal dump truck, and whip it around as hard as I can, nailing him across the face, a nasty sound echoing across the park. That puts Baldy on his back.

"My kids," I pant.

Calhoun staggers toward him, spreads his arms out, wheezes, "Belly flop."

Baldy yelps and rolls away just before Calhoun crashes into the sand.

I gasp. "Don't . . ."

Baldy struggles to his feet.

". . . you . . ."

Calhoun rolls over, props himself up on his elbows.

". . . ever . . ."

The man bolts for the parking lot.

Sirens.

". . . come near my kids again."

Calhoun fingers the leather string around his neck, pulls a whistle from under his shirt, blows loudly, yelling into the air, "I've fallen"—tits jiggling from laughter—"and I can't get up."

Of course, not until I'm sitting in the back of the squad car, handcuffed, coming down from the rage, regaining a ration of logic and reason, do I realize how much shit I'm in.

Calhoun is outside with the detectives, telling his story, loving every second of it. He's got that stupid look on his face, and his little arms are flapping about as he sings God-knows-what into the air. The detectives glance at each other and take notes.

Why am I the one in cuffs and he's out there making nice with the cops?

Then I realize: I have assaulted a man. I have hit a man with a Tonka truck—for playing with my kids in the community sandbox. This will not look good to the San Carlos Police. And it might look worse to some ambitious county prosecutor. At the moment, it doesn't really matter that the "victim" was the same guy who attacked me a few hours earlier in a Menlo Park grocery store, the same guy Calhoun saw prowling around my house.

No, what matters is that I'm facing a night in jail. From my days as a crime reporter, I know that much.

I look over at Calhoun, who's got his shoulders pulled back, no doubt mocking my attack stance. And now my boys are standing there looking at their daddy sitting handcuffed in the backseat of a squad car, everyone watching, and I know this will be a memory they'll never shake.

Ben stomps up to the car, pounds on the glass, yells, "Daddy, you're supposed to use your words." He frowns, balls his fists. "You always tell us to use our words."

I fight the urge to vomit.

Harry approaches next, with troubled eyes. "Calhoun says he's coming to my birthday party next year."

"We'll talk about it, honey." I take a deep breath, try to calm down. "That's a long time from now."

Harry stares into my eyes. "Why'd you hit that man?"

"I'll tell you later, kiddo."

"He was nice."

I look down. "No, honey, he wasn't nice. He was pretending to be nice."

Suddenly, Harry looks a little scared. Brows crinkle.

"Before today, has that man ever spoken to you? Have you ever seen him?"

Slow head shake.

"Good, Harry."

He's staring at me.

"Listen, honey. Mommy is gonna be here any minute, I'm sure."

He nods.

Where the hell is Kate? Someone call Kate.

"You're gonna come home tonight, right?"

A lump forms in my throat. "Of course, honey. I need to talk with the police, then I'll be home." I force a smile. "When you wake up tomorrow, I'll be there."

His face lightens, and he lets Stacey walk him away, looking back at me. I gaze back, force another smile. I'm sure I look like a freaking psycho, sitting there cuffed in a squad car, smiling like a Hare Krishna.

I try to calm down.

I look back at the huddle around Calhoun, still flapping his arms, and I close my eyes. *When Kate gets here, it'll all be better.*

Sitting there, breathing deeper and deeper, I finally allow the obvious to sink in: This is no mistake, none of it.

This guy, this maggot, is no chance acquaintance. Some guy decides, out of the blue, to knee me in the nuts—on Vasectomy Day, of all days? That's no random act of rage. Same guy shows up in my neighborhood and hanging around my children?

I feel like my face is about to separate from my head.

A uniform gets into the driver's seat and shuts the door.

"Call my wife," I gasp. "They need their mother."

"Someone's gonna take 'em home."

The cop pulls the car out. I turn back to the boys, see that

Stacey has managed to walk them away. I swallow hard and force myself to look calm, just in case they turn around. I want to show them, through the bulletproof glass, that everything is gonna be all right.

Then I turn around and throw up on the floorboard.

Two

Fighters.

I understand fighters. I understand their determination, their passion, their need to press on, to resist the current pressing against them, to refuse to give up. If you're a fighter, chances are you're sticking up for something: yourself, your little brother, your country, your family, maybe even something stupid. And, hell, that's a lot better than all the other pussies out there who won't fight for anything, who just don't care enough, those folks with distilled water running through their veins.

Yeah, give me a fighter any day.

This is probably why Rod Stone and I are still friends. Rod is a fighter—literally. And every time he walks into the cage to fight, he pours his heart into it, leaving everything on the mat. He's still not sure exactly why he fights, and neither am I, but if I had to bet I'd say it's because when he does fight, it's him on his own, standing up for himself, just like in childhood, when his dad was long gone and his mom was either at work or passed out drunk on the couch. By exhausting his body and soul to save himself, Rod has created a roundabout way to love himself. Bottom line: Rod cares—cares about something. I like that a lot.

Rod can see the Little Fighter in me. It's always been there—not like Rod's Big Fighter, but it's there. Rod's Big Fighter is happy to come out for any number of reasons. But there's really only one thing that gets my Little Fighter going: Someone is fucking with my people.

"Kate?"

"Dan? Where did they take you?"

"Kate, do you have the boys?"

"Where are you, Dan?"

It sounds quiet at the house. I'm not hearing any of the boy noises I've grown so accustomed to the past six years— the incessant hollering, the toy trucks slamming into walls, the pounding of little feet on our chapped hardwood floors.

"Kate," I plead, "where are the boys?"

"They're here." She sighs. "They're passed out."

I feel sick again. I gulp back a surge of bile.

"Where are you, Danny?"

Damn, she sounds tired.

"Police department." I'm about to cry. "They might move me to County."

There's a long pause, and then, "What the fuck, Dan. I mean, what the fuck is going on with you?"

I swallow hard, trying to keep it together. "The guy I attacked?"

She's silent.

"It was the Safeway guy, Kate. The guy who kneed me at the Safeway. And the same guy Calhoun saw prowling outside the house today."

Silence.

"Did they tell you that, Kate? Did they tell you he was the same guy?"

Long pause. "All they told me is, you went psycho and Calhoun stopped it all."

"What?"

"They're saying Calhoun was like a hero."

I pull my hair back.

"Something's wrong, Kate. Things are happening here. The nerds in the van, the bald guy at our house, then at Safeway, then at the park with the boys."

Kate sounds confused, uncertain what to believe. "You sure?"

I close my eyes and shake my head. "I saw this guy with the boys, I just went crazy."

"Did you tell the cops this?"

"They're reviewing the Safeway tape now."

Another pause. "Stacey said she'd never seen you like that. She said it was like you were another person." A second later she whispered, "Thank God for Calhoun."

What? Calhoun? Thank God for Calhoun?

I lower my head and rub my brows.

"She said he seemed like a really decent guy."

"Calhoun? Is she nuts?"

"No, the bald guy."

"A nice guy *with a switchblade*?" I sigh.

I let the line go silent, giving Kate time for it all to sink in. In a day, things have gone crazy, and it doesn't take a genius to realize it's all related—and most likely centering around my all-powerful employer.

"I want you home, Dan." Her voice cracks. "I just want you home."

"Kate, when we hang up I want you to call Rod. I want you to have him spend the night at the house. I don't want you and the boys alone."

She's crying now.

"We're gonna get through this, Kate. The Menlo Park Police brought the Safeway tapes over. Calhoun gave them his statement. The detectives are gonna verify my story, and we're gonna be all right."

"Okay," she says, and sighs.

"Just call Rod, okay?"

"Okay."

"Tell him what's going on."

We're silent on the line again, and it's the closest I've felt to her in a long time. Finally, she sniffles and says, more like a prayer, "We're gonna be okay."

"Kate, we *will* be. I promise. I just need you to do one more thing."

Another sniffle. "Okay."

For the last several hours, I've just realized, I've been in deep, deep denial about something. Now I can feel my pulse pounding in my head, my blood racing like an eighteen-wheeler passing on the freeway. "I just need you to go to my car, Kate. On the shotgun seat you'll find a bottle of Vicodin and my prescription papers. I need you to have someone run it over here to the police station."

"Vicodin," she mumbles, as if to herself.

By now I'm gripping the table with my free hand, gritting my teeth.

"Sooner the better."

They bring me into the interrogation room. Again.

Bryant and Topeka. Two of San Carlos's finest—or perhaps only—detectives. My sandbox fight is probably the most action they've seen this year. In this peninsula town of highly educated technology professionals and pedicured East Coast expats, the cops are lucky to pull a nanny-jaywalking, maybe an extra-loud milk steaming.

Bryant has the face of a grandpa and body of a twenty-five-year-old; he probably logged a few decades in some city like Oakland before landing this cushy gig. Topeka looks like a kid: buzz cut, pink skin, doughy body. If they were real estate agents, I'd take them as a father-and-son team, but right now I can barely look at them. My mind is devoted to two primal thoughts: My crotch needs relief, and I wanna go home.

Bryant is glaring at me. I turn away and grit my teeth as my crotch releases yet another wave of agony; they're coming every few minutes now. Looking back at his gray eyes, square jaw, and salt-and-pepper mustache somehow intensifies the pain, sends it all the way to my temples and down my neck.

"Okay," Bryant says, his voice deep and dry, "first things first." From his front pocket, he pulls out the orange prescription bottle of Vicodin and practically slams it onto the wooden table between us. I grimace and reach for it, grunting, and he swipes it away.

Topeka snorts, smiling.

"Hold on there, partner." Bryant studies me as he slides the bottle to the far corner of the table, out of my reach. I stare at the bottle. "We have someone double-checking the prescription. Until it's confirmed, try meditation."

I lean back and stare at him.

Bryant studies his notes and fingers a red file folder. Topeka is leaning in on his elbows, watching me, still smiling.

I squint in pain. "You guys review the Safeway tape?"

Bryant doesn't look up from the notes. "We sure did."

"And?"

"We had Calhoun come over and take a look."

"And."

"He says it's the same guy."

"Which means I can go home."

Bryant turns a page, casual, like he's on the lido deck. "Don't think so, partner."

My heart sinks. "I don't get it."

Bryant glances at me, then returns to his notes.

"You saw me hobble in there, minding my own business."

"Yep."

"You saw me back into this guy, and the guy going ballistic."

"Yep."

"Throwing me into the freezer."

"We did." Bryant sighs and finally looks up from his notes. "We sure did."

"You have witnesses who saw him pull a knife on me at the park."

He nods.

"And you have Calhoun saying the guy was prowling outside my house."

Nod.

"So you know this guy was the instigator."

Bryant looks so calm. "*That* we don't know."

What?

"You rushed this guy at the park, Jordan. Unprovoked." He fans a few pages. "Wasn't for Calhoun, you might be in an even bigger heap of trouble."

I open my mouth and catch myself. Count to four. "Sir." I exhale. "He was playing with my kids. The same guy who'd prowled around my house and later attacked me unprovoked was now playing with my little boys. That's no coincidence. *He pulled a knife on me.* My sons were in immediate danger."

Bryant and Topeka exchange glances. "Tell you the truth, Dan, what we don't know is whether there's history here or not." He pauses. "Do we?"

I feel a wave coming on, and my crotch hardens into a block of pain. I grip the table, lean forward, and glance at the Vicodin bottle. The fuckers. I imagine siccing an overly aggressive, gelatinous attorney on them.

"Say that again?"

Topeka says, "How do we know you guys didn't know each other? How do we know you guys hadn't been feuding?"

I push back from the table. "Like I said, guys, go through

all my stuff. Go through my house, my phone records, whatever." I feel like I'm about to cry. "I promise you I've never seen that guy before all this."

Bryant waits, probably hoping I'll start to cry and confess to something. I take the moment to draw in a few deep breaths.

"Now tell us what the fuck is going on here."

"I've told you." *Shit, Danny. Hold it together.* "There's nothing."

"Tell me how you know this guy."

"I don't." I gasp. "I have no fucking clue."

"You're lying," he yells, his face flushed. "And you're wasting my fucking time."

I look away, shake my head.

Bryant pushes away from the table, releases a low grumble. Topeka moves in. Calm voice. "I think what Detective Bryant is trying to say is, there must be *some* reason this guy picked you out, found your sons at the park here."

I look up, can feel my eye twitching. "No shit. That's what I've been saying the past six hours."

They exchange glances.

"Then tell us," Topeka says. "Tell us what the hell is going on here."

I look at him and think about it. I know this must have something to do with the geeks and Stephen Fitzroy, and I realize that small-timers don't fuck with major CEOs like this, tracking down their speechwriters the way this guy has. I'm dealing with something far more dangerous.

I look back at Bryant, then Topeka. I have no idea what I'm dealing with, and I won't risk my life with these two assholes.

They can't help me with something like this. They might even make things worse.

Topeka says, "You're right. We can't charge you. Assistant D.A. already came in and took a look at the tapes, read the witness testimonies from Calhoun and the moms at the park, looked at the knife. Justifiable force. Self-defense."

Bryant sighs and turns back, facing me again. He seems to have cooled.

"You think we're idiots?" He pauses, watching me. "I've been doing this a long time." He waits a second. *Maybe he's handled assaults someplace else.* "We all know there's more to this, and I know you're withholding something." He pauses again. "Maybe it's something someone said to you . . ."

We stare at each other, and suddenly I want to tell him. I want to be taken care of, put to bed like a little kid after a cold, rotten day, knowing that all the bad stuff will be gone when I wake up the next morning.

". . . or maybe you think this involves someone you know, or something you did a long time ago."

I look up at him, shake my head.

"Well," Bryant says, "this won't be the last time you see me." Another pause. "Just the beginning. I'm gonna be all over you."

I look at him.

"And do you know why?"

I wait for more.

"Because I don't like knife fights in my children's park." He glares at me, his eyeballs nearly shaking with rage. "Not here. Not in San Carlos."

I struggle to stand up. "Give me my bottle, guys."

Bryant snatches the Vicodin and tosses it to me. So much for that bullshit about checking my prescription. I pop it open, finger two pills, and swallow them dry.

"Now, you guys wanna start actually doing your job?"

Topeka stirs, Bryant jolts.

"What'd you say?"

"You wanna do your job," I snap, "and get some protection out at my house?"

The first time I saw Kate, I was at Alta Plaza in San Francisco.

Saw her sitting with a girlfriend on the north end of the hilltop park, a six-pack of Tecate and a bag of Las Palmas tortilla chips between them. I was sprawled out on a blanket, trying to return to Bukowski's *Women* and failing badly—all on account of her, this bewitching individual sitting nearby, laughing with her girlfriend as they looked out at the breathtaking view of the city. I kept staring and smiling, and she kept glancing back with a grin.

There was a cuteness to her. A freshness. She was barefoot, sandals kicked off, jeans rolled up.

She hollered, "You want one?"

"Huh?"

She yanked a can of Tecate off its plastic ring. "You want one?"

I still have that can.

Two years later, Kate and I sat right where we'd first met. She had her head on my lap, and I was running a finger along her hairline, looking down at her, determined to reassure her.

We were getting married in a month, and we'd just had our worst fight ever—about my career as a reporter, its inability to provide stability for a family, and the difference between chasing a dream and being responsible. The conversation—or yelling match, as it turned out—in my Toyota had quickly disintegrated into a nasty attack-defend flurry in which everything from "You always wanted to change me" to "You don't really love me" came flying out before we could think to stop.

It had been a great two years, except for the past three months. The closer we got to the wedding date, the more things between us had unraveled. Of course, it had taken all that time to realize what was happening here. We were getting married, and Kate was horrified that someday we'd end up just like her parents—divorced, with a child.

Kate spent her childhood alone, with a TV.

She looked up at me, sniffling. "You're not gonna leave me?"

I stroked her head. "Kate, I'll never leave you."

She started to cry. "Even when things get shitty?"

I wiped the tears off her cheeks. "I'm in this for the rest of my life."

"Even if you get sick of me?"

"Even if I get sick of you."

She looked up, those blue eyes melting me, the purity drilling into the center of my heart, and I was certain of two things: I loved this woman more than anything, and I would never let her down.

•　　•　　•

Seven years later:

ANNE:	OMG, my face is so flushed right now
DAN:	That's because you know I'm turned on
ANNE:	Well that and the fact I can't stop thinking about you
DAN:	God, you are so bad
ANNE:	Whatev . . . ;)
DAN:	So did you think about me?
ANNE:	Okay, now my face is getting like cherry red
DAN:	Did you?

[long pause]

ANNE:	Yeah
DAN:	The big moment
ANNE:	Yeah?
DAN:	Did you have one?
ANNE:	Um . . . yeah
DAN:	And were you thinking of me?
ANNE:	I can't believe I'm telling you this
DAN:	You were, huh?
ANNE:	Uh-huh :)
DAN:	And??????
ANNE:	IT . . .
ANNE:	. . . WAS . . .
ANNE:	A
ANNE:	M
ANNE:	A
ANNE:	Z
ANNE:	I

ANNE: N

ANNE: G

DAN: Whoa

ANNE: It was like you were inside me last night

DAN: Whoa

ANNE: Uh-huh . . .

DAN: God, I want you

ANNE: Are you still hard, Dan?

DAN: Oh, yeah.

ANNE: Good :)

My worst moment, hands down.
God, I am scum.

Driving home from the police department in the predawn mist, I'm thinking about it all, realizing how close I've just come to letting Kate down. Writing that crap with Anne. Soiling the spirit of my marriage. Jeopardizing a million dollars just to leak gossip to a reporter. Not to mention nearly getting locked up for assault and battery. I can't imagine anything more destructive, anything that would destroy the trust Kate had developed over the past nine years, that would send my boys along the same damaging trajectory their mother experienced as a child.

I need to keep my family intact. I just don't know where to start.

I open the front door a crack and peer in. The faintest hint of dawn has crept through the blinds, the colors muted. In the corner, in my leather armchair, is Rod's silhouette, his heavy brow profiled prominently, his posture upright but relaxed, his legs planted open on the floor.

"Hey." I open the door a little more. "It's me."

"No shit." He doesn't move. "Could hear your car two blocks away."

I have to admit, it feels good to see Rod in my front room. Rod is never afraid of anything, and being around that confidence, that strength and courage, is reassuring. These assholes, whoever they are—they're in for a surprise if they haven't accounted for Rod.

He nods to the back of the house. "Go." His voice is cool as granite. "I'll pour you something." He rises and strides toward the kitchen. "Coffee or a cold one?"

I limp across the living room. At the hallway entrance I nearly trip on a toy motorcycle. My house is a freaking minefield of boy toys. Coffee sounds pretty damn good, but after everything that's happened, all that's racing through my mind, I know what I really want.

"Cold one," I whisper.

In the boys' room, I stand between their beds and gaze down at them. Ben is stretched on his side, twisted blankets snaking through his legs, his back arched dramatically, his belly coming through the pajamas, belly button showing, his chin up—just as he slept as a newborn. I squat down, bite my lip from the pain, and run the back of my hand along his cheek—smooth, warm, and perfect. He's brought to bed a small truck, a plastic lion, and a framed photo of me from the living room. I kiss him lightly on the temple.

My boy Benny.

I turn and look at Harry—at his blond hair, fair skin like his mom's—and start to tear up. I've come so close to scarring him. *Daddy attacked a nice man at the sandbox.* The thought makes my stomach turn.

I gather myself in the hallway, taking deep breaths. I hear Rod opening beer bottles, the caps bouncing on my counter. I take another deep breath, exhale slowly. I hobble down the hallway to our bedroom, inadvertently kick a Hot Wheel down the hallway, where it slams against the baseboard. I look in; Kate is asleep, surrounded by extra pillows, the phone a foot away from her face.

Loyal Kate. I back out, careful not to wake her.

When I get the kitchen, Rod is sitting at the table, nursing a Modelo. When he sees my eyes, he walks over, grabs my shoulders, and shakes me. Affection, Rod Stone style. "It's gonna be all right, Danny." He shakes me harder and brings me in for a hug—an awkward man-hug, chests pushed out to limit the intimacy, big hard thumps on the back. "Whatever this is, we'll figure it out."

We sit down and take our beers, leave the lights off. A sliver of sunlight streaks through the kitchen blinds and crosses his face, illuminating a gray eye and the scar on his left cheek. I take another deep breath, trying to regain my composure. He takes a swig and studies me, eyes narrowing, neck and head going rigid, as if he's saying, *Who did this to my buddy?*

Of the many times I've seen Rod fight, one of the few times I've seen him get emotional was in high school, more than twenty years ago.

It was actually one of my fights.

Ninth grade. I'm a lowly freshman still getting lost trying to find my locker. Two juniors sneak up behind me, lift me up by the legs, laughing. A longhair with tinted glasses keeps yelling, "Freshman . . . freshman," like he's proclaiming me to the school. They're laughing, I'm laughing, students are laughing. Not a big deal. Easy hazing. Until I lose my balance, grab for leverage, and end up stabbing my No. 2 pencil into the forearm of the longhair. Unintentionally.

"What the fuck?" The longhair looks down at me and pushes me hard, bringing his fists up. "Fucking stabbed me, you little fuck."

Kids swarm around us. My heart spasms.

Oh fuck.

An English teacher with a surfer cut saunters to his door, leans against the frame, and watches, arms folded. Guys are hollering, "Fight! Fight! Fight!" Big circle around us. Pretty girls watching from a distance.

"Dude, it's cool." My heart is pounding. "I don't wanna fight. It was an accident."

"Like hell it was." He comes toward me, and I back up. "Fucking stabbed me."

FIGHT! FIGHT! FIGHT!

"Little fucking new-wave piece of shit."

FIGHT . . . FIGHT . . . FIGHT.

"Hit him."

"Waste him, Mark."

He charges and takes a swing, and I duck. He misses badly, and I roll behind him on the asphalt, scramble back up. I feel like I'm about to cry, but I can't.

God, please don't let me cry.

People are screaming, happy about the excitement. Long-hair turns around and comes after me, at which point someone yanks me back. It's Rod, my best buddy. Goes straight for Longhair, swipes away a punch, lands a right into his glasses, cuts the guy in the eye, sends shards of tinted lens into his brow, grabs and slams him onto the ground. Place goes silent as my freshman buddy Rod puts this junior into an "arm bar," ready to make his elbow do unnatural things.

Longhair groans and struggles.

Rod's eyes are wild. I've never seen him so angry. "Say you're sorry, burnout."

Longhair struggles again.

Rod applies more pressure. "Say you're sorry."

Nothing.

Snap.

It took three minutes for the English teacher and two seniors to pull Rod off the screaming Longhair. And when they did, all Rod could say was, "My family."

I was Rod's family. No one else. Just me.

I've just told Rod the whole story. He's walking back to the fridge, fingering two more Modelos. "I know a guy at the gym." He pops the caps. "Does some side work for the suits. You know, security."

Rod himself used to do that kind of work. He had a nice gig doing weekends for some of the biggest names in technology and venture capital. Easy work. But it wasn't him. Now he's a full-time mixed martial artist signed to a six-figure contract with the UFC—a premier athlete training with some of the best MMA fighters in the world.

Rod glances at the clock on my microwave. 6:10. "I'll call my buddy later this morning."

I take a sip. The alcohol and the Vicodin seem to be mixing nicely because my crotch feels okay for the first time in nearly a day. "What are you thinking?"

Rod looks out to my backyard. The lawn is littered with toy trucks, balls, and plastic dinosaurs. "I'm thinking, this bald guy? Probably has some connections to the security crowd, and someone in that circle is paying this guy to fuck with you." Rod pauses, thinks about it. "Doesn't sound like an amateur." He glances at me, stoic, and returns his gaze to the yard. "You got lucky, Danny. Real lucky." He shakes his head, exhales hard. "Never do that again."

I take a pull off my Modelo. "I wasn't thinking."

"You're lucky your friend Calhoun was there."

I roll my eyes.

"Screwed things up for you, but probably saved your life."

It's hard to accept it, but I'm starting to realize: No Calhoun there, it would have been just me and Baldy, and chances are I would've been pounded to jelly.

"Guess I can't blame you." He takes a swig, keeps his gaze on the yard. Rod loves my boys—more than anything, maybe. "I'd have killed him."

"So I'm not crazy."

"'Course not." He sighs. "Problem is, with a guy like that, if he's what I think he is—a pro? If you redid that sandbox fight twenty times, he would've killed you the other nineteen."

My stomach sinks.

"I mean, the guy pulled a knife. But, hey." He lifts his Modelo toward me. Instinctively, I clank my bottle with his. "You took care of your people, and he's beat up."

My mind is swimming, but I have to admit it's satisfying, knowing I got the best of him.

Rod says, "What about the guys at FlowBid?"

"Which guys?"

"The security team for Fitzroy."

"Yeah?"

"You think you could trust them? Maybe they'd tell you if they're having problems on their end." He pauses. "You know, if someone sent a guy like that asshole after *you*, what are they pulling on the big cheese himself?"

I hadn't thought of that. Fitzroy's security team consists of two relentlessly congenial guys with law-enforcement and military backgrounds. I've always joked to Kate that they're the nicest guys you'll ever meet . . . who are ready to break your neck should you endanger the merchandise, i.e., Fitzroy. I've never witnessed one incident that even remotely required their services, but ever since we went public and amassed those billions, the FlowBid board of directors has required the security detail. Unlike other companies with deeper "bench strength," FlowBid is seen by many analysts as a one-man show. In other words, if Fitzroy bites the dust, so will the company's market cap, not to mention the investments of all our shareholders, which includes a handful of very heavily invested (and rich) people. Regardless, the fact that the board thinks Fitzroy needs security always gave me a chuckle. Until today.

"Check them out," Rod says. "See what kind of information they volunteer. Hell, maybe you'll feel safe telling them about this bald guy."

I shake my head. "Can't do that." I almost laugh, because I don't think Rod realizes how easily rumors travel in corporate. "I have to last two more days without creating a stir. Those guys hear about Baldy, the fact I attacked a man? . . . No way."

Rod frowns, and a deep growl rumbles inside his chest. "So that's what this is about—money. That's the problem with this place. Everyone is obsessed with money." He glares at me, looks away. "What the fuck happened to you, Danny? What the fuck happened to the guy who just wanted to chase the truth? The guy who wouldn't get caught dead in a suit? Now you're playing games with millionaires and hired security pros." He pauses and shakes his head. "Taking huge risks with your family."

I put the Modelo down a little too hard. "Don't give me that again," I say. "It's easy to be idealistic when all you have to worry about is yourself. Everything I've done, everything I've given up, it's been for Kate and the boys. Even now, it's for the family."

"You mean, for the money." He glares at me again. "You realize how fucked-up that is? One screwup, and Kate and the boys are in serious danger." He thinks about it. "Must be a lot of coin."

There's no way I'll tell him how much.

"What am I supposed to do, Rod? You think telling those cops would accomplish anything more than getting me fired, maybe even killed, depending on who's behind this thing?"

I take a sip. "You think those IT guys in the van aren't ready to destroy my life if I don't play along?" I wait a second. "You understand the pressure I'm under to provide for my family? Mortgage? Medical? Schools? Food? Safe neighborhoods? You understand how much I've given up to get here, to be just days away from our cash-out?"

He grumbles and looks away.

"Two more days. Then I change my life."

He looks disgusted. "Well, then, until this shit blows over, I want Kate and the boys up at my place." Rod lives twenty-five miles away in an oversized flat in San Francisco, in the gritty, industrial-bohemian neighborhood south of Market. "There's no way they're staying here."

I nod, and I feel better already.

"But first . . . it's dawn."

Oh, fuck. That's right. It's dawn, and I'm with Rod.

Rod gets up, pours the rest of his beer into the sink, opens the door to our backyard, glances at me, still frowning. "Come on, bub. It's dawn."

"Yeah, I heard you."

"You know the routine."

I do.

It started the summer before our junior year in high school. Rod was already fully obsessed with martial arts, and I just couldn't say no to my best friend. So every Friday at dawn, Rod would run to my house, crawl through my window, pull me out of bed, and drag me out to the football field a few blocks away, where he'd slap me around till I'd start yelling to "fucking stop it." Even as I was protesting, though, I knew what it meant to him—hell, Rod was out there solo the other six days of the week. And once I got my blood rushing, I loved it. The fresh air, the surrounding silence, the reminder that we were doing something special.

Every Friday at dawn, until I left for college.

Rod never stopped, but over the years the routine has evolved with him. Physically, it's become more intense; he continues to push his body and self-discipline to new heights. But it's also come to reflect his own evolution. Where the Rod I knew back in school couldn't care less about the harmonic balance of nature and its creatures, Rod the adult integrates his newfound love for all things natural into his routine. He's also developed an interest in spirituality, with an emphasis on Zen Buddhism. He insists that "the complex duality of the universe" allows him to pursue both spirituality and cage fighting.

My best friend, the Zen Buddhist cage fighter.

Between the beer and the Vicodin, I've almost forgotten my vasectomy. "Go easy on me." I widen my legs and square myself. "I'm not exactly sure this is a good idea."

Rod squints. "I'll be gentle."

"I really don't think—"

He explodes toward me, flips me over, and sprawls across my body, his armpit covering my face, his upper body weighing me down. The impact knocks the wind out of me.

Rod chuckles. "Trying to stay clear of you down there."

Finally I get a lungful of air. I struggle to get out from under him, but it's hopeless. He swings around, his knee brushing against my nose, my eyes suddenly watering. I struggle to my knees, at which point he slides me into a Peruvian Necktie, my neck trapped in a constricting mass of legs and arms. My defense instincts take over, and I flail my arms, trying to hit him.

He laughs. "There we go," he says. "That's what we want." He releases me, and I gasp for air. I stagger to my feet, the anger from yesterday surging like an electric current into my arms and legs, taking control.

"Hit me," he pants.

This is what he wants. He wants me to take a swing. This is what he had me do all those years on the football field. It's what they pay his sparring partners to do all day at his gym.

I'm practically wheezing, and suddenly I feel the pain in my crotch. It's like someone snaked barbed wire through my scrotum and down my legs. *God almighty.*

He snarls. "Just hit me."

The anger has my chest heaving. In my mind I hear Dr. Heidi's voice: *Are you acting like a man, Dan?* I see Detective Bryant yelling at me in the interrogation room, calling me scum. I hear the laugher of the geeks. I see that look on Baldy's face just before he knees me in the crotch. I'm ready to explode, and I know Rod won't let me go until I let it out, so I throw a hard right. He deflects it, slaps me hard across the face, picks me up and body slams me onto the grass. My insides rattle.

He growls. "Faster next time."

We get back up, and I know what I have to do. He won't stop until I do it.

"No more half speed," he snaps. "Faster."

I go for it. I throw everything I have at him. Rights. Lefts.

Kicks. He deflects the punches, steps away from the kicks. Finally, he catches my left foot and spins me off-balance, and doesn't let go until I've crashed to the ground. He comes at me with a cocked fist, stops, opens his fist, and slaps me hard on the face, grinning.

I'm panting so hard, I see stars.

"God, that brings back good memories." His eyes water as he pulls me back up. Sniffles. "Remember how hard you'd work just to land one punch?"

I don't think I've *ever* landed a punch on Rod. "I'm too old for this," I say.

He laughs, slaps me on the back, and brings me in. "I love you, Danny."

"Love you, too, man." I swallow hard. "Just glad you're here."

He looks away and nods. "Come on," he says, "we need to meditate."

We're sitting cross-legged in a field of toy trucks, plastic T-Rexes, and a dozen Wiffle balls. Rod's eyes are closed, and it looks like he feels The Light: head cocked, an eyebrow arched, corners of the mouth up, eyelids nearly fluttering.

"Just listen to the nature."

Rod isn't someone who's always loved animals, insects, and plants. I have friends like that, people who've been true naturalists since grade school, guys who've been camping and fishing all their lives. Rod, on the other hand, is a relative new-comer, which is fine with me because he's not doing it to be cool. He's doing it because he really feels it at the core of his heart. And yet something saddens me about Rod's newfound love for nature, about his determination to find authenticity and meaning.

Rod says, "I want us to think about this bald guy."

My eyes are closed, and Baldy's big nose and narrow-set eyes flash before me. I breathe out hard. "I don't know, man. This is . . ."

"Trust the Zen process," Rod says. "Find your answers within."

I try my best to let go, the Zen meditation way. At first I keep getting the same images: Baldy kneeing me in the frozen-food section; playing with my kids; pulling a knife on me.

"Try to imagine him as a little boy, a kid someone loved."

I try, and all I get is the image of Baldy's adult head on a child's body, pushing another boy around. I shake my head and try to let go, and just like that I get an image of a little boy cuddling with his mother. Within seconds, I can actually feel the love coursing through my veins. I feel like I'm about to cry. I see a woman's hand stroking a boy's arm. I shudder, and a blast of cold shoots through my body.

I feel Rod's hand on my foot. "We ask for wisdom in this bald man's life."

I know it's supposed to be a meditation, not a prayer. It's just that Rod likes to fuse things. He's Californian; it's what we do.

It's hard to pray for Baldy, but I get it.

"We ask for clarity and meaning in our lives." Rod's resolute voice gives me comfort. "And we ask for wisdom."

In front of my house, a van door rolls open.

·   ·   ·

Rod's eyes are closed. Mine aren't.

"Listen to the birds," Rod whispers. "The scamper of squirrels in your pines."

I hear the sounds of a van door slamming shut.

"Imagine you're inhaling the serenity."

I whisper. "*Rod.*"

He's practically humming. "Can you feel the harmony?"

"That car out there?" I pause, listening for more. "I think those are the geeks."

His eyes fly open, and he jumps to his feet. "Who?" He stretches his neck and listens for more. "The guys who jumped you after the snip job?"

My heart pounds. "This hour, who else could it be?"

And just like that Rod is striding to the side of the house, headed for my driveway. "Geeks?"

I hobble after him, whisper-yelling. "Wait . . . wait."

Rod opens the side gate, squints, and points at someone. "Hey," he snaps. "Stay there." He explodes out of view, and I hear a body slam against the van.

A high-pitched moan, an even higher-pitched shriek.

I limp around the corner, and sure enough, it's the geeks. Rod has the muscular guy, Little Red, against the van, one hand pinning his neck against the sliding door, the other holding a chrome revolver by the barrel. Little Red is wide-eyed, struggling to breathe. I look for his sidekicks and finally spot High Rider curled up inside the van on the floorboard, shotgun side. No sign of Star Trek.

Rod says, "You some kinda tough guy?"

Little Red gurgles.

Rod whips the butt of the revolver straight into his nose. Blood sprays onto Rod's face. High Rider tries to suppress a yelp. Little Red is heaving now.

"Hold this." The revolver flies toward me, hits me square on the chest, and I manage to grab it before it hits the ground. It's cold and heavy, and I don't know what to do with it, so I shove it down the back of my sweats like I've seen in the movies.

Rod puts Little Red in an upright choke hold, from behind, and whips him toward the side gate. "Backyard," he snaps. "Danny, get the other guy."

And then I notice my next-door neighbor, Louis, standing beside his midnight-black Saab, briefcase slung over his shoulder. Staring at us.

Louis is a few years older than me. He does product marketing at NetApp—he's worth millions now, no doubt—and has managed to avoid eye contact with me for the better part of four years. I give him a stoic hey-dude nod and grab High Rider by his collar shirt, yanking him out of the van. I look back at Louis one more time and realize he's hypnotized by the revolver sticking out of my sweats.

The rising sun warms us.

We've got High Rider and Little Red sitting cross-legged on the grass. Rod is squatting in front of them, holding the revolver. Little Red has blood running down his lip. He nods to the revolver. "I didn't pull that on you."

Rod snorts. "I don't like pricks who reach behind their backs when I'm talking to them."

High Rider glares at Rod. "If either one of you ever touches us again, we'll release the details of Dan's terminable offenses."

Rod straightens. "You screw up my friend's life, I'll release myself on you."

High Rider looks at Rod, then at me. "We instructed you to tell no one."

"Hey," Rod snaps, "do you have any idea what's happened to this man since you took him for that little joyride?"

They look back, waiting.

"Danny here had some asshole attack him at a Safeway. Then the same prick pulled a knife on him a few hours later." He pauses. "In front of his kids."

Little Red loses his smirk, and High Rider goes pale. And I'm thinking, either these two are great actors or they have nothing to do with Baldy.

"Yeah, that's right. We have a problem." Rod glares at them. "And it's your problem."

High Rider says, "We don't know this individual."

I ask, "What are you doing here?"

"We told you we'd come with action items."

"C'mon, out with it." I think of my neighbor Louis, who's probably dialing 911 right now. "Quickly."

High Rider nearly closes his eyes. "Tomorrow night your CEO will arrive in Tampa, Florida, for a speech he will deliver the following morning. As you know, he will speak to an audience of investors and analysts." There's pleasure in High Rider's voice. "Currently, you are not scheduled to join him, on account of your recovering testicles." He pauses an extra-long time. "You will rectify that."

Rod leans back and rolls his eyes.

My heart sinks.

"You need to be on that jet tomorrow morning. Find a reason; it shouldn't be hard. And you need to be with Stephen Fitzroy the entire evening preceding the speech." He looks over at Little Red, who's grinning. "Mr. Fitzroy will be staying in an executive suite at the Grand Hyatt Tampa Bay." High Rider's upper lip curls; his eyebrow arches. "It's going to be interesting." He looks at Little Red and snickers as he reaches into his pants pocket. "You will find a way to be with Stephen Fitzroy that evening, and you will have this on your person."

He pulls out a small black box tangled in wires, slings it onto my lap. I squint at the contraption; one wire is attached to the box, and another is attached to a black shirt button. Rod leans over, gives it a look. "Micro video camera," he announces, glancing at me. "They want you to tape him." He squints at High Rider. "What's happening in Tampa?"

High Rider is stoic. "You don't need to know that."

Little Red widens his eyes and smiles. His eyes are huge behind those glasses.

I look at the camera and sigh. *How in the hell am I gonna pull this off?*

"What are you gonna do with the tape?"

High Rider says, "Again, you don't need to know."

Rod turns to me, squints. "Well, their motivation has to be either blackmail or some kind of humiliation."

High Rider smirks. "Don't hurt your little walnut trying to figure it out."

Little Red snickers.

"All you need to know is that Mr. Fitzroy won't know about the footage until *after* Danny's precious options vest. It's only fair." He turns to me, narrows his eyes. "And if you do this right, he'll never know it was you."

I feel blood rushing to my face, my breathing getting shallow. I close my eyes, count to five, and open them. "You understand that if something bad gets out, it could destroy the dreams of thousands of hardworking people?"

High Rider puts his hand up. "We're not doing that," he intones. "This is not about destroying livelihoods." He waits, narrows his eyes. "But of course, the dreams and livelihoods of these hardworking colleagues were hardly a concern when *you* leaked all that damaging background to *BusinessWeek*." Long pause. "You sound like a hypocrite, Mr. Jordan."

My heart sinks. *Shit. He's right.*

Rod says, "If it's not about blackmail, then what is this?"

"Again, it's not your concern."

I'm staring back at High Rider, wondering what they want from Fitzroy. Money? A favor? A change in corporate strategy? Ethical business behavior? A cancellation of his outsourcing and offshoring policies that got these guys laid off? Something else that I couldn't possibly imagine?

"Any chance that some third party is monitoring you guys?"

They look at each other, pause, and burst out laughing.

"Impossible." High Rider beams with pride. "No one is monitoring *us*. Nobody hacks *our* systems."

Impossible? Arrogant prick. When it comes to hacking, nothing is impossible.

High Rider reaches over, grabs the black box, flips it over. "This red switch here activates the power." He points to an orange button. "This activates the recording mode." He points to a black button beside it. "And this stops the recording." He pauses, looks at Little Red, who nods. "The unit is fully charged. The batteries will last ninety minutes, the tape will last thirty."

Rod's face is contorted. "What's he going after?"

"Before the night is over, he'll know," High Rider says. "We want nice, clear footage of that mucus plug you call a leader." He turns to me. "And if you return with poor material, you know what we'll do."

I look at him.

"All that IT history goes public."

Little Red adds, "And you can say bye-bye to all your big ladies of the night."

High Rider turns, squints at the grass, and snaps, "Stop it."

Little Red glows. "You never know."

High Rider mumbles, "You and your big ladies." Then to me, he says, "The lens in that shirt button is wide-angle. It'll capture anything within ten feet. Be sure it's installed correctly, preferably in a black collar shirt, and make sure it's not pointing up or sideways. The best way to ensure a good shot is to stay as close to Mr. Fitzroy as humanly possible."

I exhale, heavy. *How the hell am I gonna do this?*

"When you return to your room that night, you will remove the cassette, deposit it in your briefcase, and place the button camera and recording pack into a plastic bag. You will take that bag with you on a late-night stroll near the hotel, during which time you will dispense of the camera in a trash receptacle." He pauses for effect. "We will know if you don't follow this procedure."

Rod looks at me, shakes his head, and chuckles. He leans over, reaches around me, and snatches the Modelo bottle I never finished. He glares at the geeks and takes a long swig.

"The following night, at six-fifteen, the jet is scheduled to land in San Jose." High Rider is gazing into my eyes. "You will deplane at the corporate jet center, get into your Corolla, and start driving north on U.S. 101, as always. At six-thirty, you will receive a call in which you will be instructed to proceed to a specified location. We will be waiting at this location, in the van, where we will review the footage."

I think of my future life on the other side of the hills: my beach-shack life, now just two days away. I think of being able to get the hell out of here, away from all the money people, away from all the opportunists like these guys, all the people who want to clamp on to the Stephen Fitzroys of Silicon Valley and suck something out of them.

"One last thing." High Rider points at me, then at Rod. "We're watching. We're monitoring your call records, your e-mails, your Web browsing—everything." His eyes widen. "If we see that you've told anybody else about this, the deal is off."

Rod gets up, shoves the revolver into the back of his army surplus pants, takes another swig of Modelo, and motions for them to follow. "I want you guys to leave," he says, "before I do something we all regret."

· · ·

Rod opens the side door to the van and shoves both of them in. High Rider yelps and scampers to the driver's seat. Little Red points at Rod and growls, then slinks further into the van.

Rod steps back, takes another swig of beer, and squints at them. With his other hand he reaches behind his back, pulls out the revolver, and empties the rounds onto the sidewalk, six brass bullets bouncing over his flip-flops. He throws the gun to Little Red, a little too hard. "Bring live rounds to my friend's house again, you'll eat them."

Little Red sneers and slides the door shut as High Rider speeds the van away. I have the button-camera contraption in one hand as I squat to pick up the bullets, thinking, *Geeks who pack heat?*

Rod is pointing. "I think we've got another visitor."

I jolt. *What now? Detective Bryant? Baldy?*

"Isn't that your neighbor?"

I look up, and there is Louis, frozen in the driver's seat of his parked Saab. He's parked away from his house, down the street, maybe hoping we wouldn't see him. He must have driven around the block and returned, parking where he'd have a better vantage point, and by the looks of him I'm guessing he's never been this scared. He reminds me of a toddler trying to poo: teeth gritted, jaw strained, brows asking for charity.

We move toward him.

He fumbles with his cell phone.

Rod breaks ahead, pointing at him. "Get off the phone, hotshot." When he gets to the driver's side of the Saab, the doors lock in a muffled click of Swedish precision. Louis lowers the cell and peers up through the window, his gaze weak, as Rod knocks the bottom of his beer bottle against the glass.

"Open the goddamn door."

Louis has these droopy eyes. They were the first thing I noticed about him the day he moved in. After the movers had left, I'd walked over and found him in his garage. Introduced myself. He glanced at my high-tops, mumbled, "Yeah, hi," ignored my outstretched hand (strike one), popped the trunk of his Saab, pulled out his golf clubs (strike two), and asked, "What do you do?" Not *Glad to meet you?* Not *Thanks for coming by.* Not *Hi, I'm Louis.*

Strike three.

We're in the Saab now—me in the back, Rod riding shotgun, crowding Louis's space. In this intimate setting, it's clear just how imposing Rod is to someone like Louis: Rod isn't huge, exactly, but he makes the car a lot smaller. I look at his glinty eyes, his cauliflower ears, his giant hands, the scar on his cheek, and it all makes me feel like some kind of country-club dandy.

Louis has his head half bowed before Rod, eyes down, hands in his lap. It's the first sign of respect I've ever seen from him.

Rod reaches over and taps the cell phone with his Modelo. "Who were you calling?" His voice is hard and even.

"What? It's just that . . . Well, you see, I just . . ."

Rod's voice gets darker. "You were gonna call nine-one-one."

Louis looks down and nods, real slow.

"I want you to stay out of my buddy's business." Slowly,

Rod reaches over and takes the cell out of Louis's hand, holds it as if he's weighing it. Louis shrinks further into his seat, wincing. "If I see you getting involved, watching that house over there, calling the police, or anything I don't like, I'll come back for you." He pauses, leans back, looks out the window. "And I will cram this piece of shit down your throat."

Long silence.

Still gazing out the window. "You hear me?"

Eyes still down. "Yes."

Seeing how much Louis is trembling, I see a great opportunity.

"Do you know those guys, Louis?"

Shakes his head no.

"So you were just parked here watching?"

Louis glances at Rod. "When they showed up, I saw you with the gun. . . . I mean, it was just a—" His voice cracks. "I didn't know what to think."

Rod squints, his jaw out. "That's not your job. Your job is to be the arrogant prick who lives next to my best friend."

Louis glances at the beer bottle, nods slowly.

I wave Rod off. "You don't need to worry about this, Louis. Seriously."

My cell rings, the number blocked. Rod turns and frowns. "Who's calling you at this hour?" He nods at the cell. "Pick it up. Maybe it's your baldy."

I take the call.

"Dan, this is Janice from Fi—"

I hang up. "False alarm."

Louis mumbles, "You're a speechwriter, right?"

"I am." I sigh.

My cell rings again, and I turn it off.

"FlowBid, right?"

Rod huffs and leans in, bringing the beer bottle to eye level. "Listen, asshole." He presses the tip into Louis's doughy cheek. "What part of *Mind your own business and fuck off* don't you understand?"

The trembling intensifies. I swear there's a whimper.

I wave Rod off. He withdraws the bottle. Then something catches his eye outside.

"Freak show at one o'clock."

I look up, and there's Calhoun in his dirty-white terry-cloth robe—dingleberries everywhere—barefoot, hair pointing in all directions, eyes puffy. Huge stupid smile on his face.

"Ah, shit."

He's pretending to tiptoe toward us, shoulders hunched, hands under his chin exaggerating each step. So happy with himself.

Louis squirms, mumbles under his breath.

"That's Calhoun, by the way."

Calhoun, still on tiptoe, getting closer, laughing.

Rod straightens, jerks around to look at me. "*This* is the guy who saved your life?"

I close my eyes, nod.

Calhoun goes to Louis's side and presses his face against the glass. Louis looks straight ahead, slumps a little more.

Light finger tapping on the glass.

"Yoooooo-hoooooooooooooooooooooo?" Laughter and giggling.

Rod says, "Open the window."

The window descends.

Calhoun sticks his head through, nearly touches Louis's nose, offers a wide-angle view of his tits. His trademark scent wafts in.

"When the Saab's rockin' . . . I *do* come knockin'."

Rod laughs, says, "You saved my best friend's life yesterday."

Calhoun beams. "Even more reason to invite me in."

"Well, I wanna thank you."

Calhoun nods, glances at Louis. "I see you're getting to know Mr. Precious here. A real down-to-earth guy, don't ya think?" He giggles. "A real charmer, so full of—what's the word?—humility."

He laughs.

Louis sinks lower.

Rod says, "Calhoun, I have a favor to ask."

Mock surprise. "From me?"

Rod nods. "Calhoun, would you mind keeping an eye on this guy?"

A squeal. "You mean, like, house visits?"

"Exactly. I was hoping you could keep him out of trouble."

Louis moans.

"Oh, yes." Calhoun inches closer to Louis's face. "You play Risk, Mr. Louis?"

Louis pulls back.

"Because I'm a tournament champion."

Rod says, "Okay, buddy. Sounds like a plan. Now, can we have a few more minutes with your new friend here?"

"Fine." He blows a playful raspberry at Rod, sprays Louis. "Little party pooper." Pulls his head out, starts to walk away, arms folded. "Car's not big enough for another stud, eh?"

Rod turns to Louis. "So, I guess you could say we'll be watching you."

Louis is staring at his dashboard.

"Listen, Louis." I hope he can tell I'm still a rational guy. "We just need you to be cool about this, okay?"

Rod bristles. "You think this guy understands cool, Danny?" He sighs, annoyed. "I don't think this asshole would know cool if it got him drunk and fucked him."

Louis straightens, fiddles with the leather lining of his steering wheel. "Nah, I'm cool, guys. I mean, I . . . You know, I saw nothing. Really. And I'll just keep this—"

"You know what?" Rod is looking at him, nearly amused. "I'd really like you to stop talking."

"Okay, I'll just . . ."

And he's wise to stop right there.

Rod has brought a small Igloo full of food. He knows he can't rely on my kitchen to provide the early-morning nourishment he's ingrained into his daily routine. He's at the kitchen table, eyes closed over a half pound of raw salmon, cut sashimi-style—thanking the salmon, no doubt, for what it is about to give him. Finally, he opens his eyes and sighs, content, grabbing the chopsticks and glancing at his large glass of carrot juice.

I'm leaning against the counter, watching him. "You think I should stop all this and tell the detectives?"

Rod drops a piece into his mouth, looks out to the back-yard, squinting. "Well . . ." He chews slowly, thinking about it, and swallows. "There's one thing I know." He drops an-other piece into his mouth. Chews, swallows, takes a sip of carrot juice. "As your friend"—he straightens, looks down at his lap—"as the guy who knows what you *could* be doing with your life, all this just proves that you need to quit that job, drop this way of living, and listen to your soul." He takes a sip. "So I'm happy you have a plan to get out."

He glances up at me, returns to his sashimi.

"So if that means you need to hang on a few more days and play along with the geeks on this thing in Florida, maybe that makes sense." Sip of juice. "Wait till the money's in your account."

As crazy as it sounds, I think I agree.

He adds, "And I don't think it's such a bad thing that you'll be out of the state a day or two—you know, considering we have no idea who's behind Baldy."

I nod. "Probably would be safer."

"You'll be safe with your CEO and on the jet, far away from here and whoever sent Baldy after you, and Kate and the boys will be safe up at my place." He downs another piece. "I'll have to keep training at the gym, but I can get some guys to come over when I'm gone."

The thought of Kate and the boys staying at Rod's place calms me. His flat is a fortress, and you couldn't ask for a better group of protectors than Rod and his cage fighters.

"And later, if you think there *is* a connection between the geeks and the bald guy, you can tell the cops."

Then a funny thing happens. I actually feel like I might have a chance in hell.

All the scheming is starting to hurt my head. I haven't slept in nearly twenty-four hours, and I can feel my logic functions grinding to a crawl. Sitting here in my boys' room, on the rocking chair, waiting for them to wake, my brain tries to pick itself off the floor, like it's drooling as it stares into space with a dull gaze. I snap into a moment of clarity, replaying in a garbled echo what Rod just said in the kitchen.

You've got bigger monkeys to corral.

You need to get yourself on that jet tomorrow.

You need to calm your family's nerves.

You need to ID that bald guy.

You need to handle your nosy neighbor.

You need to prepare for Fitzroy and Florida.

My heart flutters as I consider it all: the guy I attacked, the guy who came after me and my family for reasons unknown. And now my best friend suggesting I've turned into a Money Guy, someone who has abandoned his passion—and even endangered his family—for Internet riches.

I used to be like Rod, so sure about things. But the older I get, the less sure I'm of anything.

There was a time I looked down on the corporate jobs. But then we brought Harry home from the hospital. I'd stare at him for hours at a time, and my perspective changed. Providing for your family is noble, period. It has universal value, and it gives meaning to life. Right?

Not to Rod, I guess. In one sense, that annoyed the hell out of me. But then again I loved the fact he was so resistant, such a purist. Hell, Rod wouldn't be Rod if he didn't scream into the deafening roar of Silicon Valley, if he didn't stand before it and throw his hips out and heave his middle fingers into the air. And of course, I'd love to join him, cashing out and giving this life the finger.

The house is silent as I begin to nod off in the rocking chair.

Then a gurgling noise. The sound of thick liquid. Choking.

A weak, muffled "Daddy."

I shake my head, my temples throbbing.

More choking. Splatter on the floor. A gasp. "Daddy."

Ben is sitting on the edge of his little bed, something dripping off his chin. I bolt over and scoop him up.

He cries, "Daddy." Holds me tight. Little hands gripping my shoulders.

I smell vomit, and I'm relieved. It's not blood.

"Daddy," he moans, and vomits again. It runs down my neck and back.

"It's okay," I whisper, and stroke his head. His forehead is a little warm—mild fever. "Daddy's here now."

I move us to the hallway, where I can get some towels. He vomits again, down my back and onto the floor. Rod comes around the corner, see us, and grabs some towels from the linen closet.

I turn on the faucet, splash cool water into Ben's mouth to get the taste out.

Afterward, he rests his head on my shoulder. "Daddy," he mumbles, and squeezes me. A lump forms in my throat, my chest expands in warmth.

Rod is in the hallway, oblivious to the sour odor. He wipes Ben's mouth with one towel, drops the other near my feet, and spreads it out with a naked foot. "Let me have him," he whispers.

I give him a look.

"I'll take care of him," Rod says. "I want you to go out front and tell me if you recognize the guy I found in your garage."

"What?"

"I tied him up," Rod whispers. "I'll stay here, near Kate and the boys."

I give him my what-the-fuck? look.

I switch Ben over to Rod, and they hug.

Rod nods toward the front of the house. "Go see."

The kitchen door opens to the garage. I open it, poke my head in—and see the nasty end of my garden shovel coming straight at my face.

I fall to my knees, kind of slow. I can't feel my nose, mouth or forehead—it's all morphed into a thick mask of pain. I look up, see the shovel coming again. I duck.

The shovel sinks into the door frame.

I look up. A man in his forties is backing up into the garage. I don't know this guy. Some of my rope is still wrapped around his right arm, my duct tape trailing his ankles. Rod may know how to fight, but apparently he knows jack about tying people up.

The man is wearing dark blue sweats and a gray sweatshirt. He looks athletic, and horrified.

No way this asshole's getting through me. I lunge for him, knock him down.

Rod's voice echoes from the other side of the house. "Danny?"

The man screams at the sound of Rod's voice, stumbles up, and slaps the garage door button on the wall. The garage door starts to jerk open, and he bolts toward it.

I struggle to my feet, slap the button. The door halts. I slap it again and it starts to jerk closed. "You're not going—"

He slides under the garage door, inches to spare.

Feeling a bit dizzy, I find myself falling to one knee. *Can't let this guy . . .*

Rod hollers, "Danny, you okay?"

"Yeah." I get to my feet, shake my head. "Just stay with Kate and the boys."

I hear Kate holler, "Dan?"

Outside, a car door opens and shuts.

I reach back into the kitchen, feel around for the key hook on the wall, grab my keys, and slap the garage door open again. I try to run, but I suddenly realize I must have strained my scrotum, which is now sinking ice picks of pain into my stomach. I hobble out, see a green BMW 325i racing past my house.

He might have the fancy German import, and I might have an old Toyota. But I *have* raced through countless neighborhoods to reach shootings, disasters, and myriad other public-safety events, and I'd bet my life that I can catch him.

To the Corolla! I think, and limp to the street.

I just don't expect to find Detective Bryant when I get

there. But there he is, leaning against my shotgun door, tooth-pick in his mouth. Sly grin.

I stop for a second and limp toward him.

"Little bloody there, Danny." Bryant pulls out the tooth-pick and shakes his head. "I'd call that a head wound."

"That guy." I shuffle up to him, panting. "You didn't stop him?"

Bryant smirks. "You ready to talk, Danny? For real?"

I stand there and think about it, wipe the blood out of my eyes.

"Okay."

Three

Bryant says, "I want in."

I squint. "What are you talking about?"

"You heard me, partner. I want in."

We're in his car, right in front of my house. Kate, Rod, and the boys are standing on the porch watching us. Across the street, Crazy Larry is on his own porch—nursing a coffee and staring.

I wipe a bit of blood off my nose. "Want in?"

Bryant folds his arms and glances at me. "I want in. Whatever this is, I want in."

"Want in," I repeat, my mind scrambling.

"I want a piece of the action."

"Piece of the what?"

"C'mon, partner. You think I'm some idiot?"

I shake my head.

"I looked you up, got your employer. Found out you've been there since the beginning, almost." He pauses. "Read a few stories. They say employees who've been at FlowBid awhile—guys like you—are worth millions."

You have got to be kidding me. "Sir, I'm not a millionaire."

"Bullshit." He wipes his mustache real fast, glances at me. "On paper, you're worth millions, for sure."

"Whatever." I look out, and Crazy Larry is still watching us, so calm. "So you want me to give you money I don't have, or else you'll make my life a living hell over that sandbox incident?"

Real slow. "No. No, that's not what I'm saying."

"So what are you saying?"

"I'm saying I learned some things this morning that lead me to conclude you're in a big mess."

I try not to freak. "And what's that?"

"I just locked down some details on this suspect."

My chest tightens. "Did you get his name?"

"Well, that's just the thing. You see, I wanna help, but my caseload is huge and I got a ton of other cases that need attention."

I laugh. "In San Carlos?"

He smiles to himself. "I'm busy."

"Oh, I see." I feel the rage building. "Too busy to investigate this guy, unless I make a donation to the Detective Bryant Fund?"

"Hell no." He laughs, folds his arms. "No, I just want in on whatever it is you've got going."

I think about it a second, realize Bryant must have something good on Baldy.

"Sir, I don't have anything going."

"Like hell."

"Well, there's obviously something going on, but damned if I know what it is."

He smiles. "You sure about that?"

I close my eyes and exhale. *Tell him about the geeks? My options?*

"Because this guy yesterday? This guy who's after you?"

"Yeah?"

"I got a positive ID on him, I think."

"You're kidding me."

"And if he's who I think he is, he's not some everyday dude."

"Who is he?"

He chuckles. "Well, hold on, partner."

I look away, shake my head. "Unbelievable."

He says, "First, I want you to understand where I'm coming from."

I sit back in the seat, fold my arms.

"Let me give you a little background." He looks down, and his face tightens. "You see, partner. I've been working my ass off all these years, barely making it."

Long pause. "Okay . . ."

"And I just sit here every day and watch you kids run around with your money. All you cocky little pricks who've done nothing, just worked a few years, and then you're set for life."

I look away and shake my head. "I'm not like that."

"And all I'm saying is, I want my shot." He sounds almost like a kid. "I want my fucking shot at the action." He's yelling now. "Been working all my life, serving the community, barely making it, watching kids like you skip right into the millions, just being at the right place at the right time, and all I'm saying is, I want in."

He turns and looks at me.

"I want in. I want a shot at making a little money. I want to pay off my mortgage. I want to stop worrying about the bills for a change."

We look at each other for a long time. There's pain in his eyes, hope in his brows.

"I don't want your money, partner. I just want a shot at the action."

I look away and think about it.

Crazy Larry is watching us, his head cocked in bewilderment, like he's a cat and I'm a new windup toy.

"Sir, I don't know about any 'action.' I have no idea why this guy is on me, and I'm not involved in any big deal or anything."

"But you have to be."

"Because of this bald guy?"

"Exactly."

"And you're not going to tell me who he is, are you?"

He shakes his head no. "I don't have to tell you. I can proceed with my investigation without telling you a thing."

"But if I decide to tell you everything I know?"

He nods. "Then I'd be more than happy to tell you everything *I* know. All you have to promise me is, once we figure out what's happening, I have a chance to get a cut. Like, if it involves insider information, I get a chance to invest accordingly."

"Fine. But why are you so sure there's any action to be had?"

He folds his arms and smiles. "With this guy? Your friend from the sandbox? This guy doesn't get involved unless there's money to be had—a lot of money."

My stomach weakens.

He whispers, "Okay, partner. You first."

So I tell him. I tell him everything.

And he tells me.

And I realize I'm in way over my head.

"What was *that* about?" Kate is holding Ben, soothing him. "You guys were out there for like an hour."

I push my hair out of my face. "We were just trading information."

I can hear Rod and Harry laughing in the boys' room.

"You look pale." She studies my face. "Are you okay?"

I look back into her eyes. Damn, she's beautiful, and warm, and I wish we could go back to that time when everything was so easy and natural between us, when I could wrap my arms around her and she'd smile to herself and fall into me. Of course, life was so much simpler back then—before kids, before corporate, before we dove headfirst into the rushing white waters of our new life.

"Not sure."

Light tapping on the front door. Kate and I glance at each other, then at the door.

From the other side: "Yoooooooooooooooooo-hoooooo?"

Kate looks away and sighs.

"What is it?" I snap.

The door opens, and Calhoun eases his head through. "Morning, sugar pops." He giggles and raises an eyebrow. "Mind if I come in?"

I struggle to get up. "Actually, this isn't the greatest—"

He pushes through, looks around. "Well, well, well, isn't this the little Taj Mahal?" He's taking it all in, his eyes working fast; it's the first time he's made it inside our house, and he knows it'll probably be the last. "Someone likes his Fancy Town."

He's still wearing the robe, and he's sipping coffee out of a plastic Goofy mug, ears and all.

"Calhoun, we're kinda dealing with a few things right now."

He puts his free hand on his hip and blows a raspberry at me, long and sloppy, spit spraying everywhere. His lower lip eases out as he waits for a reaction.

"Calhoun, we just—"

"So you decide to have a little party over here, and you don't even invite little ol' Calhoun, the man who saved your life?"

Kate laughs, says, "Does this look like a party? Okay, sure, there's vomit in the hallway. And, yeah, the cops came. But this isn't that kind of party."

He closes his eyes. "One would have assumed you'd have me over for waffles and bacon this morning"—he tucks his chin, hopeful; opens his eyes, pleading—"considering I saved your little lover's life."

"Well, we're sorry, Calhoun. We just have—"

"Calhoun!" It's Harry in the hallway, waving him over. "Come see the LEGO city I built with Rod."

Calhoun looks at me, says, "I'd love to." He marches toward the boys' room, stops, and turns back to Kate with those pleading eyes. "Not even a little plate of Eggos?"

Like scolding a dog: "Calhoun, no."

"Fine." He gives us a final raspberry, real quick, and turns to Harry. "Your mommy no leggo her Eggos."

Harry smiles, not getting it.

"But let's see your LEGOs." They laugh and pad down the hallway.

Kate turns to me. "What did he tell you?"

"Who, Calhoun?"

"What? No, the detective."

"Oh."

She feels my forehead with the back of her hand. "I'm worried about you."

"I think I'm losing it." Then again, I think, an hour ago some guy broke into our garage and tried to take my head off with a shovel.

"Just stay focused a little longer," she softens, "and then I'll put you down for a nap." She's talking to me like I'm one of the children, and I have to admit that, on this day, I like it. "Danny Boy needs some sleep."

I nod.

"And maybe some more Vicodin?"

Another nod.

"Mama's gonna take care of you," she says.

Ben snuggles closer to her, sighs, "Mommy."

"Now tell Mommy what the detective said"—her voice hardens—"so we can get a plan going."

Down the hall, I hear Calhoun announce, "Potty break."

I shake my head, will myself to focus a little longer.

"Long story short . . ." I lower myself onto the couch, hissing in pain. "The cop gets a lead on the bald guy, gets a positive ID on him, tells me he's employed with a firm called Stanislau, which has offices in Grenoble, Munich, New York, LA, and San Francisco."

"And?"

A loud noise in the bathroom. Heavy porcelain.

Internal alarms go off. "What the . . ."

"Danny, stay with me. What about this Stanislau?"

I plod ahead. "I guess they're some kind of high-end private firm—personal security, intelligence gathering. Like a CIA for top-tier companies—capital investment firms, venture capital funds, even some family trusts. Big money. Really big money."

Kate sits down with Ben, gazes at the wall. "Whoa. What the F?"

"Bryant said he'd heard about a guy like this who'd turned some heads in San Jose—got detained for suspicious activity around a tech campus down there, but got himself released. So Bryant sends the Safeway pics down to San Jose PD—he's got a buddy there—and they send back a fax of the guy's business card."

"What's his name?"

"He wouldn't tell me."

A loud crash from the bathroom.

Ah, fuck.

Calhoun. In my bathroom. Making too much noise.

Kate says, "But he works for this security firm?"

"Well . . ." I get up and hobble to the hallway. God, my crotch hurts. "It looks that way."

She sighs hard, falls back on the couch. "What do we do?"

I turn and head down the hallway. "We take care of a more immediate crisis."

I'm pounding on the door.

Calhoun grunts, "Goaway."

I shake the door handle with both hands.

Grunt. "Ineedsomeprivacy."

Rod joins me, squints at the door. "What's the deal?"

I yell, "Calhoun, are you upper-decking?'

From the bathroom, a big sigh of relief.

Rod juts his jaw out, tenses. "You want me to bust it open?" He steps back, ready to kick.

I wave him off. I don't need a broken door on top of everything else.

Calhoun grunts, "Onemore."

"Calhoun, I'm gonna kill you."

"Antisocial"—big grunt—"ingrates." Big sigh. Then another grunt. "Notevenawafflebreakfast—ahhhhhhh."

Kate arrives, carrying a hairpin. Rod snatches it and begins to pick the lock. In seconds it clicks, and Rod steps back, waves me in. Kate turns away, closes her eyes.

I open the door a little.

Grunt. "One-nnnnnnnn moooore." Sigh and a grunt. "Justalittle"—grunt—"guy." Big sigh.

I push the door open. Calhoun is sitting on the exposed upper water basin of our toilet, his open robe covering the sides, his feet on the seat, his elbows on his knees, his face grimacing.

Rage courses through me. "*Calhoun!*" I roar. "Off."

Harry runs into the bathroom and freezes in wonderment. "Wow."

Calhoun tries to close his robe, yelps, "Privacy! Privacy!" Closes his eyes, sticks his chin out. "Someone help me."

I want to throttle him, but I don't want to get near him. Rod backs away, grumbling, "Gross." Kate barges past us, her nostrils flaring. She grabs the plunger next to the toilet, winds up for a swing.

Calhoun recoils, squeaks, "Don't hit me, Mommy."

"*Get*"—she whacks him hard across the face— "*off*"—another whack, right in the chops—"*right*"—she swings again, he ducks, and she loses her balance a little, but comes back with a direct attack, covering his face with the plunger and pushing his head back—"*now.*"

He whimpers.

She keeps the plunger over his face, pushes harder.

We all see his pickle. *Didn't need to see that. Really, really didn't need to see that.*

With her free hand, she grabs the lapel of his robe, and yanks him forward. He loses balance and tumbles off the upper deck, crashes to the ground, a mound of whimpering jelly.

Kate takes the hard end of the plunger and jams it into his ribs. He stiffens in pain, yells out, "Mommy."

Kate screams like she did when she was in labor with the

boys. "Out!" Jabs him again, even harder, and he balls up. "*Out!*"

Rod takes Kate, and we lead her out of the bathroom.

Slowly, Calhoun rises from the floor, pulls up his orange boxers, closes his robe, and makes baby steps toward the hallway. He stops and looks at us, eyes hopeful.

"No Eggos?"

Four

I won't describe the cleanup in too much detail.

Suffice it to say that it involved an old pasta strainer and yellow rubber gloves, and that I nearly threw up in the process. Suffice it to say that, when my work was done, Kate had me deposit the strainer into a triple-layered plastic bag system which then was dropped into a paper grocery bag, which then was stapled and walked directly to the garbage. And suffice it to say, it made for some really weird dreams during the fitful two hours of sleep that followed—dreams in which Detective Bryant is leaning over me, repeating, "I want a piece of the action," and then he turns into Crazy Larry, who leans in closer and says, "You *will* tell Kate I said hi," and I straighten up and tell Larry to go away, and I turn back to my work, only to find Little Red upper-decking on my tank, snickering and snarling, repeating, "Fat hookers, fat hookers," until I swat him on the head, which is when High Rider comes from behind, his eyeglasses enormous, says, "You have three days to clean out that tank, otherwise we will be forced to . . ." and Rod comes in, squinting, announcing that Crazy Larry is slow-dancing with Kate in the hallway.

At which point, Harry bounces atop me, hollering, "Wake up, wake up."

"Ah, Harry." I open an eye and moan. "Come back in ten minutes, kiddo."

Harry bounces harder. "No, Mommy said to get you up no matter what you say."

"Oh yeah?" I groan. My temples constrict, my crotch aches, and my body begs for more slumber. "Just a minute."

"No." Harry is firm. "Mommy said she made a list for you, and that you need to *get crackin*'!" He claps, hard.

I push him off and sit up, run a hand through my hair. "List?"

"Yeah." Harry is so fresh, so full of energy, and somehow seeing this makes me feel even more tired. "A list of things you need to do today."

Actually, that sounds okay. My mind is reeling, I'm confused and overwhelmed. My writer brain can only take so much before it really starts freaking out, like a hose that's left spraying and flapping uncontrollably, chaos taking over. I need Kate's sharp mind, her ability to stay cool during crazy times, her gift of supreme executive function, all those first-class leadership skills of hers that I wish I had.

Harry looks at me. "Mommy says she's going to give you a list that'll make everything better." He tenses, puts his hands out. "Stay right there."

He bolts out of the room.

I wiggle to the edge of the bed. And then, out of nowhere, ripples of pain shoot down the insides of both legs, and up into my abdomen. I get a flash of Baldy kneeing me in the nuts at Safeway, that look on his face, those eyes too close together. I hiss and grunt as I ease my tighty-whities off, and let the gauze roll down my leg. *I'm way overdue to ice my crotch*, I think. *Guess I got sidetracked.*

I don't want to look down, but I know I've got to. And when I do, I wince.

It's a trippy sight. I'm bald, like a boy, but my scrotum is purple with yellow swirls, and it's enormous. Testicles the size of peaches. I look away, but the damage is done. Nausea courses through my body; my head feels like it's floating.

I take two Vicodin, swallow them dry. "Honey, can you send Harry back with a bag of peas?"

She hollers back, "Okay."

On the nightstand, my cell rings. I look at it; blocked number. Probably Fitzroy's office calling about his speech for Florida.

"Dan Jordan."

"Dan, this is Janice from Fi—"

"Janice, I need to call you back."

Long pause. "Dan, I have some special instructions for how you need to execute the L18 as it relates to putting the P6s into the FOD."

"Janice, I'll talk to you later," I say, and end the call.

I put the gauze back in place, pull up my tighty-whities, moaning through gritted teeth. *Holy shit*, I think. *Thank God for Kate and her list, whatever it is.*

A minute later, Harry returns with a bag of peas under an arm, holding a pint glass of café latte in both hands, biting his lip as he stares at his payload.

"Just what I need." I bring him in and kiss his forehead. Love that kid.

"Mommy says drink up and take a shower, then come out to the kitchen."

"Thanks, honey." I take the glass, and its warmth soothes me. The aroma steams my nose, and I take a sip.

He watches me. "Daddy? What are those red lines on your eyeballs?"

"Don't worry about that, honey. That just means I'm really tired."

He studies my face. "You look like you did when Ben was born."

I put the latte on my nightstand. "Let me see those peas, kiddo."

Harry hands them over, sticks a lip out, pouting hard.

"Daddy?"

"You okay, kiddo?"

"I'm sad."

He holds his arms out for a hug, and I drop the peas and grab him. I *knew* that whole Daddy-in-the-squad-car scene would be too much.

"What's going on?"

"No one's letting me be me."

Huh?

"What do you mean, kiddo?"

"Like Mom . . . the other night . . . not letting me . . ."

Harry buries his face into my chest and mumbles, "pick my nose."

"Harry. That was at the dinner table. You can't pick your nose at the dinner table."

He pulls his face off my chest, looks at me. "Why not?"

"I'm not having this conversation with you."

We hug a little more, and then I ask, "Who else is not letting you be you?"

He tells me about school. Apparently, some of the rules and procedures and curricula don't jibe with my expressive, language-oriented, naturalist son.

Penmanship? The banal work of simpletons who obviously don't care about more important things, like how volcanoes happen or how his "bug club" might someday be able to undermine the insecticide industry.

Math? Don't even go there.

He says, "I wish school had just two subjects: talking and reading."

I nod in concession. He's right—that would be nice.

The caffeine and Vicodin kick in, and the shower feels great. I put on my FlowBid clothes—"hip jeans," as Kate calls them, with a collar shirt tucked in—and reach for the peas.

"Wait a second." It's Kate in the doorway, arms folded. "Maybe I should see how things are down there."

"You can't be serious."

She closes the door and approaches with a straight face. "Let's see what the fuss is about."

"Believe me. It's not something you want to—"

"Sshh." She's already unbuckling me, her hips easing forward. "I was thinking, if it's too nasty, I should call the doctor."

"No doctors," I say. "Just peas and Vicodin."

She squats, pulls down my briefs, and gasps. "Oh . . . you poor thing." After the initial shock wears off, she begins to inspect me like a concerned lab scientist—lifting, analyzing, craning for a closer look. "Does it hurt?"

"Not right now, thanks to the Vicodin."

Still inspecting. "Maybe I should call the doctor."

"Honey. There's no time for doctors."

She's so gentle. "You poor thing."

After a while, I say, "You keep doing that, and I'm gonna get—"

But it's too late. My transformation has begun, and Kate shakes her head with a chuckle. "Oh yeah," she mocks. "You're *really* hurt down here. I can see that."

"You know it's got a mind of its own."

I pull her up to me, fumble with her jeans. She laughs, grabs my hands. "No way."

"Honey," I plead.

Her lids are lower, and she's looking at my hair, then my chin. "You're a piece of work, you know that?"

I laugh. "And what about you? This little inspection?"

"I was worried about you, and *this* is what I get." She pushes away, but lets me pull her back in.

"Honey. C'mon."

She laughs, then whispers, "You're awful."

I return to her belt buckle. "Don't mess with the bull if you can't handle the horns."

"I was thinking . . ." She grins to herself, then looks me in the eyes again. "What if I told you I kind of liked that?"

"Liked what?"

She lets me pull her jeans down and loop my fingers under her panties. "That badass side of you."

"Huh?"

I tug at her panties, and she slaps my hands away.

"What if I admitted I kind of liked that? The fact you beat up that tough guy? Protecting me and the boys?"

I stand there, dumbfounded. All that time and money spent on Dr. Heidi Douglas, when all I had to do was beat up a hard man.

"You sure this won't hurt?"

Okay, maybe it hurts a little. But do you think I'll tell her?

Afterward, in the kitchen, Kate gives me a spoonful of cod liver oil. "For that extra juice," she says, and drops a handful of vitamins into my hand. "You'll need every bit of it today."

"Where's Ben?"

"I gave him some Motrin, and he's napping. Just a little fever. And I'm keeping Harry home from school so we can leave for Rod's place."

I lower myself onto a chair like a ninety-eight-year-old man. Not that the sex wasn't worth it, but now that it's over, things hurt more than ever. "So you have a list?"

Kate spoons protein powder into a bowl of Raisin Bran. She turns and hands it to me. "Have that, and I'll debrief you."

"Thank God," I sigh, looking out to our backyard. "I don't know where to start."

"I know." From her back pocket Kate pulls out a three-by-five card, hands it to me. Her handwriting is perfect. "This is what you're going to do, okay?"

I glance at the card, then at her. I think about what we just did in the back room, and I guess my face shows it.

"Dan, stop thinking about that. It's time to get cracking. Dan, listen to me. I'm making it really simple." She flips the card over so I can't read it. "Just listen to me first, okay?"

I nod again.

"Here's the thing, Dan. I want you to focus on taking care of the work stuff. Get yourself on that flight tomorrow, keep that job for another two days. And if you have time, look into this Stanislau place. But that's it."

"But what about—"

"Don't worry about the other stuff. I'm handling it."

"All of it?"

"All of it."

"I mean, how—"

"Dan," she soothes. "Just worry about those two things. First, your job. Second, Stanislau. That's it."

"What about all the other stuff?"

"I'm handling it," she says.

"Baldy and the shovel guy?"

Stoic face. "Handling it."

"Employment lawyer?"

"Handling it, and I won't be going to Crazy Larry for a reference."

"But what about the geeks? How am I supposed to find out why they want me to tape Fitzroy in Florida?"

"I'm looking into that," she says, unnervingly calm. "All you need to do is focus on your two items."

I can do that. I really think I can. It's like someone's taken a sack of sand off my shoulders.

"I feel guilty."

"Don't feel guilty," she says. "Feel smart."

I nod, but I don't feel smart.

"We need to work as a team, Dan. None of this macho I'll-do-it-myself crap, okay?"

How I wish I have what Kate has—that ability to multi-task effectively, to be a field general in a crisis, to make valid assessments and set a course of action. I could live a thousand years and never be able to handle so much so gracefully—to be the badass that is Kate.

The kitchen door opens, and I jolt.

"Relax." It's Rod coming in from the garage, holding a black metallic box no bigger than a deck of cards. "After finding that guy in there, thought I better scour the garage."

"Shovel Man?"

He nods. "Looks like he came in through the window. Found him on his knees near Kate's minivan."

I nod to the device in Rod's hand. "What'd you find?"

"This was under the right front fender." He flips it over, brings it closer so we can look. "Magnetic plate on this side." Flips it over again, shows us a rubber protuberance. "Antenna on this side."

Kate and I glance at each other. The first thing I think is, *Remote-controlled bomb*, and a cold chill hits my extremities.

Kate says, "Tracking device."

"Exactly," Rod says.

Oh.

"Mommy, Mommy." Harry darts in, slides to a stop in his socks. "Crazy Larry is throwing his buck knife again."

"Okay, honey."

Hopeful eyes. "But don't you wanna see? We always watch."

"Not today, honey. We're trying to figure some things out, okay?"

He slumps his shoulders, turns, and mopes back to the front room.

"We hand it over to Bryant?" I ask. "See if the cops can lift some prints off it?"

Kate and Rod look at each other and shrug. "That guy sounds like he's more interested in getting rich," Kate says. "Plus, Rod's prints are all over it now."

Long silence, and then Rod says, "Whoever is behind this, it would be great to send them in the wrong direction."

"What do you mean?"

Kate says, "He means, put that thing under someone else's car."

Kate and Rod exchange smiles.

"But someone who can handle the heat."

"Can't be you, Rod. You're gonna have Kate and the boys at your place, and I don't want them near there."

He's squinting at the floor, thinking, mumbling, "I know, I know."

Kate says, "It should be someone who lives nearby, so they think I'm still here."

Outside, a loud thwack. In the front room, Harry says, "Whoa."

We join him by the front window.

Crazy Larry is in his Speedo and flip-flops—nothing else. He's sunken his buck knife so deep into the garage door that he has to plant a foot on the door and yank with two hands to get it out.

Rod whispers, "Damn."

Kate nods to the Chevy Malibu station wagon parked on Larry's curb. It's old but pristine. "And that's his car."

We all glance at each other, smile, and look back at Larry. He yanks the knife loose, turns around, takes ten steady paces, then pivots and heaves the knife back into the door.

"We'll need someone for diversion," Rod says. "And a runner."

"You're sure you're okay with this?"

"No, I'm *not* okay with this. But that's life."

"Then you don't have to do it, Kate. No one's making you do it. It's just that Larry's crazy about you."

"Exactly, which means I have the best chance of distracting him. I don't see another option. We need them to think that thing's on my van. Otherwise, someone will come back."

"We could put it on someone else's car."

"No. Larry's perfect. Look at the way he throws that thing."

"But you can change your mind, Kate, and just let Rod and me do it."

"It's fine. Just signal me once Harry makes the plant."

"Like I said, put your cell in your back pocket, and I'll text you when Harry's done his thing. Just put it on vibrate."

"Just promise me you'll watch Harry like a hawk. I swear, Dan—something happens to that kid . . ."

"Nothing's gonna happen to him. Rod and I will be watching the whole time."

She holds up a skirt. "What about this?"

"Try the jeans. Let him see your figure a little."

"That's disgusting."

"And be sure you get him with his back to the car."

"I see that knife, I'm out of there."

"Of course. They're on knife watch right now."

"How in the hell did I ever get involved with you?"

"Have you thought of a conversation starter?"

"Dan, these jeans are the conversation starter. All I have to do is stand there."

"Well, don't do that."

"Of course not."

"Just don't encourage him."

"Maybe I should tell him I have a boil on my back."

"Don't do that. He'll want to lance it."

"With the buck knife."

Harry slides into our room, his blue eyes like saucers. "He put the knife away."

Rod and I watch from the front room as Kate and Harry walk across the street.

Crazy Larry puts his book down, rises from his spot on

the porch, and adjusts his Speedo. The closer they get to his porch, the more Larry straightens.

She's wearing a tight T-shirt with her jeans. Her hair is blown.

Rod nudges me, says, "Hot mama."

"Tell me about it," I whisper.

Larry pushes his chest out and cocks his head, smiling. Forcing it. You can tell he's actually a little nervous. Imagine that, someone making Crazy Larry nervous.

Her back is to us.

He's facing the station wagon, staring at her. "Turn him around, Kate," Rod whispers. "C'mon."

Kate tosses her hair back and walks toward the driveway, motioning to the garage door, looking back at him with a big smile.

Larry stares at her ass.

She pivots and motions to the door, pointing to the knife marks, making some comment with a big smile.

Damn, what an actor.

Larry turns to face her. Finally.

Kate motions to Harry, as if she's telling him to go home.

"C'mon, buddy," I whisper.

Harry heads straight for the station wagon.

"Look at him," Rod gushes. "What a little stud."

I prepare to send the text, my thumb rubbing Send.

Kate puts a hand on her hip, smiles as Larry imitates throwing a knife.

Harry darts to the back of the Malibu, reaches into his back pocket, and pulls out the tracking device.

Kate runs a hand through her hair, steps closer to Larry, luring him in.

Harry holds the device, looks around.

"C'mon, buddy. Quick."

Kate smiles, gazes into the air, like she's saying, *What am I gonna do?*

Larry baby-steps closer.

Harry looks at the device, gazes back at Larry.

"C'mon."

Kate pushes a hip out, throws her arms up, laughs.

Harry kneels down, plants the device under the Malibu's back fender, and bolts.

I send the text.

Larry cocks his head and turns to face Harry, who's already standing a safe distance from the Malibu, hands at his side, feet together, scared shitless.

I think, *I am the worst parent in North America.*

And I'm out the door.

Larry is staring at Harry like he's a nasty math problem.

From my porch, I wave and holler, "Larry!" like he's a long-lost friend.

Larry's still staring at Harry, steps toward him. Kate follows.

I trot across the street, make it to Harry's side, pick him up. He grabs me and holds on for dear life.

Kate stands behind Larry, hand on her forehead.

Larry is staring at the back end of the Malibu.

"Hey, Larry."

Still staring at the Malibu. "Your child interrupted my time with your wife."

That sounds so . . .

Kate says, "I was just telling Larry about my uncle Bo who used to throw knives, only he had a cabin in the woods."

Larry says, "And I heard something." He gazes at the sky. "A click."

Harry buries his face into my shoulder.

Rod emerges from our house. Nursing a glass of carrot juice. So casual. But prepared to turn Larry into a pile of bloody, cocoa-butter-scented jelly.

Kate says, "I think Harry may have stumbled and nicked your car." She walks over to the back of the Malibu, makes a big production of searching for any nicks on the wagon's original, mud-brown paint job. "I don't see any marks, though. Guess we lucked out this time."

Larry looks like he's listening for a faint sound. "But I heard a click." Squints into space. "It sounded almost metallic."

Crap.

Harry lifts his head off my shoulder, announces, "It was my mythical creatures ring," and brandishes a fat plastic ring Rod gave him last year.

What a kid.

Larry turns to Harry and says, "I don't like mythical creatures."

I give Harry a squeeze. "Okay, Larry. I hear ya. Sorry about that. I'm gonna give this kid a snack and head on out."

Kate says, "I should go, too."

Larry stops her. Says, "Not yet." His voice is so cool and even. "You were telling me about your uncle Bo."

Five

At work, I decide to tackle the toughest thing first. I drop in on my old instant-messaging friend, Anne.

Anne is long and lean, sandy-blond hair down to the middle of her back. Freckles on her face. Big blue eyes. Pretty woman, for sure, my kind of look and all that, but ever since we cooled it—came down from the insanity and the high that came with it—I can barely look at her. She is the symbol of my seediest, darkest side—a reminder of my worst potential realized.

And I have to see her daily.

When I get to her cube, I gesture that I need to speak with her.

"You okay?" she whispers, scanning my face.

"Just come with me."

The FlowBid facility is designed to stroke the ego and retain employees. It's 2008, after all; the dot-com bust of just a few years back is already a distant memory. These days, the skyrocketing real estate market and the new frenzy around tech companies like FlowBid and Google and Facebook have pumped more cash into the Valley than ever. Add the funds pouring in from frothy investors, skyrocketing user statistics, and astronomic NASDAQ gains, and you have the recipe for the typical 2008 Silicon Valley workplace: a hip interior design with cement floors and exposed air ducts, bottles of Pellegrino in every conference room, an on-campus masseur to rub away stress, a free concierge service that will find you anything from a new nanny to concert tickets, heavily discounted on-site dry cleaning, free lunches at the cafeteria, and a world-class fitness center with a staff of six.

Anne and I find an empty conference room.

"I'm sorry, but someone's got hold of those IMs."

Her face darkens and her brow crinkles. She looks down and covers her eyes with a trembling hand.

"Ohmyfuckinggod. *Ohmyfuckinggod.*"

I flatten my hand on the table. "But I think it's gonna be okay."

She's taking big breaths.

"Seriously, Anne."

She looks up. "Is it Kate?"

"God, no."

"Someone here?"

I pause.

"Well, sort of."

"Fitzroy? Is it Fitzroy? It's Fitzroy, isn't it? You should see the way he looks at me." She shudders. "Please tell me it's not Fitzroy."

"It's not Fitzroy."

Huge sigh of relief.

"It's—"

The door opens, and it's Janice from Finance, poking her head in. She's wearing a gray blazer with this scarf thing wrapped around her neck, and her hair is paralyzed by a gallon of Aqua Net. Classic Janice.

"Dan?" she whispers.

I clench my jaw, say nothing.

"I still need to talk to you about putting those P6s into the—"

"Janice," I say through gritted teeth. "Can you tell that I am having a closed-door conversation here?"

She looks at me, then at Anne, and pulls her head back, shuts the door.

Anne says, "It's not someone from Mark's office or something, is it?" Mark is her husband.

"No, no. It's these guys you don't know. I don't know them, either, really."

"Guys?" Anne huffs. "As in *guys*, plural?"

"Afraid so."

"Dan, I just can't . . . Holy shit." She begins to cry. "This is my marriage."

"I'm sorry, Anne."

"Who are they?"

"A bunch of laid-off IT guys."

Her voice cracks. "So a bunch of guys are reading all that stuff about my—"

"Anne, listen to me. It's not going to get out. These guys

just want a favor from me, and I'm gonna do everything I can to give it to them. I should be able to."

She sniffles and shakes her head in disbelief.

"I just thought I should let you know, in case the whole thing blows up."

"Blows up?"

"In case I can't deliver what they want."

"And what is that?"

"I can't tell you."

"And if you can't deliver it, they do what?"

I pause, trying to come up with a gentle way to tell her. "Well, they claim . . . They say they'd send the IMs to everyone at FlowBid."

Anne goes pale, takes some big breaths.

"That's not gonna happen," I say. "I'm ninety-nine-point-nine-nine-nine percent sure I can handle this, and they'll destroy the records once I deliver my end of the bargain. But if something screwy does happen and they do send those IMs out, you should be prepared."

She scans the room. "They want money?"

"No."

"Because if they want money, I can help with that."

"No, it's something else. And I can't tell you."

We sit there a long moment, thinking about it.

"Anne, I'm really sorry I brought you into this."

"No . . ." She looks away, takes a big breath, and exhales. "No, this is my bad, too. The way I remember it, *I* was the one who started it."

"It was crazy, that's for sure."

She sighs, looks down. "I love him, Dan. I love Mark with all my heart."

"I know. And I love Kate."

"We're just bad news, you and me. We just shouldn't be around each other."

"Maybe." I look away and mumble. "I don't know."

She says, "It was such a slippery slope."

She's right. The whole thing unraveled so quickly, and easily—from friendly chitchat to harmless flirting to full-blown porn chat in a matter of days.

"We made a big mistake," I say. "But we did stop way before the big no-no."

"As if that would matter to Mark or Kate." She closes her eyes. "Those IMs get out, I guarantee everyone will think we were doing it."

"Well, it's not going to. I'm on it."

She sniffles, glances at me. "I want to know who they are, Dan. I have a right."

"I don't even have their names yet. When I get them, I'll let you know."

She covers her eyes again. "Fuck."

"Have faith, Anne."

She looks up, examines my face. "I think this finally did it."

"Did what?"

She makes a look like she smells something foul. "Killed my crush on you."

I force a chuckle. "Aw . . ."

She gets up to leave. "Don't take it personally when I go back to my desk and remove you from my IM list."

"You haven't done that already? Damn."

She walks to the door, and I don't even take the opportunity to glance at her butt.

"Oh, yeah," she says, and turns back to me, her eyes shaky. "What?"

"Do you think I could take her?"

"Take her?" I frown. "Who?"

"Kate? If she comes after me, do you think I could take her?"

I don't have the heart to tell her.

Time to unload the peas. The bag has been defrosting, and my crotch is starting to get wet. I take a stall in the men's room, pull the bag out. I don't want to walk out of here with a bag of peas in my clutch, so I rip it open and turn to the toilet. They spill out, and it sounds like a giant rabbit on the toilet releasing a thousand pellets into the water.

I hear something, stop.

Someone's at a urinal.

Fuck.

I wait awhile, hoping he'll finish, but Christ, he's taking forever. *Fuck it, I don't have time for vanity*, I think, and recommence the pouring: more rapid-fire kerplunks, followed by a few stragglers, which sound even worse.

I flush the toilet, realize I should've been flushing all along, then fold the pea bag and slip it into my back pocket. Now it's a matter of waiting the urinator out.

The urinal flushes. *Finally.*

I stand at my stall door, spy through the crack. It's this guy from Web marketing—big jaw, bigger nose, small eyes. Can't remember his name.

He looks into the mirror, sees my feet at the stall door, scans up and meets my gaze—looks away quickly.

Major awkwardness.

Only one thing to do now, unless I want to be known as the guy who spies at people from inside the stalls. I open the door and step out. "Hey, man."

Scrubbing his hands hard. "Hey."

I take a sink on the opposite end. "What's new in the Web cave?"

"Just manic, as always. Was here till three A.M." He glances at my shoes. "You okay?"

"Me?"

He straightens, pulls a paper towel, glances back at the stall. "Just hoping you're okay."

"Oh, I'm fine. It's just that I had a minor procedure yesterday and—"

He waves for me to stop. "No worries, man. You don't need to explain."

"No, that was just a bag—"

"No sweat, man." He turns and heads out the door. "Take it easy."

That went well. Wonder how long it will take before half the Web team has heard that Dan Jordan is crapping mass volumes of pellets and spying on people from bathroom stalls. If only I had the time to care.

I hobble toward Fitzroy's office until Danzig from PR comes up behind me and grabs my shoulders, scaring the hell out of me. "You gotta see this," he says. "The new guy's putting on a show in the break room."

"Wish I had time for it."

"You won't believe it, Danny. The guy's eating a rat on a stick."

That gets me. "Rat?"

"Like a kid at the fair polishing off a corn dog."

"A *rat*? You sure?"

Danzig leans in; his breath is like sour milk. "Dude, it has legs. And the new guy's eating it. Fitzroy's new genius."

I press forward, toward Fitzroy's office. "That's some trippy shit."

Finally, Danzig says, "Ask Fitzroy about that guy, dude."

People always want me to do things like that, but I never do. I hate office politics. Plus, the minute I start passing along comments from Fitzroy is the minute my reputation tanks.

Danzig grabs my shoulder, stops me. "At least come check out the new guy. You'll never see anything like it again."

He has a point.

The new guy is, indeed, sitting in the break room poking his tongue through a rat on a stick. Just like Danzig said, and it's pretty disgusting. Carlie from Legal walks in, gives him a double take, drops her Swedish meatballs, and trots away. We can hear her retching in the restroom.

We watch him from afar, through the glass. And I suddenly wonder if this new guy possibly could have something to do with the upheaval in my life. I mean, what are the odds of all these crazy things happening at once?

"It's a stunt," Danzig says. "He's trying to psych us out."

"Maybe," I say. "Maybe not."

"Oh, c'mon, you think he just loves rat?"

More people join us. Gasps abound.

"Well," I say, "in Africa, a field rat is a real treat. Millions of people eat them."

"But this guy isn't African."

"So you're saying only Africans can eat rats?"

Carol from the second floor says, "But Fitzroy loves him."

Barbara from Analytics joins us and squints into the break room. "That's Fitzroy's new guy." She watches him. "Some kind of rugged genius."

Danzig snaps, "Genius? Who said that?"

"Well . . ." Barbara watches. "They say Fitzroy loves him." And then after a pause she asks, "What's he eating?"

"Rat."

"Rat?" Barbara straightens her blazer and clears her throat. "We'll see about that."

She charges in. We all look at each other and decide to follow.

"So you're the new guy," she says, hands on her hips.

The new guy looks up, licks his teeth, and grins. "Yeah," he says, nice and slow—lazy-California-surfer style. "That's right."

Barbara seems unfazed by the glistening rat skeleton on the napkin in front of them. "Where are you from?"

The new guy pulls his head back, grins. "All over."

Barbara frowns. "No, I mean, where were you working before this?"

The new guy grins wider. They're nice teeth. "Long story."

I like this guy. It's like he's saying, *Fuck you, lady*, smiling nice and easy the whole way.

Standing behind me, Danzig must be feeling brave. He leans in and says, "So what's the deal with the rat?"

New guy turns and looks up at Danzig. Long silence.

"Well . . ." The new guy waits a long beat. "What do you think?"

Danzig studies him. His voice is high from the stress. "They say you're some out-of-the-box thinker."

He smiles and nods, like he's saying, *Okay, man, it's cool. I hear you.*

Barbara bursts out, "What are you going to do here?"

Slowly, the new guy turns to her. "Are you familiar with the California stink beetle?"

Barbara squints. "What?"

"Well, the stink beetle can thrive in some of the world's harshest environments—like the world's toughest deserts— even though it's this big, juicy insect. So the question one might have is, *What gives?* How can this black beetle thrive in a place like that?"

Barbara is still squinting.

"So here's the deal." The new guy straightens. "The deal is, the stink beetle innovates. At dawn, it 'drinks' from the moist air simply by positioning its rear into the breeze and opening its anus." His smile is gone. "Now that's innovation."

He looks up at Barbara, an eyebrow emerging from behind the shades. "So the thing is, maybe it's time to open your own anus to the moisture that breezes over you every day."

Barbara is frozen. Speechless.

Danzig says, "So it stinks or something?"

The new guy turns to him. "You fuck with the stink bee-tle, it'll stand on its head and expel some seriously nasty gas."

Danzig mouths the words.

The new guy folds his arms. "Yeah, I seriously dig the stink beetle."

And I'm realizing: I *do* need to ask Fitzroy about this guy.

Stephen Fitzroy's office is at the end of what we call Executive Row. Anytime you visit, you must walk past a series of executive offices and admin stations. It's a long hallway, and it's always an awkward journey—like walking up the center aisle of church as everyone watches, nodding as you bring the sacraments to Fitzroy's altar.

Fitzroy's admin, Sharon, is at her station right outside his office. She's in her late fifties, with vibrant green eyes, a square chin, and short, salt-and-pepper hair in big curls. You wouldn't guess it by looking at her, so unassuming and gentle, but she puts all the other admins to shame with her world-class speed and grace.

When I approach, Sharon gives me the please-help-me look.

"What?"

She motions with her head, whispers. "She won't leave."

I look in. It's Beth Gavin, Fitzroy's executive assistant, talking with the boss. I roll my eyes, mumble to Sharon, "What's new?"

Beth Gavin does everything she can to be attached to

Fitzroy's hip. I've learned what a big deal it is for some folks, to be there constantly with the top dog. *Check me out, look at who I spend my day with.* As long as Beth is with Fitzroy, she has access to a wealth of information and power—she's *in the in*, as they say, and she has the opportunity to influence Fitzroy. One of her best-loved sports is giving the boss her color commentary on just about everyone—and it's usually not pretty. When you realize how avidly she feeds this bullshit to one of the most powerful people in the Valley—paralyzing careers along the way—you realize just how dangerous she can be.

Can you tell I don't like Beth Gavin?

I've watched her misrepresent people and their contributions. I've seen her blame her mistakes on them. I've watched her seize a quiet moment to drop in a comment to Fitzroy about someone else's screwup—always careful to make her tattling seem incidental.

And I've been there during concalls, when it's just the three of us in his office and some poor bastard in Sales is talking on the Polycom, and Beth mutes the speakerphone and says, "This guy's an idiot."

Fitzroy looks at her. "Really?"

"Big time."

Happens every day.

Sharon says, "Will you go in there and break them up? I need to get him in the sedan by one."

"Of course. Where's he going?"

"San Diego for a quick meeting, then back up in time for dinner."

Classic Fitzroy. The man uses the jet to achieve feats that

otherwise would be impossible—day trips to locales as far out as Tennessee, thanks to one of the easiest, most luxurious ways to travel.

"Speaking of the jet," I say, "do you think I could get on that flight tomorrow to Tampa?"

"Shouldn't be a problem. It's just him and Beth tomorrow."

"I'd appreciate that."

"No problem." Her brows wrinkle as she thinks about it. "I thought you said he wouldn't need you on this one."

"Yeah, but now I think I should join him. There's some new content in this one, and he's probably gonna have some questions."

"No problem." She jots a note on a piece of paper. "I'll add you to the manifest."

"Thanks, Sharon."

"You need a room at the Grand Hyatt?"

"That'd be great, Sharon. Thanks."

"Wheels up at nine-thirty."

"I'll be there at nine," I say, and pause. "And, oh, one more thing. Do you know Janice?"

"Janice?" She seems surprised. "From Finance?"

"Exactly."

"Oh yeah." She rolls her eyes. "The tunnel-vision lady."

"Yup," I say. "So you know what I'm dealing with."

"What's she doing?"

I lean in and whisper. "For some reason, she thinks I'm the one who's supposed to fill all these data points into all these reports—something about putting P6s into an FOD. I don't even know what the hell she's talking about."

"Lord."

"And she says—get this—that *Beth* told her I'm the guy for this."

Sharon blows out a loud gust and types Janice's name into her computer. "Let me get her number."

"Thanks, Sharon."

"This kind of stuff needs to stop."

"I know."

"We need you focused on his speeches. You're working too much as it is."

"I know." I look down at my feet, wait a moment. "I'm sorry to even bug you about this."

She looks up at me, eyes hard. "You need to stick up for yourself, Danny."

"I'm going to. I'll bring it up on the flight tomorrow."

She dials, waits, looks up at me. "Yes, this is Sharon in Stephen Fitzroy's office."

I imagine Janice's eyes when she picks up the phone. Most people at FlowBid have *never* gotten a call from Fitzroy's office—have never even met the guy. I'll bet Janice's heartbeat just jumped from seventy-two to one-forty-four.

"I'm calling to let you know that Stephen needs Dan Jordan to join him on a trip tomorrow for a critical speech. . . . Yes, and so we need you to find someone else who can do those reports for you."

She looks up at me, smiles. I bow to her in a silent *thank you*. I can almost hear Janice backpedaling through the phone.

"Yes, well, he's very busy supporting Stephen."

She listens.

"Yes, well, maybe you and Beth had a misunderstanding. Dan is Stephen's speechwriter, and you're asking him to do data entry for Finance." She glances up at me, purses her lips, listening. "Beth told you that? Well, nothing could be further from the truth. . . . No, no apology necessary. . . . Okay, thanks, Janice."

Sharon hangs up, gives me a motherly look, nods into Fitzroy's office. "You need to find a way to call her off."

I nod. I'm pissed, but I hate confrontations. There's something building at the base of my throat, and I can't tell if it's anger or anxiety or both.

Sharon says, "Not tomorrow on the jet. Right now. You need to stick up for yourself. For your own self-esteem. Don't let it go another hour." She nods toward Fitzroy's office. "Now's your chance."

"Okay."

"And get her out of there so we can get him to the jet center."

I square myself to his office door, trying to summon the spirit of Rod Stone, the Big Fighter. If Rod were here, he'd swat me over the head, finger-push me in the chest, ask, *What the fuck is wrong with you, Jordan? Putting up with assholes like this? Haven't you learned anything after all these years?* I can almost see him in front of me, his jaw jutting out, his temples throbbing.

Time to get out of the comfort zone.

You saw Beth Gavin on the street, your jaw would hit your chest. On paper, she's gorgeous. Enormous blue eyes, high cheekbones, full lips, long snow-white hair, silky skin, legs till next year.

And yet, midway through my first day with Beth Gavin, I was kind of turned off. Not sure why—I usually find strong, smart women sexy—but I'd say it has something to do with the fact that she seems so one-dimensional, as if there's nothing there beyond ambition. She's not passionate about Finance, like Janice; she's not passionate about finding a better way for people to connect, like the engineers; she's not passionate about making deals, like our sales teams. Beth is passionate about herself, and that's her problem.

Beth once told me she prefers job candidates who are "forward-looking," as in, driven to get lots of promotions, to earn tons of money, and to lead larger and larger groups of people. These people are like her, she said: hungry, willing to bust their asses to do whatever it takes to get ahead.

Don't get me wrong. I like people who bust their asses, and I like people who want to succeed. But I prefer them to be busting their asses and succeeding because of their love of something other than their personal advancement—whether it's Rod's love for mixed martial arts, or Steve Martin's passion for humor, or Brad Mehldau's love of the piano, or even Janice's love for finance. Point is, what drives their success is their belief in something else—something other than themselves.

The way I see it, rabid ambition intoxicates your moral equilibrium. It fuels bad behavior, encourages you to screw your friends and colleagues, and justifies your lies and misrepresentations. These people want their promotions so bad they're capable of doing anything—like throwing you under the bus or smearing you—to advance themselves.

So I have a hard time trusting ambitious people.

There, I said it.

I take another deep breath and step in.

Stephen Fitzroy's office is enormous—windows everywhere, looking out on a sweeping view of rolling hills. He's slouching in an armchair; Beth is on the couch, legs crossed at the knees. From the stack of papers on the coffee table, it looks like they're prepping for sales meetings he'll have in Tampa.

Beth is trying to soothe him. "You're the reason. Everyone knows it."

Fitzroy tightens, looks away. "Which is why *Fortune* is doing another profile on another member of my staff?"

"No," Beth says. "Everyone knows it's you, Stephen. Everyone knows you're the reason this place is white-hot. A *Fortune* story on one someone else won't change that."

Fitzroy seems satisfied. He looks up, raises his eyebrows. "Danny Boy!"

Beth gives me the slightest of smirks, glances back at Fitzroy as if they're in on some joke.

"Hey," I say, big smile, "your new guy's eating a rat in the break room."

Fitzroy lights up. "Perfect. That's perfect." He looks up at me, eyes hopeful. "Are people freaking out?"

"Oh yeah."

"That's great. We need to knock folks out of their comfort zones, Danny."

"Who is he?"

He waves away the thought. "I have a question for you."

Beth looks away, tries to suppress a smile.

"Okay."

Fitzroy snatches a sheet off the coffee table, stands up, and brings it in close, invading my space. It's hard to focus on the drawing on the sheet—some rudimentary scribbling of a tiered pyramid—when I'm getting this up-close view of those bloodshot eyes, those dark teeth, that lifeless skin, that pink scalp with its odd collection of stray hairs and plugs.

"What you see here, Danny, is a breakdown of the general population."

"Okay."

Fitzroy leans in, coffee breath hitting me hard. "Down here at the bottom of the pyramid are the morons. I've got it all labeled here so you can follow along."

Beth releases a short laugh, nearly a snort.

"That's the majority of the population, actually." He's saying it in an exaggerated, professorial tone. "And they're hopeless."

He looks at me for a reaction, the sunken eyes bulging and twinkling as he gets near my ear, bringing the breath closer. *Lord, that's nasty.*

"And then, above the morons, we find the schmucks." He exaggerates a turn toward me, still in that instructor voice. "If you're a schmuck, at least you can say you're not a moron."

Beth laughs again and looks away.

"So the glass is half full, you're saying."

"Exactly. Very good, Danny." He bats the sheet with his index finger. "Then, above the schmucks, are the idiots."

"Nice."

"People take offense to the word *idiot*. But the truth is, Danny, you're not doing that bad if you're an idiot. You could be much worse."

I decide to say nothing.

Fitzroy studies my face, mocks concern with bewildered brows. "Are you okay, Danny?"

"Yeah, I'm fine. Don't forget, Sharon has the sedan waiting out front."

"It can wait." He studies my face. "You're not mad or anything, are you?"

I *am* getting mad. I mean, only Fitzroy would come up with a pyramid like this, and only Beth Gavin would find it hilarious. This is how they see the world, how they see me and the others here. But of course, I don't want to register any kind of reaction, because that's what they want—a reaction.

"You have a little cut there." He's looking at it. "Above your right brow there."

"Oh, yeah. Just Harry, getting a little aggressive with his light saber." I think of the shovel coming at my face, feel my body tense for a moment.

"Looks like it's bruising."

"Harry swings hard."

Beth has turned to her notes. Any mention of children usually repels her.

"Okay," he says, straightening up and shaking the paper in front of me. "So you have the idiots."

"I see."

"Which leaves us with the last group, at the top of the pyramid."

I squint at the sheet. "That little dot at the top there?"

Beth laughs hard. Fitzroy shows his coffee teeth, giggling. "What does that say?"

"Leaders." Fitzroy is so proud of his little comedy routine, puffing his chest out, smiling so hard he's showing gums. "These are the leaders."

I force an embarrassed smile. "Interesting view of the world."

He loses the smile. "Realistic view of the world."

I give him my subdued oh-yeah? look.

"It's that tiny group of leaders at the top that make the world go around, Danny."

"Hmmm. Interesting."

"Not interesting, Danny. Realistic."

"Okay."

Beth sitting there looking at me, her eyes gleaming.

"So the question I have for you is, where are you on this pyramid?"

I glance at Beth. She's so calm and comfortable there on the couch, watching me with amusement.

"I don't know. Haven't really given it any thought, Stephen."

Of course, I know where Fitzroy and Beth place themselves on the pyramid. I wish I could bring myself to ask them what happened to the missing layers—the liars, cheats, assholes. Not to mention all the honorable people.

"Where are you, Danny?"

I look at the ground, feeling my anger rise. "Well, I'm not a moron or an idiot or a schmuck."

When I look up, they're exchanging glances.

Maybe this is what I needed, this fucking pyramid routine to fuel my anger, push me into action. I turn to Beth, feel my face harden.

"By the way," I say, "why do you keep sending people like Janice my way? All these people who say you've told them I can do all this data-entry bullshit."

Beth loses what little color she does have. "Huh?" She wasn't expecting this. "What? Janice?"

I stare at her. "Yeah, Janice from Finance. She's been bugging me incessantly about these data-entry clusterfuck projects, says I'm supposed to handle them."

Long silence. Fitzroy takes an exaggerated step back, looks at Beth like he's saying, *Interesting. You're gonna take that from him?*

"Which doesn't make any sense," I add, "since I'm Stephen's speechwriter and I'm sure you don't think I should be taking time away from his needs."

Her face turns cherry-red. She says, "You said you wanted to do new—"

"Beth, it needs to stop." I look over at Fitzroy, his eyes bulging as he watches his usually amiable speechwriter giving Beth Gavin hell. "I've got more than enough to do with my real responsibilities, and I don't need people coming to me for these time wasters. It's wasting everyone's time."

"I didn't know what—"

"Beth . . ." I try not to look mad, force my eyes to soften a little. I just need to seem firm and in control. "No more."

Beth looks away and mumbles.

Fitzroy looks surprised, almost impressed. "Well . . ." he says, and pauses. "I like this side of you, Danny. You're already moving up the pyramid there."

Whatever, asshole.

Sharon pokes her head in, looks at Fitzroy. "You need to get to the jet center."

Fitzroy gathers his stuff, shuts down his laptop. "We're witnessing the birth of the new Danny, Sharon." He grabs his cell, slides his laptop into his briefcase, glances at the shell-shocked Beth. "And I think he's rendered Beth speechless."

"While she's speechless," I say, grinning, "I wanted to let you know Sharon's added me to the flight tomorrow."

He turns to look at me. "You're coming to Tampa?"

I nod and shrug. "It's a new deck—I put some new notes in there, so I thought we should probably go over the speech on the way out. That way I can take care of all the AV stuff for you, too."

He makes for the door. "Excellent."

Beth says, "I can do that, Stephen. He doesn't need to come for that." Vintage Beth move.

He never looks back, just says, "You guys figure it out."

I meet Beth's squint and say softly, "I think we just did."

So this is the problem.

People see me walking and talking with Fitzroy, imagine me whizzing around on the jet and all that. They see me in his office. They can almost see me and Fitzroy walking into some fancy European hotel lobby, encircled by a gorgeous security detail. They can imagine us crouched over his coffee table as

I sketch out the latest crazy idea on a scrap of paper. They can see me sitting in on board meetings, where big decisions are made.

The problem is, they haven't a clue.

I'm more of a parlor boy: a lackey who crafts speeches and ghostwrites op-eds, a guy who isn't above anything when it comes to supporting the boss. The man wants me fetch him a coffee? No problem. The man needs slide-deck work that's so irritating it would drive Gandhi to road rage? Fine, bring it. The man needs me to write up some thoughts on the future of the Internet and then recede into the shadows of the jet? My pleasure. I do that well.

Then I go home in my fourteen-year-old econo car.

Has the man ever asked me to join a FlowBid board meeting? Never.

Do I care? Absolutely not.

You see, I never was all that concerned about the prestige of the job. It was just a job I was qualified to do; it found me and promptly sank its hooks into my flesh. Not the other way around. Some people have a hard time understanding that. They're usually the status and prestige fiends—the ones who are taken not by the fact I might be a straight shooter who does good work, but by the fact that I work with the living legend, Stephen Fitzroy. In this culture of status, pedigree, and over-achievement, I confound them.

Take George in Corporate Development, who stops me in the hall as I hobble back to my cube.

He hollers, "What's new in FitzroyLand?"

"I don't know what you're talking about."

"Sure you do. You guys know all that stuff."

"No, I don't."

"They're thinking about another stock split, right?"

This is news to me—not that George would believe it.

"Don't know a thing, George."

He smiles but kind of grits his teeth, mumbles, looking me over. "Sure you do."

If it were simply a matter of George overestimating my involvement, I could forgive the man. But with this guy, it's more than that. He has grossly overestimated his own abilities and emotional intelligence, which means that people like me must stand there and watch as his muscular ego 'roids out on a daily basis—veins popping, pecs twitching, eyes bugging, muscle grease spraying onto our faces. With him, the conversation always seems to settle on the same topics: how smart he is, how superior his education is, how successful his father is back East, how gifted and talented his son is. So it's no surprise that he thinks I have the dream job he deserves—me, a state school kid, hanging out with Fitzroy, wasting the opportunity of a lifetime.

"How are the boys?" he asks. "Your oldest having a good time in first grade?"

Sure, I think. *He's majoring in planting tracking devices under station wagons.*

"He's doing fine, George. I better get go—"

"Well, you should see Maximo. I swear, he has his teacher stumped. I mean, he's bored, really." George is smiling at the ceiling, whispering, "I told the teacher Maximo was reading at the third-grade level in preschool. And now he's in first grade.

And math? The kid's *insane* with math. I mean, he just needs to be challenged." George blows a hard gust, frowns at the floor. "They just don't understand him. Those aggression issues? Just 'cause he's not being challenged."

I start to walk away. "Okay, George. I gotta—"

He hollers, "Your little guy doing T-ball?"

"Yeah, but I—"

"You guys having fun?"

I stop, take a breath, and turn. "Harry's okay. He's still a little apprehensive."

"Is he taking pitches yet?"

"Oh, nah. It's T-ball. The whole team is—"

He waves his arms, stops me. "Maximo is a little beast out there. He started taking pitches in the first inning of the first game. You know, and this is *T-ball*." George smiles at the ceiling again. "So some of the parents get a little worked up, say Maximo's going to make the others feel like *they* should try taking pitches, too. Told me to cool it a little, stop bringing the private trainer to games." He laughs. "But I really think the real issue is that everyone should know their limitations."

"Okay, George, I'll see you—"

"Or, I should say, their kids' limitations."

"Yeah, I know. Okay—"

"Reminds me of when I played ball at Yale. Where did you go again?"

He knows the answer. He just likes to hear me say it.

"State."

"Oh, right. Do they have athletics at places like that?"

I start to walk away. "Okay, man. I gotta get ready for this speech."

"Hey, Dan," he hollers. "You heard about Fitzroy's new guy? He's brilliant. Be sure to schedule some time with him."

My back to him, walking down the hall. "Okay, George."

He's nearly shouting. "Smart, smart guy, Danny. He ate a rat at lunch."

One thing I've learned about folks at FlowBid—everything is about being smart. Hell, I admire smart; don't get me wrong. Smart is good. But I really think it should be about more than smart. Shouldn't it be about *developing and executing* great ideas? Shouldn't it be about being decent? For that matter, shouldn't it be about results? Maybe it bugs me that half these people, despite all their Web-hype luster and smarts, never quite figured out how to turn in even one quarter of profitability at the start-ups they came from.

Hell, who am I fooling? At FlowBid, who's thinking about profits when everyone is telling you how brilliant you are, how bright your future is? Who needs cost control when millions of users just keep pouring in? And who needs modesty and common sense when you have a never-ending supply of irrational investors pumping more and more money into your stock as they announce to the world that you're a living genius—which only spikes the share price higher?

I'm just reaching my cube when I hear a voice:

"There he is."

It's Tracy, the events manager who works across the aisle. Ever since she returned from maternity leave three weeks ago, she has worn nothing but black. Tracy would much rather stay at home with her newborn boy and three-year-old daughter.

She sounds sad, almost muted. "Spend some time with the family this morning?"

I stop, glance at her. "Sort of." My crotch pinches in pain. "I'm a little under the weather."

"Kate can take care of you." She lets out a little laugh. "Being home and all, she has the time."

I hear this all the time.

"Not really," I say. "Kate is pretty swamped with the boys."

She closes her eyes. "It's not work to me. I'd stay home in a second, if I could."

What can I say to that? I bite my lip.

"You guys are so lucky," she says, shaking her head.

God, I'm sick of hearing this. Fortunate? Sure. But lucky?

Lucky for being at the right place at the right time, putting me just a few days from completing an insane cash-out? For sure.

Lucky for being able to keep one parent home these past six years? No way.

We didn't get lucky. We made choices.

We chose my beater Toyota over Tracy's $65,000, fully-loaded Audi sedan with microclimates and leather seats. We chose our tiny house with paper-thin walls and old appliances over Tracy's Menlo Park compound with copper roof gutters, two Nordic dishwashers, a rec room, a pool house, and a small fortune in Pottery Barn appointments. We chose camping trips to Mount Shasta and Big Basin over Tracy's wintertime pilgrimages to the Maui Ritz Carlton and her monthly weekends at spa resorts in Sonoma, Big Sur, and Mendocino.

"I don't know how you guys do it," she says, still shaking her head.

I count to three, walk over.

"Can you cash out? You know, sell your options and quit?"

She shakes her head, looks away. "I've only been here a year, nothing's vested." She looks up at me, pained. "By the time they vest, God knows if they'll even be worth anything." She pauses. "I'd rather just quit, be home with Holly and Spencer."

"But you can't?"

Shakes her head, real slow. "The budget doesn't flush." She pauses. "Jared just doesn't make enough."

But Jared has a great job. Makes a lot more than me; I'm sure of it.

"So lucky," she whispers.

I've heard all this before, but now I'm finally going to let it out.

"I'm not sure it's luck, Tracy." I give her a moment. "I mean, what about cutting your expenses?"

She acts like she didn't hear me.

"You know, what about your car? What if you sold the Audi? You could buy a commuter car for a fraction of the price."

Total silence.

"Okay, then what about Jared's race boat? Sell that thing and you could stay home for a year at least."

"Nah, Jared would never do that." She sounds even more deflated than before. "Never."

"Then what about that vintage car he has in storage? Sell that."

"Nah, it's like his baby."

I can't stop. I don't want to stop.

"Okay," I say, "well, what about the weekend house in Rio del Mar? Sell that thing and you could quit next week, stay home for ten years, and still have money left for the kids' college."

She looks down, says slowly, "Nah, we've got so much equity in that house, there's no way we can sell now."

"Okay," I say, forcing the upbeat voice, "last suggestion."

She looks up at me, hopeful.

"Sell the Menlo Park house. Downsize. Use the extra cash and reduced living expenses to make up for the loss of your salary."

"Nah, we love that house."

Who wouldn't love that house? *Sunset Magazine* would love that house. That's not the point.

"Well . . ." I mosey back to my cube. "I think I'm out of ideas."

"See," she mopes. "I mean it. You guys are so lucky."

And that's when I realize it. I *am* lucky, very lucky. Just not the way Tracy thinks.

At my desk, I manage to finish the Fitzroy speaker notes and slide deck, print copies to review on the flight tomorrow, and even make a few calls about Stanislau. I feel like I'm a reporter again, calling around and asking questions, trying to get closer to the real story. I get their address in San Francisco easily enough, but it takes a little longer to find someone who's had firsthand experience with the firm. Finally, I reach Barry Devine, a corporate intelligence expert who is recommended to me by a buddy at my old haunt, the *Oakland Tribune*.

Barry runs a consulting boutique not too far from Sand Hill Road in Menlo Park, the main drag for the valley's venture capital and private equity firms. To get through his assistant, I mention, almost unconsciously, that I'm Stephen Fitzroy's speechwriter.

Within ten seconds, Barry's on the line.

"How's Stephen?" he asks, like he knows the guy.

"He's fine, Barry. I really appreciate you taking my call."

"I met him once, after he spoke at the DPN One Conference in Napa."

"Yeah?"

"But I'm sure he doesn't remember me. It was just a few seconds."

People say this all the time. I wish I could say, *I'm sure he'd remember you, he'd totally remember you*, but we'd both know it would be total bull.

"I'd be happy to tell him you said hi, Barry. I'll be with him tomorrow."

"If it comes up, sure, that would be nice. So what can I do for you?"

I explain that I'm interested in Stanislau, that I'm looking for people who've had direct experience with them.

Barry pauses for a moment. "Stephen has his speechwriter doing research on Stanislau?" The disbelief is heavy.

Damn, time to lie. God, I'm such a jerk.

"Well," I say. "Not for his speeches, of course." I pause for effect. "I guess all I can say is that I've been asked to get some third-party testimonials on Stanislau."

He doesn't need to know this action item came from my wife.

"Interesting," Barry says slowly. "Interesting."

"Yes, and we'd really appreciate it if you'd keep our conversation confidential."

"Of course, of course." A trace of glee in his voice. "I'm happy to share some thoughts with you. And if Stephen thinks I could be of service in this matter, I'll be happy to come in for a consultation."

"We'll take that into account, Barry. Thank you."

"So what kind of information are you seeking?"

Hell, I'll take anything, but I can't say that. "Well, as you know, they're kind of mysterious. There's not a lot of information about them."

"Exactly."

"So we're interested in hearing where you think they're the strongest—in terms of their capabilities—and maybe even some background on who does what over there."

And so he tells me about Stanislau, says they excel in corporate intelligence gathering, for which they employ a cadre of top-flight attorneys in the lawful acquisition and evaluation of information affecting the investments of very rich people.

"So, if you've pumped millions of dollars into a small start-up, and you're concerned about anything ranging from their customers to the actual leaders of that start-up and their behavior, this is where Stanislau comes in."

"So they're kind of like the Secret Service for the millionaires and their investments."

He laughs. "Usually, more like billionaires." He pauses. "But if Stephen Fitzroy has you calling for third-party testimonials, you should already know this."

Shit—busted.

Or nearly, anyway. "Oh, well, Stephen may know all this, but I sure don't."

He chuckles. "So, I don't know about the Secret Service. Maybe a little more like the CIA."

Okay, assume the guise of a lackey collecting customer-satisfaction survey results. "So, you generally hear good things from their customers?"

Long silence.

"They're happy?"

"That's the thing, Dan. One rarely knows who their customers are. Ever. That kind of information is heavily guarded."

"So you don't know of anyone—individuals or firms—who've used them?"

"Well, I wonder if it would be better if I came in and discussed this with you and Stephen. I could tell him about my services, and maybe we could talk about how I could help FlowBid with this."

That didn't take long. Already soliciting.

"Well, we're not at that point, Barry, but I really appreciate the offer. Maybe when we get a little further along, Stephen could have you come in." And I'm thinking, *I'll be gone in less than a week, buddy.*

"I'd appreciate even just coming in to tell Stephen about my services, how I can help."

Not a chance in hell. "For sure, Barry. Maybe next month."

"I'd appreciate that," he says, "because I think I know why he has you calling around about Stanislau."

I force a laugh. "Oh yeah?"

"Yeah," he says, pausing a moment. "The only Stanislau client I *do* know about is a group that Stephen knows pretty well."

"Yeah?"

"Knowland, Hill, and Davis," he says. "You know, KHD."

Damn, I do know about KHD. They're only the private equity investment firm that has sunk $2 billion into FlowBid—not to mention getting two of its own executives appointed to our board.

And then it hits me. KHD, a very serious group of people who have invested billions of dollars into my employer, has hired a firm that is screwing with me. A firm that sent a goon like Baldy after me.

I choke on my own spit. *And what about the geeks? Who are they with?*

"You still there, Dan?"

"Oh, yes. I'm just writing all this down. Important background."

"That was news to you, huh?"

I chuckle. "Well . . ." And I let it die. "Just one last question, Barry. In its intelligence work, does Stanislau also engage in covert activities, or attempt to, you know"—I search for delicate language—"correct situations?"

Long pause. "I'm not going to answer that on the phone, Dan."

Aw, man.

Not that I have any time to freak about it.

Seconds after I hang up with Barry, I get a call from High Rider. I know it's him; his voice is unmistakable, like an elf holding his breath.

He squeaks, "Where is he?"

"Who?"

"You know who."

"No, I don't know who."

Tracy glances at me, so I swivel my back to her.

"Our associate? . . . You met him in the van?"

"Oh, Star Trek. The Star Trek guy."

He whispers, "No, the other one."

"Little Red?"

Tightening the words, he says, "Little Red?"

"He never introduced himself, so I just came up with that . . . You know, it just made . . . " *Stop, Danny. Just stop right now.*

Finally, he says, "Yes, that's him."

"And I'm supposed to know where he is?"

Snaps, "He's missing."

"Well, what happened to him?"

"That's what I want to know."

"And you think *I* know?"

He pauses. "I can do it anytime, Dan. I can pull the trigger on all your material, right now."

"Wait—"

"I *will* do it if you don't help us find him. In fact, if something happens to me, your private information goes out. We have a JavaScript all set up, and if I'm unable to update it on a regular basis, the system will distribute your material."

"Listen," I say, "I have no idea where the hell your buddy is."

"What about your people? What about your cage fighter?"

"He's with my wife and kids."

"Which is exactly why—"

He stops himself, and I get the hint I need. Little Red obviously had been trying to locate Kate, Rod, and the boys so he could keep tabs on them, report their whereabouts back to the Enterprise, or whatever they call their war room. If High Rider is so confident that Little Red had been near my family when he disappeared, it's only because he thinks the tracking device is still on our minivan.

It all makes sense.

These guys were the ones who'd sent Shovel Man into my garage, planted that tracking device under the van. The tracking device my six-year-old then replanted under Crazy Larry's Malibu.

So the geeks have a fourth conspirator? Shovel Man?

Maybe Little Red had been tracking the car remotely with a GPS device or something, saw that the car was going someplace weird—because you just *know* Crazy Larry goes to weird places—and decided to go check it out.

And just like that, I realize that maybe I *do* know what's become of Little Red. Crazy Larry must've "taken" him. Maybe he's even discovered the device under his car—given the fact that High Rider has no idea where his buddy is.

But I don't want to say anything. Don't want to tell him what I do know: that he's the one behind Shovel Man and the tracking device.

"Listen," I say, "you're not going to tell me your name, are you?"

Silence.

"I can go and ask around FlowBid."

"That would be a really incoherent thing to do, Dan."

I chuckle. "But you know I'll find out afterward."

Silence.

"Okay, listen . . ." I want to say *High Rider*, but I know I shouldn't. "Okay, listen, pal. Let me see what I can find out. But I'm telling you, Kate and Rod don't have your little friend. We're just trying to get through the next few days here."

"You find him," he snaps, his voice quaking. "Or you lose everything."

I reach Kate on her cell.

"You guys don't have Little Red, do you?"

"Who?"

"He's one of the IT geeks."

She huffs. "God, no. We're on 101."

"Where's Rod?"

"Right behind us."

"Anyone in the car?"

"No." She sounds annoyed. "He's basically giving us a cage-fighter escort to his place. He's solo."

"Okay, that's all I needed to know."

"Everything okay?"

"Everything's fine, honey. How's Ben?"

"Gave him more Motrin, so the fever's down."

I think of Stanislau, get a chill. "Okay, honey. Tell the kids I love them."

"I will. They love you, too."

"Oh, by the way. When you were leaving, did you see Crazy Larry around?"

She thinks a minute. "I didn't."

"Ask Harry. See if he was doing any Larry-watching."

She puts the cell down, then comes back. "Harry saw him drive away in his station wagon."

"Ask him how long ago."

Murmurs, and then, "A couple hours ago. Is there a problem with Larry?"

"Honey, there's always been a problem with Larry."

Little Red. High Rider. Star Trek. Shovel Man.

The future of my family is in their hands, and I don't even know their real names.

Hell, if I knew who they were, I could see if they're connected to this Stanislau stuff. As for getting their real names, sure, I could start asking around IT, concoct some excuse for my interest, but then my snooping might get back to High Rider, and that could be it for me and the family.

But maybe there's another way.

I take one more look through my blue speaker cards for Fitzroy, print out the hotel information Sharon sent me, and slide my laptop into my briefcase. I pack up everything I need for the Tampa Social Net Conference and fire off a note to Fitzroy, attaching the preso.

Then I hobble to the stairway, descend a floor—with substantial pain—and limp onto the second floor, home of Creative Services, Engineering, and IT.

In an office packed with gear—three wide screens on the walls, stacks of CDs on the desk, neat rows of Beta cassette holders, and humming computers everywhere—I find Oscar Mendes, our video editor. Oscar makes Fitzroy look and sound a lot smarter than he actually is. He can take a thirty-minute studio borefest, suck out all the *um*s and *ah*s, cover up the strained goofball looks, cut out the redundant chatter (and there's a lot of it), and turn it into three minutes of compelling video.

Oscar Mendes is paid very well.

As we're the only brown-skinned people in the entire building—rare California natives in an office of out-of-state fortune seekers—we've also bonded pretty well. I love the fact he's not afraid to talk like a real human being around here; it's like a blast of fresh air off the Pacific.

He waves me in. "Dude, did you see that e-mail I just forwarded?"

"What e-mail?"

He giggles, stops short. "Someone was shitting rabbit pellets in the men's room."

"That's bullshit."

"Hey, by the way." He swivels and rummages through his cluttered desk. "I've got some shit that's gonna fucking blow your mind. This shit—" He fingers through a stack of discs, each encased in frosted plastic. "I'm telling you, this shit is gonna knock you on your ass."

He pulls out a disc, glances at me.

I nod at it. "You score some good shit?"

He swivels back, his brown eyes serious. "Dude . . ." He grabs my forearm with his free hand, squeezes. "Just wait till you take a hit of this shit."

He hands it over. I pop the case open, glance at two discs. He's written, *Afro Cuban* across the top of each.

"Thanks, man. I love Afro Cuban."

"Forty-seven tracks."

"Forty-seven?"

He nods, grinning.

"That's a lot of Afro Cuban."

"I've got a connection, dude. Guatemalan buddy of mine came into town last night, laid this music on me, blew my fucking mind."

I hold the case with both hands to show my appreciation. "Aw, man. This is monumental."

Oscar points at the case, raises an eyebrow. "This isn't poser shit, either." He waits, for emphasis. "We're talking about original shit from the forties, fifties, sixties, and seventies."

"Aw, dude. I can't wait."

He's nodding to the disc. "There's Benny Moré in there."

"Sweet."

"Manny Oquendo."

"Nice."

"Ray Barretto . . . Pérez Prado . . . Willy Colón."

"I can't wait, Oscar."

"Tons of Africando, tracks like 'Yay Boy.'" He pauses, blinks hard, like he's taken a hit of Humboldt skunk. "Some really early Tito. I put some Cachao in there." He lays the accent on, hard. "You know, 'La Negra Tomosa.' 'Son Montuno.'"

With the exception of Tito Puente, Benny Moré, and Ray Barretto, I've never heard of these guys. Nor do I understand anything more than the very limited amount of Spanish my Mexican grandmother taught me as a kid. But it doesn't matter. I do love the music, love the way it makes me feel.

He slows down, takes a good look at me. "You don't look too hot, dude. You okay?"

"I've been—"

A heavily bearded man with thick eyeglasses pops his head in, releases an awkward smile. "Hey."

"Hey, Roger." Oscar nods to me. "You know Dan Jordan?"

We nod to each other.

"Roger's on the system design team, works around the corner."

I nod. "Cool."

Roger steps into full view, hands a DVD to Oscar. "Thanks, man."

"You liked it? Told you that shit would blow your mind."

"Loved it."

"Music?" I ask.

"Documentary."

Oscar says, "It's about the health care industry. PBS? The networks? They'll never have the balls to broadcast something like this, dude. You should take this home, too." Classic Oscar.

"You got anything else like that?" Roger asks hopefully.

"I do," Oscar says, stretching to finger through a stack of DVDs. He pulls out a disc, hands it to Roger. "This shit takes it to another level."

"Yeah? More on health care?"

"Nah. The influence of peyote on twentieth-century California politics. I'm telling you, this shit will make you run for the mountains, dude."

Roger looks like a kid on Christmas morning.

Afterward, Oscar says to me, "You're not okay, dude."

"I'm not."

"What happened?"

"Long story."

"You look beat-up," he says. "Worried."

I laugh. "Well . . ."

"You need help?"

I look away. "I'm fine."

"Just let me know, okay?"

"Of course." After a moment, I say, "There is one thing I need help with—the IT guys."

His eyes nearly pop out of his head. "IT guys did this to you?"

I shake my head, chuckle. "You remember that little guy with the high-rider pants?"

He squints, thinking about it. "Yeah, yeah. Serious little dude. Major high-riders. Got laid off with the others."

"You remember his name?"

He thinks about it, sighs hard. "I can ask around."

"No, please don't. Seriously."

Studying me. Trying to figure me out. "Okay."

"Yeah, it could get me in more trouble."

He leans back, pinches his chin. "What the fuck is going on with you?"

"I'm fine. I just can't have High Rider know that I'm asking about him."

We stare at each other.

"I'll explain more once I get through this. I promise."

"Dan, I can get his name in a very casual way. You know, like I'll refer to him in conversation or something, say I forgot his name. Keep you out of it."

"Thanks, Oscar." I slip the Afro Cuban into my briefcase. "And if you get a name, don't call my cell or office line."

He smiles at me, like I'm nuts.

"Just call my buddy Rod."

"The cage fighter?"

"Exactly." I scribble Rod's cell on a scrap of paper, hand it to him. "Call him here. Just avoid my numbers entirely."

"What are we, in a movie here, dude?"

I chuckle. "I promise I'll explain when I can."

"No worries."

I back out of his office. "I better jet."

"You headed for the airport?" Then he throws a hand into the air. "Not that you have to tell me."

"Nah, I have to go home, find Crazy Larry."

Now he's really studying me. "Crazy Larry?" He laughs, pauses. "You need to go find someone named Crazy Larry?"

"Long story, but basically I think Crazy Larry has Little Red."

He laughs again. "Crazy Larry has Little Red?"

I nod. "So now, if I disappear, you'll know who to mention to the cops."

"Yeah, Crazy Larry, Little Red, and High Rider."

He laughs and I laugh with him. Till the tears are rolling down our cheeks.

Finally, Oscar takes a deep breath, sighs hard. "Seriously, dude. You go home, you may wanna take a nap."

I stand in front of Larry's house. No station wagon. The street is empty.

Where is everyone?

I look back at my house. By now, Kate and the kids are in the city, safe with Rod, but just about anybody could be in that house waiting for me. Baldy? Shovel Man? Crazy Larry? Crazy Larry with Little Red? Someone new?

I feel myself swaying.

Oscar is right, I do need a nap.

And, fuck, do my balls ache. My whole midsection aches.

Something's screwed up down there. For sure.

I reach into my pocket, pull out the bottle, pop another Vicodin, stare at Larry's garage door, squint at the knife marks. Crazy Larry. If he goes wacko on me today, in my current state, there's no way I can handle him.

All of a sudden, I hear an electronic buzzing and snapping coming from Larry's garage.

Fuck, is that him in there? With Little Red?

I pull my hair back, look around the neighborhood, try to think. I need a plan. I walk across the street, hear the tap of a hammer, metal rustling, heavy panting. Then that buzz-snap sound again.

Faint trace of someone growling.

Something rushes up behind me, gives me a hell of a jolt. I yelp and turn, realize it's little Luke Burns, the nine-year-old from down the street, zipping up on his Razor scooter, big head of blond hair shooting in all directions.

"I wouldn't stand there."

"Oh yeah?" I say. "Why's that?"

Luke steps off his Razor, leans in, whispers. "Larry."

"Yeah?"

Luke looks around, adds, "Extra cuckoo today."

"Yeah? Tell me."

"I was playing out front when Larry pulled up in his station wagon."

"Uh-huh?"

"But it was weird."

"Weird?"

"The back windows were covered with cardboard."

"Yeah, that's odd." *Did he have Little Red back there?*

"And then he backed it into his garage." Luke stops, looks at me with some serious eyes. "Larry never backs his car into the garage."

He's right.

"Did Larry see you?"

Luke nods. "He saw me, but I kept watching, and he lowered his head like this and glared at me. So I say, 'Bye,' and he says, 'Yes, that's right, bye-bye.'"

"Did you go tell your mom?"

Nods. "She said Larry's just being Larry, and to leave him alone."

"Wise advice, Luke. Listen to your mom."

"But I was riding around later, and he came out, so I rode by and he was just squinting into space with this weird smile, like his mouth was just pretending to be happy."

"Did he say anything?"

Luke nods. "He asked me about the 'scent of bacon frying in the wild.'"

"Bacon?"

"He said, 'Does that affect you, Luke?' And I said no. And he said. 'Bacon scent in the woods drives me nuts.' Then his arms and legs got all tight, like this." Ben shoots his arms out, crosses his eyes. "I didn't know what to say, so I just said, 'I like bacon.'"

"Good for you, Luke."

"And Crazy Larry says, 'Well, I think I smell bacon.'"

"So then you left?"

Big nod, serious eyes. Whispers, "If Crazy Larry smells bacon, I don't think it's a good thing."

"You're probably right, Luke."

"But after a while I came back."

"You should keep clear of him, kiddo."

He shrugs. "He didn't even notice me. It was like he was in his own world."

"Did you see anything else?"

"He opened the garage door, pulled his station wagon out, and went to the store."

"The store? How do you know he went to the store?"

Luke huffs and throws his hands into the air. "All the stuff he came back with. Duh."

"Stuff? What kind of stuff?"

"All kinds of stuff. Big metal bars, chicken wire, a whole bunch of twine, propane canisters—the kind my dad uses for the barbecue."

I mumble, "Wow."

"Those big cement square things."

"Foundation blocks?"

"I think so. Oh, and then a big bag of cotton balls, a bunch of that silver tape, and a bunch of buckets with some kind of dark wet stuff inside."

"Wow."

We stand in silence a second as Luke squints into the air. "Oh, yeah, he had car batteries and those thick wires for when your car is dead."

"Jumper cables?"

He nods. "And then a roll of fabric, an ironing board, a power drill, I think, and a bunch of beer."

I laugh.

Still squinting into air, thinking about it. "Oh, and on the sidewalk he left a can of shaving cream, a thing of Vaseline, and some cans of WD40. That stuff's awesome."

"Don't play with WD40, Luke."

"I know." Then he brightens. "But Larry does."

"But you don't want to be like Larry, do you?"

He concedes the point, his eyes serious.

"Did you see anyone else with him? Maybe a little man with really red hair?"

Thinks about it, shakes his head no. "But he did say something else weird."

"What's that?"

"The last time he came out, I asked what he was doing, and all he kept saying was, 'Larry needs some time to himself.'"

"Hmmm." We stand there awhile. "Last question, Luke."

He peers up at me.

"Do you swear you're telling me the truth?"

"Totally." His blue eyes pop. "It's totally true."

"Okay, I believe you."

He nods to Larry's house, smiles with hope. "Are you gonna sneak in there?"

A loud buzz-snap from Larry's garage.

"Um, don't think so. If I need something from Larry, I'll just knock on his door."

Luke fails to suppress a grin. This astute little guy knows I'm full of shit.

I open my garage door, grab Harry's aluminum baseball bat, and enter the house through the kitchen, ready to take anyone's head off.

And what do you know?

No one.

Windows locked. Everything secure. Peaceful silence. In my house.

At this moment in my life, how rare.

I return to the kitchen, lean against the counter. I'm so tired my eyelids hurt. My mind is swimming. I need a beer.

That'll settle me down, add a little juice to the Vicodin, put me on course for a much-needed nap, a sweet block of blackout thirty minutes from now.

Assuming that's enough time to figure out the Crazy Larry situation.

I limp to the fridge, finger a bottle of Sierra Nevada, pop the cap, and pour it into a pint glass. Call me a fancy boy, but that beer is so much better in a glass—tastes better, looks better, sounds so lovely going into the glass. I stand in the kitchen, look out to the backyard as I take a sip.

Ah, man. Just perfect.

Say to no one, "Damn, that's good." Take another sip, feel it settle in my stomach.

Go sit on the front porch and keep an eye on Larry. That's what I'll do.

I bring the bat with me, use it for leverage as I lower myself onto the front step of my porch, put the pint down beside me. The beer and Vicodin start mixing nicely, and I find myself gazing skyward as I listen to the odd noises coming from Larry's garage—the hammering, the buzz of a saw or drill, those periodic buzz-snaps.

And I realize that I probably look pretty crazy myself about now.

From Larry's garage, a wet slap against the pavement.

My cell rings.

"Yo."

It's High Rider. "Do you have an update?"

"I do." *Am I slurring?* "I talked to Kate. She hasn't seen your buddy, I'm afraid. And Rod's with them, so . . ."

"Anything else?"

"How about you? Why don't you admit it was you who sent Shovel Man into my garage this morning, tried to plant something under my wife's minivan?"

Long silence.

"C'mon. Fess up." *Oh yeah, I'm buzzed.*

Finally, he says, "It was you who removed the tracking device."

I imagine High Rider in a dimly lit basement, placing a trembling finger over the Enter button of his keyboard, ready to destroy my life.

"Now, wait," I say. "We thought it was someone more powerful, someone connected to the guy who attacked me in the Safeway."

Silence.

"Hell, if you wanted to track Kate, you should've just asked. We've got nothing to hide."

Long silence. And then, "We found the tracking device, Dan."

Oh shit. Larry's car.

"On a station wagon," I say.

"No." Long, irritated sigh. "It wasn't on any station wagon."

"What are you talking about?"

"Do any shopping today, Mr. Jordan?"

"Me? . . . What? . . . No. Why?"

"Well, it seems our tracking device made a trip to the grocery store."

"Okay."

"Lunardi's, to be precise."

"Inside Lunardi's?"

"Under a neat stack of cucumbers."

I get a vision of Crazy Larry fucking with a pile of cucumbers in the produce section, everyone keeping clear.

"Before there, it was up in the hills."

"Hills?"

Silence, and then, "Which is where we lost contact with my associate?"

"Little Red?"

Annoyed. "My associate."

"Okay, well—"

"We know you were at work at the time. Irrefutable. Your IT activity bears it out."

"Good. See, I was—"

"And from what we now can tell, your wife and the cage fighter had nothing to do with this."

"Beyond a doubt."

"And yet you knew about the tracking device."

"True."

"And it clearly wasn't on the minivan."

"Yeah, we removed it."

"And you placed it on a vehicle, judging by the fact the signal had us zigzagging up and down the peninsula."

I think of Crazy Larry. "Really?"

"Whose car, Dan?"

"What?"

"I'm getting ready to release your information, Dan. This isn't funny."

"Okay, okay." I blink, and my vision blurs. "We put it under my neighbor's station wagon. Thought it would be harmless."

"Your neighbor across the street?"

"Yeah."

I wait for a reaction, trying to think of what to say next, when Larry's front door opens. It's Larry, in his skin-colored Speedo and shiny black army boots, with a faded orange tank top. Nursing a pipe, glancing at me as he takes a seat on his porch.

"What's his name?"

"Don't worry about that."

"Is he home?"

I squint back at Larry. "He is."

Silence. *Fuck, he's deciding what to do. I know it.*

"Like I said, we thought that device came from some serious dudes, not you guys. We just wanted them off our tails."

"Who are *those guys*, Dan?"

"That's what I'm trying to figure out."

Not gonna tell him about Stanislau. Not yet, at least.

"So, does he have my associate or not?"

Larry takes a puff, watches me. A buzz-snap echoes from his garage.

"Probably, but it's a matter of where."

"You have an hour to retrieve my associate, or this thing is over."

Larry watching, puffing, stroking his beard.

"Okay," I say, "but you need to tell me where his car went this morning. That might help."

High Rider huffs, ruffles papers. "The signal was everywhere. First the library, then to the wetlands, then up and down 101, back and forth, over and over, between Redwood City and Belmont, for ninety minutes."

I imagine Crazy Larry driving up and down the freeway with that look on his face, the radio turned off as he thinks about God knows what. Creeps me out.

"So when did your buddy attempt to follow the car?"

"Well . . ." His anger is palpable. "He began the pursuit on 101, but couldn't find the car, because he was looking for a minivan. He followed the signal up and down 101 for twenty minutes, at which point the vehicle got off the freeway and headed for the hills."

And I'm wondering, *Daily routine for Larry?*

"My associate followed the signal all the way to the top of the hills, proceeded south on Skyline Boulevard, Highway 35, which is where we lost contact."

"In the woods," I whisper, gazing back at Larry. "He obviously realized he was being tailed and lured your guy into the woods, snagged him there."

A pause. "The signal returned to your neighborhood. Remained there for a while, then proceeded to dart around town, to stores, we think, and then settled, apparently, in the produce section."

"Okay." Gazing back at Larry. "So, I think your buddy is over here at Larry's house."

"You will need to provide a welfare status."

"Well . . ." I watch Larry as he puffs and stares. Another buzz-snap from inside. "He might be a little rattled."

High Rider yelps, "Get him."

"But that might be—"

"You have one hour to get him, or your life is ruined."

Dial tone.

Fuck, I'm buzzed.

That Sierra Nevada had sounded like such a good idea. But now I want balance, a clear head.

I wobble toward Larry. He sits there assessing me, his mouth frozen in an odd smile—and I realize he actually has a nice face, a face the ladies probably liked at one point, when he was saner. Hell, maybe they still do.

"Hey, Larry."

He stares at my feet like they baffle him, looks away, exhales a puff.

Buzz-snap.

"You've been busy over here today."

He turns and stares at me. He nearly whispers, "I made a friend."

"Oh yeah?" I play it straight, like he's just won five hundred dollars in the Lotto. "That's great, Larry."

"You could say . . ." He's gazing into the air, then turns to me, forcing that weird smile. ". . . we're having what you yuppies call a playdate."

I offer an awkward laugh. "Yeah?"

He brings the pipe to his mouth, produces a cloud of smoke, studies the swirls, follows their ascent until they dissolve into nothing.

"You think the playdate is over?"

More smoking.

"Maybe your new friend wants to go home now?"

Crazy Larry gives me this look like I've morphed into a porcupine.

Another buzz-snap, and a faint growl.

Human growl.

Larry cocks his head, like he's he listening to Bach.

And I realize: I'm hosed.

A funky beat thumps out of Calhoun's granny unit.

I recognize the beat, those lyrics.

"My Humps."

Black Eyed Peas. They love the humps.

Hell, these days, the whole world loves them.

Including Calhoun.

The windows are fogged a little as I inch closer, the beat getting stronger, Fergie belting it out high and breathless.

> *I drive these brothers crazy,*
> *I do it on the Daily . . .*

I peek in, see Calhoun in his open robe—arms snapping, pelvis thrusting, belly shaking, feet working hard, head cocking and snapping.

Whoa.

Calhoun.

Serious moves.

Calhoun sings along, "She's got me spending."

> *Spendin' all your money on me and spending time*
> *on me.*

Calhoun wails, *"What you gon' do with all that junk? All that junk inside that trunk?"*

I stumble to his door. *Fuck, I'm light-headed.* But, hell, I need help. I need to get Little Red out of that garage within the hour or I'm hosed, and Calhoun is the only way I can think of to gain entry to his landlord's house and spring the little guy loose. Or at least talk Larry into cooperating.

I'm a make, make, make, make you scream
Cos of my hump, my hump . . . my lovely lady
lumps

Calhoun wails, *"What you gon' do with all that ass? All that ass inside them jeans?"*

I move closer, reach the door.

Push it open.

Whoa.

A visitor.

A woman.

An older woman—very short, very bottom-heavy.

Dancing for Calhoun.

In a thong.

Backing it up toward him, swinging it, seconds from grind time.

Calhoun turns, still shaking it, grins at me, and sings along, *"I met a girl down at the disco. She said hey, hey, hey yea let's go. I could be your baby, you can be my honey. Let's spend time not money."*

And then after a few beats, he hollers, "Mr. Danny likes to watch."

No, I don't.

She looks over her shoulder, sees me, and drops her lids as she backs into Calhoun, his robe hiding the friction.

Touchdown.

Calhoun grabs her sides, points his chin into the air, lets his eyes turn to slits.

I feel the beer coming up.

Step away, lower myself to the ground beside one of Larry's cacti. The earth starts to spin. I close my eyes. I should probably spread out on Larry's rocks, take a breather, and let the spinning stop as I wait for them to finish.

And I fade to black, Fergie's anthem washing over me like an echo.

I awake in someone's arms.

Rocked gently, back and forth.

It's nice, reminds me of simpler times. *Is this a dream?*

I blink hard—and look up to see Calhoun's gray little eyes peering down at me, a droplet of sweat falling from his brow to my chest. He smiles and whisper-sings, extra-high, "Rise and shine, Mr. Danny."

It sinks in, and I jolt out of his arms, roll onto the rocks. But I'm weak, and he gathers me back into his embrace, holds me tight.

Cradled. By Calhoun, in his brown boxers and white tank, stinking of sex and sweat.

Oh God, I'm gonna pass out.

"Easy, boy," he whispers, like I'm a horse. "Easy."

I give up.

"There we go," he soothes, "there we go." After a few moments, he adds, "You've been out awhile."

That gets me. "What?"

"Shshhh." Soft and gentle. "Easy, boy . . . Easy."

I look around, notice the lady friend watching from his doorway. She's wrapped up in his robe, arms folded, unimpressed. She must be at least thirty years older than Calhoun.

"Ellie and I thought you left," he says. "A long time ago."

I moan.

"We would have halted the coitus had we known. I swear."

I break loose and sit up, scamper away from him.

"You don't look so hot, Mr. Danny."

"I know."

"Actually, I think you're ripe for a paradigm shift."

"Yeah, well I have bigger fish to fry right now."

Ellie steps forward, rasps, "Listen to him. He knows what he's talking about."

"What? Do you even know this guy?"

She smirks at me. "He's my life coach."

"Life coach?"

She gives me the this-shit's-for-real look. "He's good."

This clears my head. I straighten, wipe my nose. "This man is your life coach?"

She nods, so calm. "I've graduated. Now he's just my booty call. Isn't that what they call it?"

Calhoun giggles, nods.

"His coaching methodology is basically teaching by example."

"Nice," I say, get to my feet. *Whoa, still light-headed.*

She proceeds to blow me away.

Turns out, Calhoun is actually a millionaire several times over. One of the first eighty employees at Google. Made a fortune and got out.

This gets me. "And you live here? In a three-hundred-square-foot granny unit behind Larry's house?"

Calhoun closes his eyes, confident. "You choose to live a large life, Mr. Danny. But you don't need it."

But you don't support a family, bub.

"I make choices," he says. "And I choose to live small."

Ellie nods, watching my reaction. "See?"

"You have millions and you live here?"

"I have made a choice to appreciate where I am, Mr. Danny."

Never thought I'd get deep with Calhoun.

Calhoun struggles to stand up. When he's finally upright, he whispers, "Paradigm shift, Mr. Danny. You need a paradigm shift." He looks at me, catches his breath, and adds, "You and Kate are livin' *la vida loca.* And where is it getting you?"

I shrug. "Actually, we're—"

He shushes me. "You should see yourself. You look all chewed up and spat out. *La vida loca* is sucking the life out of you, Mr. Danny."

"I know. But all I need to do is last another—"

"That's what they all say."

"But we're—"

"You and that sweet little family of yours need to cash out, Mr. Danny. Cash out and live small."

Live small. Not bad, actually.

"Calhoun, listen to me. This is exactly what I am trying to do. I *want* to live small. I *want* to cash out. But believe me, to do it, I need to hang on a few more days."

Calhoun nods, says, "That's good, Mr. Danny. Set a date."

"But I need your help."

He shakes his jowls. "I don't do loans. But I do give investment tips."

"No, I mean—"

"In fact, I have a friend who just told me about this little company that lets you put short mess—"

"Calhoun, no." Now I'm the one whispering. "I need your help with Larry."

I tell him about Little Red. "I need to spring him loose."

He wheezes. "You're not going to spring that man loose, Mr. Danny. You'd need a Sherman to get into that house."

I turn and cuss. I've forgotten about the time. Look at my watch. *Holy shit.*

I have five minutes.

"I gotta go," I huff. "I'm so fucked."

Calhoun says, "Think, my little one. Think."

I turn back and squint at him. "I'm not thinking too well lately. Just tell me."

Ellie turns back into his place, fiddles with his boom box, starts up the "Humps" song.

Eyes twinkling, he rasps, "Think."

Again, that silly beat, those raspy *ha-ha-cha*s over and over.

I keep squinting. My brain is empty.

"You're not going to spring anyone out of Larry's house." He waits. "But you *do* hold power over him, don't you?"

Ha-ha-cha, ha-ha-cha

"I do?"

Slowly, he nods. "By virtue of your little lover."

And the music blares, calling for Calhoun.

"Now it is time for us to part." He closes his eyes, sighs. "My own lover is calling."

My cell rings. I recognize the number. *Aw, man—High Rider.*

I take the call, and he says, "It's over."

"What?"

"I have released the data."

I don't want to believe it. "What?"

"Dan." So calm, in control. "I've released your personal information."

Six

I have to sit down to take the news.

"You released my information?"

"I warned you, Dan."

The world swirls.

Holy shit.

My life is over.

I think of the chats with Anne, the e-mails with *Business-Week*, and I can nearly see the people of FlowBid reading it all, gathering in each other's cubes, giggling, giant scandalized smiles on their faces.

"You asshole," I yell. "You *fucking* asshole."

Shit, where's Kate? I need to reach Kate before it gets to her.

He says, "I gave you an hour, Dan."

I want to rip his lungs out. "I was working on it, you . . ." I swallow hard. ". . . little bastard."

"Good, so there is hope."

I sit there along the side of Larry's house, stare at this brown little trap door connected to the garage, but it's not registering.

"Hope," I yell. "There's no fucking hope. Not now."

"You said you were working on retrieving my associate, so there is hope."

"No, this is your problem now. You ruined my life, asshole. I'm done. I have to get to Kate."

Long pause. "Dan, I don't think you comprehend what's happened."

I stare at the trap door, feel like getting up and kicking it in out of anger, but realize it's metal and would probably break my toes. "You just released all that personal information, you said. My life is ruined. Which means it will now be my mission in life to tear yours to fucking shreds."

He laughs, like an elf on helium. "You don't understand." He composes himself, adds, "Yes, I released your personal info to the employees of FlowBid."

My head goes cold. *I'm gonna throw up.*

"But I did not release all of it."

What?

"I just released your porn activity to the top floor of the headquarters building. Nothing else."

My vision narrows, and I feel faint as the particulars of my situation reassemble to present what might be a new future— one not nearly as awful as the one I just had, but disastrous on its own level.

"All employees on the top floor of the headquarters building, including those inhabiting Executive Row, have just received an e-mail from an IT mailbox labeled 'Browsing Activity Reports/Browsing History of Daniel Jordan, Employee Number 452.'"

I think of the people on the top floor. People I know. People I work with daily. Everyone in Legal. All those young ladies in Finance. Fitzroy's assistant, Sharon. Beth Gavin. Fitzroy himself.

"In said e-mail is a listing of what is termed 'Questionable Browsing Activity.'"

Cold sweat. Spreading rapidly. "Lovely."

"If you say so."

What is that, geek humor?

"And that questionable browsing history includes, well . . ." I can hear the joy in his voice. "Well, let's just say it's apparent you enjoy a certain part of the female anatomy."

Oh yeah. He's outed me. The whole building will know what kind of man I am.

An ass man.

Just little breaks from the day, they were. Ladies in bikinis and thongs and all that. Half the time I sent them to Oscar for jobs well-done. And he'd send some back for me. Now, what a nightmare.

My stomach tightens. "You're such a dick," I mumble, running a hand through my hair.

"I can read the list, Dan, but I think you know these sites. The number one destination, a sweet little site called Assathon dot-com. Another one called—"

"Stop," I yell, compose myself, and mumble, "God, you're such a prick."

Another call comes in. I look at the display—it's Sharon from Fitzroy's office. I click Ignore.

He says, so calm, "I could have truly destroyed your life, Dan. But I chose not to. . . . Not yet."

I close my eyes, shake my head.

"I could have effectively eliminated your options by releasing other information. I could have ruined your marriage, too. And I will, if I have to. If you don't do as I say, and that starts with retrieving my friend." He waits a second. "And then proceeding to Tampa to execute our plans . . . to a T."

I stand up, take a breath. "My Humps" beats from Calhoun's place. I'm thinking, *I still have a chance to salvage this.*

My cell beeps again. Look at the display; it's an unknown FlowBid number. Press Ignore again.

"Let me get your little buddy out."

"So just to be clear, Dan: You will call me within the hour and put my associate on the phone, or I will release more of your personal data to the entire FlowBid building." He pauses for effect. "And let's just say it will make this first installment seem as interesting as an NPR discussion on rice subsidies."

"Okay."

"And no police."

"Okay."

I think of the IMs with Anne, feel a wave of nausea. "Okay," I say, and hang up.

Gotta get that geek out of Larry's garage.

I stumble to the front of Larry's house, thinking of what Calhoun said—I hold power over Larry, by virtue of my *little lover.*

And finally I get it.

My cell rings. Another FlowBid number. *Ignore.*

I'm so screwed. The whole building is reading my porn history.

Cell rings again. FlowBid. *Ignore.*

I find Crazy Larry on his porch, still blowing clouds of smoke with his pipe.

Cell rings. FlowBid. *Ignore.*

"I meant to ask, Larry. Do you ever get to San Francisco?"

"The city?" He turns and looks at me, interested. "You mean, civilization."

I nod. "Yeah, the city. Just up the freeway. Kate's there now, in fact."

He fingers his beard, studies me. "So close," he mumbles, thinks about it, "and yet so far away."

"Yeah, she's in the city for a few days. I was thinking maybe you and I could meet her someplace for a drink."

His eyes enlarge. "Kate?"

"Yes, Kate and you . . . and me. In the city. A drink or something. Someplace in Cow Hollow, maybe. There's a nice place on Union. You know, a nice visit, just the three of us. In the city. A little date."

"Date?" His lips quiver. "Date with Kate?"

"And me."

His eyes tighten. "Just Kate."

God, she'll kill me.

"Well, maybe I could join you in the beginning."

He studies me, turns his head like a curious cat.

"Then, I suppose I could leave you guys for an hour or so and go take care of some errands."

And I'm thinking, *Rod and I will never leave the bar.*

He whispers to himself, "Kate," and gazes into space.

"Yes, a date with Kate."

Man, I gotta stop using that word.

He sounds like a poet, his voice so delicate. "I'd like that very much."

I'll be paying for this for years. Decades.

"Only one condition."

His eyes tighten.

I nod to the garage. "You need to release him."

Crazy Larry glances at the garage, looks back at me.

"Date with Kate?"

I nod.

"In the city?"

Nod again.

He looks into space and strokes his whiskers.

Cell rings. Oscar. *Ignore.*

"What do you say, Larry? . . . Deal?"

Larry stands up, rearranges his Speedo, smoothes out his tank top. He turns and leaves me standing there, saunters into his house, disappears.

"Larry?"

Silence.

Buzz-snap.

Cell again. FlowBid's head of HR. *Crap. Ignore.*

"Larry?"

Finally, he appears in his doorway holding what looks like the remote control for a garage-door opener.

"Date with Kate. Tonight."

"Well, you know, a visit. Call it what you want."

He smiles to himself. "I prefer to call it a date."

Larry brings the pipe to his mouth, produces a cloud of smoke, stares at me through the swirls. Clicks the device, triggering from inside the garage a series of rapid mechanical clicks. Metal contraptions collapsing to the ground. Hydraulic hissing. An intense series of pops and snaps, followed by the longest buzz yet.

From the side of the garage, the sound of the trap door blowing open, and a second later a high-pitched yelp.

And then a streak of flesh: Little Red, naked, shaven bald, and greased up. Darting down the street, yelping.

Crazy Larry says, "I don't like red hair."

My cell rings.

I start to hobble after Little Red.

"And tell your child . . ."

That gets me. I stop, turn to him again.

". . . that tracking devices interfere with my cerebral frequency."

"Okay, Larry. Believe me, it won't happen again."

Big puff. "He's lucky that sweet little mom of his put him up to it."

"Okay, Larry. We appreciate your tolerance."

And he fades into the smoke.

I find Little Red around the corner, hiding behind a cluster of junipers.

I pull him out and drag him back to my place, aware the whole time of the scene I'm making. Cars slowing. Kids stopping on their bikes, watching from a distance, as this neighborhood daddy drags a hairless, greased-up, naked man down the street and into his house.

Someone must be calling the cops.

"It's nothing," I tell passersby. "He's just a little confused. Just scared."

Let them think Little Red is a psycho. Hell, he probably is.

In the house, he grunts and growls. His whole body shakes, and his teeth won't stop chattering. Not a word out of him. Just glares—daggers, aimed right at me.

I wrap him up in a blanket, start the shower.

"You *do* realize I was the one who sprang you loose, right?"

He snarls at me.

I look at my cell. Thirty missed calls, all from FlowBid folks. I think of Assathon dot-com and God knows what else. Not a terminable offense, but what an embarrassment.

I shake my head. Can't think about that right now.

I find High Rider's number, call him.

"Do you have good news, Dan?"

"Here." I put the phone to Little Red's ear. "Say something. Tell him where you are."

He grunts.

I can hear High Rider say something.

Little Red growls, "Yes."

Something else from High Rider. Another yes from Little Red.

I take the phone away. "So we're back on?"

"I was minutes away from distributing your instant messaging, Dan."

•   •   •

I know Little Red was never quite right, but now he's even worse. He can't stop twitching and blinking. Every time I try to inspect the marks and bruises on his body—the razor cuts on his shaven head, the welts on his legs, the hundreds of pinch marks over his chest and back, the Vaseline smears everywhere—he swipes at my hands like an angry kitten. Practically hisses.

He keeps twitching.

Damn, this isn't right.

"What did he do to you?"

Just that snarl, then a twitch.

"Do you need to see a doctor? Urgent care, maybe?"

He bristles and twitches.

Steam eases out of the bathroom.

"Your buddy is coming with new clothes. Why don't you take a shower?"

He whimpers, turns and heads for the shower.

My cell rings again. It's Oscar, and this time I pick up.

"Dude," he says.

"I know. Someone already told me."

With emphasis. "Dude."

"I heard it only went to the top floor."

"Three different people forwarded it to me, dude, and not one of them is on the third floor. It's everywhere."

I'd figured as much, but hearing it from Oscar makes it real. Nausea washes over me, and I close my eyes.

Oscar says, "I'm freaking, dude."

"Don't worry about it."

"No," he says. "About me. I'm freaking about me."

"No, you're fine. There's no risk."

"But Assathon dot-com? I sent you a *ton* of pics from Ass-athon dot-com." He moans, worried. "Maybe I'm next."

I close my eyes tight. *Fuck, my head hurts.*

"No, I don't think it's like that. This was just about me."

He sighs, relieved. Then, with a trace of amusement: "Dude, you've been busy."

"What does it say?"

Extra slow. "There's a list here, dude. Sites you've visited."

"Like what?"

"Beach Butts dot-com . . ." He giggles, stops himself. "Camel Toes dot-com."

"Camel Toes?" I yell. "*You* sent me that one."

"Says you spent twenty-seven minutes there. So you can't really blame me."

"Yeah, whatever."

"There's one here I've never heard of. . . . Rate My Ass dot-com." He pauses. "Five hours."

"Nice." I take a Modelo from the fridge, take a huge swig. "I'll never enter that building again."

Another big sigh. "Dude, I have to tell you. This looks bad. Two more people just forwarded this list to me. It's all over the place."

"Oscar," I say, closing my eyes tight, "I need to get off the line. I can't handle this anymore."

"Okay, dude. I'm gonna respond to these. I'll say you told me it's someone's idea of a bad joke. That it's all bullshit, not true."

I take another huge swig. "Thanks, man." I feel my body sway. My mind is floating away, it seems, and maybe that's not such a bad idea. "I gotta go."

We hang up, and my cell rings again. My head wobbles as I look at it. Another FlowBid number.

Fuck it. Pick it up, Danny. Tell them it's all a lie, some prick's idea of a practical joke.

"Yo?" I say.

"Dan?"

"Yo?"

"Dan, this is Janice from Finance."

"Yo?" I press my butt against the fridge, let go, allow gravity to slide me down to the floor. Hard landing. "Yo, Janice."

That stops her only a second. "You don't have time for P6s in the FOD, but you have time for three hours at Golden Buns dot—"

"Listen for a sec, Janice." I let the words slur a little. "That's all bullshit. That's all a lie."

"It looks pretty authentic to me, Dan."

"Well, it isn't," I snap. "And regardless, I'm never gonna do your goddamn P6s in the FOD."

She huffs. "Something's not right."

"Oh, really? You finally figured that out, Janice? Good for you. In fact, why don't you enter that into your FOD?"

I hang up as I lower my head to the kitchen floor.

More freaky dreams.

Crazy Larry escorting Kate down a busy San Francisco

street in his Speedo. High Rider carrying Little Red in his arms like a sleeping toddler, leaving the house. Calhoun cradling me again, only this time he's topless and trying to make me "latch" on to one of his tits, his nipple long like a pinkie, and I'm like a newborn, fussing and resisting.

That wakes me.

My cheek is wet from the drool.

My cell is ringing. *Damn . . . Modelo and Vicodin. Whoa.*

I pick up the cell. "Yo," I slur. "It's all bull. All a bunch of bullshit."

"Dan?" It's Kate. "Dan, where are you?"

Head bobbling. "Kitchen floor."

"Dan, are you okay?"

"Now? Now, I'm just fine."

"What's going on?"

"Nothing," I yell, almost lazy. "Nothing. I'm fine. Just had a beer, okay? I'm just on the kitchen floor, if that's okay with your sweet little face."

"Dan, I've been thinking." She pauses. "There's more, isn't there?"

"What?"

"There's more you're not telling me."

"Stop it," I slur.

"I knew it. I mean, with all our problems, I wouldn't be surprised."

"Honey, enough."

After a long pause, she says, "You shouldn't be there."

"I'm fine," I slur, arching an eyebrow. "Fiiiiinnne. Fine."

She's annoyed. "I can't believe you're drunk."

"I'm not," I say, slow about it. "Just a Sierra, then a Mod-elo."

"Make yourself a coffee, take a shower, pack your things for the trip tomorrow, and when your head's clear, get up here to Rod's."

"Fine," I say.

"Dan," she says, softer. "Just keep it together a few more days, okay?"

Staring at the cabinets, glazing over. "Yeah."

"I found an employment lawyer," she says. "He was very helpful."

This clears my head a little. "Yeah?"

"That *BusinessWeek* stuff gets out, you're toast. The options are toast."

The news bounces off my face. "Okay."

"So we just have to hang tough a little longer, okay?"

Staring at the cabinets.

"Dan, just have that coffee and get up here, and we'll get you ready. Okay?"

"Honey?"

"Yeah?"

"Honey, you have a date tonight."

She laughs. "Oh yeah?"

"I'm serious. I'm bringing Larry. He has a date with you."

Silence.

"You see . . ." I pause, arch an eyebrow, as I recall my predicament. "You see, honey, Crazy Larry? He wouldn't let Little Red out of his garage. So I needed to ne-*go*-tiate with him."

Long silence.

"Otherwise, High Rider would've released my info, all my info, and that would've been it for us."

Nothing.

"But the deal is, he can't be alone with you, and it's just an hour . . ." I fail to suppress a burp. ". . . or something."

Nothing.

"Sorry, honey."

Silence.

"The good news is, I got Little Red back." I pull my head away from the cell, realize the shower is silent. "I think High Rider came and got him, carried him out like a baby," I say. "Only I thought it was a dream."

Nothing.

"You there, honey?"

The cold shower clears my mind a little. The coffee steaming in my face helps, too. But the beer and painkillers still have me floating. It feels like I'm gliding through it all, like I can do anything I want.

Like call my mom.

For the first time in years.

I stumble down the garage steps, cordless in my hand, as I thumb her number—same number for twenty-five years.

Shit, I'm doing it.

Ringing.

I glide to the shelving, glance over my sander and power drill . . .

Heart pounding.

. . . past my dad's shelf of old Yuban cans filled with nails and screws . . .

Swallow hard.

. . . and settle in front of the family Coleman. Dark green metal with white plastic trim, a chrome latch. Forty years old, easy.

Ringing.

All those family vacations at the beach. Pajaro Dunes. Every summer. Sweet and gentle times, in a simpler world. Feels so long ago, I wonder if it ever even happened. Or was it a fantasy? But here's the proof—the Coleman. Spent all those days sunken crookedly in the sand, full of Welch's Grape Soda and Coors and pretzels and oranges and PBJs.

So long ago. And yet here it is.

"Hello?"

Bet I could find sand under the plastic trim.

She clears her throat. "Kate?"

"Mom?"

"Danny?"

It's been two years.

A lump forms in my throat. "Mom, I miss you."

She starts to cry, and I let her.

"I love you, Danny."

"I know I haven't called."

"Oh, Danny." She sobs, fights to control herself. "It is so nice to hear your voice."

And to hear hers brings back a thousand memories, all of them washing over me in a warm rush, all at once. I start to cry.

"Kate calls me," she sniffles. "And Rod. They tell me you're okay, but I worry."

I wipe a tear. "I'm sorry, Mom."

She cries, "I'm sorry, too."

After a while, I say, "How did it get this bad?"

"We say too much, you and me. We say way too much."

I know she's right. My mom and I, we've always said too much, hurt each other too deeply. And it's always about the heaviest stuff, too—who did who wrong all those years ago, who didn't do enough during my dad's last days, when he was withering away from cancer. And the words, they crush.

The truth is, we both cared so much.

"Are you okay?" she says. "Why are you at home in the middle of a workday?"

I'm staring at it, swaying just a little. "You remember all those times at Pajaro?"

"Of course," she sniffles, her voice weakening. "Those were the best days of my life." And they were. The three of us, together and happy. With the Yakamotos, the Piersons, Tommy and Betty Sims. I reach out and touch the cooler, just glance it with the back of my index finger. "You ever go back there?"

"No." She sighs, her voice so soft. "No, I can't. It would just—"

"Mom, we're going to move there, or somewhere nearby. As long as I can hang on a few more days."

"A few more— You're moving?"

"And I want you to come visit us. And we'll go to the beach, and we'll pack some stuff in the cooler, spend all day on the beach, play with the boys. Like old times, okay?"

She clears her throat, sighs. "Are you okay, honey?"

"Promise you'll come."

"Of course, I'll come. But you don't sound—"

"Mom, I just wanted to let you know I love you."

"Danny—"

"And that we need to start making new memories, and just let go of that other crap."

I can hear my doorbell ring. I know who it is.

"Danny, tell me what's—"

"Mom, Crazy Larry's at the door. I need to take him to the city for his date with Kate."

Damn, that—

"Danny, are you okay to drive?"

If only I could worry about that.

Larry actually looks pretty decent. Light brown hair washed and blown. Nice pair of black slacks, solid-blue collar shirt opened to reveal puka shells against honey skin. Black leather shoes, unscuffed.

"*Whoa.* Larry."

His eyes are serious. "I'll drive."

In a car? With Larry?

I scratch my head, look away. "You know, actually . . . We should take our own cars, because I'm gonna stay up there tonight and then head straight to the airport tomorrow."

Larry blinks hard. "Your car. I'll drive."

"Yeah, but you need to get home tonight." Translation: *There's no chance in hell you're staying with us.*

He turns and walks away. "I'll be waiting in the car."

"Okay, Larry."

"I'll drive."

"Well, we'll see, Larry, we'll see." I pause. "I mean, maybe I should drive."

He stops and turns back, gazes at me, his eyes hardening. "I'll drive."

I try to maintain the eye-lock, try to let him know I can't be bossed around. He stares back, his smile freezing. And I realize, number one, that I probably am too buzzed to drive. And, number two, that Larry can—and will—do this all day.

"Okay, Larry, you'll drive."

Five minutes later, I'm holding on for life.

"Slow down, Larry."

We weave in and out of traffic on northbound 101.

"This is a necessity." His voice is so soft. "It's calming."

He takes the Ralston Avenue exit, hits the brakes hard, considering the fact we're going ninety-five.

"What are you doing? Why're you getting off?" My voice hardens. "Pull to the side here, Larry, I'm driving."

He drives us over the overpass, takes the southbound on-ramp, hits the accelerator. The engine reaches a high pitch.

He soothes, "I'm getting centered."

My cell rings. *Fuck. It's Fitzroy.* I pick up.

"Danny?"

"Hi, Stephen."

"Where are you?"

"I'm just—"

"You making margaritas, Danny? I hear a blender."

"Oh, that's just my—"

"You okay, Danny?"

Larry jets around a Range Rover, sends me against the door.

"I'm fine, sir. I'm just—"

"I got this e-mail, Danny."

"Oh, that's—"

"I thought you told Beth you're busy." He sounds amused.

"Sir, that e-mail is a bunch of BS. I think IT is investigating who sent that out."

Larry tails a Hummer, bangs on the horn.

"That you, Danny?"

"Yeah, that was just—"

"No need to turn to road rage, Danny."

"No, I'm just—"

"Danny, I'll see you on the jet tomorrow."

"Yes, sir."

"Unless you need to take some time off, to get your personal life in order."

"No, sir. I'll be ready."

"And Danny?"

"Yes, sir."

"We're taking the new guy."

"New guy?"

"Yeah, the rat eater."

"Oh, the new guy. Okay."

"He's got a lot of ideas, Danny. Out-of-the-box thinker. He wants to join us, so I'll have you guys dope out this pitch."

The only thing I can think to say is "Sounds interesting."

Larry takes the Holly Street exit, hits the brakes, launches me into the dashboard.

"And Danny?"

"Yes, Stephen?"

"You're not alone."

"Sir?"

"You're not alone."

I wait, unsure where he's going.

He pauses for effect. "I'm one, too."

"And what is that, sir?"

"An ass man, Danny. Just like you."

The line goes dead.

Larry takes us over the overpass, gets on the northbound on-ramp.

"Larry, what is this?"

"This . . ." He hits the gas hard, bangs on the horn, and speeds onto the northbound lanes. ". . . is how I attend to my frequency."

Oh yeah. He did this earlier today, when the geeks were tracking him. They're like warm-up laps, only it's more like wind sprints up and down the 101.

"I want to hit the right frequency," he says, staring at the road. "For my date."

I grip the side handle and slide down as he executes a dramatic lane dive. My stomach rises, and my crotch aches with each jerk.

"Larry," I say, "I'm sorry, but it's not a date."

Larry's silent until we reach the Ralston exit once again. "No . . ." We speed over the overpass, coast onto the southbound on-ramp for another lap. "No, it's a date."

This could be a while.

I look at my briefcase, then at the CD player on the dash-board, and figure, *Might as well put on some Afro Cuban.*

In all, we do eight laps until Larry finally slows to a tolerable speed and we coast past the Ralston exit. I loosen my grip and ease up, whispering, "There we go."

The car beats with Africando's "Yay Boy."

Larry gazes at the road with this frozen look, the slightest of grins, an eyebrow arching.

"You centered now, Larry?"

Voice so soft. "Yes."

I pull out my mobile. "I'll tell Kate we're on our way."

He nods, pulls out his pipe from his shirt pocket, then a yellow lighter. He uses his knees to steer as he lights his bowl, gets a good smoke going. "Tell her I knew this day would come," he says, and blows out a cloud.

Kate picks up on the second ring, but says nothing.

Oh yeah, she's pissed.

"Honey?"

Silence.

"Honey, we're about thirty minutes away. So why don't we meet you at Betelnut?"

Silence.

"Kate?"

"Whatever," she says, and hangs up.

Can't blame her.

Larry slams on the brakes, and I crash into the dash. Cars sail by, horns blaring. I look over at him, and his eyes tighten as a BMW 325i sails past us and pumps the brakes. Larry executes a lane dive, falls behind the 325i, jerks me forward when he hits the brakes. The 325i slows some more, and so do we. It changes lanes, and so do we.

Larry's not letting this guy go.

"Larry, road rage is really pretty dangerous."

"This isn't road rage." The 325i accelerates, and Larry hits the gas, pulls the pipe out of his mouth. "This is a counteroffensive."

I press against the dashboard as Larry makes the Toyota scream.

"Larry," I growl.

Larry hands me his pipe. "Take that." He pumps the stick shift, jerks me back.

"Hold on," he says crisply, and floors the gas.

We rocket toward the Beemer.

"Stop."

He squints at me through the smoke, turns back to the road. "I thought I made it very clear."

The Beemer pulls a lane dive for the ages, nearly crashes into a pickup as it crosses the slow lane toward the Third Street exit.

"Holy shit, Larry." I slide down my seat, brace for impact as we dive across three lanes. Horns blare and tires screech. "Slow the fuck down."

We're right up on the Beemer as we curl around the offramp, to Third Street. The driver glances back a second, and I recognize him immediately despite the bruises and cuts on his face.

Baldy.

Oh shit.

"I thought I made it very clear." Larry cocks his head, like he's been hit with a high pitch that's hurting his ears. "I don't like people following me."

We chase Baldy across the overpass.

"No," I yell. "This is different."

Larry comes up on Baldy, pounds on the horn, bumps his back bumper. The contact makes the Beemer fishtail a little.

"Larry," I yell. "Please."

We follow Baldy toward downtown San Mateo, blaze through a set of red lights. A Land Rover coming right at us skids out of control, flips over, and slides untouched across the intersection.

"Holy shit. Stop it, Larry."

"Different, you said?"

"Yes, yes. Please stop, Larry. You're gonna kill us."

"I need your context as it relates to 'different.'"

The Beemer weaves through traffic. We follow.

"This is the guy who beat me up yesterday. He has nothing to do with the tracking device."

Larry comes up to the Beemer, rams the back again.

"And what about our Kate?"

I feel dizzy. Holy shit, I'm gonna die.

"Kate?"

Larry grabs the pipe from my hand, takes a few puffs, hands it back to me, squints at the Beemer. "What does our Kate think of this individual?"

"Kate?" I yell. "Kate?"

"Yes," he says, his voice calm and delicate. "Kate."

I'm ready to blow. "What do you think she thinks? He scares the shit out of her. We think he's with a corporate security firm or something."

"Corporate?'

"Big money, Larry."

"Big money," he says, more to himself.

"Scary money, Larry."

"And this frightens Kate?"

He hits the gas, changes lanes.

"Larry, watch it. This guy—"

"Daniel?"

"Larry, I think— What?"

We pull up to Baldy on my side. I slide down so only my eyes are showing.

"Daniel," Larry says, his voice crackling, so in control. "I think I smell bacon."

We're speeding down Third Street, side by side with Baldy.

I look over, and Baldy is showing us his handgun, this black number.

God help me. I slide down some more.

Larry steers with his left hand, freeing his right to tug up a pant leg and pull out a buck knife. I let out a little yelp as he waves it around and puts it in his mouth, like a rose, and glances over at Baldy, grinning.

I swear, I'm gonna faint.

"Hol' onsh." Larry slurs through the blade and speeds up. We lane-dive in front of Baldy and slam on the brakes, forcing Baldy to spin out as he tries to avoid hitting us.

And fails.

The collision is hard, the Beemer slamming into my side of the car, behind me. The buck knife flies out of Larry's mouth, onto the dashboard. My head bobbles around in a very unnatural way—so unnatural that everything goes silent. And dark.

From blackness I awake.

It's so quiet now, so peaceful.

The car bounces hard, and the trunk slams shut.

My head throbs, my neck stings, and my crotch radiates hate.

I straighten up, look around.

What the—

"Twine." Larry comes around to my side of the car, so calm. "We'll need twine."

Slowly, I mumble, "Wha— Larry, what's . . ."

Larry leaves me. I moan as my head wobbles. It hurts to look, but I do, using the side-view mirror. In a second, Larry's at the stranded Beemer, pulling at his buck knife, which is sunken into the driver-side door. A metal screech sears my senses as he pulls it loose.

Had no idea someone could throw a knife into a car.

Passing motorists slow down, but no one stops.

Where's Baldy?

Larry reaches into the Beemer, pulls out Baldy's handgun, and shoves it down his pants. Cool as ice.

Sirens in the distance. *God. My car—totaled. My life—*

Larry drops into the driver's seat, slams the door shut, and we jerk forward, take an immediate right into a residential area.

"We need twine."

"Larry, let's stop and wait for the pol—"

"Oh yes," he says, to himself. "Wisnom's Hardware. On First."

Major thump in the trunk.

"Larry, what'd you do?"

Larry stares at the road. "Twine," he whispers. "Twine rope, twine. What else?" He hums to himself. "Well, we'll see what they have."

A big kick against my backseat. Another one, even harder.

"Larry, what'd you do to him?"

"Nothing." Larry taps his fingers to the Africando, jerking his head to the beat. "The collision left him a little dazed, so I just popped your trunk and walked him over."

We pull into the Wisnom's parking lot.

"Larry . . ."

"Our Kate will need to wait a few more minutes."

"Larry," I slur. "We need to stop."

"Don't let him out."

"Larry," I snap.

He's gone.

The next few minutes, the kicks get harder, louder. I ignore them as I try to think of what to do—rubbing my head, trying to ignore the sirens coming from various directions and clear my head, and I realize:

I can't let him out. He could get me arrested. He could kill me.

Plus, this is probably the best chance I'll ever have to make Baldy sing, tell us what he knows.

Lord, what have I become?

From the trunk, a muffled, pissed-off "Hey."

I hear myself yelling, "If I have to pop that trunk, you're getting the baseball bat."

He quiets.

Larry returns with two bags of supplies, opens my door, drops them in my lap.

I poke through the bags. "What is all this stuff? Turpentine? What the hell do you need turpentine for?"

Larry steps behind the wheel, looks at me, gazes at the dashboard. "Let's find a quiet spot." The Toyota jerks backward. "Nice, quiet spot."

"Twenty-gauge metal wire? Pliers? Wood clamps? Rags?" I poke some more, frown. "Lawn fertilizer and polyurethane?"

Larry whizzes us down the street, away from the sirens. "Quiet spot," he whispers, turning us left onto a tree-lined street. "Quiet spot."

"That guy back there is dangerous, you know? Think about this, Larry." I pause, scratch my head. "I mean, maybe we just pop the trunk, let him hop out and we speed away."

Larry scans the neighborhood.

"I'm serious, Larry. This is getting crazy."

Larry pulls us to the curb under a low-hanging elm, behind an old camper. I scan the neighborhood of older homes. Not a soul.

Larry leans over, fingers through the bags, and pulls out the wire and turpentine. Then he pierces me with those eyes.

"Would you like to know why this man is harassing you and your family?"

I look away and tilt my head. Yes, I would.

"Would you like a brief and controlled intermission from your recent insanity?" He pauses, studies my face with those eyes. "For Kate?"

Larry's peering right into me, it seems. His eyes are beautiful, I must admit. "Do you like answers, Daniel?"

I hear myself whisper, "Yes."

He steps out of the car, shuts the door, and leans back in through the open window. "Then follow me."

And just like that, I place the bags on the floorboard and step out of the car.

In front of the trunk, Larry hands me the twine and turpentine and retrieves the buck knife from his shin holster. Without hesitation, he stabs the trunk door with all his might. A loud boom cracks the silence. Baldy yells out, muffled by the trunk.

"Larry," I whisper. "Easy on my car here, okay?"

Larry pulls the knife out, resheathes it, grabs the can of turpentine from my clutch, twists off the cap, and pours a generous amount through the new hole.

The scent reminds me of my father, and I'm transported to my childhood. It's the end of a Sunday, and we're dipping paintbrushes into an old bucket. I'm just a kid, squatting there beside him, watching him run the brushes through the turpentine, the sharp odor hitting me hard, the day fading, the scent of browned hamburger coming from the kitchen.

It's like a sock in the gut.

From the trunk, like a voice in a jar: "Hey."

Larry's eyes enlarge just a tad.

"*Hey!*"

I feel myself getting wobbly again.

Larry pours more in.

"Hey, what the fuck, dude?" A big kick from inside the trunk. "Hey." A big cough, then some wheezing. "Let's be reasonable here."

I wobble forward, touch Larry's forearm. "Larry," I whisper, "what's this going to do to him?"

Holy shit, I'm gonna faint. I put my hand on the trunk to hold myself up.

Larry looks at me, his eyes so alive. "Rashes. Shortness of breath." He cocks his head, thinks about it, and allows the slightest of grins. "Eventually, a nap."

Baldy rasps, "Dude. C'mon. Let's talk."

Larry raises an eyebrow, says into the air, "Oh, we'll talk," then turns and pours more turpentine through the hole.

Which is when I feel myself falling backward, into the sweet sticky realm of nothing.

Such a sweet memory.

A day in the city with Mom and Dad. Afternoon around the Embarcadero and along the piers, then a few shops up around Hyde Street, and then Mexican down in the Mission: chile rellenos and huevos rancheros and Spanish rice. And orange soda and chunky guacamole.

And then that sweet moment when I'm half awake in the backseat, stretched out for the ride home, bounced awake for

just a second, just long enough to note the drool, the moist seat
fabric on my cheek, the hum of the motor soothing me back to
sleep, all so familiar and safe, the memory of the dinner juke-
box playing "Soy Salsero" still in my head, the beat relentless,
the timbales and trumpets dancing so happily as I sink back
into sweetness . . . a distinct blend of cocoa-butter body lotion
and vanilla-scented pipe smoke washing over me.

The music ends, and a new song starts up. Bongos and
trumpets and piano and more timbales, someone singing, "Al-
abanciosa."

Blink my eyes open.

Crap.

I sit up.

Splitting headache.

The beat picks up.

Larry's at the wheel jerking his head from side to side,
tapping the steering wheel as we speed north up 101. Outside,
south San Francisco is a blur.

Larry eyes me through the rearview mirror, blows out a
puff. "I'll need directions," he says. No emotions—like he's a
bank teller.

I frown and rub my forehead. "What?"

"Our Kate," he says. "Our Kate. I'll need directions to our
Kate."

Pain is everywhere—at the back of my head, in front of my
head, in the depths of my eye sockets. Most of all, in my crotch
and spreading to my legs and abdomen and curling around to
spiderweb up my back. I try to stretch, but it hurts too much. I
close my eyes and wish I were dreaming again.

I lean back and squint, trying to keep the light out. "Just take 101 all the way to the end, take a left on Fell Street, take an immediate right on Laguna, and you're good."

The beat intensifies.

Larry leans forward and slaps the top of the dashboard with an open palm, humming to the rapid-fire Spanish.

"Larry, where's the bald guy?"

Still slapping the dash. "You know where he is."

"Larry," I say. "We need to have a plan. I mean, we need to release Baldy. I'm not doing kidnap—"

A black wallet hits me in the face. "It's Anthony," Larry says. "And he's mine, until I get some answers for our Kate."

I stare at the wallet on my lap. With a thumb, I flip it open, glance at it, and look away.

"Larry, we can't do this."

"*We?*" Larry chuckles. "No . . . *I'm* doing this."

"Well, I can't let you do this. We have to give him back."

Big cloud of smoke. "Why was this gentleman following me?"

I sigh, look away. "I don't know, Larry."

"Precisely." He sounds like he's just put the finishing brushstroke on a masterpiece. "Which is why I am going to do some extraction."

"Extraction?"

Larry nods.

"But this has nothing to do with you."

"You said the same thing about the little man who followed me this morning."

I plead. "That was a whole other thing, Larry."

"No . . ." Larry pauses. "No, this is all one big thing."

We cruise in silence awhile, the wallet untouched on my lap, until Larry pulls a right onto Laguna. "You will have to let him go, Larry." I bite my lip, thinking about it, and pick up the wallet, weigh it in my hand. "Eventually."

Larry scans the area. We're driving through Hayes Valley, an interesting cross-section of junkies, hipster merchants, and yuppies in industrial urban wear. "Ah, yes," he sighs, almost a whisper. "Civilization."

"Larry," I yell. "Larry?"

"What?" he snaps.

"You *will* have to let him go. You hear me?"

Larry is annoyed, says, "Of course."

"And I'm not going to lie to the cops."

"The last thing that individual in there will ever do is contact the police."

Damn, the crazy fuck has a point. Still, not on my watch.

"Larry," I beg, my voice cracking, "don't hurt him. It'll just make things worse."

The smoke swirls from the front of the car.

"Are you gonna put him in your garage, Larry?"

Long pause. "Daniel?"

"Yes, Larry?"

"Daniel, I'm about to become agitated."

"No one wants that, Larry. Seriously."

"Daniel, why was this man following me?"

We cross Geary, into Japan Town.

"I don't know, Larry. That's just the thing. I just don't know."

"Well . . ." Larry's voice is rising. "Tell me what you *do* know about this individual."

Don't cry. Hold it together. I take a big breath, let it out slowly. "Only thing I know is, he's connected to big money."

"Big money?"

"Really big money."

"Daniel," he says, so soft I can barely hear him.

"Larry?"

Real long pause.

". . . I do not like big money."

We park the Toyota on Union, right in front of everyone—all the young professionals walking home from work, the fashionista shoppers strolling past, the locals walking their dogs. A woman about my mom's age walks past us with a St. Bernard, a giant drool towel hanging under its collar.

Larry gets out, stretches, smiles to himself as he looks around. "Cow Hollow," he says, motioning to the pedestrians, the boutiques, the restaurants. "I've always admired Cow Hollow, although I see . . ." Larry watches a yuppie brush past us as he barks into a mobile phone. ". . . it has changed."

He's right.

Gentrification.

Like a lot of the more affluent neighborhoods in the city, Cow Hollow seems to have been overrun by young, college-educated fortune seekers from the East—a critical mass of them just a little too smug, a little too status-conscious, a little too sure of their place in the world at such young ages.

I work with some of these folks at FlowBid. One of them loves to refer to San Francisco as "my city." It's not her city.

For it to be her city, she'd have to recognize Cecil Williams in a crowd. She'd have to be able to identify a Santana ballad within the first two chords. She'd have to be interested in her nontech neighbors—the teachers and city workers and artists and merchants. She'd have to know where the city of Fremont is. She'd have to ride Muni.

This isn't her city.

During the holidays, Kate and I like to come to Cow Hollow because all these folks are back home with their parents in New Haven and Boston and Albany, which makes the parking a dream and the remaining population a complete delight.

Betelnut is one of our favorite places—great Asian fusion, great vibe—and now I'm wondering why we agreed to meet here. Not the right kind of energy for Larry, I'm thinking, as I watch him circle the sidewalk in front of the restaurant.

I lean against the wall. When Larry passes, I say, "Not a word from the trunk. Not even a kick."

Larry slows, looks down, and says, "I used the twine. I used all of the twine."

God, my head aches.

"Yeah, but not even a moan or anything."

Larry looks into the air, says, "It's amazing how one has so much less to say when one has a sock in one's mouth."

My heart races. "Larry," I whisper-yell. "He could be dead."

A passerby in a blue blazer glances at me and keeps walking.

"He's napping," Larry says, the irritation high. "I know what I'm doing."

I hobble to the car, pull out my keys, and unlock the trunk. Crouch down, peer in. Can't see a thing.

"Daniel," Larry says, like I'm a disobedient spaniel. "Daniel . . . Don't you dare interfere with my work."

"I'm just checking," I say, and open the trunk a little more, letting some light in.

It would be impossible for someone on the sidewalk to see in my trunk, but I block the view anyway. I squat and squint into the trunk. There's Baldy all wrapped up, twine everywhere, metal wire reinforcing everything, white masking tape wrapped around his jaw, allowing a black sock to hang out of the small opening in front of his mouth.

And he's snoring.

Thank God.

I straighten, look around, and shut the trunk door quickly.

Larry smiles at me. I look down at his feet. One of his socks is missing.

A yellow cab pulls up, double-parks beside my car. Kate steps out, and she's beautiful—a trace of makeup to accentuate her eyes, that silky hair in a ponytail, her black leather jacket and tight jeans, and those boots I love.

"Kate!" I sound like a restaurant greeter, forcing the happiness. "Perfect timing."

I glance at Larry, who has gone rigid, his body paralyzed, his mouth frozen into a smile.

"Larry's here, honey."

Kate looks down, her face taut, and steps past me. She stops a good distance from Larry, spins, and scans the neighborhood. "Okay, where are we doing this?"

Perfect opportunity to steer them away from Betelnut. "How about La Boulange?" I say. "Just down the street."

Larry loosens, says, "Go for a little walk, Daniel. Give us a few hours."

Kate glares at me.

"No." I motion them toward La Boulange, a mellow café and bakery down the street. "Remember the agreement? I need to stay nearby."

Kate walks ahead of us, crosses the street.

We stay on our side, watch her.

Larry says, "You need to get your own table."

Kate reaches the other side, turns, and barks at us, "C'mon."

Larry steps onto Union without looking, causes an Audi to screech to a halt and lay on the horn.

He doesn't care.

I wait a second, glance at my trunk, and limp after him.

La Boulange is basically deserted. I'm in the corner nursing a grossly oversized cup of latte that looks more like a cereal bowl. Kate is at the other end watching Larry pull apart a cinnamon roll with two forks.

Poor Kate.

Her legs are crossed in that proper way—her hands resting on her lap, her back straight—as she watches him work the forks. He looks up at her a second, says something that makes her smile a little.

I mean, to put her through this.

He looks so earnest there with his forks, pulling the swirls apart, stabbing the soft dough, whispering one-off comments to Kate. And she's forced to sit there and engage him with whatever insanity he dishes out.

My wife doesn't deserve this.

I did this to her.

To my relief, at least she doesn't look pissed off. There's a slight warmth to her expression—a kind of quiet amusement, maybe. She lifts her chin, her eyes trained on the forks, and says something to Larry. He stops, glances at her, and eases a forkful of cinnamon roll toward her mouth. She pulls back, nearly laughs. Shakes her head no.

Larry shrugs, slides it into his mouth.

She glances at me, and I offer a see-this-ain't-so-bad smile. She gives me a long, blank stare and returns to Larry.

So much for our rekindled sex life, only a few hours old.

I look at the black leather wallet resting beside my bowl-cup. Baldy's wallet. Still haven't opened it. Not sure why. I mean, hell, now I can find out who this guy is, maybe even who at the equity firm is paying him.

And yet, I let it sit there, unopened. Maybe I'm just too tired. Maybe I'm afraid of what I'll learn.

C'mon, Dan. Get a grip.

I stand up, wobble to the counter, look at the clerk—this twentysomething woman with short black hair and a pierced upper lip—and ask for a pen and piece of paper. She gives me a long look before turning and disappearing into the back area.

Yeah, I know I look awful.

Kate laughs, says to Larry, "Well, I bet."

I look over, and Larry is beaming. Kate's body language is softening. Are they connecting? Is that possible? A well-adjusted mom and a crazy man? Connecting? At some level?

And I realize, *Of course it's possible.*

"Sir."

I jolt, turn around. It's the clerk, reaching over the counter with scratch paper and a pen. "Here you are."

I thank her and turn away.

"Everything okay?"

I stop, turn back. "Huh?"

She glances at Larry and Kate, comes back to me. "Is everything all right?"

"Oh yes." I meet her eyes, smile. "I think so."

She's looking at Larry and Kate again. "I've seen you and your wife in here before."

Embarrassment creeps in. I close my eyes a sec, smile. "Yeah, we love it here."

Still watching Larry and Kate. "I can call my manager, if you'd like, or—"

"No, thanks. But—"

"Or ask Johnny Two Forks over there to leave." She glances at my table on the opposite end of the café. "You know . . ."

Her concern softens me. "Thanks, but we're fine." I begin to shuffle back to my spot. "I'm sure it all seems weird, but believe me, everything is perfect."

Now that really sounded wrong.

I'm lowering myself onto my seat when my mobile rings. It's a 650 number. I stare at it, thinking maybe it's one of the geeks. Maybe it's another coworker calling to report that the entire Western world knows I'm a "butt man." Hell, maybe it's one of Baldy's associates calling with a death threat.

It's Calhoun. Laughing so hard it sounds like panting.

"How'd you get this number?"

"Silly Mr. Danny. You think I can't call FlowBid, ask for Pretty Boy Jordan, and jot down the cell number on your voice mail greeting?"

I glance across the café. Larry sits back, straightens, and scratches his throat with one of his forks. Kate acts like it's the most natural thing in the world.

"What's up, Calhoun?"

Larry continues with the fork. Kate is stoic.

"I just thought you'd like to know I saw a big beefy gentleman walking around your house. And he doesn't look like a policeman."

Larry puts his forks down and gazes at Kate.

Kate motions for him to finish the cinnamon roll.

"Really?"

"He looks like he could be a friend of that mean little cuss."

"Friend? . . . Who?"

"You know, that bald little cuss I belly-flopped."

Kate leans in, tries to stop Larry from lighting up his pipe.

"And you're sure he's not a cop?"

"No, those little rascals came for you earlier."

"Who?" I snap. "Who? The cop from before?"

"He wants you to call him." Calhoun affects a mocking tone in a low, guttural voice. "He said something about a hit-and-run in San Mateo."

Crap.

I say nothing.

In a low baritone: "He asked me about your little car."

"What?" My heart pounds. "What did he say?"

"Oh . . ." Calhoun emphasizes the lackadaisical tone with a long, bored sigh. "He just wanted to know if there were any big dents in your car, and if I'd seen you driving away with—how did he put it?—an older, physically fit Caucasian man with sandy-brown hair."

I feel my latte surge. "What'd you tell him?"

"Well . . ." He giggles like a baby, milking it for all he can.

"C'mon," I snap, earning a glance from the clerk. "What'd you tell him?"

"Well, first, I *would* like to talk with you about some investment opportunities. I can help you, Mr. Daniel. My friend Michael is funding another start-up, and they're accepting buy-ins."

"Calhoun," I snap, "the cop. What did you tell the cop?"

"I'm going to invest in a few of these little companies, and I really think you should consider the same, Mr. Daniel. Michael swears by these kids."

I close my eyes and take a deep breath. "Calhoun, the cops."

"Fine," he snaps, exaggerating his annoyance. "Little Danny doesn't want my investment tips. Fine."

"Later, Calhoun. Seriously. Just tell me what you told the cops."

"What do you think I told him, you silly little cuss? I told him nothing. I told him I saw nothing. And I said not one peep about you and Mr. Larry leaving in your little car."

Larry produces a cloud of smoke, and Kate pushes her chair back. I glance at the counter, where the clerk offers a why-me? look.

"Thanks, Calhoun."

The clerk is coming toward me, scowling, pointing a thumb at Larry.

"Gotta go, Cal—"

"Remember what I said, Mr. Danny. Paradigm shift. You need a paradigm shift."

"Bye," I say, and end the call.

The clerk leans in, motions to Larry, says, "Can you help me with this?"

A voice rumbles, "I'll take care of it."

It's Rod Stone, standing behind me.

The clerk takes Rod in, wide-eyed. And can you blame her? He's quite a sight, the kind of guy who looks amazing in old, raggedy clothes, which he's wearing today—gray threadbare T-shirt, brown thrift-store pants, and worn-in Docs. Seeing him makes you want to try the same look, but you know those old clothes would look awful on mere mortals.

"Thank you," she says, her eyes gleaming, and heads back to the counter.

I look up at him, squinting into the sunlight shining over his shoulder. "How'd you find us?"

"Dude, we need to take charge here." Rod is glaring across the café. "This is ridiculous." He glances down at me. "You're letting that guy have a date with your wife?"

I look away, nod in concession.

"And why?"

"Well," I say, looking up at him again. "Crazy Larry had Little Red in his garage, and High Rider got—"

"Dude." Rod takes my shoulder, squeezes it. "Dude, you need to take charge. I know you need to play nice a few more days, but this is insane."

"Okay," I say, and stand up with a grimace. "You're right."

The clerk stares from behind the counter.

"C'mon." Rod starts for Larry, but I stop him.

"Just one more thing."

He turns, squints at me. It's that look he's always made when I disappoint him, when I fail to live my values. It's like he's trying with all his might to stay positive and understanding.

I get closer. "You know Baldy, the guy who kneed me in the Safeway, threw me into the Eggos, found Harry and Ben at the park?"

He nods. "Yeah, the guy who could've killed you, if not for Calhoun."

I glance at the clerk, whisper, "He's in my trunk."

Rod stiffens and squints. "What?"

"Baldy," I say. "Larry put him in my trunk."

"In your trunk?" Rod says, a little too loudly. "Is he alive?"

"Shshhh," I snap, and glance at the clerk, who's suddenly lost her smile. "Watch it." I stop, look around for eavesdroppers. "Of course he's alive." I look around again, whisper, "Larry just put him down for a nap."

Rod sighs and shakes his head.

"Rod, he was chasing us. We crashed and I got knocked out."

Rod examines my face, focuses on the shovel marks on my brow, the bruise on my left temple, which I must have gotten when we slammed into Baldy's car. I can only imagine what he's thinking.

My eyes are saying, *Help me . . . Please.*

Then Rod says to the clerk, "Throw me that wet rag, will you?"

The rag comes flying, and Rod turns and snatches it out of the air. "We're taking charge, right now," he rumbles.

"Rod," I whisper. "*Watch it!*"

He turns, looks at me, stoic.

"That's Crazy Larry," I say.

"Is he carrying anything?"

"Buck knife in a shin holster."

We look at the clerk, who's watching Larry, her arms crossed over her chest, her teeth biting into her lower lip.

I follow Rod to their side of the café.

"Okay," Rod says, his voice hard. "Date's over."

Larry examines him through the smoke.

"Thank you," Kate says, and stands up to leave.

Rod takes the pipe out of Larry's hand, covers the bowl with the rag, looks down at him. "All right, dude. Let's go."

Larry stares at the pipe and rag, looks around the café, leans forward, and drops his right hand. His other hand grips a fork, ready for attack.

Kate says, "Rod? Umm, who's with the boys right now?"

Rod watches as Larry's hand slides closer to his left shin, where the knife holster should be. "They're still at my place," Rod says, easing me out of the way. "Damian and his sister came over to watch them." He stares at Larry, his jaw tightening. "And we're going to take you back there now."

Larry lowers his hand a little more.

I feel myself back up.

Get ready.

"Larry," I say, "you better watch it with Rod here."

Kate says, "How'd you find us?"

Rod waves her off, keeps his eyes on Larry.

"Larry," I say, "I told Rod about our friend in the trunk."

Rod steps closer, towers over him, and drops the pipe onto the table, lets it bounce. "And we're gonna take care of that right now."

Larry scratches at his left pant leg.

Rod says, "Where's your restroom, miss?"

The clerk, her face pale, motions to the back hallway.

"Thanks," he says, and turns to Kate. "Excuse us a second."

Larry fumbles with his pant leg.

Rod reaches down, grabs his arm, and spins him off his chair. In a second, the fork sails across the café and Larry is immobilized in one of Rod's mixed-martial-arts holds, his arms helpless, pointing in unnatural directions. Rod kicks Larry's leg, and the buck knife clangs to the floor.

"Get that, would you?"

I obey.

Rod rushes Larry down the hallway into the restroom.

The buck knife is heavy and cold. I look around, decide to wrap it up in the dish towel, and clamp the whole thing under my right arm. I meet eyes with the clerk, who's backing up slowly.

From the restroom, hard thuds and muffled grunts.

From behind the counter, the clerk picks up the phone, dials three numbers.

Nine-one-one. Fuck.

Kate grabs my arm, tugs. "C'mon. Let's get the car."

The clerk whispers into the phone. Great—squad cars will be here in minutes.

"Rod," I holler. "Time to jet."

The door pops open, and Larry walks out gingerly, his movements a little disjointed, his head a little wobbly, his shirt stretched and torn. Rod strolls after him, says, "I think we understand each other now."

Sirens in the distance.

Kate is gone.

"C'mon." I walk to the counter, drop two twenties into the tip jar, and point Rod and Larry to the street. "We're here when they show up, they make us pop the trunk."

Suddenly, Larry quickens the pace.

Rod strides past me, looks straight ahead, says, "Take us to The Spot."

"The Spot?"

Sirens getting louder.

He stops, looks back, and nods.

"You sure?"

He leads Larry down the street, to my car. I follow them, the San Francisco breeze cooling my skin.

"You think that makes sense?"

"This guy in the trunk. He got a name?"

I stop short. *Crap. The wallet.*

I turn and run back into the café, knock over two chairs in my scramble to my table, snatch the black leather wallet, and pivot back toward the entrance.

The clerk is waiting, a baking pan in both hands.

Sirens a little closer.

"C'mon," I plead.

Shakes her head no. "You have someone in your trunk. I heard you."

"Move," I snap.

Shakes her head no. "You think I can just stand there and let you get away when you have a human being in your trunk?" She raises the pan above her head, ready to whack me.

Sirens getting louder.

"It's not like that."

"Oh, sure. I stuff people into my trunk all the time."

I slide Baldy's wallet into my pocket. "C'mon."

Shakes her head. "*You* I can handle."

Probably.

I shuffle toward her, cringe as I approach.

She steps aside, yells a war cry, and whacks me hard across the face as I stumble out of the café and onto Union Street, where my Corolla skids to a stop.

It's getting dark.

Kate's driving, Rod is in shotgun, and Larry and I are in the backseat, the can of turpentine and the other "supplies" on the floorboard between us. We sit silent as Kate speeds us out of the city, onto 280 South, toward Daly City. "Tell me where to get off," she says.

Rod acts surprised. "You don't know The Spot?"

From the trunk, Baldy thumps against the backseat.

"The Spot?" Kate repeats. "Is this another high school thing?"

Rod turns back to me, releases the tightest of grins. Returns to her, says, "Take the John Daly Boulevard exit, head west, toward the ocean."

Kate gives me an unreadable look through the rearview mirror, her jaw taut. Is she pissed that I failed to take charge, watched as Rod did what I wouldn't do? Did someone send her the butt-lover e-mail from FlowBid? Or does she know there's more where that came from? Can she see it on my face?

Rod looks out the window, smiles to himself. "Been a while since I've been to The Spot."

I glance at Larry, who seems to be in a trance, and close my eyes.

The Spot. Late summer night, the eighties. What I'd give to go back to that moment, just for a sec.

I take a deep breath, let it out slowly, and I can almost hear Journey beating slowly on the boom box, can almost see the silhouettes around me, just as they were all those years ago, when we were thirteen and ready for high school, that night when Rod and I tagged along with my older cousin and his friends, ended up here on the bluffs over the Pacific, a girl in my arms in a very real and soft way for the first time in my life, dancing really close for the first time, a virtual stranger, the long bangs and nighttime dark shading her eyes and grin as "Feeling That Way" eases from the speakers, looking back to Rod and a girl, bumping into them and laughing, the older kids sitting on car hoods, talking softly, letting us be, the soft clank of beer bottles over easy talk about friends and surf, no one breaking our balls for being over here dancing and hugging, our cheeks sliding against each other ever so lightly, over and over, her body feeling so new and different against mine as Journey bleeds into "Anytime" and she lets me keep her close. I look over to Rod and his friend, realize they're back with the others, leaning against my cousin's AMC Eagle. Rod seems to be watching us a second before leaning in to his new friend in that flirtatious way, chuckling about something, and it occurs to me that I've never seen him happy this way, included, brought in from the cold.

I open my eyes. It's dark out, and we're nearly there.

Rod says, "You sure you want to do this, Katie?"

Kate's face tightens, nods.

Rod glances back at me a sec and says to her, "Let me start with him. Okay?"

She nods, looks like she's about to cry.

Larry stammers, strains to say, "He was mine."

Rod turns and looks back at him, grins, amused. "Oh yeah?"

Larry says, "I need to rationalize him."

Rationalize?

Kate says, "Is this it?"

Rod nods, points to the far end of the gravel parking lot. "Take us over there."

When we come to a stop, Larry sits up. "He's mine."

"He's not yours, Larry." Rod hardens. "We decide."

I rub my forehead. *Shit, whatever happened to the cops?*

Then I think of my options, of all the dirt the geeks have on me, of that detective demanding a piece of the action.

Just thirty-six more hours, Danny.

Larry says, "He's like a rag, engorged with the milk of data and background, and I can wring that rag in an effective, systematic manner that will extract every ounce of that milk into my chalice." He stops, squints into space. "*Our* chalice."

Rod frowns, looks at Kate. "Chalice?"

She shrugs, looks away.

Larry draws a breath. "Our chalice of knowledge, our chalice of . . ." Slowly, he exhales. ". . . intelligence."

Rod and I glance at each other.

"I've already wrung the milk out of the diminutive individual who tried to follow me this morning."

Ah, Little Red.

And then it clicks. Crazy Larry wasn't simply "playing" with Little Red in his garage; he was "extracting" background, getting to the bottom of it all.

"You know, don't you?" I grab Larry's arm, squeeze. "You know why Little Red and his buddies are harassing me?"

Larry cocks his head like he's picking up an irritating, high-pitched noise. "Not harassment," he snaps, his voice crisp. "Forced collusion."

"But you know everything?"

He turns to me, narrows his eyes. "I had him for hours." His voice softens, goes extra delicate. "I wrung out every droplet." He thinks about it, hums and whispers. "A thorough wringing. Or, to use an agricultural euphemism, a harvest."

"Larry," Kate snaps, "just tell us what you know."

His voice crackles. "All you had to do was ask," he hums, and motions his head toward the trunk. "But I wouldn't want our new friend to hear."

I whisper, "He's not in cahoots with the geeks?"

Slowly shakes his heads no.

Rod rumbles, "Then what's his deal?"

"And that is the question." Larry's voice drips with want. "Which is why I'd like to take him home and . . ." He hums to himself—Chopin, I think, or maybe Bach. ". . . and harvest the knowledge."

"Nah," Rod says, opens the door, and gets out. The cold Pacific blasts in, digs under my shirt, jolts me, and I hunch my shoulders and shiver. "Nah, we'll take care of this right here."

Kate retrieves my flashlight from the glove compartment and steps out, too. "I'll start with him."

"Let me start," Rod says. "I need to make sure he and I . . ." He loosens his neck like he's about to step into The Octagon, cracks his knuckles. ". . . understand each other."

Before I follow them, I lean over to Larry and whisper, "What's their deal?"

Larry turns to me, squints like I'm an annoying noise.

"The geeks," I snap. "The geeks. Why do they want me to tape Fitzroy? You know? In Florida."

Larry examines my face, his eyes settling on my chin. "People." He opens his door, turns to get out. "It's about people."

I reach to grab his shoulder but think better of it, pull my hand back. "But what is it? What is it they want me to tape?"

"You don't need to know."

Same thing the geeks told me.

"But, Larry—"

He turns, faces me. "I told you." His eyes go dark, seem to sink deep into his sockets. "I told you I don't like big money."

"But—"

"Listen to the little people, and do as they say."

I nod to the trunk. "But what about this guy?"

Larry touches my hand softly. "You tell your cage fighter to retreat, and I will take him to my place and harvest the intelligence."

"No more garage time, Larry."

I step out into the frigid cold. The fog has come in, dimming the moonlight and distant parking lot lamps, seeping under our collars, shooting down our backs, chilling us. I look around and listen—nothing but the cold wind, the crashing of the waves, and the fog making the night even darker. I hug myself and hobble to Kate and Rod behind the car, grimacing with each step as bolts of pain shoot through my crotch and stomach.

Rod looks at Kate, then me. "I need to know."

"What?"

He eases closer. "Before I pop that trunk, I need to know how badly you need this info."

Kate says, "Rod, it's important. We hold on another day and a half, we can walk away forever."

Rod says, "A lot of coin? Life-changing coin?"

"For us, yes." I look around, step closer. "If I screw up these last thirty-six hours, Kate and I lose everything. So I just need to play along a couple more days."

Rod nods, looks away.

"And this guy?" I nod to the trunk. "It's like he wants to stop me. And if he succeeds, we lose it all."

Rod whispers, "We're talking about a lot of money?"

Kate says, "Rod, we last a couple more days, we can live the way you've always wanted us to live."

Rod sways to the trunk, looks back at us. "You're cool if this has to get ugly?"

"Rod, this guy was following my boys."

He's lingering over the trunk lock, fingering through my key chain. Kate steps closer, clutches the unlit flashlight.

Larry joins us with the can of turpentine.

Rod gets the key in, prepares to pop the trunk, motions to the flashlight in Kate's hand. "Get that ready."

Larry lifts the turpentine, steps forward.

"Hey," Rod says, putting a hand out. "Cool it."

Larry stops.

Rod whispers, "Me first," and pops the trunk.

Door eases up in silence. Nothing but the scent of turpentine.

Kate flips the light on, shines it into the trunk. Baldy is still curled into his forced fetal position, constrained by the metal wire, the sock still hanging out of the slit where his mouth should be. His eyes are wild, his chest rising and falling. He looks exhausted and terrified, but his vitals seem fine. I sigh in relief.

Rod snarls, reaches in with both hands, rips the tape off Baldy's face, and pulls out the sock. Baldy heaves and spits, sucks in big breaths, his eyes still wide in fear. He convulses once, then moans and shudders.

Rod takes the flashlight from Kate and puts it under his chin.

"You see this face?"

Baldy looks, his eyes in terror, and nods.

"Is this the face of someone who plays games?"

Baldy shakes his head no.

Rod plows his elbow into the trunk, getting Baldy in the mouth. Brings it up again, drops it again, into Baldy's nose.

"You fucked with the wrong people, asshole."

Baldy cries no.

Rod puts the light on his face again, smiles. "I'll fucking maim you, brother. I'll maim you for life."

Baldy sputters. "No, it's just— Let's try to—"

Rod drives his right fist into Baldy's throat.

Baldy stiffens, chokes, spasms.

"You think you're some kinda tough guy?" Rod's jaw juts out. "You think you scare us?"

Kate creeps forward, touches Rod's shoulder. He eases her back.

Finally, Baldy regains his breath, starts to whimper. Never would have believed it if I hadn't seen it myself. Baldy the bulldog, the guy who decked me at Safeway just yesterday, is now tied up and whimpering in my trunk.

"It doesn't have to . . ." He gasps. ". . . end this way. I have money."

"Money?" Rod lowers his head into the trunk, yells, "You think I want money?"

Baldy winces, preparing for impact.

"Give me his wallet, Danny."

I dig into my front pocket, hand it over. Rod opens it, pulls out the driver's license, eases it under the light, leans in and squints. "Anthony Altazaro." He pauses, looks into the trunk. "Of Brisbane." He fans through Baldy's credit cards and IDs. "This is perfect, Anthony. Or can I call you Tony?"

Silence.

"Regardless, this is everything I need to destroy your life, and those of the ones you love. Assuming you're capable of love." He stands there, thinking about it, jutting his jaw out again. "Assuming you get through this."

Baldy spits more cotton.

"You want to live?"

Baldy nods.

"Then tell me why you're harassing my friend and his family. And if you lie, I will find out. I have all your info. And I will—God as my witness—fucking kill you."

Long silence. "Not here." He sighs. "Not like this. I want guarant—"

Rod slams the trunk lid down, hollers at it. "It's about to get much worse, Anthony." He waves Larry over. "Your turn, Larry." Then, to the trunk: "You remember Larry from earlier, don't you, Anthony?"

A distress call from the trunk.

Rod mumbles to Larry, "Do your thing."

Larry twists off the cap, pours the turpentine into the knife hole, then stops and waits.

From inside the trunk: "Hey. *Hey!*"

Larry pours more in.

Coughing. "Okay, okay."

Rod stops him, pops the trunk. Baldy gasps for fresh air, spasms again.

Rod grabs Larry, pulls him to the maw of the trunk, shines the light above his face, illuminating his beard and nose, leaving his eyes in shadow. Baldy glances up at him, screams.

"So you do remember Larry?"

Larry says, "I need my pliers."

A whimper.

"Larry would like to take you back to his place and—what was that word?—wring . . ."

Larry coos, "Or *harvest*."

". . . the details out of you."

Baldy squirms.

"Point is," Rod says, "I don't think he's gentle like me."

Larry hums and crackles. "I'll take him."

"Or we can pick you up as you are—all tied and restrained, compliments of Larry here—and drop you off at the pool, so to speak." He nods to the black expanse before us, cups his hand to his ear, listening to the waves. "It's your choice."

Baldy coughs, gasps, "Give me a second."

Rod slams the trunk shut, nods to Larry.

More turpentine. More shouts from the trunk.

Larry hums another classical melody—Bach?—as he continues to pour.

Kate says, "Pop the trunk."

"But—"

"Just pop the fucking trunk."

The trunk door rises again. Kate snatches the flashlight from Rod and climbs into the trunk, squats over Baldy. "Listen, you little fuck," she growls. "You beat up my husband, you come after my boys, and now you think you can follow us?"

He looks away, cowers.

"Either you start singing, or we drag your pathetic face down to the water." She climbs out of the trunk. "Starting now."

Baldy rasps, "It's not that simple."

"Oh yes, it is," she snaps, and turns to us. "Guys, let's take him for a dip."

The roar of the surf drowns out his screams.

As Baldy rolls around in the ankle-deep water, pleading for his life, Larry and Rod stand over him arguing.

"Let me harvest," Larry snaps. "In my lab."

"He's not going to your garage, Larry. Too much evidence."

Baldy yelps and tries to rock himself to dry sand. Rod puts a foot out, pushes him back into the froth.

"If I get him to my lab, I can harvest the intelligence. Every last droplet."

Rod turns, squats down to Baldy, tries to make eye contact with him. "Plus, we don't have the time."

Baldy coughs on icy seawater.

"C'mon, c'mon." Kate paces, squinting into the fog, looking for witnesses. "Let's do this already."

"Kate's right," Rod says. "It's time to roll."

He rolls Baldy farther into the water. Baldy screams.

Kate takes my arm, pulls me back. Concern in her eyes.

"Don't worry," I whisper.

Rod rolls him deeper, until a wave crashes over them, submerging Baldy. When the wave recedes, Baldy is rocking back and forth, heaving and gasping for air. Giant breaths.

"Oh," Rod says, backing up. "Here comes another one."

The wave breaks, sending a wall of white water toward Baldy.

Rod sings, "Incoming."

The water submerges Baldy.

This time, for longer.

The water recedes again.

More spasms and choking and gasping.

Rod squats, rolls him toward the water, looks up. "Oh Lord. This one's a big boy."

Rod backpedals.

The wave engulfs Baldy, pulls him out a little more.

I can't see him. Holy shit, I can't see him.

I pull off my shoes and socks, bolt into the water, frantic, my crotch exploding.

"Don't worry," Rod says, pointing to a blotch of black in the foam. "He's right there."

The wave recedes.

Baldy is rocking violently, trying to roll away from the water. More heaving and spasms.

"Please," he chokes. "Please."

Rod walks over, squats down, "You feel like talking now, Tony?"

"Yes, please," he cries. "Please."

Rod motions for me to help roll him to higher ground.

"He feels chatty now, Danny."

Baldy cries.

Larry emerges from the fog. "I get him after you."

Rod says, "Just make sure no one comes over here."

Larry disappears into the fog.

We roll Baldy so his face is up. The bone-chilling water has drenched him. With the sharp gusts blasting us, he's shivering uncontrollably, his whole body vibrating, his teeth chattering like a cartoon. "Puh-puh-puh . . . p-p-p-p-p-puh-lease."

Rod squats, gets close, asks, "Why are you harassing my friend?"

Kate arrives, squats behind me.

"It-it-it-it's a j-j-j-job."

"No shit, Beatrice. What was your assignment?"

"Just . . . j-j-j-just scare him a l-l-l'il. R-r-r-rough him up."

"And following his kids to a park, playing with them. What's that all about?"

"Wa-wa-wa-wa-was g-g-g-going to have th-th-the-the b-b-big kid pass along a m-m-message."

"Oh yeah?"

"I'm sup-pup-pup-pup-posed to scare 'im into stayin' he-he-he-here."

"Here?"

"The k-k-k-k-kid wa-wa-wa-was supposed to t-t-t-t-tell him to n-n-not go to T-T-T . . . Tampa."

Kate and I glance at each other.

I say, "You're not working with those IT geeks from Flow-Bid, are you?"

Shakes his head. "They're th-th-the p-p-p-problem."

Kate says, "Why shouldn't he go to Tampa?"

"N-n-n-no idea."

We look at each other. I believe him.

Kate says, "Who's calling your shots at Stanislau?"

Baldy stammers.

"Does this have to do with Knowland, Hill, and Davis?"

Baldy shudders, nods yes. "All I-I-I kn-kn-know is, he's not sup-p-p-posed to go to Tamp-p-p-pa."

Rod says, "You're withholding information." He tugs on Baldy, adds, "Time to take another dip."

Baldy screams. "No . . . *no*."

Rod tugs him toward the ocean.

"No-no-no-no-n-n-n-no."

"Who gave you this assignment? Someone at Stanislau, or someone from that other place?"

Baldy stammers. "The other place, th-th-the other p-p-place."

"Knowland, Hill, and Davis?"

Nods yes.

"Tell me his name right now, or you're going for a swim."

He whimpers. "It's comp-comp-comp-complicated."

Rod stands up, starts rolling him back to the surf.

"Ser-seriously."

Rod rolls him onto the wet sand. "Bet you wish you brought your nose clips, huh?"

Baldy whimpers, "F-f-fine. Fine. It's David D-D-D-Duncan."

All I can see is Rod's silhouette. "David Duncan? With Knowland, Hill, and Davis?"

He makes a yes-whimper.

"Your client?"

Another yes-whimper.

Larry steps out of the fog. "Now I get him."

Rod stands up, stretches. "Danny, help me get him back into the trunk."

Baldy cries.

Larry steps toward Rod, thinks better of it, steps back.

Rod straightens, sighs. "Tony was a good boy, Larry. He decided to talk. I think it's our responsibility to take him home, remove the wire that's been digging into his flesh, and tuck him in bed."

Baldy makes a noise that sounds like *Yes, yes, please, please.*

"But of course," Rod says, "he will need to give us the home address of this David Duncan."

Seven

This much I know . . .

David Duncan is in his $3 million home on Jackson Street, near Broderick–Pacific Heights. He's in the office, tapping on his laptop, a glass of '92 Colgin cabernet sauvignon from the Herb Lamb Vineyard on the desk, Coltrane's "My Favorite Things" pulsing low, adding to his glow. The wife is already asleep, and the au pair is upstairs handling the bedtime ritual with the kids. David *hates* dealing with the kids at night.

He's looking at the stocks.

In a day, his portfolio has appreciated by $270,000.

Google.

Salesforce.com.

Genentech.

VMware.

And then all those inside deals he engineered as a partner with Knowland, Hill, and Davis. Deals to fund an elite crop of start-ups, most of which have gone public and amassed extreme fortunes on the wings of the second tech bubble in a decade.

As a partner at the firm, and as a shrewd private investor, David Duncan boasts a portfolio north of $79 million. But he wants more. Much more.

Hell, he's only forty-one. By forty-five, he wants his own jet, with his own pilots, and not some Citation X piece of shit, but a Gulfstream 5. He wants homes in Kauai, New York City, Paris, London, and of course his hometown outside Hartford, Connecticut. By the time he's fifty, he wants to be able to establish trust funds for his great-great grandchildren. He wants to be on the *Fortune* list—a list of the smartest winners of the Internet era. He wants everyone to know he's winning, and that he's winning more than they are.

He wants at least half a billion.

FlowBid has made a big difference. Since the IPO, the stock has increased fourteen times its original share price. If everything holds together a few more months, Knowland, Hill, and Davis will be allowed to start selling its FlowBid shares on the open market—portal to millions of investors who are, once again, frothy—and could walk away with more than $1.3 billion.

As long as Stephen Fitzroy can keep it together.

As long as those stupid downsized geeks don't make it worse.

Which is why David Duncan picks up his cell and dials his guy at the corporate intelligence and security firm, Stanislau. Tony, or Anthony. The compact, muscular bald guy who kind of gives him the creeps. The guy who's supposed to be keeping the geeks in check, keeping them from recruiting more people—people like Fitzroy's speechwriter.

He rings Tony's phone.

Hears something at the front of the house. *Knocking?*

Gets Tony's voice mail, again. *Shit, where is he?*

He gets up, walks toward the front of the house, squints through the glass door.

Two tall men in dark clothes are standing at his porch. At their feet, balled into the fetal position, is Tony, his problem solver.

Getting Baldy out of my trunk the second time is harder. Probably because his clothes are soaking, his body vibrating. Or maybe because my own hands are shaking so hard.

Rod ends up doing most of the lifting and pulling.

"You okay, Danny?"

"Yeah." I scan the street—no one. "You sure this makes sense?"

Larry watches from the sidewalk.

"What's this guy gonna do? Call the cops?" Rod huffs. "He can't." He thinks about it a second. "And we need answers."

I look at the house. It's a fully restored Victorian, four stories, perfectly manicured and appointed—lights illuminating the landscaping, crystal-clean windows releasing a perfect glow from within. Small spiked entry gate opening to a cobbled path leading to a beveled-glass door. I look at it all, notice the security camera on the porch, feel the jolt in my gut.

This could be it. This could be the moment I become a criminal—and have it all captured on tape. Thank God we dropped off Kate at Rod's place to be with the boys. This thing here goes tapioca and I end up in prison, at least the boys will have Kate.

"Help me with this guy." Rod is squatting over Baldy, who's curled up on the sidewalk, the metal wire still digging into his flesh, still forcing him into the fetal position.

Larry watches.

By the time we reach the front door, I'm panting and Baldy is pleading.

"D-d-d-don't do this, guys. I'll lose my job."

"Oh, did you hear that, Danny? Tony here may lose his job on account of stalking your young boys and attacking you unprovoked in the frozen-food section of an otherwise fine establishment. Hmmm. Maybe I shouldn't ring the doorbell. I mean, poor Tony here may not be able to harass and endanger more families if I ring this doorbell."

"P-p-please. My rep will be de-de-destroyed. We can take this offline."

Rod looks at me. "I tell you what. Maybe I shouldn't ring the doorbell. Maybe I should just tap the glass here on this pretty door. Like this."

David Duncan looks like a 1970s TV cartoon. Meaning, when you get past the broad strokes of his appearance—no wrinkles, soft chin, pasty-white complexion with zero color, unscuffed hands, and a perfectly fashioned block of blond hair—nothing else really stands out. Everything on him is uniform.

He's standing there in his work clothes—the standard venture capital outfit of light-blue button-up, midnight-blue slacks, and shiny Kenneth Coles—examining us through the thin, delicate glasses on his nose.

Rod says, "You David Duncan?"

Duncan stares down at Baldy.

"Hey." Rod juts his jaw out, steps across the threshold and into Duncan's personal space. "You hear me?"

Duncan backs up, stammers. "What is this?"

Duncan is looking at Baldy again, his mouth puckering. Baldy shakes, stutters, "S-s-s-s-sorry, David. They had me in the ocean. I h-h-h-had to talk."

Rod says, "Good. So you *are* David Duncan. We're making progress."

Duncan backs up, quivers. "I have video surveillance. You're being recorded."

Rod says to me, "Help me with Tony here." He squats over Baldy, and I join him. "Ready? . . . One . . . two . . . three."

Larry follows, puffing on his pipe, watching, making an enormous cloud in Duncan's entryway, which is where we lower Baldy.

"I have cameras."

"We heard that," Rod says, pleasant. "And I'm happy for you, David."

Duncan steps back again, touches his glasses. Rod invades his space again. "And I bet you have panic buttons, too. Would you like to press one? It's fine if you do. We can talk this out with a few of San Francisco's finest."

Duncan peers up and settles on the scars racing up and down Rod's face—the cauliflower ears, the thick brow and square jaw.

"Go ahead," Rod says, pleasant. "Push your little buttons."

Duncan motions to a perfectly lit room toward the end of the entryway. "Let's take this to my office."

"Sure," Rod says. "That sounds real nice, David."

Duncan motions to Baldy. "Ummmm. Guys?"

"Oh, well, our backs are kinda sore from lifting and rolling Tony around."

Duncan studies Rod, swallows hard.

"So why don't you roll him in yourself?"

Duncan looks at us, frozen, then at Baldy. Puts his hands on his hips, stares at the floor.

"Heck, maybe Larry here would be willing to give you a hand."

Duncan looks up at Larry for the first time. Larry stares back with hollow eyes.

"Granted, Larry doesn't like big money." Rod sighs, mocking concern. "So I'm not sure he'll want to help."

Larry is still staring at Duncan. "Let me have him."

"You see," Rod says. "Larry's the one who did this to your pal Tony here. He's very creative. He did this number on the fly—on the side of a road, I hear. Put Larry in his garage, with all his tools and a little bit of time, and . . . well, he's a fucking artist."

Duncan looks to Rod, then at Larry. "Who are you guys?"

Rod ignores him. "An artist with his own medium. Not with clay or watercolors or even scrap metal. With assholes like you."

Duncan seems paralyzed.

"Larry, would you like to help David here with his friend?"

Larry produces a fresh cloud of smoke, steps over Baldy, and saunters into the office. "After this . . ." He nods to Duncan. ". . . I take him to my place."

Rod smiles. "See?" He wants to take you to his garage."

"Where I can extract," Larry says, so soft, "every droplet."

"Oh yeah." Rod shakes his head, laughs. "Larry gets information—"

"Extracts," Larry corrects.

"Okay, extracts information—intelligence—from his subjects while he uses them to . . . Well, to be honest, I'm not sure what he does with them in there. All I know is what happened to one of the geeks today when he met Larry."

I clear my throat, add, "But we're betting we won't need to send you to Larry's place."

Duncan looks at me, wide-eyed and submissive.

"We're betting you'll talk with us tonight. Right now."

A child's voice. "Daddy?"

We all turn and look up the staircase. A girl, four maybe, is standing at top of the stairs, in her nightgown. She's clutching a stuffed animal. A unicorn?

"Veronica, go back to bed."

"Daddy?"

"Go to Maria's room if you need something," he snaps. "Just stay up there."

She doesn't move. "Daddy, why is that man on the floor like that?"

Duncan hollers, "Maria?"

Rapid footsteps.

"Maria, take her, will you?"

A soft female voice says, "Yes. Sorry, sir. Come here, honey. Come."

Rod turns back to Duncan. "I can tell you're the involved type of parent."

Duncan looks away, motions to the office. "Let's talk."

Rod nods to Baldy. "We wouldn't want to make Tony here feel left out."

Duncan looks at us, and we stare back at him. Until David Duncan, young master of the universe, squats over his shivering, wet, sandy associate and begins the awkward task of sliding him toward the office.

We're all in chairs, except for Rod, who's sitting on Duncan's solid-oak desk. He looks at Duncan and nods to me. "Do you know who this guy is?"

Duncan glances at me. "I don't know what—"

"Answer the fucking question."

Duncan glances at me again, returns to Rod. "No, I don't know him. But I'm gathering he's the speechwriter."

"Oh yeah?"

"Stephen Fitzroy's speechwriter." Duncan seems annoyed, huffs. "He spends a lot of time with Stephen."

Rod acts surprised. "Wow, lucky guess."

Duncan sits back, folds his arms.

"Now here comes a really important question. See if you can answer this one the first time I ask."

Larry whispers, "I get him."

"David." Rod's voice hardens. "Why are you having a corporate security guy like Tony here—from Stanislau, no less—beat up my man here? Harassing his family and even stalking his children?"

Duncan chokes on his spit, swallows hard. "I don't know what this—"

Baldy rasps, "You said to get his att-tt-attention."

Rod nods. "Good. We're getting somewhere." He studies Duncan. "You wanted to get his attention. You wanted to scare him."

Duncan looks away. "Well, I just—"

"Does he look scared?" Duncan glances at me. "Do *we* look scared?"

Silence.

Rod nods to Baldy on the floor. "Who in this room looks scared?"

Duncan concedes the point, mumbles to himself.

"Why were you doing this, David?"

Duncan bites a nail, thinks about it.

"Okay," Rod says, "seeing as you seem to be a little tongue-tied, and seeing as I'm running out of patience, I think it's time I tell you about your choices."

Duncan looks up at him.

"Think of them as doors, really."

Larry hums the theme music from a game show—I'm not sure which.

"Yeah, that's right," Rod says. "*The Price Is Right*. What's behind the big doors?" He studies Duncan a second. "Only we'll make it easy for you. We'll tell you."

Larry still humming.

"Let's assume you just keep mumbling and we don't get any answers. In that case, you'll get Door Number One."

Larry intensifies the humming.

"And what's behind the big door?" Rod waits, then affects a booming MC voice. "*Well, Bob, it's a trip to Larry's garage.*"

The humming stops. Larry stiffens, makes a clicking noise, like a cat staring at a rodent.

"So that's one option."

Duncan straightens, says, "I'm sure we can work this—"

Rod stops him. "Now, assume you do talk, but not to my satisfaction."

Larry booms, "What does he win, Bob?"

Rod loses the MC voice, lowers his voice to that rumble. "Door Number Two."

Duncan waits for more.

"Do you know what I do for a living, David?"

"No, I—"

"I fight people." Rod's eyes twinkle; his voice goes soft and gentle. "In a cage."

Duncan tries to maintain eye contact, and fails.

"So." Rod chuckles to himself. "*Behind Door Number Two . . .*"

Larry says, "No, just Door Number One."

Rod blinks. "Door Number Two . . . Well, that's just me. Or, I should say, me and you. Right here in this office. With the door shut. Our little cage."

"Guys, we can work this out."

Rod smiles. "Good, because the other option is Door

Number Three. And that one is a lot less physical, I guess, isn't it, Danny?"

"Yeah," I say. "It's just me contacting some of my old co-workers from my newspaper days. Just me telling a few choice business writers—or maybe my crime reporter buds?—about David Duncan, the partner in a major private equity fund, who is having employees of FlowBid, *a company in which he has heavily invested*, stalked, harassed, and attacked by a high-priced private security operative."

Duncan says, "Guys—"

Rod says, "No, David. I'm going to ask you a simple question, and you are going to answer it. And if you don't, well, I guess I'll let Larry here choose a door."

Larry clicks, produces a cloud of smoke. Baldy chitters and moans.

Rod leans in. "David, why did you have this asshole attack Dan here and harass his family?"

Duncan freezes, says, "It's about Fitzroy."

Rod and I glance at each other.

"What about him?"

"Well, it's what some people want to do to him."

"What? Hurt him?"

Duncan looks away. "No, they want to— You know. They just want to humiliate him." He huffs, shakes his head, looks away. "They want to expose some things."

"About Fitzroy? Or about the company?"

He looks down at Baldy, who's stopped shivering. "Well, Fitzroy *and* the company. They're kind of the same thing. FlowBid is Fitzroy, and Fitzroy is FlowBid."

"What do they want to expose?"

"I'm not quite sure." He fidgets with his cuff link, looks up at me. "But I know they're talking with you."

Rod says, "They want Danny's help with something."

"Yes, but I don't know what it is."

"But you're concerned."

"Yes, well . . ." He looks at us, and his face sags a little. "We've invested heavily in FlowBid, and . . . well, we can't afford anything to erupt these final two months. That's all this was about."

"Erupt?"

"With Fitzroy. You know."

"No, I *don't* know."

Duncan shrugs. "Fitzroy's behavior. You know, his extremes."

"Extremes? You mean, extreme business practices?"

Duncan shakes his head. "All I'm saying is, if Fitzroy goes down, the market cap of FlowBid will plummet, and—well, a lot of people would lose a lot of money."

Rod rumbles. "Including Knowland, Hill, and Davis."

He nods yes. "Including hundreds of thousands of investors. Millions of investors."

"But especially you guys."

He closes his eyes, nods. "Yes, yes. Especially us."

Rod says, "So tell us about these guys."

Duncan puts out a hand. "Guys, I really don't think it's going to help—"

"Larry and Danny." Rod stares at Duncan. "Can you excuse us for a second? I think David here has just won Door Number Two."

I get up to leave.

Larry says, "Then I get him."

Duncan snaps, "Okay, fine. They're laid-off sys admins."

Rod lowers his head and yells in his face, his veins popping. "*No shit, Maxine.* We already knew that."

Duncan winces and braces for impact.

"You know more about these guys. And you're gonna tell us or we'll do a round in the 'cage' here."

Duncan recoils, shuts his eyes.

"NOW."

"All I know—" He chokes on his spit again. When he recovers, his voice cracks, like he's seconds from crying. "All I know is, they were laid off four months ago."

"Yeah," I say. "Just four months before their own options would have vested for millions. Real nice move."

Duncan winces again. "It wasn't personal. The board agreed that FlowBid needed to align the cost structure appropriately, due to market conditions."

"Market conditions?" I explode from my chair, stand over him. "*Market conditions?* The company's never been more profitable. The stock's never been higher. Our op-ex has stayed flat. And to lay off original employees—people who have been with the company since the beginning, people who built this company—just months before they can vest their share of the profits?"

Duncan looks away, blinks.

"For an even higher stock price?"

Silence.

"Because when those layoffs were announced, the stock price went up another thirteen percent, didn't it?"

"Guys, that has . . . I mean, that's the way it . . ."

"Big money." Larry blows out a cloud, crackles. "I don't like big money."

Rod says, "Okay, so what are the geeks doing, David?"

"We just know they're—" He sighs. "They're trying to get evidence of Fitzroy's being— I don't know. Fitzroy doing things that would have negative material effect on FlowBid's market cap. They want him to lose his fortune, but doing so would destroy everyone else's investments."

Rod looks at me, returns to Duncan. "Who else at Knowland, Hill, and Davis knows about the geeks and what you're trying to do here?"

"No one. I swear. No one."

Rod thinks about it. "Good."

Duncan looks at me. "I don't know what they have on you, what they're threatening, but I can help."

Rod sneers. "Which is why you had your buddy here . . ." He taps Baldy with a Doc Marten. ". . . beat Danny up in a grocery store."

Duncan blinks hard. "All I know is, whatever those guys are offering you, whatever they're threatening, I can handle it. Or I can double your take."

Silence.

"I know you have options that will vest soon." He looks at me, eyes hopeful. "If you work with me and drop the IT guys, I can double your take."

I stare at him, look away. *God, I want to hit him.*

Rod says, "What's happening in Tampa?"

"I don't know. Something, but I don't know what."

Rod stands up. "But you know enough that you don't want Danny joining Fitzroy there."

"We just know those guys are pretty wound up about Tampa. So it's just a precau—"

Rod says, "We're done here. And I'm afraid you haven't been as forthcoming as I'd like."

Duncan looks up at him. "No."

"Oh yes." Rod looks down at him, twinkles. "Oh yes. You've won a prize."

Duncan whimpers. "No."

Larry whispers, voice delicate, "Yes."

"Yeah. And not only have you failed to meet my expectations tonight, I'm also worried about what you might do if we leave you here. I mean, you could get Danny here fired, just days before his options vest."

"No."

"Yes, you could. And you probably would."

"No." Duncan looks at me, eyes straining. "Never."

"You had *no* problem laying off those geeks. From what Danny tells me, as a partner of Knowland, Hill, and Davis, you sit on the FlowBid board of directors . . ."

"Which means," I add, "he approved those layoffs."

"Guys. No. Please. C'mon."

"So it's obvious you'd do just about anything to preserve your absurd fortune, wouldn't you?"

"No. Guys." He holds his breath, blows out hard. "No."

"The problem is, Danny here wants to cash out. He wants to get away from people like you."

Rod and Duncan look at each other.

"And I can't tell you how much I support that plan." He looks at Duncan, disgust taking over his face. "His plan to get away from people like—"

"Guys. Please."

". . . a crock-pot of pus like you."

They look at each other.

"And I'm not gonna let you get in the way, not during these last few days."

"No. Guys. Tell me how much you want."

"Dude." I feel my temples throbbing. "I don't want your dirty money. I just want to last two more days and get out."

Duncan straightens, throws an arm out. "Then that's fine. That's fine."

"But the geeks," Rod says. "The geeks could ruin it for him if you and Tony here get in the way. You see, they're asking for a favor, and it doesn't seem like such a bad favor. Problem is, if he doesn't grant that favor, or if you and Tony here get in the way, my best friend here is toast."

"But wait. I can—"

"Which means, I'm afraid we need to hole you up. You know, pull you from society for a few days. Until those options vest and Danny can cash them out, get the funds into his account."

Larry stiffens, clicks, and produces a billowing cloud.

Duncan cries. "No. Guys."

"And as I understand it, Motel Larry . . ."

Larry clicks. His mouth is frozen open.

". . . has a vacancy."

•   •   •

Rod walks David Duncan upstairs so he can tell his nanny he'll be gone for a few days, and ask her to tell his heavily medicated wife and their kids in the morning. Back downstairs, Duncan paces his office, hugging himself and staring at the enormous framed Dartmouth degree hanging on the wall.

I'm using Larry's pliers to untie Baldy.

"Not even my cell phone?"

Rod says, "There's no time for that at Larry's place. Consider it a gadget-free retreat."

Duncan glances at Larry, his upper lip pulled back in fear and loathing. He looks to Rod. "What about you? What if I stay with you?"

Slowly, Rod shakes his head. "Sorry. I gotta get back to the gym. But if you'd like, Larry can bring you over tomorrow, for some sparring . . ." His eyes twinkle. ". . . in the cage."

Duncan sticks his lower lip out, looks at the floor. "Anything happens to me—like, I'm gone too long, or, you know . . . never come back?"

"Yeah?"

"Well, the police will have the video surveillance."

"Nice point, David. Larry, did you hear that?"

Larry cocks his head, gazes into space. "Extraction."

"But, Larry." Rod sounds like a stern father. "We do need to return David here in one piece. So, no disfigurement. You hear me?"

Still gazing into space. "Extraction."

Duncan looks at his cell, thinking.

"Yeah, I'll hold all that stuff. Your wallet. Your cell. Your laptop. In fact, let's go pack your suitcase, so no one starts thinking something bad has happened."

"But my wife. She's sleeping in there."

"Don't worry. We'll tiptoe."

I finish with the wire. Baldy moans, tries to stretch his legs.

"Danny, I don't trust Tony here. I mean, I know he's kinda spent at this point, but I also know he can be an ornery pistol. Do me a favor and tie him up at the ankles and wrists with that wire. Have Larry help you." He looks at Duncan. "David and I are gonna go pack up, as soon as he sends an e-mail to work saying he'll be out a few days."

Larry darts around my car like a pilot inspecting his plane.

Rod sounds amused. "God, he's excited."

I nod. "He knows he's scored the mother lode."

We stand there awhile.

"Well," I say, "the thing is, he's made it very clear. Larry doesn't like people following him."

We watch as Larry walks in tight circles and flattens his beard with his fingers.

"And he hates big money."

Larry opens the driver-side door and takes a seat.

Rod shoves his hands into his pockets, nods to the car. "And those guys bound and gagged in the trunk? They're like the personification of big money."

"Big money," I add, "that was literally following him."

We stand there a second, letting it all sink in.

Which is when my eyelid twitches. *Reality is setting in.*

"This is kidnapping, you know."

Rod scrunches his face. "That's a matter of opinion. The video surveillance in the house would show him leaving his home with three reasonable men, and doing so under his own free will."

I offer a dry laugh. "And the footage showing a heavily restrained man curled up on the floor begging for mercy? That wouldn't look like kidnapping to a cop?"

Rod nods, bites his lip. "Hey, here in San Francisco, we're tolerant of people's extracurricular activities. I mean, if the man who is tied up is refusing to press charges—and we *know* he'd rather have his thumbs lopped off than have this whole thing go to the police—why should the law care?"

I feel my throat tighten, my skin cool. *This is all too much.*

"But what about the footage of Duncan walking to my car under his own free will—only to get sucker-punched, tied up, gagged, and shoved into a small car trunk with his friend, the so-called consenting participant?"

"Role playing," Rod offers with a big smile. "David Duncan has paid us to do some role playing. Hell, he wouldn't disagree. He'd rather admit to role playing than come clean about this FlowBid shit."

I turn, scan the street for pedestrians. No one.

"Hope you're right."

"Danny, he's in this for hundreds of millions of dollars. You think he cares about getting detained—"

"Kidnapped."

"— whatever, for a couple days?"

"Dude, I'm gonna shit my pants if we keep talking about this."

Rod steps away, looks back at me. "You said this was important, Danny. Life-changing for you and Kate."

I throw a hand out, let it fall to my side. Defeated. "Yeah, but . . . You know. All this?" I motion to the car trunk. "This is beyond. I mean . . ."

"You said you needed to last a few more days so you can cash out."

I mumble, "I know."

"And live a better life."

I sigh, irritated. "Yes."

"And these assholes have gotten in the way. Singled you out."

I look away, shrug. "Yeah."

"So you've been forced to protect yourself and your family, without the cops. Otherwise, you'd lose a ton of money." He studies me. "Money for which you've worked very hard the past two-plus years. No?"

I gaze at the car trunk, nod.

Rod eases closer. "Listen. If you've changed your mind, we can stop this and call the police right here, right now."

I look at him, roll my eyes.

"See what they say about the kidnapping, the hit-and-run with Larry, the various instances of battery. See what FlowBid says about it all."

My stomach weakens. "Okay, okay. I get it."

He smiles down at me, puts a hand on my shoulder, and shakes me hard. "Just hang in there." There's amusement in his voice. "I'll make sure Larry goes gentle on those guys. I promise."

"Okay."

Rod looks at me, his face softening. "I'm doing this because I believe there's something better for you, Danny. This start-up venture capital shit, it's not you."

I nod, break the eye contact.

"That Duncan guy in the trunk there? Dickheads like him are the reason you got into journalism back in college." He studies me. "Exposing the risk they pose to the rest of us."

I look down. *Fuck, he's right. It hurts to hear it.*

"Remember that judge you nailed in that campaign-funding investigation?"

Mumble, "Yeah."

"That was a public service, Danny. That was your passion."

"I know. I just—"

Rod scrunches his face into disgust. "All these people with their fancy cars and IPOs and catered meetings and extravagant parties?" His eyes narrow. "That shit rots, and it rots fast."

I close my eyes, nod.

He slides an arm around me. "And it's not you. This is your chance to make a break for it, and I'm not gonna let those assholes get in the way."

I take a deep breath, let it out slowly.

"Now . . ." He raises his shoulders, looks around. ". . . you think you have this secret-video thing doped out for tomorrow night?"

I blow out a gust, and my stomach sinks. "Yep. It's all packed."

"You think whatever it is you tape will cause the stock to plummet or something?"

"That's the thing." I look away, glance back at him. "I have no fucking idea."

He studies me.

"And if it's something I think will damage the share price . . . I mean," I sigh hard. "I just can't . . . Even if it means that I . . ."

His face softens, and he nods.

"I just can't do that to all the FlowBid people. To all the investors—I mean, people—who've sunk their savings into this company."

Rod bites his lip a moment. "But what if Fitzroy is doing something awful? Breaking the law or something? What if you're being asked to document something important that needs to be reported or disclosed? Something that could save even more people even more money down the road?"

I look down and shake my head.

"What do you do? Do the right thing, turn the tape over, and watch the stock sink?" He thinks about it, adds, "Turn all those lives upside down?"

"I don't know."

"Or keep it to yourself? Let the geeks get you fired? Lose your fortune, but save the livelihoods of everyone else?"

I close my eyes. "I don't know, man. I'll just have to. Dude, I just can't think about that right now. I just— I mean, I just need to get through the next twenty-four hours, come up on the other side. Then, depending on what I get on tape, I'll have to make a decision."

He shifts, looks into the shadows, nods.

"I mean, there's a chance they want me to tape something that won't have any kind of material effect on the stock."

Rod smirks. "And that's why one of FlowBid's largest shareholders was trying to scare you into staying out of Tampa?" He looks out, laughs. "Yeah, right."

"Okay, okay. I'm sure it could affect the share price. Okay?"

"I'm just saying—"

"Yeah, I hear you. I can't discuss it any more right now."

"Okay, and I'm just saying you should be prepared for the dilemma."

Larry taps the horn, calling for Rod.

"Kate coming?"

I nod. "We're gonna get a bite, head back to your place."

Rod starts toward the car. "Good. Larry's gonna drop me off at my place. I'll make sure he understands my rules before I send him off."

"What about Baldy's friends? The guys casing my house? Larry's house?"

He stands over the shotgun seat. "Something tells me Larry here can handle it. Go get a bite, Danny. Maybe a drink, too—loosen up, take a couple of big breaths, get your bearings. And when you come home, take my bed. I'll sleep in the front room with the boys."

"Rod, c'mon."

He points at me. "Don't you dare offend me." He drops into the shotgun seat, slaps Larry on the shoulder, hollers out to me, "Be safe, Danny."

Safe? I laugh to myself. *We'll see how safe I am after I tell Kate what I have to tell her.*

And, just like that, I feel like I'm about to faint.

I wait for her at the corner of Jackson and Fillmore.

She pulls up in our minivan, unlocks the doors, and looks down the street as I ease in. My heart pounding, I glance over and look away.

"You okay?"

Her voice is tight. "Sure."

"Where should we go?"

"The Haight." She starts down Fillmore. "I need some-place easy and chill."

God, I don't want to do this.

We cross California.

The tone in her voice is heavy. "Do I want to know?"

Oh shit. "What?"

"The bald guy."

"Oh."

"Do I want to know? Is he okay?"

"Oh, yeah. Well. We're letting Larry take him—"

"You know," she says, her voice tightening, "actually, I don't think I want to know."

"No, honey. Seriously. He's fine."

"With Larry? That guy's fine with Larry? Are you nuts?"

"And David Duncan, actually. The guy who hired Baldy. I mean, I guess Larry has him, too."

We drive in silence for a long while.

"Dan, assuming this thing doesn't blow up in our faces

sooner . . ." She glances at me. ". . . what do you think guys like that are going to do once Larry lets them go?"

I twist my lips, look straight ahead, and nod, conceding. "Well . . ." I'm drawing a blank. "Yeah, that's a good question."

"I mean, so what if that man was following you guys?"

"Yeah. Well, yeah. Yeah, Larry doesn't like people fol—"

"That's the problem, Dan. Larry." She grips the steering wheel with both hands, leans forward in frustration. "Larry's involved."

"Yeah, I know. That was . . . I mean—"

"But, hey, I sure enjoyed my date with him." She pauses, forces a chuckle. "Oh yeah, that was a real treat. Thanks for setting us up, Dan. You're a real swell husband."

"Yeah, yeah," I snap.

"I mean, not every gal has a husband who sets her up on dates with violent sociopaths."

"It wasn't a date," I snap.

We cross Oak.

My steam is rising. "Listen, I'm doing the best I can here. This whole thing is crazy."

"No shit. And it's all—" She stops herself, bites her lip.

"Sure," I snap. "Say it. I knew that's what you're thinking. It's all because of me and my big mouth, talking to *Business-Week*, doing all that stupid shit at work."

"And doing God knows what on the Internet."

Shit.

She waits a long while. "It's just that the geeks should have had nothing on you. I mean, we should have been celebrating right now."

"Kate," I start, but can't think of anything to add.

We reach the top of the hill, and Kate pulls right onto Haight. "And now I get a call from Julie at FlowBid telling me there's an e-mail flying around listing your porn activity." Her voice quakes. "Some e-mail to all of FlowBid's—"

"Well, just the top floor, actually."

"Whatever. The point is, every person in the company has seen it. And according to Julie, it's all a bunch of ass stuff."

My stomach is surging again.

She takes a parking slot near Steiner.

"Well, it's not like you have a bad ass."

She scrunches her face. "What?"

"What I mean is, it's not like you have this disgusting ass and I had to look at nice butts on the Internet. You have an amazing ass."

She looks at me, the disbelief piercing me. "I can't believe you."

"I'm just saying, hopefully it's a little less embarrassing for you. This is not because there's a problem with you or—"

"Oh, I *know* it has nothing to do with me."

"It has to do with my problems."

A momentary tone of sympathy. "Your ass problems?"

"It's not like you're chubby and I was looking at skinny girls or something."

"Oh, gee, Dan. That makes me feel so much better. It's not like I have a disgusting ass. So why should I be hurt and humiliated? Is that what you're saying?"

"I'm just . . ." And my brain freezes.

"Dan, what if I worked someplace where lots of people

knew I was married to you. And, one day, thousands of my co-workers learned that I was spending hours upon hours looking at boners and balls on the Internet? Bonerssandballs dot-com?"

"Well—"

"No, think about that."

I do, and I can literally feel the humiliation.

"How would that make you feel?"

I'm such an asshole.

"Would you feel hurt, like there must be something wrong?" She looks at me, her eyes hurting. "Would you take it personally?"

There's a lump in my throat, and it's so big I can barely swallow.

"You know it's more than this sex shit, right, Dan? The fact we don't do it like we used to. You know that's just a symptom of bigger things."

"No."

"Yes." She shakes her head, looks away. "We don't connect anymore. We're like robots, running around trying to catch up, trying to do it all, and all the time we're running right past each other."

"I'm so sorry, honey." My voice breaks. "You deserve . . . so much more."

This softens her. "I mean, I know you're a man, and men like to look at girls, and that's okay, I guess. But this e-mail thing was . . ." She looks out onto Haight, shakes her head with a dry chuckle. "This was a lot."

"I am so sorry, honey."

She's looking out the window. "Like I said, it's symptomatic."

I close my eyes, shake my head. "Honey, listen, it's not like—"

"You're obviously horny. I mean, the whole company knows you're horny. And now they're all thinking you're obviously not getting what you need at home."

"No, listen."

"And then I'm thinking—you didn't even *tell* me the geeks had this on you. The ass activity. I had no idea."

"Neither—"

"So, now more than ever, I'm wondering what else they have on you. Things you're not telling me." She turns, looks me in the eyes, and my heart sinks. "Something you'd do anything to keep from me."

"No."

"Something so bad, you'd rather see people kidnapped and sent to Larry's house."

And I know, I have to do it. I have to tell Kate about those instant messages. Those fucking stupid messages with Anne. If I tell her, I take that bargaining chip away from the geeks. And I can tell her on my own terms, not through a company-wide e-mail.

I look down, take a deep breath. "Honey." I can't look at her. "There's something . . ." I force myself to look up, meet her eyes. ". . . I have to tell you."

Kate is crying when she spins on her rear, pulls her feet from under the wheel, and lands the heel of her boot into my nose. The back of my head bounces off the window.

I'm crying, too.

"I'm so sorry," I wail.

"I"—she kicks again, gets me in the arm—"*knew*"—another one, in the gut—"it."

Blood drips off my upper lip. "Honey."

She drops her head, sobs.

"Honey." I wipe the blood off my lip. "It's just that stupid IM'ing. I mean, it got out of control. But there wasn't anything else."

Oh my God, how did I become such an ass?

"We never touched, I swear."

She squeaks, "Do you love her?"

"Love her? Honey. Never." I quake, teeter on losing it. "Honey, I love you. *Only* you."

I do lose it, start to sob.

She shakes her head, covers her face. "I can't. I just can't"—she opens the door, wobbles onto Haight, her mascara-streaked face caught in the headlights—"do this."

She stumbles toward the sidewalk.

I roll down the window, shout, "Honey."

Her shoulders fall as she walks away.

I stumble out of the car. "Katie."

She quickens her steps.

I try to run after her. *Shit.* My crotch feels like hardened plastic.

"Honey."

"Leave me alone."

I touch her shoulder. "Honey, just wait."

She turns with a look of utter disgust, swipes away my hand. "Leave . . ." She pushes me back, follows. ". . . me . . ." She pushes again. ". . . alone."

I stand there, watch as she turns and heads down the side-walk. A spindly homeless man wrapped up in countless layers of clothes meets my eye, says, "Whoa," and giggles.

I follow her. "Kate."

She turns and rushes me, slams me against the metal gate of a shuttered vinyl shop, bites her lip, looks me in the eyes, and knees me hard, right between the legs.

My face freezes in shock.

My midsection explodes, and my legs nearly give. I feel my eyes roll back. But I won't let go.

I can hardly breathe. It feels as though every nerve ending in my body has been redirected to my crotch and plugged into an electrical transformer. With one swift kick, Kate has cut through all my layers of defense—all the distractions, all the denial, all the Vicodin—and brought me to my knees.

"I'm so sorry." It's the only thing I can say. "So sorry."

Finally—maybe at the sight of me crumpled on the ground—she softens a bit.

"I don't know what happened to me, honey."

She takes a big breath, exhales slowly. "I thought it might be something like this," she says, her voice heavy with resignation. "You've been . . . You weren't acting like the guy I married. You've been . . . You've been an asshole, Dan."

"I need to get back," I sniffle. "Back to the real me. That's what this whole thing is about—quitting this life. We can get back together. I know it."

She looks down at me. "*You* need to get back. I'm right here."

I try to stand up with her. It takes me a while.

"I need a drink."

She takes off down the sidewalk. I hobble after her.

We're at the Gold Cane on Haight.

I'm at one end of the cocktail lounge, pressing a bloody napkin into my nostrils. She's on the other end, all alone.

Except for the two guys she's talking to.

One of the guys has bought a round of tequila shots. Kate hoists hers, smiles up at the guys, and downs it. She looks up to the taller guy, smiles up at him, and straightens. Then she looks my way and glares.

"Want another?" The bartender on my end has nose studs, straight bangs, a tight, ripped black T. The loud voices, laughter, blaring music all bounce off my face. "Huh?"

"You want another beer?"

I shake my head. "Shot of Cuervo."

She looks at my nose. "You want some ice for that?"

I nod.

Kate and the guys are laughing about something. She takes another shot, lifts it into the air. The tall guy eases closer, exchanges a huge smile with his buddy as she drains her shot, grimaces, and signals for another.

My bartender returns with a shot glass and a Ziploc full of ice. She tosses me the ice and pulls a bottle of Cuervo, glances at me as she pours. "You okay?"

I glance at Kate and the guys, nod yes.

Now Kate seems to be leaning back on the tall guy. He's lean and narrow and blond, like he's just gotten off a flight from Stockholm. Is he the kind of guy she really finds attractive? Someone completely different from me? Or is he just the first opportunity she had to piss me off?

I take the Cuervo, down it, and my nose explodes all over again. I shake my face, hunch my shoulders, and narrow my lids, glancing over. Kate smiles to herself, catches me looking, and glares again.

"Don't forget your ice, dude."

I look up, and the bartender nods to the Ziploc.

"Oh yeah," I mumble, pull it off the bar, and slide it down my pants. Through gritted teeth I exhale, "Thanks."

Bartender watches, mumbles something to herself, and turns away. I say to her back, "I have a bigger problem area than the nose."

The tequila warms and dulls my head. The ice pack cools and numbs my crotch.

Stockholm is beaming. Surely, he thinks it's his night of blind luck, to have this gorgeous creature fall into his arms, to have this woman with a modest ring on her wedding finger lean into him and laugh.

I nod to the bartender, and she shifts over and pours me another shot. "You sure you're okay?" There's a trace of amusement in her voice.

I nod, hoist the glass to her, and she nods back.

"Going through a rough patch, looks like?"

I down the shot, shudder, and try to ignore my throbbing nose.

She nods to Kate and the guys. "One of those guys rough you up?"

"Huh?"

"They don't look the type."

"No. It's— I mean, the lady did."

She squints at me and turns back to look at Kate. "She kicked you?"

I look down, nod.

"What, you get a little fresh?"

"No, I— Well, actually . . ." I rearrange the ice pack. "Yeah, a little too fresh. But with someone else."

She smiles, eases away. "Such a dude."

Stockholm is leaning over Kate, his mouth practically in her ear, whispering something, his lips almost brushing against her ear.

Okay, that's enough.

I swivel off my stool, weave through the bodies toward them. Everyone else in the bar is having such a great time. Everyone else is on a different planet.

Kate looks up again and notices my seat is empty. Stockholm tries to nibble her ear and she brushes him off, stumbles off her stool, heads my way.

I emerge from the crowd, shuffle toward her. "Honey."

She reaches out, yanks me to her, lets me hug her. "You asshole," she slurs. "You *fucking* asshole."

I wrap my arms around her, look her in the eyes. "Never again, babe. I swear."

"Hey." Stockholm stands behind her, his hands out, brow creased. "Dude."

Kate announces into the air, "Dude . . ." She fights off a burp. ". . . it's over." She swallows hard. "Scram. My asshole husband is begging for forgiveness."

I'm staring into my girl's eyes.

She chokes on something.

"Dude," he says, takes a step closer. "Totally not cool."

Kate sways, moans and burps.

"Dude."

Then, like an unexpected slap across the face, she vomits down my chest and over my shoulder. Warm, rancid wetness rolls down both sides of my body. Some of it splashes onto the floor.

Everyone *eeeeee-ewing* and shrieking.

Everyone making room for the drunk parents on date night.

I'm driving shirtless down Baker Street, Kate riding shotgun.

"Food," she rasps. "I had all that—" She gasps, moans. ". . . on an empty stomach."

"Just hold on, babe. Keep that bag close."

"Honey." Her fingers latch onto the plastic grocery bag I'd salvaged from the back of the van. She gasps, closes her eyes. "I need to get—" She exhales hard. "Something . . ." She pauses, blows out a gust. ". . . in my stomach."

"There's a McDonald's at Fillmore and Golden Gate. It's got a drive-through."

She covers her face, exhales. "Fine."

I pull a right onto Golden Gate. "Just hold on, babe. We'll get some food in you, sober you up a little." And I realize I'm probably drunk myself, shouldn't be driving. "We'll do the drive-through, find a place to park and sober up a little."

She reclines her seat a little. "Why?" She takes a big

breath, lets it out slowly. "Why . . . aren't we connecting like we used to? Thass . . . That's the problem, you know?"

"No. No. Honey, I was just stupid. I just got pulled into it with those IMs. I mean, we told a few stories, I guess."

"You tell her how I sucked you off behind that rock that time?"

"Kate."

"Did her stories give you a . . ." She pauses, swallows, and sighs. ". . . a hard-on?"

"Kate. C'mon."

"Well, I got news for you." Tiny burp, long exhale. "What if I told you Alec and I have been back in touch? We've been e-mailing?"

Alec? Kate's old boyfriend? The guy she always says she hasn't heard from in twelve years?

"What"—*burp*—"would you think of that?"

Is she kidding? My brain constricts. *She's been lying to me.*

"Guess I don't feel so bad about that anymore."

We pull into the McDonald's drive-through. "That's nice," I say. "You're mad at me for having a few horny instant messages with a coworker? When you've been off reconnecting with your old boyfriend?"

God, that sounded bad.

"Stop it . . ." She exhales. "A couple of e-mails—"

"Welcome to McDonald's," says a female voice.

". . . with an ex doesn't compare to . . ."

"May I take your order?"

". . . boner and vagina talk."

Long silence.

"Ummmm." The attendant pauses. "Can you repeat that?"

"Hold on," I holler.

I turn to her. "Have you seen him?"

Her eyes closed. Annoyed. "No."

"So, what, you're having one of those *emotional* affairs? Missing him or something?"

The attendant says, "Sir?"

"He's just a friend." Kate blows out a gust. "When there's no one else who'll listen. That's the problem with you and me. Who am I supposed to talk to?"

"Sir?"

"Hold on. So you're saying, because it's not boner and vagina talk, that's okay?"

"Dan," she gasps, quiet, "I'm not feeling so hot. Just get me something starchy."

"Sir?"

"Obviously your little e-mail affair was wrong, too, or you would have told me."

Eyes closed. "Order the . . . fucking . . . food."

I order her a cheeseburger and fries, and a Double Quarter Pounder with Cheese and fries for me. When we get to the window, the pimply-faced attendant acts like everything's normal. Hell, at a late-night drive-through, maybe boner talk is normal.

I can't help myself. "Does he still have feelings for you?"

"Oh God. I don't feel—"

Kate sits up, opens her door, leans out, and throws up onto the asphalt. The bitter, acidic stench cuts through the air.

"Here." I reach into the glove box, pull out the last napkin, hand it to her. "Hang in there."

She dips her head, groans.

I rub her back. "It's okay."

I turn to my left, and the attendant is handing me a hot bag of food. I look up to her and produce a happy, grateful smile.

"Could we . . ."

More retching and splatter.

". . . have some extra napkins."

The attendant smiles, turns away, and returns with a massive wad of napkins.

Kate closes the door and releases a long groan as I ease away from the window. I hand her a few napkins. "We'll turn out here and find a spot, get you cleaned up."

"Water," she rasps.

I turn onto Fillmore, hand her the water bottle from the cup holder between us. "I think . . ." She takes a sip. ". . . that food will come right back up." She sighs hard. "All that grease."

Crap. She's probably right. "You need something bland."

"Exactly." She sighs, wipes her mouth. "Pancakes. No butter or syrup. Just pancakes."

I head north on Fillmore, toward Cow Hollow and the Marina. "There's a Mel's on Lombard." I shove a bunch of fries into my mouth. "They serve breakfast."

"Fine." She reclines her seat, closes her eyes, moans. "And no."

We cross Geary.

"No?"

"No." Gasp. "I don't have feelings for Alec."

That's good to hear.

"I'm just . . ." Her voice cracks. ". . . so lonely sometimes."

My heart sinks. "Lonely?"

"It's just nice to have someone to listen."

That hurts, like a sock in the gut. "I don't listen?"

She sniffles. "I can't tell you anything negative—my concerns, my fears, my frustrations. You don't like hearing that stuff."

"But I want to hear it, Kate. I do."

We cross Sutter.

"I don't want suggestions or solutions, but that's what I get from you. I just want you to listen."

"Don't I do that?"

Shakes her head. "When I start talking about that stuff, your face says it all." Sniffles. "You don't even realize you're doing it."

There's nothing more maddening than knowing you're hurting the one you love, but not knowing how you can change. We've gone through all this with the therapist, and it's still a problem. How am I supposed to change my facial reactions when I don't even know I'm having them? How am I supposed to know when Kate's venting is just venting, and when she's trying to tell me about her deeper problems? I want to be there for her—I do. I just need to figure out how to get there.

"I want to get better, Kate. I want you to be able to share this stuff with me."

"I guess I don't feel so bad about Alec anymore." She pauses. "Considering your sex-talk buddy."

"That was just . . . so fucking stupid." My throat weakens. "And I'm so sorry."

She thinks about it, starts to cry. "You slept with her, didn't you?"

"Oh my God. Honey. I never even kissed her."

"How am I supposed to know?" She sniffles. "For sure?"

"And how can I know for sure whether you haven't met up with Alec?"

We hit the top of the hill, surrounded by mansions, and start coasting down toward Lombard.

"Okay," she says. "I'm sorry, okay? I should have told you." She sighs. "And I probably shouldn't have been e-mailing with him anyway."

"He wants to meet you someplace, doesn't he?"

"Don't worry about that." Annoyed. "Because I said no."

I get light-headed. "He wants to fuck you, you know?"

"Stop it, okay? I told you everything. I just want you to listen, be there for me."

And that's the problem, I decide. This fucking job of mine. This hyperventilating life in the valley. Nonstop. Unrelenting. Monster hours. When there are millions to be made, only the weak slow down.

"We cash out, I'll have more time, honey. More time for us. To be there for each other." We hit Lombard, pull a right. "I know it. I know things will get better."

She sits up and vomits into her bag.

At the nearly empty Mel's, Kate is in the restroom dry-heaving. I sit in our booth wearing her jacket, my bare chest and stomach exposed. I'm finger-padding my nose when my mobile rings. It's a private number I don't recognize.

"Yes?"

"Dan, it's Detective Bryant."

"Working late, aren't you?"

"Looks like you are, too."

The waitress delivers Kate's pancakes, slides a plate of grilled cheese and fries and a giant, perspiring, aluminum cup of vanilla milk shake in front of me. I nod thanks.

"Well," I say, taking a fry. "Crazy time right now, I have to admit."

"Yeah, I guess you could say that. They had an impressive little car chase in San Mateo today, climaxing with a hit-and-run and some type of motorist abduction."

My stomach tightens. "Oh yeah?"

"Wouldn't know anything about that, would you?"

"I've been up here most of the day."

"Dan, where's your Corolla?"

"What?"

"Your car. A witness gave a description of a car that fled the scene, scribbled down a few of the numbers on the plate— not all, but a few. They scanned cars registered in the area, sent us the matches in San Carlos, and I saw your name there."

"Well . . ."

"So I came over to check you out, and you and your car are nowhere to be found."

"Well, we're up in the city right now."

"Can you come in to answer some questions?"

Kate returns, eases into the booth, stares at the pancakes.

"I'm sorry. I can't right now."

"There's a man missing, Dan. This one isn't going away."

Kate picks up a pancake with her hand, eats it like a tortilla.

"Well," I snap, "I don't have him. I'm here in the city having a late dinner with my wife. And I'm getting on a plane for Florida first thing in the morning."

Kate gives me a lazy sneer.

Bryant says, "The missing motorist is the guy we think attacked you at the Safeway. I thought that was an odd coincidence." The sarcasm is heavy. "A guy named Anthony Altazaro."

I play along. "That does sound odd. But, you know, maybe no one took that guy. Maybe he fled the scene. Maybe he didn't want to speak to the police. Maybe he was juiced up and ran away, wanted to avoid a DUI. You know that happens all the time. I covered a ton of those stories."

He laughs. "Well, I still want to see your car."

"Sorry," I say. "My neighbor has it."

"Larry? Would that be Larry?"

"Yeah."

"That's funny, because a witness reports seeing—and I quote—'a spry, bearded crazy man' darting around at the scene of the collision."

Kate takes another bite.

"Hmmm. That's weird."

"I've checked on Larry's place several times today. Can't find him."

"Yeah, I don't know what to tell you, Detective. I think Larry might be on a road trip."

He laughs. "With your car?" He laughs some more. "That's pretty good."

I look at Kate. She's still staring into space, chewing slowly, the pancake still pinched between her fingers.

"Listen, sir. I need to get off—"

"Dan," he whispers. "Remember our conversation. I can make all this hit-and-run shit go away. I just want a piece of the action."

"Calling from a private line, are we?"

"I want a piece, Dan."

"The action?"

"Whatever it is. Because I know there's something going on. I'm not an idiot."

"Listen," I say, biting my lip a second. "Listen, I'm getting closer, but I still don't know what this is about. If there is some action to 'get into,' I'll let you know. Okay? Just so long as you keep me and Larry out of this hit-and-run thing."

"I can do that," he says, "as long as we know Altazaro is okay. I can't redirect a kidnapping investigation. Nor would I want to."

"Good." I dip my long spoon into the milk shake and pull out a dripping heap of vanilla. "Suppose someone called and said they saw this Altazaro guy flee the scene. It wouldn't be a kidnapping anymore, would it?"

"But I'll need to get that witness account, and I'd like to know Altazaro is alive and safe."

"Well, what if I were to tell you that it *was* Larry and me in that chase, and that once the cars collided, this bald, beefy dude jumped out of the car and fled the scene, and that Larry and I were so scared, we took off? Remember, this is the guy who not only attacked me in the Safeway but also stalked my young children."

Long pause. "I can work with that." Another pause. "Only thing fishy is why you and Larry didn't stick around for the cops."

"Hey," I say. "We were scared."

He chuckles. "Scared. Okay." More chuckling. "But I'll need to know this Altazaro guy is okay. And we still need to press charges for the battery at Safeway."

"Fair enough," I say. "What if I assured you that someone will personally deliver Altazaro to you within forty-eight hours, safe and healthy?"

"And I get a piece of the action?"

"Yes, yes. You get a piece of the action." I roll my eyes. "If there is any."

"With people like this guy involved, there *has* to be action. Just has to be."

We hang up, and I look over at Kate. She's still holding her pancake. "What the hell was that?"

"What?"

She closes her eyes. "You trying out a career in human trafficking?"

"Listen. I think I need to go home tonight, leave you with Rod and the boys."

She takes a big bite, looks away, and chews. "Fine."

"I don't manage this thing right, we'll have a kidnapping investigation on top of everything else."

Still looking away. "*God.*"

"I just don't want Larry going overboard." The thought makes me shudder. "We can't afford permanent maiming."

"Nah," she says. "Wouldn't want that."

I watch the cars and trucks scream by on Lombard.

"Sure. Our marriage is flying out of control . . ." She yells into the air. "But Crazy Larry has gotten himself in trouble and the cops are calling. Better give *that* your full attention."

We sit there awhile.

"I can stay with you guys tonight."

"No." She flicks the last bit of pancake into her mouth, allows a lazy glance in my direction. "This is better. This way, I can think."

"Fine."

"I'm thinking, maybe you need to find an apartment."

"Apartment . . ." My face freezes. "What?"

She sits back, looks at me with that lazy cocked eyebrow. Her movements are slow and drunk, but her mind seems pretty clear. "You're having IM sex with PR sluts. I'm letting my stupid high school boyfriend flirt with me . . ."

I swallow hard, look away.

". . . so maybe it doesn't make sense to cash out and buy a beach shack together. I mean, these kinds of problems . . ."

"Kate."

"No, I'm serious. Buying a shack isn't going to change anything."

"Kate. C'mon."

"Dan . . ." She's about to cry. "Take me to Rod's."

Eight

It's close to two in the morning when I finally roll up to our house. The whole ride down here, I've thought of nothing but that comment.

Maybe you need to find an apartment.

Was that real? Had my wife, my only true love, just told me to move out? Was it the Cuervo? The emotions of this one crazy night? The prospect of Alec, that smug-nosed little twerp?

Of course I have no defense—no one to blame but myself. If I'd done the right things all along—avoided the IM'ing with Anne, decided not to squeal to *BusinessWeek*, protected my equity in FlowBid—the geeks would've had nothing on me, and Kate wouldn't be hurt. Sure, we'd still have our issues, but our lives wouldn't be like houses teetering over an eroded beach cliff during a violent storm, seconds away from collapse.

Yeah, it's my fault. All of it.

Bare-chested once again, I ease myself out of the van, my

midsection throbbing, and glance across the street to Larry's place. No sign of my Corolla. Larry's house is dark.

God only knows where he's—

Then, from his covered porch, a red ember.

I squint into the blackness. "Larry?"

The ember fades.

This is what Larry does most nights—turns off the lights and sits on his covered porch facing our house, smoking and drinking. You can't see *him*, just the glowing red ember of his pipe.

I start to cross the street. "Larry?"

Faint traces of Alvin and the Chipmunks slip from his garage, their high-pitched squealing just barely cutting the silence.

> *All around the mulberry bush,*
> *The monkey chased the weasel*
> *The monkey thought it was a joke,*
> *Pop goes the weasel*

I bite my lip, take a few more steps.

"Larry," I whisper. "The detective called me."

The ember glows.

From the garage, an electronic buzz-snap, followed by hissing and popping and the high-pressure release of liquid. Muffled distress.

"Larry?"

The ember fades.

"Larry?"

The ember glows. "Come here." His voice is strong, like he's not asking.

Wet, squishy noises echo from the garage.

The ember fades.

I come closer, but I still can't see him.

"Larry." I step closer. "We can't get too crazy with these guys."

The ember brightens, and finally I see the outline of his face. Just a moment, a glimpse of his cheekbones, his brow, his chin, the contours of a mouth that seems paralyzed.

The ember fades, and he returns to darkness.

"Larry, listen. We need to cool it with these guys, okay?"

Nothing.

"I know you don't like people following you, and I know you hate big money. But if these guys don't come back fully functional, we're wearing orange jumpsuits for ten to twenty."

Nothing.

"Plus, I think we'd regret it."

"Daniel."

"Larry?"

"Daniel, I have never regretted anything." The ember brightens, then fades. "Ever."

The sound of splashing in the garage.

I look back at my house. It seems so sweet and cute from Larry's place, the porch light on, the bushes trimmed. "Calhoun said some shady characters were snooping around my place. Maybe Baldy's buds. Did you see anyone?"

Silence.

"Go easy on 'em, Larry. I mean it."

Larry says, "It's been a while."

"While? What while?"

"Since Mr. Wetty has had visitors."

"Mr. Wetty?" My heart thumps hard. "You have someone in there with them?" My breathing goes shallow. "We can't have more people in on this, Larry."

The ember brightens. "Mr. Wetty is an Adirondack."

"A chair?"

"Mr. Wetty likes visitors, and he likes to get wet."

"Larry?"

"So I think he was quite pleased to have company tonight." The ember fades. "Which is why it will be my pleasure to give the boys turns on Mr. Wetty."

Okay, maybe I don't want to know this.

"Larry?"

Silence.

"Larry, where's my car?"

The ember glows.

"Larry?"

Finally, peace.

My face has melted into my pillow. A warm blanket of black comfort, this sweet nothing, seeps through my skull and soothes my brain. It's thick and black and solid, and it halts everything—dreams, radiating aches from my nether regions, outside stimuli.

The slumber is so sweet.

Until someone lifts me off the bed.

I jolt awake, look at the clock. 4:57.

A large figure twirls me in the air and crashes us into the wall. When I open my eyes, on my back, the shadow looms over me.

"Where is he?"

When I open my mouth, he forces his hand in, fingers my tongue, and pulls it out just enough to make me convulse.

"Where is he?"

My tongue twitches in his grip.

"You're gonna answer." The shadow lets go, whips me around so my head is sticking out of two enormous, hairy, interlocked arms. "Where is he?"

I feel absolutely helpless. Hell, I *am* absolutely helpless.

"I am not going to ask you again."

"Where's who?"

The arms tighten. "I'll take you . . ."

I gurgle.

". . . and leave you where archeologists will find you." He squeezes, and I moan. "A long . . . long . . . time from now."

I claw at the arms. "Please."

The arms constrict like a hairy boa, and I shut my eyes in overwhelming pain. "*Please?* That won't buy you the morning paper, hotshot. Where is he?"

"The bald dude?"

The arms hold tight. "There you go. See, you *do* know who."

"I . . ." Tiny breath. ". . . don't know."

"Oh yes, you do." He squeezes harder, takes a breath. "You know exactly where he is."

I'm starting to feel dizzy. I'm not getting the air I need, and the pain is paralyzing. I gasp, "Please stop."

"You control that." The arms tighten and bulge. "Where is he?"

Saliva bubbles from my lips.

The arms tighten. "Where—"

Then, in a flash, some overwhelming force seizes control of both of us. Together we stiffen and shudder, frozen into paralysis. I feel his head jerking, his jaw shuttering, as a current of spiked pain shoots through my body and stays there, launching bullets of agony to the core of my chest.

I can't even moan or open my mouth.

Finally, it ceases. He releases and topples over as I slide to the floor, my twitching limbs so heavy I can't move. But I can smell something. That smoky hint of vanilla and rum. And then the cocoa-butter lotion. From my angle, I roll an eyeball for a view of the ember. The red ember brightening over us.

Larry pulls the Taser probes off us. "There we go," he says in a soothing voice.

Larry cuffs my attacker and throws a pillowcase over his head. "The probes did not align," he says.

I whimper on the hardwood, try to get a look at my attacker. He's massive—maybe six foot five, three hundred pounds—with hands the size of catcher's mitts. His power had been overwhelming, but now he's a mound of dead weight.

"One probe landed on you, and the other on him. The current danced between you." Larry reaches behind his jeans, pulls out an extra-large choke collar, something for St. Bernards. He pulls the pillowcase tight, collars his captive with the choke, and attaches a leash. It's a move he's obviously done before. He yanks on the leash, and his captive shrieks and scrambles to his knees. "A simple conduction of electrical current from his body to yours."

I roll on the floor, moaning.

He says softly, "That was not my intention."

The smoky vanilla wafts through my room.

He yanks again, and the captive follows. Larry leans against my dresser, and the captive settles at his feet like an obedient dog. "Some pets," he says, looks down at the massive figure kneeling before him, "learn quite quickly."

I sit up. My skin feels like it's on fire. I scratch uncontrollably. "Larry," I rasp, and lower myself back to the floor. "How'd . . . ?"

"I've been watching him . . ." He pauses. ". . . watch you . . ." He produces a cloud, studies me through the haze. ". . . for hours."

I try to sit up again, decide against it.

I moan, "Why didn't you tell me?"

Larry puffs, stares at me. "This is better."

"Larry, we need to think about this a second."

"I've decided." Larry gazes down at me. "I'd like another date with Kate."

"Larry. A date? Larry, you're not dating my wife."

He softens and whispers, "It would please me."

"Let's just focus on the matter at hand." I nod to Larry's captive and shudder at what I'm about to ask. "You have room for him, Larry?"

He allows the slightest of nods. "I can introduce him to . . ." His eyes seem to moisten. ". . . Mr. Wetty."

From under the pillowcase: "We can pay you. A lot."

Larry stiffens, looks at me and yanks the leash as he turns toward the hallway. "I do not like . . ." He yanks again, harder. ". . . big money."

"Larry." I sit up, rub my face. "We'll need him back."

Larry hums his little snippet of Bach as he leads his captive down the hall.

"Larry," I snap.

Distant humming. I hear the door open, the choke collar snap.

"I need all those guys back, Larry."

The door clicks shut.

I squint at the clock. 5:12 A.M. My head throbs, my left eye twitches; my energy is at an all-time low. I crawl back into bed, every inch of me aching, and let my head sink back into the pillow, thinking, *Two more hours of sleep before I really need to get up*. And realize—for a millisecond—the absurdity of it all, that I've grown so comfortable with all this insanity that I'm able to drift off just minutes after getting Tasered. But the thought vanishes as the absolute requirement for sleep dismisses all analysis in short order.

A sing-songy whisper. "Rise and shine, Mr. Danny."

It pulls me out of the slumber. I am so tired—my head throbbing, my eyes burning, my limbs heavy. I open an eye, look up . . . to Calhoun's puffy, pink face. He's curled around me, stroking my arm. "There's my sleepyhead," he soothes in full-on baby talk. "There he is."

I scramble out of his embrace. Daylight is streaming through the blinds. *Holy shit*. My heart hammers. *I've overslept*. I look at the clock, squint—7:45 A.M.—and exhale. It takes a few seconds for my brain to unscramble the confusion. *Just fifteen minutes late. Okay. I can make that up. Just need to be at the jet center by nine. I can do that.*

Calhoun bounces off my bed, straightens his robe. "I made you waffles."

"Calhoun." I scratch my head, glance at him. "What are you doing?"

Calhoun mocks offense. "Your little lover sent me."

"Kate?"

"She tried calling you this morning, to wake you for your little plane ride. I guess she thought little Danny Boy might be so tired that he'd oversleep. But it seems like someone cut Mr. Danny's phone lines, and his little cell-phone battery was dead because her wakeup calls kept going straight to Mr. Danny's voice mail." He looks at me, does the silent laughter thing that makes his tits shake and quiver. "So Kate called sweet ol' Calhoun to the rescue."

I rub my face, think about Larry leaving my house with the big guy. "Was the front door unlocked?"

Silent laughter. "Yes," he wheezes, "which gave me the opportunity to start charging your cell phone and make some big, fluffy, juicy waffles for my Mr. Danny." He tiptoes to me, slaps me on the butt, and gives me his side. "You go get ready, and Uncle Calhoun will keep those waffles warm."

I head to the bathroom, but the entire middle region of my body—from thighs to abdomen—feels about as flexible as a two-by-four. So I shuffle into the bathroom, search for my Vicodin. "Fine, fine. Waffles. Fine. I just need to be in the car in twenty minutes."

Calhoun jumps for joy and dances down the hallway singing in baritone, "Danny's gonna get his waffles on," then in a
high tenor, *"Danny's gonna get his waffles on."*

The thing about showering when you're severely sleep-
deprived: It takes longer. Your brain is slower, and your body
works at half speed, which you really can't afford, because if
you didn't *have* to be up showering, you'd be back in bed with
your head in a fluffy pillow. Today I shower in cold water, yelping and yipping and shuddering as I race through the routine.

When I open the shower door, I'm confronted by an enormous wedge of moist waffle, dripping long strands of but-
tery syrup. Calhoun makes an airplane noise, says in the baby
voice, "Open wide for Mr. Waffle."

Either I open wide, or my face is smeared in syrup. I
choose the former.

Calhoun pads closer with his waffle plate. "Tell me it's not
absolutely delicious."

I snatch my towel, wrap myself up and swallow. "Just give
me a second."

Calhoun follows me as I put a dab of gel in my hair, slide
on some deodorant, and waddle back to my room. I slowly
step into a pair of black slacks, pick myself out a pair of black
leather shoes and a dark blue dress shirt. I grab my blazer, pull
a huge wad of cash from my cedar money box on the dresser,
and scan the room for my travel bag and the recording device
it contains. *Oh yeah. Left it in the van out front.*

Calhoun darts up to me, shoves waffle into my mouth.

"Cahouuu." I grab my suitcase, look for my keys, try to
swallow. "Enoughh."

My cell rings in the front room. Calhoun darts out of the room, slams into something, and gallops back with the phone. I take it, look at the screen. It's Fitzroy.

"Hi, Stephen."

"You okay for this trip, Danny?"

"Of course."

Calhoun gets closer, giggles to himself, and shoves waffle into my mouth.

"I'm not so sure."

I chew hard, swallow. "No, I'm fine. It's just been—"

"I looked at what you did for this pitch tomorrow."

Calhoun presses his face up to mine, makes the airplane noise as he forces another piece in.

"Mmmm-hmmm."

"And I don't like it."

Calhoun watches me, laughs through a closed mouth, his tits shaking.

Big swallow. "Okay, we can—"

"It's not the right pitch." His voice is rising, the irritation heavy. He always gets this way before a speech. "These guys are expecting thought leadership, not the same old babble." He pauses, collects himself. "Let's dope it out on the jet with the new guy. He's got some new ideas we can use."

New guy. That's right. The new guy.

"Okay, Stephen. I'm sorry about this. We'll get it right on the plane."

Calhoun comes at me with more waffle. I swat it away, send everything sailing across the room. Calhoun stomps a foot, blows a raspberry at me, and giggles.

Amusement in Fitzroy's voice. "But if you're not doing well—you know, if you're dealing with some issues at home after yesterday's fiasco—you can skip this trip, Danny. The new guy and I can dope this thing out on the flight."

"No, I'm goo—"

"Okay," he mumbles, and hangs up.

Calhoun dances toward me, forces me into a corner, fingering a piece of waffle. "You're not getting away this time . . ." He scrunches his face in mock annoyance. ". . . you little pistol."

I grimace and grunt to the van.

Larry lazes on his porch, nursing a coffee, observing me.

I throw my stuff into the van, cross the street to Larry. Streaks of water darken half his driveway as tiny ripples escape from under the garage door. I glance at the garage as something inside hisses and pops and sprays; a larger ripple of water eases from under the door and down the driveway.

Larry sips his coffee, gazes into space.

"Hey, Larry." I make it pleasant, as if he hadn't been in my bedroom and Tasered my home invader. "Still at it with Mr. Wetty?"

Larry looks up at me, thinking, his mind a thousand miles away.

"Listen, Larry, I can't emphasize this enough. Those guys in there? I'm going to need them back. I mean, in about twenty-four hours."

Larry says, "We'll release them in the high country."

I think of park rangers tranquilizing a bear and relocating

it hundreds of miles away.

"Well, maybe it's time to give Mr. Wetty a rest."

Larry shifts, sips, and squints into space.

"Larry?"

Slowly, his eyes turn to me. They seem hollow.

I look at my watch, realize I need to hit the road. I can't worry about Mr. Wetty. But I'm hoping he can help me with one last thing.

"Larry, you said you extracted the details out of that little guy."

Still staring at the ground, thinking.

"It'd really help me if you told me what he said about Tampa. So I'll know what I'm walking into out there."

Still staring.

"Larry?"

Stroking the whiskers.

"Larry," I snap, "tell me what that guy said about Tampa."

He stands up, glances at my shoes. "Just do as they told you."

"They?"

"The little people."

"Larry. C'mon. I need more than that."

Larry opens his front door, then turns and looks me over one last time, nearly deflated. "I have work to do," he says, and shuts the door.

No matter how many times I fly with Stephen Fitzroy, the spectacle never ceases to strike me.

I leave my tiny peninsula house of chipped hardwood

floors and battered, stained furniture; step into my old Corolla and merge into the hordes of commuters on U.S. 101; pass the long-term parking at SJC and drive to the opposite side of the airport, to another world. I park the Corolla in front of Atlantic Aviation, the operator that provides support services to the dozens, if not hundreds, of private jets that fly in and out of San Jose each day. And just like that I'm in another world, one I never thought I'd see.

I waddle through the doors, nod to the familiar faces.

"You can join the others on the plane if you'd like, Mr. Jordan."

My heart stops. I turn to the young attendant with her fresh face, her freckles and giant green eyes. "He's here? Don't tell me he's here."

She smiles, her pleasantness unflappable. "No, he's not here."

"Thank God." I push through the doors and begin to waddle across the tarmac, headed for Fitzroy's Gulfstream 5, enormous and gleaming, the morning sun giving it a glossy blue-and-white sheen, its engines idling in a high-pitched purr. A smiling male attendant in a dark blue windbreaker takes my bags and walks me to the jet, which always gets me—I'm not some fancy boy who needs someone taking my bags and treating me like royalty—but I know it's his job, and the last thing I want to do is come off as an unappreciative prick.

"How are you today, sir?"

I make eye contact with him, nod and smile. "I'm doing great." A flash—Larry lazing on his porch this morning, gazing into space. "Beautiful day for a flight."

He nods eagerly. "A perfect day, sir."

As we approach the G5, the engines drowning our voices, I think about the family van just fifty yards away with the ripped seats and sun-bleached dashboard, think of my simple little house on my modest little street, and shake my head in disbelief.

How in the hell did I get here?

I climb the stairs, greet the pilots—Jim and Earl, Fitzroy's own—and turn into the cabin. Everything here is beyond luxurious: leather recliners, polished cherry paneling with recessed lights, gleaming tables offering fruit, coffee, tea, and the morning papers, a dining area and a long couch that turns into a bed.

Beth Gavin is seated in the second most prestigious spot on the plane—the left-front, forward-facing chair, directly across from Fitzroy. She's bent over her cell phone, punching numbers and listening to voice mail through an earpiece, scribbling onto a notepad, probably recording the very latest adjustments to Fitzroy's schedule—or, as I sometimes suspect, listening to old messages to make herself seem busy and important. Hell, I've felt that urge.

She doesn't look up.

Facing her is the new guy. Shiny black jeans and a skin-tight, solid-black, cotton long-sleeve, dark shades still in place, dark brown hair wavy, and extreme, lean, veiny hands covering his knees.

I look down at him and nod, no idea if he's staring straight ahead or even awake. Finally, he looks up at me, betrays his stoic look with the smallest of grins. "Ah . . ." The grin widens a little, nods slowly. "The lover of the buttocks."

I shrug, roll my eyes.

Beth looks up from her phone, glances at me, then at the new guy. "That e-mail was disgusting." She looks at me a split second. "If you reported to me, you'd be fired."

The new guy pulls his head back, puckers. An eyebrow rises from behind the shades.

I stop, lower myself to Beth's level, let her see how red and saggy and tired my eyes are. I stay there a second, stare at her wide mouth and long teeth, allowing the disgust to contort my face, and harden my stare. "Let me tell you something, Beth. I will never, ever report to you." I study her wide-eyed reaction. "*Ever.*" Her face darkens as I get up and walk away.

I head for the dining table, where I plan to set up—we always leave the seat opposite Fitzroy open, to give him leg room.

The new guy smiles wide, gets up and follows me. He comes in close, slaps an arm around me, and whispers into my ear, his breath like fresh pine. "There are worse fates than being an ass lover." He pauses, shakes me around for emphasis, and nods to the back of Beth's head. "You like her ass?"

"It's got no personality," I mumble. "Just like the rest of her."

The new guy grins, nods to himself. "Speaking of no personality, we need to pull that speech apart and rewrite it completely. I spoke to Fitzroy about it."

I roll my eyes. "Do you even know anything about the audience for this event? For that matter, who are you again?"

Grin widens. "I'm helping Stephen out."

I grin back. "You're a consultant."

Grinning. Slightest of nods.

"Someone with Hill, Knowland, and Davis send you over? Little twerp named Duncan?"

The grin fades. He shakes his head. "I'm with Robards International."

Liar.

"What's your practice at Robards?"

"Paradigm rationalization." He places a hand on my shoulder, like he's saying, *This is above you.* "High-level stuff. Tectonic-plate-shifting stuff."

Yeah, whatever, dude.

"David Duncan hooked you up with Stephen, huh?"

He puts his hands out, steps back.

I look at the shades. "You're an executive chaperone, disguised as some kind of hip business mind fluent in catch-phrases. 'Paradigm rationalization,' my ass."

"Listen." He chuckles and comes in closer, so I can feel his deep, calm voice. "I'm here for Stephen these next two months, like it or not."

"Two months, huh? Gee, that's a coincidence. It's just two months until Knowland, Hill, and Davis can sell its first block of FlowBid shares."

The new guy chuckles, looks away.

"You're a babysitter."

He shakes his head.

"Are you with Stanislau?"

The new guy turns back to me. "I think we're finished, dude."

Earl, the pilot steps into the cabin, announces, "He's here."

Beth straightens her things, glances over her notes—ready, no doubt, to rattle off all the items she's managing for him. I stoop and squint out the window. Fitzroy has pulled up beside the jet in a gray Porsche said to be worth $110,000. He hands his bag to one attendant, tosses the keys to another, points out something on the dashboard, a big stupid smile on his face.

I step in to the new guy. "Either you tell me if you're with Stanislau, or I go to Stephen before these wheels are up."

The grin freezes. "I can call Duncan right now," he says. "Get you fired." He bites his lip, thinking. "Get you off this plane before that door shuts."

"I'm afraid . . ." I poke him in the chest, get him in the sternum. "David Duncan . . . isn't taking calls the next day or so."

His forced grin disappears.

"And neither are his goons."

Fitzroy climbs up the stairs.

The new guy says, "I don't know the first thing about Stanislau. I mean it."

I look at him, thinking, *Could be. Stanislau is the muscle. This guy? He's intel. Duncan's high-priced babysitter.*

"What's your assignment?"

"Danny!" Fitzroy enters the cabin, hollering, happy. "My ass man."

The new guy grimaces. "The same as what yours should be." He nods to Fitzroy, who's plopped into his chair. "Keep this guy out of trouble another two months, save thousands of people millions of dollars. Not just Knowland, Hill, and Davis, but everyone—investors, employees, partners."

Fitzroy yells into the air, "Wheels up, gomers. Let's go."

I will say this about Fitzroy: As much as he might abuse you, there's a soft side to him.

He'll call you names. He'll shred your work to pieces. He'll do that pyramid routine on you as you hover over his speech with the new guy, rewriting a perfectly good pitch just because the new guy has to seem like he's adding value. He'll make you sit there and nod and smile and look away as he speculates on your ass preferences to Beth, the new guy, and Sally the flight attendant, everyone laughing. He'll run you ragged with work and harassment.

But then he feels guilty.

You can see it softening his face, deflating his glee. Soon you're the recipient of rare bottles of wine, backstage passes to the hottest acts, sometimes even spot bonuses. Which explains why, somewhere over Texas, Fitzroy has Sally set up the bed in the back so I can I slip my aching body into its silk bedding, lower my throbbing head into an enormous down pillow, close my cherry-red eyes, and slip slowly into three of the sweetest hours of airborne slumber I will ever know, melting in this bed of Big Money, the absurdity of it all striking me in these final moments of lucidity, swaddled in opulence some forty thousand feet up, dozing off in this flying luxury suite like it's the most normal thing in the world.

If Crazy Larry saw me now in my Big Money bed, I'd be in his garage, too.

And then, thick black nothing.

Until a light slap to the face rouses me. "Danny," Fitzroy whispers. "Wake up."

I open an eye, grunt. "Hey."

Fitzroy is sitting beside me, like a parent. "We're descending."

I rise up on my elbows. "Okay," I rasp. "Thanks."

He puts a hand on my chest, pushes me down gently. "It's okay, we have a second." He studies my face. "You feeling better?"

I nod, realizing how long I slept. "I needed it, I guess."

He looks at me. "You're not doing so well, kiddo."

I look away. "I know. It's been a tough couple—"

"You're walking funny, too."

"Well, that. I got a—" The last thing I need is for Fitzroy to know I've been snipped; I'll never hear the end of it. "A little injury."

He whispers, "You sure you're okay, Danny? Because if you're not, you gotta let me know. I could help."

I open my eyes, sit up "No, I'm good, Stephen. Thanks."

"I've got IT investigating that e-mail. We'll nail 'em, whoever did it."

"That's okay, Stephen. I just want to put it past me."

"It *is* past you. Doesn't mean we can't nail 'em, quietly. Let 'em go."

I get a memory flash of my e-mail to *BusinessWeek*, shiver. "Thanks, Stephen."

"Listen." He looks around, scoots closer. "Do me a favor tonight."

"Sure."

He glances back to the front of the plane. "Keep that clown away from me."

"The new guy?"

Fitzroy nods. "Tonight. Take him out or something."

And here I was thinking Fitzroy loved him.

"Sure, Stephen." I rub my eyes, straighten up a bit. "Yeah, whatever you need."

He nods, looks back at the new guy.

"So why do you let him shadow you and coach you and all that?"

Fitzroy leans in. "Because I'm doing 'the dance.' Something you need to learn."

"The dance?"

He leans in for emphasis. "The dance. The act of humoring folks."

I look at him, nod.

"Humoring folks you need to humor."

"Okay, but . . ." I swing my feet off the bed. ". . . who are you humoring here?"

Fitzroy looks away and blinks, like he's trying to ignore a foul odor. "A couple of bozos on the board."

I'm thinking David Duncan and his partners at Knowland, Hill, and Davis.

Fitzroy adds, "And Beth."

"Beth?"

He whispers. "She brought him on, but I know where this originated. Beth is working with these guys on the board."

I'm tying my shoes. "Knowland, Hill, and Davis?"

Amused. "Not bad, Danny. Not bad."

"So you're doing the dance with these folks? Beth, too?"

"I've got multiple sources telling me she's pumping them for outside investment opportunities."

"You mean, she passes along tidbits about you and they give her a chance to sink some dollars into the next Google before everyone else knows about it?"

He nods and rolls his eyes.

"And you have to do the dance with these guys?"

He sighs. "They own more of this company than anyone, Danny."

"They want you to follow the new guy's counsel?"

"Nah, he's full of shit."

"Then?"

He looks away, deflated. "They're just trying to keep tabs on me, make sure I don't screw up in these final two months."

Just like the new guy said.

"And they don't know that you know?"

He sighs again. "Who knows?"

"So they have Beth planting spies, basically?"

"It's like my entire circle has been tapped." He turns to me. "No one's reached out to you? No one from Knowland, Hill, and Davis, or even outside?"

Oh man.

I meet his gaze, shake my head.

Fitzroy looks at my mouth, thinking. "Did you know this guy Duncan called me the other day and suggested I let you go?"

"What?"

"That's what I said."

My face reddens. "I mean, why?"

"I just don't think they trust anyone, Danny."

I look away, my mouth open. "Me?"

And then it makes sense: If Duncan pushes me out, I'm useless to the geeks.

Fitzroy picks at a cushion, shakes his head. "They have no faith in me, Danny Boy. No faith."

I don't know what to say to that.

"So do me a favor. Keep him away tonight, okay?"

"Sure. Of course." We sit there a second, and I add, "You think bringing security along would give you some separation?"

"Nah. That'd just muddy things up more."

We sit there until I can't stand it any longer. I can't help it. I have to ask. Hell, I need to videotape Fitzroy tonight, and I still have no idea what to expect. This is my best chance.

"You have something planned tonight? A customer meeting or something?"

He blinks hard, swats away the question. "Don't worry about that. Just handle the new guy for me, all right? Keep him busy."

"Yeah, of course."

He leans in closer, the coffee breath hitting me hard. He whispers, "I had Sharon switch my hotel. You three are still at the Grand Hyatt, but the driver will take me to another place. Just to get some separation from those two." He looks to the front of the plane, adds, "Don't tell them. I'll say something in the car."

I give him my earnest look, nod. "Good for you, Stephen. I'll keep the new guy away."

My gut surges.

Now, how am I supposed to end up with Fitzroy tonight if I don't even know where he's staying? I swallow hard, feel my heart pound. *I'm toast.*

He nods, squints into space. "Beth won't be a problem. She'll be working in her room." He nearly mumbles. "I loaded her up."

Long silence as we sit there.

"Stephen?"

He turns, looks at me.

"Where will you be staying?"

Still looking at me, settling on the shovel cut on my forehead.

"You know," I say. "I was thinking. You know, after I take care of the new guy, maybe I should come over so we can review tomorrow's pitch one last time. You know, with all these changes."

Looking at my chin, then back to my cut. "Nah," he says. "We can take care of that in the morning."

Damn.

As we come to a stop, a large, black Escalade waits thirty feet away. A thin, middle-aged chauffeur in a black suit packs our luggage into the back as Fitzroy, Beth, and the new guy pile into the vehicle.

I'm last to emerge from the jet. Having never been to Florida, I'm struck by the tropical humidity. Squinting from the sun, I saunter over to the chauffeur at the back of the SUV, the roar of the jet engines silencing my steps. I reach into my front pocket and finger my roll of cash. When he shuts the back door, I approach, pull out my roll, and peel off two twenties, tuck them into the front pocket of his suit jacket. I have to admit it feels pretty good, like I'm a wise guy or something.

He's unfazed. "Thanks."

I look into the SUV. Beth and Fitzroy have cell phones pressed to their cheeks, and the new guy is watching the ground crew service the jet. "There's more, if you can help me."

He glances into the SUV. "Yeah?"

"You sticking with Mr. Fitzroy tonight? Taking him to his evening appointments?"

He nods. "I am at his call. All night."

"You have a card with a number I can reach you?"

Nods.

"I'm hoping we can stay in touch tonight."

Slight nod.

"You know, I'll call you and you will tell me where he's at, who he's with."

He's looking me up and down. "Oh yeah?"

I look around, pull out my roll again, and peel off two more twenties, stuff them into the same suit pocket. He looks down at it, offers an exaggerated I-don't-know look.

Bastard.

I peel off two more, stuff them into his pocket.

"Okay." He reaches inside his suit jacket, pulls out a business card. "We're in business."

By the time I get settled in my room, it's nearly six, three in California. I call Kate's cell, get sent immediately to voice mail.

"Hey, honey. Just wanted to let you know I'm here." I pause. "I'd tell you all the crazy shit that's happening, but . . . Anyway, I just wanted to let you know I've been thinking. You're right; the IMs were probably some kind of symptom. I know we never see each other. All I know is, life's gotten lonely these past few years, and I miss you. So maybe it just felt good to have somebody—" I stop myself, take a breath. "So maybe that whole thing caught me at a weak moment. If you want me to move out or stay someplace for a while when I come back, let's talk about it. But just know I love you more than ever, and if that little twerp ex of yours contacts you again, tell him to leave you alone or I'll find him and beat the shit out of him. Okay, honey. I love you, okay?"

I end the call, roll my eyes, and sigh. *Yeah, that was smooth. Nice job, Danny.*

Next I pull out the chauffeur's card, dial him up.

"Randy."

Long silence. Annoyed. "He's still here."

"And where's that?"

"The hotel."

"Yeah, but which hotel? That's the whole point. I don't know where he's staying."

He pauses. "I don't want to get caught up in something illegal here."

"No, no. Nothing illegal."

"Nor do I want to ruin my reputation. This gets out, I'm out of work."

"That won't happen, Randy. I promise. Now c'mon. I paid you."

Long sigh. "The InterContinental."

"InterContinental?"

"And I don't think he's going anywhere."

"Okay, that's all I need to know."

"We're square now?"

"Almost."

He grunts.

"Just text me if you take him someplace."

He grumbles, clears his throat. "Just be aware—sometimes these guys sneak out on their own. You know, take a cab? They're a lot less noticeable that way."

"Don't worry about that. Just let me know if there's any action over there."

After the call, I pick up the hotel phone and ring the new guy's room. His voice is heavier, like he's in bed.

"If I've caught you rationalizing paradigms, I can call later."

A chuckle. I can almost see him lying back in his hotel bed, shades still on.

I can hear the grin in his voice. "You're not well, you know?"

"Actually, I was thinking maybe we could get some food, start clean over a beer or two."

"Yeah? Now that Fitzroy has ditched you, huh?"

"Well," I say, "I've been thinking. Maybe we have the same interests after all."

"Finally realized that, eh?"

"Meet you in the lobby in fifteen?"

Lazy voice. "What about Beth?"

"Dude," I say, "she'll never sleep with you."

He chuckles, but it's unconvincing.

"You don't have nearly enough money."

"Women are drawn to more than money, Dan."

"Not that one."

"I'll call her," he says, and hangs up.

Knowing I may never make it back to my room tonight, I shuffle into the bathroom with the button camera and its taping apparatus. As I stand there bowlegged, stringing the wire, I realize that I've forgotten to bring my black collar shirt with the black buttons. All I have is a dark blue shirt with off-white buttons.

The button camera is black. *I'm hosed.*

I find the roll of Scotch tape I packed, tape the wire along the inside front of my shirt, and secure the small tape box against my waist. I'll have to wear my blue blazer and hope it will hide the bulge on my lower back. I button up the shirt but leave the top button undone. Sure, it looks like I'm trying to bring back the seventies, but at least this way my black "button" isn't showing. I'll have to fasten it into place before I see Fitzroy later.

As I'm heading out, I catch a glance in the mirror. Eyes dark-rimmed, sunken, and bloodshot. Face fatigued and sagging. Shoulders slouched. Hair a little disheveled. I should be in a zombie movie.

I take a deep breath, close the front door. Down to the gift shop.

Then my date with fate.

• • •

Emerging from the hotel gift shop with four packets of laxative powder, I spot the new guy lounging on an enormous white chair. He's wearing loose brown cotton pants, with huaraches and a short-sleeved white collar shirt.

I walk over to him. "No Beth, eh?"

He grins. "These things take time."

I look around the lobby, finger the packets. "Why don't we just order something from the lobby bar? I'm exhausted."

The shades study me. "You do look awful."

I ignore him, walk toward the lobby bar, glance back. "C'mon."

We sit near the grand piano and suffer through the awkward silence, sipping Amstel. Finally, after a salad for him and sushi for me, he stands up, stretches, and scans the lobby. "Be right back," he says. "Need a restroom."

If my plan works, he'll need one all night.

I look around, then pull out the laxative packets, rip open all four in one motion, and dump the powder into his beer glass. To mix it in better, I pour some of my beer into his glass, which causes his ale to foam over.

Fuck.

I try to soak up the suds with my coaster napkin.

I look up. The new guy is sauntering my way, his head down, studying his cell phone. Thank God. I force myself to lean back and act cool and relaxed.

By the time he sits down, the head on his beer has deflated. Still looking at his cell, he says, "You really know how to live it up, don't you, Danny?"

I notice an older lady at the bar. She's devouring him.

"Yeah?"

"It's your first time in Florida—like, ever—and you're chilling in the Grand Hyatt lobby bar in your uncle's blazer, getting ready to turn it in." He reaches over and takes his glass, hoists it toward me. "Danny's going crazy-town."

"Yeah, well, like I said . . ."

He takes another drink. "Actually, I suspect there's more to you than meets the eye."

I force a laugh. "Really?"

Another sip. "I called David Duncan." The shades regard me. "You were right; I couldn't find him."

I cross my legs and smile. "So what's the deal? Duncan wants you to report in to him about Fitzroy and his 'behaviors'?"

He shrugs.

"And what kind of behaviors are we talking about?"

"You tell me, hotshot." He takes another drink. "You're the one who knows where he is tonight."

I look back at him, grin.

"So you're really gonna hit the sack, eh?"

Shit, he really has no idea what I'm going to do. He's lost.

I wait a moment. "Dude, you said it yourself. I'm wiped out. I need some rest. And that room up there? You have no fucking clue. Absolute silence, no crying kids, no crazy neighbors. And I intend to take full advantage."

He polishes off his beer.

"Well." He smacks his lips. "In case you change your mind and try to slip out of here, just know I'll be right here with my friend, watching those elevator doors and waiting for you."

The lady at the bar is still staring at him.

"Friend, huh?"

He stands up and cracks a happy grin. I've got to admit he looks pretty striking—thick wavy hair, the strong facial lines, the long athletic body, and that indefinable charm.

"Soon-to-be friend."

The lady at the bar smiles coyly as he sways toward her.

At which point I notice I've left the empty laxative packets on the table. I palm them, shove them in my pocket, and head for the elevators. "Hittin' the sack, dude. Behave."

Standing in my room, still wired, I gaze out at the view of the bay. Any other time, it would have been breathtaking: the expanse of blue dominating my vision, the orange hue glowing from the west as the sun sets. But tonight it all sails through me.

My mind is racing with questions:

Do I call Fitzroy first or just show up?

How do I get his room number?

How do I prepare for something I know nothing about?

And how long before the laxative kicks in?

Plenty of questions. Not a single answer.

My cell rings. It's High Rider. He says, "It's time to mobilize."

I look at my watch. 7:37. "Do you realize he's at the Inter-Continental?"

Silence.

"Hello?"

High Rider muffles his phone, says something to someone. Finally, he says, "Make it work, Daniel. Just make it work."

"Dude," I shout. "How am I supposed to get to his room without calling him and blowing the whole operation? It's clear he doesn't want me or anyone else from FlowBid with him."

More muffled noises. He's snapping at someone. Then: "Proceed to the InterContinental, and call me when you arrive in the lobby."

"You'll have the room number?"

I can hear him pounding on a keyboard. "Let us try a few things."

"And if that doesn't work?"

The keystrokes stop. "Then you find a way to join him in his room. Otherwise, our arrangement is dissolved and we will be forced to—"

"Okay, okay." I hang up and rush out the door.

Here we go, baby.

I walk past the lobby bar as quickly as possible, glancing over once—the older lady is sitting solo, smirking, glancing at her watch. No sign of the new guy. I stop, pivot, and run-walk to the woman.

She gives me a blank stare.

"My friend? The guy you were talking with? Do you know where he went?"

She shifts on her stool, regards me with narrowing eyes. "He just stood up, practically midsentence, and said he needed to use the restroom. That was fifteen minutes ago."

I back away, ready to bolt for the front door. "And he seemed okay?"

"He was more than fine, until he stood up and walked away."

I keep walking. "If he doesn't return, send someone in there, okay?"

She nearly yells to me. "How about you?"

"How about no?" I say, and turn the corner.

I dial High Rider.

"I'm here," I say, and finger the button camera hidden in my shirt. "You have a room number?"

High Rider says, "Are you ready?"

"Uh-huh."

"Eleven eighteen," he says, and hangs up.

Okay, here we go.

I head to the elevators, mumbling to myself, "Eleven eighteen. Eleven eighteen. Eleven eighteen."

In the elevator, an older couple studies me as I reach behind my back, lift up the back flap of my blazer, and try to fiddle with the tape deck through my shirt.

"Shit," I mumble to myself, a little too loudly. "I'll do this in the can."

They look away, and I mumble, "Sorry."

They get off on the seventh floor. The doors close on me as I hear myself whispering.

"Eleven eighteen. Eleven eighteen. Eleven eighteen."

Bing. Doors open.

It's like I'm on autopilot. One foot in front of the other.

My face feeling fat and puffy, my brain in the clouds, the reptilian part taking over.

My vision narrows as I search the doors, looking for his suite.

"Eleven eighteen. Eleven eighteen."

The sounds of music and laughter bounce toward me.

I stop and squint at the door.

"Eleven . . . eighteen."

I step closer, force myself to snap out of it, blinking hard, squeezing my fists.

Here we go. Here we go.

Laughter and hip-hop music.

I knock hard.

The laughter stops, then the music. Total silence, then a few giggles. Finally, Fitzroy's voice behind the door. He's looking at me through the peephole.

"Danny?" He's angry. "*Danny?*"

I gaze into the peephole. "Stephen, I need to come in."

Long silence. "Danny?"

I plead to the peephole. "Stephen . . . Please."

"How'd you find me?"

"Stephen, it's a long story."

"Go back to your hotel, Danny."

I reach out and nearly stroke the peephole. "I really need you to let me in. Kate's not talking to me, and I might have to move out, and all this crap with the board of directors is freaking me out. . . . Plus, there's other things."

Silence.

A young woman's voice: "Aw, he looks sweet."

Fitzroy is cussing in the background.

"Better to bring him in than have him outside your room whining like a stranded puppy. That'll *definitely* draw security."

"Fine," Fitzroy snaps.

The door swings open, and I am hit by a wave of fruity perfume.

Fitzroy is buzzed, maybe drunk. His lids are low, his speech is slurred, and his head is wobbling.

"Don't ruin this for me, Danny."

His suite is packed with college girls. At least a dozen—all of them pretty, all of them in either bikinis or panties and bras. He's fully dressed on the couch, reclining into a tangle of giggling girls. It's nearly too much to comprehend.

A hotel suite of sexed-up college girls?

I mean, how did he . . .

I watch as the girls pet his scalp, stroke his arms. He burrows in deeper and coos.

What are they gonna . . .

"You hear me?" he says, his voice lazy. "Don't ruin this, Danny Boy."

"Of course not," I say. "I'm just so confused. I knew I had to find you."

Fitzroy sounds like he's about to pass out. "Danny," he lazes. "Not tonight."

He sinks deeper into the girls.

"Huh?"

"No marriage crap, Danny." He eyeballs a slender brunette in a blue bikini as she pads toward him. "Not tonight."

The brunette sits at his feet, snakes a hand up his leg, and strokes his calf, smiling. Fitzroy frees a hand, digs into a front pocket, and pulls out a hundred-dollar bill. The brunette slips it into her bikini top.

Fitzroy watches my reaction, smiling. "They know I have a lot of those. A lot."

I nod, still not quite believing.

"So don't go thinking I've got a bunch of desperate souls here," he says. "Every one of these young women is a college student, and they're all smarter than us."

I nod.

"Each of them is receiving a base payment of eight hundred dollars."

The girls cheer and laugh.

"And each is eligible to receive hundreds more if they play nice."

A smattering of giggles.

"But if you're gonna stay here, Danny Boy, you need to join the fun. No judgment from the sidelines."

"No judgment," I assure him.

"You can never tell a soul about this. Never."

"Of course."

A freckle-faced girl with silky red hair swings over to me in a flimsy orange two-piece, plops down real close, smiling as she sips on a drink, and whispers, "You okay?"

Fitzroy says, "That's what this whole night is about. It's about taking a delightful . . ." He reaches into the tangle of flesh and squeezes two knees. ". . . break from reality."

"Fine." I look away; I have to. "I just need to use your bathroom."

I stand up, and the redhead pouts. "Hey," she says, the girly voice scaled up for effect, and sticks out her lower lip.

"Don't worry, honey. He'll be back." Fitzroy cackles. "He likes girls, believe me." He cackles harder. "We all learned that this week."

In the bathroom, I twist and reach and fiddle until I'm sure I've activated the taping device. I can almost hear High Rider's instructions echo in my head: *This red switch here activates the power. The orange button activates the recording mode.* I secure the box back into place, then snap the tiny lens into my final buttonhole. I check myself in the mirror one last time; the button camera is darker than the other buttons but it'll have to do.

When I get back, Fitzroy is splayed out on the couch. The girls are all over him, rubbing themselves against him and petting him. He slides his face against someone's arm, his face red and shiny and grinning, releasing a strange throaty sound.

Swear to God, he's purring.

And it's disgusting, the sight of this sickly, bug-eyed, balding man pressing himself into this tangle of young, sexy sweetness, this mass of fresh faces, perfect skin, toned bodies, and healthy hair. I grimace as I study the scene. Some girls seem to be enjoying themselves, drunk from the booze and cash, perhaps; others seem amused, and others are clearly trying to stay back and limit the contact, their faces tight in strains of disgust.

"Daddy likes," he moans, chin in the air. "Daddy . . . likey soooo . . ."

They giggle.

". . . goodie."

I realize he has his cash roll in his hand.

Another girl rubs near his crotch. He makes the kind of happy noise you'd expect from a cartoon squirrel, peels off two hundreds, and slips them to her.

"C'mon, Danny," he says, his eyes nearly closed. "No judging. Just fun."

I return to my seat near the redhead. It's a perfect spot, as I can sit there and point my chest in Fitzroy's direction.

As the hands get closer to his crotch, he purrs louder.

"C'mon, Danny."

The redhead gets real close, whispers into my ear in a way that sends shivers throughout my body. "You're cute."

"Thanks," I say, "but I don't have his kind of money. And I'm married."

She produces a bored look.

"I'm married, and I don't wanna screw up again."

"Well," she says, "he paid me three hundred to stay here with you, so don't ruin it for me."

"Ruin it?"

From the flesh tangle, a female yelp followed by a Fitzroy cackle.

"I need this," she whispers. "This is like serious rent money for me. Money for something besides PBJ dinners."

"Fine, it's just that I'm married and . . ." I feel my throat tighten. "I love my— I just want to be good."

She's looking at me different. "Aww."

My voice cracks. "It's just been a tough couple of days."

She scoots closer, takes an arm. "Just let me sit close to you, so Mr. Perv over there doesn't demand his money back."

I finger the button camera toward Fitzroy. "Fine."

We watch the spectacle before us. One of the girls is running her fingernails over his crotch, stopping to scratch his boner, which is unmistakable through his slacks. The redhead nods to her and says to me, "Bethany will do anything for money."

"You're all here for money."

"I'll put on a bikini and dance around with a bunch of my girlfriends for one old man in a luxury suite—for eight hundred dollars. Yeah, I'll do that. If I'm cool with going to the beach and being ogled by a bunch of gross old men, I can certainly do this with my girls."

From the tangle, another yelp.

"And how exactly did you all come to be here?"

"Bethany," she says. "She organized one of these for this guy when he came down here last year. She dances to pay for tuition, and he met her there, told her about his 'fantasy,' gave her this ginormous tip, asked her to make it happen."

I shake my head, smile to myself. *Fitzroy.*

"So this year she asked me to join. I guess he wanted more girls." She cuddles closer, adds, "I just can't do everything they're doing over there, not with an old man like that." She touches my knee. "But you're cool."

"And married," I say, and look into her eyes. "With kids."

She breaks the stare and nods to Fitzroy. "Who is he? He won't even tell Bethany."

I shrug.

"He must be *somebody*, to be able to drop this kind of money, to have this suite with all this booze. To afford all of us."

From the tangle, Fitzroy hollers, "Danny Boy looks bored."

"No, no, no, no," I say. "I'm fine with . . ." I whisper to the redhead, "What's your name?"

"Krista."

"I'm fine with Krista here, Stephen."

Fitzroy emerges from the girls, sits up, and regards us. "No, you're not."

"Yes, I am."

Fitzroy gives Krista a long look. "Come over here a sec, honey. I think I know what Danny wants."

Krista pauses a second before getting up and walking over, her tush shifting sweetly right in front of my face. I force myself to look away.

"Danny likes the hindquarters," he says, peeling four bills off his roll. "Why don't you give him a lap dance?"

Krista looks back to me and smiles. "Nah, I think his heart's at home."

A collective *awwwww* from the flesh tangle.

Fitzroy thrusts the money above his head. "Who wants to make four hundred dollars lap dancing for Danny here?"

Half a dozen hands shoot out of the tangle.

"Me."

"Me! Me! Me!"

"No, me!"

Finally, a hand reaches out and snags the money. It's a big-boned blonde in a peach bikini. She easily has the largest, most muscular buns in the room—burly buns, you could say—and she's already dancing in front of me, popping her buns, bouncing hard as she backs them toward my devastated crotch.

With the exception of Krista, the girls cheer her on.

"No," I cry. "No. . . . Please, no."

Burly Buns isn't listening. She backs in closer—a huge, toothy grin on her face—reaches down and uses my knees as handrails, pushing them apart, the cheering of her friends intensifying as she thrusts her monsters into my firepit of a crotch.

Fitzroy slits his eyes, yells, "The Eagle has landed."

Holy shit, the pain. The pickax blows shooting from my swollen, traumatized testicles. The pain nearly paralyzes my body, makes my bile surge, makes me see stars. I try to push her off, but she only shakes her head no and pushes harder, nearly grunting as she presses her burlies into my groin.

Fitzroy says, "Either you sit there and enjoy it, Ass Boy, or I'm gonna pay three more girls to go over there and strip you naked."

They cheer.

"And you know I'll do it."

I can only imagine the looks on their faces when they tear off my shirt and find the camera wire streaking across the fabric, the lens in my shirt, the tape box under my belt. Not to mention my shaved, purple-and-yellow genitals. The thought makes me queasy. "Fine," I grimace, and push against her lower back. "Just ease up a little."

Burly Buns looks back, her lids low, and grinds harder.

"Please," I moan.

Her crushing dance continues, and I feel like I'm seconds from passing out. The room narrows and the sounds go hollow. I lock my jaw and growl.

Fitzroy hollers into the air, "He's gonna blow."

From the tangle, a collective "*Eeeeeee-eeeeew.*"

I lean forward and try to close my knees, reducing the contact for a few seconds until Burly Buns pushes them open again and burrows back into the center.

"On the knee," I whisper. "On the knee. Grind on the knee."

"What's wrong?" she says, and laughs. "Gonna blow?"

Krista watches, her arms folded, her brows low, her mouth tight. "That's disgusting," she mumbles and looks away. "He said he was married."

I quiver and moan. I feel tears welling.

Fitzroy says, "Here he comes."

More *eeee-ews* and cheers.

I decide to go with it. Hell, might as well fake it and end the torture now. So I hiss and *oooh* and *ahhhh* and shudder, to a chorus of louder cheers and *eeee-ews*, until I cross my eyes and force myself to go limp. Louder cheers and louder *eeee-ews* as Burly Buns stands up, picks her bikini out of her crack, and struts away. "Got 'im."

Krista notices the tear streaking down my cheek. "Hey, you're . . ."

I crawl to the bathroom.

I'm hugging the toilet, about to retch. The pain is still launching convulsions of agony through my body, and I feel my stomach surging.

The door opens and shuts. "Hey." A gentle whisper. "You okay?"

I look up. It's Krista taking tiny steps toward me, her face drawn.

"You're *not* okay, are you?"

I sniffle, wipe my eyes. "Been better."

"What are you doing here?"

I feel it coming, so I lean into the bowl right as I vomit.

Krista is touching my shoulder. "It's okay."

I retch again, and she flushes the toilet.

"C'mon," she says, tugging at my blazer. "Let's get this off you before it's ruined."

I let her do it, and spit into the bowl, gasping, "I gotta . . ." Spit. ". . . get . . ." Spit. ". . . out of here."

She hands me a wad of tissue, and I wipe my mouth and spit again. Finally, the pain is fading a little, and maybe that's why I'm able to hear my cell vibrate and ding with a new text message. Shit, it's probably High Rider with more instructions. I struggle to pull it out, glance at the message.

This is an automated reminder from Dr. Douglas to be a real man and meet your commitment tonight: Don't forget to make Kate a proper full-course meal—and remember, NO MEAT PLATTERS.

Krista flushes the toilet again, kneels beside me, and rubs my back. "Who is that guy?"

"An asshole," I gasp, and pocket the cell. "A very rich asshole."

Her hand settles on the small of my back, and before I have my wits about me, she's untucking my shirt . . . and pulling on my tape box.

Her voice sharpens. "What's this?"

I try to swat away her hand, but it's too late.

"What the fuck is this?" She yanks the wire. "You're taping us?"

I struggle to stand up right as she lands a roundhouse into my mouth. "That's . . ." I manage to yank the tape box from her before she uses her other fist to land another roundhouse into my nose. ". . . mine."

My nose explodes, driving nails of pain into my eyes.

Empty-handed, her face cherry-red, she turns and runs out of the bathroom. "He's got a camera. He's got a camera! He's been taping the whole thing!"

Nine

Fitzroy pulls himself out of the flesh pile and stands up, his pants bunched at his ankles, his black boxers propped up by his boner. He looks at me, then at Krista.

"Camera?"

Krista darts toward the girls, yanks a vase off the end table, and heaves it at me. I duck, and it bounces off the bathroom doorframe.

I hunch down, ready for attack, one eye on the door.

Fitzroy stands there. "Camera?"

"Stephen," I hobble toward the door. "It's . . ."

"Danny, what are you doing? A camera?"

Krista heaves a huge picture book at me—pages fluttering—and misses badly.

"Danny, what is this?"

The girls are way ahead of him. They start to shriek and scatter. A can of Coke sails wide right, but a glass coaster nails me in the gut, brings me to my knees.

"Stephen." I get back to my feet. "It's just . . ."

Fitzroy sees the shame on my face, realizes something is really wrong, and takes a step, only to trip on the wad of gabardine around his ankles. He crashes to the ground and struggles to look up at me. "What the hell is she talking about, Danny?"

"The camera." Krista nearly growls. "Get it."

Burly Buns booms, "Perv."

Another one yells, "Stop the perv."

But they all back up.

Fitzroy sits up, kicks his slacks off, and gets right-sided. He gazes at the contraption in my hand, mumbles wide-eyed, as if in a daze, "Camera?"

"Stephen." I stick the tape box in my back pocket, bunch my shoulders. "It's a long story. Little Red and High Rider."

"What?"

"They made me do it."

Now it's really sinking in. His face reddens. "You've been taping me?" He steps forward, realizes my size advantage, and halts.

"I'm sorry, Stephen. . . . This thing . . . I mean."

Fitzroy glares at me, then springs into action, shouting: "Four thousand dollars to the girl who brings me that tape." He points to Burly Buns. "Lock that door."

At which point, more than a dozen half-naked college girls spread out.

Encircling. Closing in. Their lips curled back, their shoulders in.

Projectiles loaded and ready for launch.

•   •   •

Within seconds I am swarmed and brought down. Hammer fists rain down on my face. Hard kicks and, worse, stomps to my chest. Legs and arms and breasts and even asses press against my face, my throat, my stomach, my arms and legs—all of it fused into a hot, sticky mass of aggression.

I twist and roll, in mad, searing pain, clenching my back pocket in a final, desperate attempt to keep the tape.

Get up, Danny. Get up now.

"Sit on him."

"No, roll him over."

From the couch, Fitzroy sounds so casual. "Okay, five thousand."

The frenzy intensifies. They roll me over. Someone pulls my fingers in opposite directions. I pull back and cry for mercy. My fingers pop, and pain explodes up my arm. I pull myself loose. But finally, of course, a small hand digs into my back pocket and snatches out the tape box.

A petite blonde thrusts the box above her head. "I got it!"

"Bring it here, baby, and claim your reward."

Burly Buns roars, "No, *I* had it."

Another girl says, "I'm the one who got him to let go."

The mob shifts off me as they follow the blonde. I sit up and cradle my hand as Burly Buns, Krista, and four others tackle the blonde.

"That was mine."

"Get off."

"We should split it."

"I said, get off me, you moose."

"Hey . . . ow!"

"Stop!"

"You stop!"

"Hold her down."

"Bitch."

The hotel room is starting to resemble a rugby scrum: bodies pressing, teeth gritting, people moaning. The blonde is in the middle, and Burly Buns and another girl have her arm. The tape box goes flying, and the girls scream. Soon it's being kicked and swatted all around the room, as each of them struggles to gain possession.

"Bring it here," Fitzroy drawls, "and get your five thousand."

Krista picks it up and darts to him, only to get gang-tackled by the mob.

Then . . . a heavy pounding on the door.

Silence.

More pounding. "Open up!"

I recognize that voice immediately. *What the hell is he doing here?*

The girls freeze, looking at each other, wondering what to do. Fitzroy gets up and reaches for his slacks.

"Hotel security. Open up now."

The girls scramble, some darting to the bathroom, others grabbing their clothes.

Fitzroy steps into his slacks. "Coming," he chimes sweetly. "Just a sec."

And I notice the tape box under an ottoman.

• • •

Fitzroy opens the door and looks down.

It's High Rider, in a powder-blue collar shirt, orange Bermudas, and yellow flip-flops. He's talking into a bullhorn, through gritted teeth.

I can't believe he's here.

Fitzroy squints down at him. "You're not hotel security."

I crawl to the ottoman, shove the tape box down my front pocket, and stand up.

Fitzroy turns to me. "Is this guy your partner? He's the brains and you're the muscle?"

High Rider steps forward and barks into the bullhorn. "Back up, Fitzy."

Fitzroy stumbles backward, and High Rider clicks the door shut.

"What are you doing here?"

Through the bullhorn: "Collecting what is mine."

"But you wanted me to—"

"Follow the plan," he snaps. "Which you obviously couldn't accomplish."

Krista steps forward, tries to pull up her jeans, and huffs, "Who's got the tape?"

High Rider yells into the bullhorn, his tiny voice gravelly. "Back up, hussies."

No one does.

High Rider bluffs a charge, and they back up a little.

Fitzroy has his cell to his ear. "Five thousand dollars, ladies."

High Rider points at him. "Put that down."

"Someone secure the door," Fitzroy says. "In fact, three

thousand dollars to the girls who can control and detain our little friend here."

I get ready to bolt.

Krista is scanning the floor. "Where's the tape?"

Fitzroy keeps the cell to his cheek and turns away from us. "Hey, Ed. It's me. Listen, I have a problem here."

"PUT THAT PHONE DOWN."

Some of the girls are creeping up on High Rider, others are searching the room.

Fitzroy glances at us. "Yeah, the InterContinental. . . . No, they're here."

Burly Buns hollers, "Now!"

Mayhem.

High Rider screams into the bullhorn, which is quickly yanked away and heaved against the wall. Within a flash he's pulled down, swallowed up by the pack.

I backpedal to the door.

Krista frowns at my front pocket and points. "He's got it."

Lamps and wine bottles are suddenly inbound, end over end.

I duck, turn, and bolt for the door.

"STOP THE PERV!"

Scrambling down the hotel stairway, grimacing, I can hear them close behind.

Get off on a random floor, Dan.

Footsteps getting closer.

The others will be waiting for me in the lobby.

Someone in heels, closing in.

Get off on a random floor, find a service closet.

Suddenly, the heel clicking ceases and I'm slammed from behind. Someone clamps on to my back and sends me stumbling forward, seconds from crashing into the stairs. Krista's red hair slides over my eyes. "Perv," she grunts, and sinks her nails into my forehead and brows. "Fucking greedy little perv."

I stop on the landing for the third floor and twirl, trying to shake her. Nothing doing. She slides a forearm under my chin.

"I got him," she yells into the air. "I got him."

She bites into my ear and growls, the hot vibration sending shivers down my body.

More footsteps in the stairway.

Oh God.

I bite into her forearm and shake violently. Krista screams and releases me, tumbles to the floor. "ASSHOLE," she yells, tugging her bikini top back into place. "You fucking ASS-HOLE."

I dash down the stairway, faster than I would have thought possible, the clamor of this cadre of motivated women in lingerie and two-pieces intensifying behind me, their cash lust and vengeance churning to a froth.

The stairway exit dumps me into a side alley, where I find three more bikinied women. One of them yells into her cell phone, "He's here. Down in the south alley."

Another one says to the others, "We split it. We get the tape here, split the money three ways."

I square myself.

They charge.

I feel my lip curl back.

Ten

One summer, as a teenager, I worked at the mall selling cheese for Hickory Farms. Most of the time, I had the evening shift, meaning I'd work the store alone and just stand there and gaze out at the empty mall as I waited for closing time. Some nights, not one person would enter the store. Even so, I was required to "dress up" for the job, so I'd tuck an oversized shirt into a pair of tight slacks, the only pair I had, and make the best of it.

One night two girls walked by, glanced in, and giggled.

Was that flirting?

A minute later, the girls returned, red-faced. The brunette with freckles and giant green eyes asked for a free sample of cheese. Her friend with dirty blond hair glanced at my crotch and grinned to herself.

Which was when I looked down and suddenly understood.

My fly was open, and out of it flowed my shirttail—like a massive, flaccid dong reaching halfway to my knees. The girls burst into laughter, turned around, and marched off arm in arm.

To see yourself as you truly are—that is tough.

I hobble to the beach, where I curl into a ball and wait for dawn.

The light breeze washes over me as I screw my eyes shut, trying to prevent the images from snaking through my head. But it's useless; the replay rolls. I see the girls charging me, one of them swinging some kind of pipe and missing by a hair, another going for my knees with a sweep, dropping me as a third comes in for a soccer kick and nails me in the ribs, sending pain everywhere. I see the bright alley opening in front of me. See the looks on their faces as I push through them and run toward the light. Nearly feel it again when one of them lands on my back and drags her nails across my throat until I toss her off, turn the corner, and hobble into the dark.

Is this all for real?

I shake my head, open my eyes. There's no way I can return to my hotel room and get my stuff—way too risky. I've become a FlowBid fugitive, curled into a ball on a deserted strip of sand, with just two critical items in my possession: my wallet and a tape worth more than a million dollars. Then again, the tape might be worth way more than that, considering how much damage it could do in the wrong hands. For the first time throughout this whole ordeal, I feel small and selfish.

I look down at my cell. I want to call Kate so bad. But I've caused her enough pain already.

Then the cell lights up in my throbbing hand. *S. Fitzroy.*

I stare at it a minute, finally answer the call.

Long silence on both sides. *Shit, I bet he can hear the waves.*

Then his voice, nearly whispering.

"Danny."

Nothing.

"Danny, listen."

He's calm, like he's brokering another $100 million deal for FlowBid, like a high-stakes play he's made countless times before. "Listen, kid, whatever this is, whatever kind of deal you struck with the little guy. You have to know I could make you solid, set you up far better than he ever could."

Nothing.

"I mean, have you thought about what you want?"

Finally, I mumble, "Cash out." I look around, see nothing. "I just wanna fucking cash out."

"Then let me help you."

Silence.

"There's no reason, Danny. There's no reason I can't make you square. Better than square." He pauses. "Whatever the little guy is offering, I can do better."

If only it were that simple.

"Danny, if it's money, that's easy. If it's something else, that's probably easy, too. You know I can move mountains. You know that, Danny."

"Stephen, listen. The little guy."

"Yeah?"

"Where is he?"

He sighs hard. "He got away."

"Stephen, he *made* me do this."

He pauses. "Does this have to do with the ass stuff? Because I can—"

"No, listen. Well, kinda. It's bigger than that."

"That's okay," he soothes. "But now we can work together on this." He waits a second. "Do you still have the tape?"

I say nothing.

He waits.

"You see, Stephen . . . The little guy? The little guy has something on me." I look out to the bay, stare at the expanse of deep purple. "If I don't play nice with the little guy, I lose everything."

Finally, he snaps. "No, you don't," he yells. "Think about who you're talking to here."

"I do lose everything."

"Danny." So irritated. "Whatever it is, I can make you solid. He's got you by the nuts some way, I can square you off with a new life, a lot of money—new everything." He pauses. "More money than you've ever had." He waits awhile, adds, "So let the little guy take his best shot."

"He'll get me fired."

"Danny." He laughs. "You were getting fired anyway. I mean, you think I wasn't going to fire you after *this*?"

"You fire me in the next thirty-six hours, that tape goes public."

He quiets, finally says, "We're coming."

"Huh?"

"Just stay there."

"What are you—"

"You're on the beach. Across the highway, right?"

I mumble, more to myself, "How'd . . ."

"I can hear the cars, Danny, and the water. And you couldn't have gone far."

I look around, see no one.

"Just stay put, Danny. We'll be there in a minute."

We?

"Ed might get there sooner."

"Ed?"

"Didn't think I'd need anything like that down here, but I was wrong."

"Anything like what?"

"Guys I can call. Guys who can solve problems."

I don't want to believe it. "What?"

"They said I could call him if there was trouble."

"They?" I rasp. "Who?"

"Stanislau."

I shake my head, blink hard. "Stanislau? You know the people at Stanislau?"

"Of course." He mumbles, like it's suddenly all so boring. "They work with the board."

"I know." I'm panting. "But you're in contact with them?"

"No, *they're* in contact with *me.*"

I mumble, "Stanislau."

"They sent me a note this morning, said I should call Ed if I had any problems in Tampa, which I thought was odd . . ." He sharpens. "Until about twenty minutes ago."

I feel my stomach weaken, and I moan.

"Just hang tight," he says, his voice strangely cheery. "He's on his way."

Which is when I see the large dark figure near the water.

•   •   •

All I see is his silhouette—the outline of a massive, broad-shouldered man. A linebacker's body. He's pacing some two hundred feet away as I sit there in the sand, a cold sweat breaking, trying to come up with a plan. And failing.

My cell flashes again. I keep an eye on the silhouette as I scoop the phone out of the sand and put it to my ear. "Call him off, Stephen."

The figure takes a few steps in my direction.

"I mean it," I say into the phone. "Call him off."

"I want my tape," a voice snaps back. It's High Rider, his voice sounding like an elf trapped in a can.

"Dude, what are you doing in Tampa? This wasn't part of the deal."

"Deal?" he snaps. "This was *never* a deal. This was a matter of *me* telling *you* *what* you'll do and *when* you'll do it."

The silhouette takes a few more careful steps.

"So you came to spy on me."

A few more steps.

"I came to protect our investment. I *knew* something would go wrong with you."

Closer still.

"I spoke to Fitzroy," I say. "He's promising more money if I give him the tape."

"And you believe him?" High Rider chuckles and sighs. "You're such an idiot."

More steps, less tentative.

"Regardless," I say, "I have a more pressing matter here."

He's getting closer, and, God, he's huge.

"I want my tape."

C'mon, think of something.

"You'll get your tape," I say. "Tomorrow at the airport— TPA. Be there by seven A.M., and I'll call you, tell you where to go."

"But I make the calls," he snaps.

"You do?" I say, and hang up, because now the silhouette is running toward me.

Sprinting, really.

Tearing over the sand like it's asphalt.

The problem is, following exact sequences is hard for me, no matter how much I try. Tell me a joke, the next day I can't repeat it to save my life. Ask me to sing my favorite song, I'll never be able to nail the lyrics. And dancing? You ask me to follow along in a class or something, my feet will screw it up. Always.

So you can understand that, despite more than a decade's worth of Rod Stone trying to teach me submission holds, I'm helpless there too.

Even so, I stand up, face the man, and try to channel Rod.

He slows as he approaches. *Shit, he's gonna shoot me.*

Deep voice. Really deep voice. "Danny?"

My breath is so shallow.

Two big steps closer. "Danny," he huffs, breathing heavy. "I'm Ed."

I take a step back.

"Danny, I need that tape."

Another step back.

"Danny." He seems so calm. "You're not going anywhere."

I'm freaking so hard, I can't feel my face. "I don't have it."

He laughs, takes a step closer, and finally I can see his face: giant chin, straight nose, and a high brow. "Is that why you're fiddling with something in your pocket there? Something that looks like a cassette tape?"

I swallow hard. "I don't have it."

He takes a step. "Danny, how do you want this to end?"

I say nothing, take another step back.

"Do you want to leave this beach upright, go back to California and see your wife and kids?"

I take another step back, resist the urge to pull out the tape and throw it away from me.

He takes a step, says ever so gently, "Do you want to see your children again?"

My legs weaken.

"I don't think you know who—and what—you're fucking with here, chief."

"I don't—"

He explodes for me, and I feel like a toddler—lifted off my feet so effortlessly, brought in the air for a moment, and tossed down onto the sand. I try to roll over and scramble away, but he grabs me by the ankles—again, so effortless—and yanks me back to him.

He rolls me onto my back, raises a fist, and tightens.

"Okay," I say. "Okay."

Too late. He lands an elbow across my face. It feels like a wall of wood has slammed my entire head. I taste blood in my mouth, roll my head to avoid the next blow, but still catch it behind the ear.

I try to move, but can't.

Fuck, he's huge.

The calm voice is gone. He rumbles, "You wanna do this?"

"No," I gurgle. "Please."

He scoots off me, lets me get to my knees, reaches for my front pocket. "Cough it up. Before I get angry."

And just like that, I can't believe it: I'm actually seeing *an opportunity.* That's what Rod Stone calls it—an "opportunity"—when an opponent opens himself to a particular submission. Ed is crawling toward me, reaching for my pocket, never thinking for a second that my best friend, a professional cage fighter, has been catching me in this very same position over and over the past fifteen years, and making me pay the price. I just might be able to resist my freestyle ways long enough to remember the moves—the sequence of steps necessary to secure a Peruvian Necktie.

"C'mere," he grunts.

I gasp under my breath, "Here we go."

He reaches for my pocket, growls, "Where is it?"

Now or never.

"You wanna leave this beach?" he yells, and shoots for my legs.

And just like that I slip into a zone I never thought I could reach, letting my unconscious take over, letting my body set it all up, my brain go blank. I push his head to the sand, slip my left arm under his throat and across his chest, reach over with the other and lock hands, and stand up. He tries to twist away, but I've got him. I've really got him. I step over his shoulders and pull up, pressing his head against the back of my leg, and fall back at an angle, pulling him with me and twisting, landing on my back and wrapping my legs around him.

All of it mindless, all of it deep-seated muscle memory I didn't know I had.

His head is torqued under my legs, his chin pressed hard against his collarbone, cutting off all blood flow to his brain.

He tenses.

I tighten for the ride, ignore the pangs in my groin.

He tries to get up, but he can't, so he tries to roll out of it.

I hold on, tighten my legs and arms.

Finally, he gets his footing and tries to stand with all my weight on his neck.

Ain't gonna happen, dude.

He collapses to the sand, and I twist and tighten.

The fight begins to drain out of him. His hands flap for me to stop, and he gurgles—trying to speak, I guess, but there's no way anything's coming out of that throat right now.

I grimace and grunt. "Nighty-night, asshole."

And with that he goes limp.

I keep the hold a little longer, just to be sure.

I kneel over him, check his pulse and breathing. They're both strong, thank God; he's just choked out, as Rod would say. Soon he'll come to, groggy and weak, with no memory of what just happened. I peer down at him, thinking about it.

Might as well make it easier to lose this guy.

I roll him on his side, pull down on his chin to open his mouth, and shovel in a few handfuls of sand. *Coming to with a mouthful of sand. That'll slow him down.*

Then I catch a clue and pull off my shirt and tie it around his wrists, tight.

Might as well relieve him of his wallet and shoes, really slow him down.

I stand there and look at him.

Wouldn't hurt to pull off his pants and underwear. A guy can't go too far naked.

I stop, scan the beach.

Which is when I notice the unmistakable outline some fifty feet away.

I drop Ed's ankles, think for a moment—then charge.

Stephen Fitzroy screams, turns, and runs for the hotel.

By the time he reaches the entrance, he's panting for help. I'm hobbling after him, sandy and bloody and shirtless, inventing curse words as we streak through the lobby.

"Help me," he wheezes. "He's killed a man."

I close in on him. "Fuckbung. You little fuckbung."

The staff are frozen.

I finally reach him, bring him down, and land on top of him.

He gets his breath, screams for help.

I call him a smegma ball.

A woman yells, "There he is."

I sit up, turn, and see Krista and the girls charging for me.

Gotta be kidding me.

I glance at the front doors, then at the charging horde.

Fitzroy lifts his head off the floor. "Ten thousand," he yells. "Ten thousand to the girl who brings me that tape."

They shift into high gear.

I roll off Fitzroy and bolt for the door, ignoring the searing pain in my groin.

"Stop him."

They're too far behind to catch me. I grunt and hobble into the night, waving down a taxi parked fifty feet away.

From behind me: "STOP THAT MAN."

I jump into the cab, tell the driver, "Two hundred dollars if you get me the hell out of here."

Driver says in a heavy Indian accent. "Cash?"

The girls close in.

"Yes, cash. Just GO!"

We pull away from the curb.

I flinch. "Watch out for the girls."

Casual: "They will scatter."

And he's right.

But the huge, sandy naked guy stumbling out of the darkness? We have to swerve to avoid hitting *him*.

In his most pleasant tone, the driver says. "And where are we going, sir?"

If only I knew.

The taxi driver hums to himself as we roll through west Tampa.

I'm slouched in the backseat, barely able to see out the window. I pull out my cell and see I have a message—from Anne.

"Hey. Listen, your wife just called?" *What?* My scalp goes cold. "We just got off the phone. I guess you told her. Thanks for the heads-up, asshole. That was a fun surprise. Anyway, she wanted to know if there was anything more between us, and when I got over the shock, I said no—I think I called it 'just some stupid horny talk'—and that the thought of hanging out with you literally repulses me. That seemed to make her even angrier. She called me a slut and hung up. So, um . . . Don't call me back—like, ever."

Lovely. I pocket my cell and slide even lower onto my seat. *Well, at least now Kate knows I was telling the truth about Anne.*

The taxi driver says, "Perhaps you would enjoy a scenic tour of Tampa Bay, sir?"

I wiggle up a little, squint at the back of his head. "None of this seems a little odd to you? A pack of angry women chasing me out of a hotel? The fact I'm sitting here in your cab shirtless, caked in bloody sand?"

He's silent.

"The fact you had to swerve to avoid hitting a large, disoriented, naked man?"

In that rich accent, he says, "I do not worry about these things, sir." After a pause, he adds, his voice calm and sweet, "Perhaps you would like me to take you to a reliable automatic teller machine at a safe location, away from the naked man and the angry ladies."

I sigh and rest my head against the door. I close my eyes. "Fine."

"Because, as I indicated earlier, I am afraid we must transact our business through cash tender."

"Fine."

I close my eyes. He hums.

I take out four hundred dollars, the maximum allowed, and give my driver half.

"I'll give you the other half if you help me find a shirt and get me to the airport."

He hums as we pull out of the empty bank parking lot. "There are several Walgreens establishments in Tampa, sir. They are open all night. Perhaps they offer a shirt that will please you."

"Fine, let's do that. Just find us a store away from the hotel."

Humming. "Of course, sir."

"And then you can drive me around until my two hundred dollars runs out."

"Have you decided on your ultimate destination, sir?"

"The airport."

He waits awhile. "You do understand that the airport is very close to the hotel out of which you came running and screaming?"

"I'll have to take my chances."

"Two hundred dollars will give you three hours in this cab, sir. That will bring us to about three A.M."

"Okay."

"Perhaps at that time, you will choose to retrieve additional funds from another automatic teller machine."

I meet his eyes through the rearview mirror.

"How much to stay in this cab until the airport opens?"

"That would be six A.M., I believe."

"Which would cost me?"

"Three hundred dollars, sir."

Give me a break.

I sigh and rub my forehead with the palm of my good

hand. "Maybe after this two hundred runs out, you can find me a nice bush out near the airport."

So calm and sweet. "It would be my pleasure, sir. There are several large foliated areas near the airport that would be ideal for you, I believe."

I limp into the Walgreens shirtless and woozy. It's past 2 A.M.

The staff and customers (and there are more than I'd expected) act like I'm an everyday sight. I find a bespectacled, middle-aged clerk stocking shelves in the personal hygiene section; he regards me with a quick glance as he loads adult diapers onto the upper shelf. "First aid kits, disinfectant, and bandages are on aisle seven."

I try to balance myself. "Looking for clothes, actually."

He doesn't look up. "We only have children's T-shirts right now. We'll get a new stock of adult garments next week."

I close my eyes and cuss under my breath.

"Aisle two."

What choice do I have? And then I realize: bandages and disinfectant probably make a ton of sense at this point.

And aspirin.

And Neosporin.

And a bag of frozen peas.

Half a mile from the terminals, my driver pulls up to a series of large bushes pressed against a cyclone fence. It's exactly 3 A.M.

"I have a newspaper for you." He peers at me through the mirror, his eyes wide and innocent. "You can sleep on it, in your bush as you wait for daylight. It will keep your new shirt clean."

Yeah, my new shirt. My pink Hannah Montana "Butterfly Girls" T-shirt, featuring the child star posing in front of a giant, girly butterfly. Children's extra large, but not nearly large enough for me: the shirt ends well above my navel, binds my chest, and digs into my armpits. I'm sure I look like a fool, but I need this shirt. Once the airport opens, I can find a shop, buy a men's shirt for some exorbitant price, and head to the ticket counter, where I'll happily pay top dollar for the first flight to San Francisco or San Jose. Until then, I'll make do with my little T, and stay out of sight.

I give him the rest of my cash and he hands me the newspaper.

I open the door and get out, the humidity hitting me even at this hour. I turn back and peer in. "You're not gonna tell anyone where I am, are you?"

He shakes his head. "Go into your bushes and curl up on your newspaper. You'll be safe. I'm going home."

I only hope I am, too.

I cry in the bushes.

No tears, really. Just dry sobbing and moaning as I lay flat on my back, atop the newspapers, bag of frozen peas held in place by my aching hand, and gaze up at the moonlight slicing through the leaves. I want to call Kate so bad, but it's midnight back in California, and I can't make it any worse on her. So I imagine her on the phone consoling me.

Did you have a bad night, honey?

"Uh-huh," I sniffle.

Things didn't work out as well as they could have, did they?

"No."

You feeling a little beat-up?

"Maybe," I say, asking for mercy.

Did those college girls hurt you?

I nod.

Bad, huh?

"There was this one. Burly Buns." My voice is weak. "She hurt me bad, babe."

I see. Well, have you come to any conclusions tonight in Tampa? Lying there in your bush?

I whimper. "Maybe."

Well, what about flirting with sluts at the office? How did that work out for you?

I pause a moment. "Not too good."

No, not too good at all. And what about looking at porn at work? Did that turn out well?

"No."

And what about gossiping to the press about your CEO? Are you happy with that decision?

I sigh long and hard. "If I hadn't . . ."

But I can't say it, so Imaginary Kate says it for me.

If you hadn't flirted with that slut—

"She's not a slut, Kate."

. . . or leaked gossip to the press, or spent countless hours look-ing at ass pics, maybe you wouldn't be so miserable right now, would you?

"But I still have it, honey. I still have the tape. Our million is safe."

Must be a proud man, she says, and hangs up.

That hits me hard. It takes a long time before I can close my eyes, listen to the intermittent traffic, and let my mind float into darkness, waiting for dawn, my good hand in my pocket holding my cash-out tape as I drift away.

The roar of jet engines jolts me upright.

Holy shit. That's some alarm clock.

I rub my eyes, trying to remove the grogginess, and look around. A trace of dawn creeps through the leaves; the cars are purring past at a steadier rate. I pull my mobile out of my other pocket, glance at it. The battery is dead.

Lovely. Now I'll need to find a kind soul to let me borrow a charger, or I'll have no way of arranging an exchange with High Rider. I gather my things—my dead cell, my muddy newspaper bed, and my plastic Walgreens bag of bandages, aspirin, and disinfectant. I'm getting ready to leave when I realize that my entire crotch is wet. The peas have thawed and moistened, leaving a giant dark circle on the crotch of my pants.

Can't worry about that now. Just need to get into that airport, find a California flight—any flight, really—buy the ticket, get some new clothes, recharge the mobile, call High Rider, set a time and place for the exchange, and board before the college girls—or, worse, Ed—manage to find me.

I emerge from the bush, straighten, and proceed along the curb like it's the most natural thing in the world.

Find a flight, I'm thinking. *Just find a flight that leaves in an hour.*

Then I see myself in the reflective doors.

I look like a wandering crazy man, stooped over in pain, hobbling along on some quixotic journey only he understands, clutching a muddy Walgreens bag as a Hannah Montana shirt three sizes too small rides up his belly. A dark wet spot circles around the crotch; his face and throat are covered with cuts, scratches, and bruises, his upper lip curled back revealing blood-lined teeth. Eyelids dark and heavy. Eyeballs wild.

No wonder everyone's keeping their distance.

It's 5:45. Businessmen whiz past me as I wander around the terminal looking for a shop that's open this early. Nothing but Starbucks. Finally, I see a Ron John Surf Shop, hobble that way until I see it's closed, too. Sign says it'll open at seven.

I look around, trying to think.

Fuck.

I turn and shuffle to the ticket counters.

Okay, buy a ticket. Any ticket.

When I reach the United counter, a young ticket agent studies me skeptically.

"Any seats left for the seven-thirty flight to Boise?"

She glances at my shirt, studies the scratches on my throat, and turns to her computer. "Only first-class, sir."

I turn and look for enemies. "Fine."

"One-way, sir?

Still scanning the faces. "Sure."

"The fare is four hundred and eighteen, sir."

"Fine." I pull out my credit card and license. "When's boarding?"

"Boarding is at seven. Gate E-seventy-four." She studies me one last time. "Any luggage to check in, sir?"

Luggage?

I just laugh and laugh.

Oh yeah, I've lost it.

I visit the ATM, pull out four hundred, and start looking for young people—the only ones who won't freak at the sight of me, who won't ignore me. The ones who could maybe use some extra cash.

I wander a bit, keeping an eye out for my predators, and find a young man in blue sweats and a black hoodie. He's slouched in his seat, his hood shading the top half of his face, his hands in his pockets, a black roller suitcase beside him.

I approach. Tiny steps.

"Wondering if you can help me."

He looks up, his brown eyes sleepy.

"As you can tell, I really need a decent shirt."

Staring.

"And, as you can see, the shops are closed."

He looks down at my shoes and wet crotch, glances up at me.

I flash my roll. "I'm willing to pay you a lot of money for a decent shirt."

He straightens up. "Going to a wedding, man." He looks around, stretches. "I need everything I packed."

I look around, and there he is—Ed. Trotting my way. *Holy shit.* I crouch down before I realize it's not him—just a big athlete with wide shoulders and that confident stride.

"You okay?"

I turn to Hoodie, my eye twitching. "I will pay you a ton, dude."

"I've got a good shirt in there, but I need it."

I look around. "I'll give you enough cash to buy three shirts . . ." I look around some more. ". . . and buy the entire wedding party three rounds of shots."

He looks around a real long time, peers up at me. "How much?"

"One-twenty."

He looks around again and rubs his eyes. "One-forty, you got a deal."

I pull out my roll, start peeling twenties. He unzips his suitcase, fingers through his clothes and pulls out the shirt; it's powder-blue, looks like it will fit me fine. I hand him the bills and he tosses me the shirt. I nod and head off for the men's room.

"Hey."

I stop and turn.

He nods to my T-shirt. "If you don't want that, I'll take it when you're done." He's smiling. "A memento for the bride and groom."

In the restroom, I splash water on my face and slather disinfectant onto my scratches. My skin sears, and I recoil in pain, hissing like a demon sprayed with holy water. I crack open the bottle of aspirin, pour out five and swallow them dry. I hobble to a stall to switch shirts; the new one fits me pretty damn well. I return to the mirrors, splash some water onto my hair, and try to pat it down.

Finally, I put bandages on the largest scratches—a deep one on my forehead, and two big puncture marks on my throat. I stand back, force a smile, see the blood-lined teeth again.

Oh yeah. Gotta rinse those off.

Afterward, I hobble past the young guy, toss him the T-shirt, and start looking for someone who will understand my need to charge a phone. In the distance, I see a slender, college-age woman in jeans and a T-shirt, with no luggage. It seems like she's looking for someone.

Was she there last night? I'm not totally sure. Just to be safe, I turn away and hunch my shoulders as she passes.

Another false alarm.

I notice a puffy guy in Dockers and a light yellow shirt, standing near the wall, talking on a Motorola, same model as mine. It looks like he's practically cooing into the phone. "Of course we deserve Hawaii," he says. "After this year? Are you kidding me?"

I hover around him.

He closes his eyes and smiles. "That's fine—I love that hotel." He listens, then adds, "Yeah, but not the credit card again. No, just use the line of credit. What? No, the home equity line of credit. It's that card in the top drawer, the one we used for the motor home. Yes, exactly."

I stand there, and he eyes me.

"Gotta get off," he says, shifting. "Someone's here."

I pull out my mobile and show it to him. "Hey, man." I nod to the socket on the wall behind him. "You got a charge?"

He freezes, then softens. "Yeah, okay." He digs though his briefcase, pulls out his charger. "I just need to leave for my gate in a few."

I squat, grimace, and plug everything in. "Where you headed? Home?"

He nods. "You too?"

I think of Boise. "Hope so."

When we part ways eight minutes later, he's on the phone talking to someone about a high-def widescreen he's going to buy. At least my mobile is powered up, the battery icon showing a sliver of black.

Better call him now.

He picks up on the first ring. "I'm here already. Where are you?"

I turn and scan the area. "Just meet me in the center of the Galleria. Six-thirty." I hang up.

I sip my latte, let the warmth soothe me. I scan the area.

High Rider's here. The girls have to be here. My beach buddy is probably here.

Nearly an hour till boarding.

Shit.

I look at the entrance to the men's room, realize it's probably my safest place.

I take a stall, pull out my phone.

In the stall to my right, someone empties his bowels.

I call Fitzroy; it sounds like he's been sleeping.

"Danny, you're killing me." I hear him stretch. "What did I ever do to you?"

A toilet flushes.

"It wasn't ever about that."

"I trusted you, Danny. Brought you in. Took you around the world . . . on my fucking plane. I set you on a course to make millions." Long silence. "I mean, seriously, what did I ever do to you?"

My throat tightens. *God, he's right.*

"Those girls? You think those girls were victims?"

I can't say a word. It's all so heavy.

"We weren't hurting anybody in that room."

"I'm sorry."

"Now they're crawling the town looking for you, ready to take your freaking head off."

Someone enters the stall on my left side. Ed? My heart races, and I struggle to take in a deep breath. My voice cracks. "I'm sorry."

"You should be."

"I had no idea what you were doing in that room. They never told me."

"You could've come to me, Danny. We would've doped it out, found a solution. Now this."

Shit explosions to my left. *Thank God.*

"You would've let that guy kill me."

"That's bullshit. I told him to get the tape, and that's it. Hell, I was coming down there to talk with you. Why would I walk down there if I thought he was gonna kill you?"

He waits.

"Danny, I was gonna try and talk some sense into you. I was gonna get you out of this mess."

I think of the college girls, think of Ed, and I shudder. *Where are they?* It feels like I'm stumbling into an intersection blindfolded, surrounded by the sound of accelerating cars.

"Let me think about it, okay?"

"You're not gonna think about it. You've made up your mind."

"I *will* think about it—if you agree to keep me on the payroll another thirty-six hours."

"Danny," he says, soft and earnest, no trace of anger. "Do you realize you've become an asshole?"

I hang up, bolt out of my stall, and hobble for the exit, but not before I see myself in the mirror.

I look away as fast as I can.

Eleven

I hide in a cluster of people preparing to board a flight to Cleveland.

Just one more day. No, just a few more hours.

I stand on my toes, poke my head out of the pack, and look around, my eyes darting from face to face. And just like that, there's Krista. No chance of mistaken identity this time; there's no mistaking the silky red hair, the enormous brown eyes, the strong brow, and the slender figure tucked into the same faded jeans and pink T-shirt from last night. She's weaving through the crowd at the next gate, fists clenched at her side.

Shit.

I duck and stay ducked, and when I realize how odd that looks I take a knee and slowly begin retying my shoelace. When I finally crouch up, wincing in pain, my head pulled in like a turtle, I feel the man to my left staring at me. I glance his way, return his smile, and nod. He's older, maybe in his seventies, a big head of silver hair, a weather-beaten face, and moist eyes that sag but twinkle.

"You've been in a scrape."

I peer through the throng and fail to locate Krista.

I return to him. "Yeah, I'm afraid so."

"And not just one . . ." He inspects my face, going from the shovel mark on my forehead to my swollen nose to the fresh scratches and indentations across my neck and head. "But many, over several days. Am I right?"

I spread my legs wide to make myself shorter, and turn back toward him. "Yeah, well, I guess—"

"Hope you don't mind me saying so, but it looks like someone shoved your face into a cage of feral cats." He stops, looks away, and squints. "I actually knew a fella who had that happen to him."

I place my hand over the cassette in my front pocket, squeeze it. "I wish it *had* been a cage of feral cats."

"Are you sure the U.S. Marshals aren't looking for you?"

I look around. "Redheads? Yes. U.S. Marshals, no."

He laughs, settles on my bandages. "What line of work are you in, if I may ask?"

I lower my head a little, look behind me. No Krista. "High tech."

He brightens. "You're a man in the right business at the right time."

I force a smile. "Yeah, I guess so."

"Who are you with?"

"FlowBid."

"Well, I'll be . . ." He straightens, ecstatic. "FlowBid."

I look around, nod. "Yep."

"I'll have you know I put half my retirement savings into you guys the day you did your IPO."

My heart sinks, and I swallow hard. "Wow."

He's beaming. "Yes, and you haven't disappointed. My adviser tried like the dickens to talk me out of it." He licks his lips, looks down, and squints at the memory. "But I'd read every word ever uttered about you guys, and it seems like you're about as close to a sure thing as they come."

"Well—"

"As long as that CEO of yours doesn't get hit by a bus."

I look away and chuckle.

"Do they take good care of him?"

"Huh?"

"Fitzroy. Your CEO."

"Oh." I scratch the back of my neck, flick a grain of sand. "Yeah."

"I'm selling next year. The wife and I, we're going to put it back into bonds and CDs. But we're also going to give some of it to . . ." His voice softens. ". . . our granddaughter, Janie."

I squeeze the tape box and try to look him in the eye.

"She's worked her tail off, and the wife and I think she deserves to go to college."

My eyes closed, my voice cracking. "You're a good grandfather, sir."

"She wants to be a nurse." He nearly hums. "You know, truly help people."

Another sock in the gut, the worst yet.

I open my eyes, force myself to meet his gaze. "You must be proud, sir."

"Well . . ." His eyes water. "I'm telling you . . ." His own voice cracks. ". . . she's a special girl."

I take another knee, pull my other shoestring loose and retie it. The tape box in my pocket feels hot and heavy, but I know it's in my head. With every second, it becomes increasingly clear. The more I think about the man standing beside me, think about the hundreds of thousands of people just like him, people who've trusted us with their savings, their retirement, their blood-sweat-and-tears money, people whose futures truly hang in the balance, the more nauseated I get.

Fitzroy's right; I've become an asshole.

My heart begins to pound.

Because I can't ignore it any longer.

I know what I must do.

The longer I wait, the harder my heart pounds.

Get up and move.

I take a step toward the restrooms, find myself light-headed.

God, I'm gonna faint.

I stumble, grab hold of a seat.

Please don't let me throw up.

I take a few more steps, grab on to another seat.

A woman's voice says, "Sir, are you okay?"

I'm floating into black.

"Sir, do you need help?"

I'm panting. "Yes."

"You need to go to the restroom?"

Cold sweat. "Thank you."

Then, off in the distance, I hear Krista.

"STOP HIM!"

I say to my guide, "Please help me."

"It's okay, I'm right here with you."

Krista's voice is closer. "HEY, STOP HIM."

"Here you are, sir. Just follow this wall, and it'll take you right to the restroom."

I squeeze my guide's forearm, nearly cry. "Thank you."

"Hey," Krista says, much closer. "Don't let him go in there."

I feel my way inside the restroom and slam into a stall door. Someone inside yells, "Hey." I sidestep along the row of stalls until I find an open door. I slip inside, shut the door behind me, and latch it. I lean against the side wall and screw my eyes shut, hoping my vision will return when I open them.

"Dude." Krista's in the men's room, breathless. "Dude, you're not getting out of here with that tape." I can hear her pacing in front of the stalls; there must be ten or twelve of them here, and she has no idea which one I'm in. "I'm going nowhere, dude." Her cell rings. "Hey, I found him. He's hiding in a stall in the men's room. What? No, near the E-gates."

I open my eyes, and finally I can see a little. I fumble with my cell, squint hard at the screen. My thumb trembles as it taps through my phone book and stops at *High Rider*. I press Call.

He picks up immediately, says, "Where are you?"

A stall door opens. A man says something to Krista, who tells him to fuck off.

"It's over," I whisper.

Long silence. "You said to meet at the Galleria."

"You're not getting the tape."

Silence.

"Have you thought about this?" I say. "Have you really thought about who this would hurt the most?"

"Fitzroy," he says. "When it hits the Internet, that tape will put an empty, narcissistic, greedy man in his place."

Krista is outside my stall, rattling it. "Dude, it's over."

"So that's what this was all about, then? This whole thing? A big slice of revenge against the man who laid you off?"

Hard kick against my stall door.

High Rider is silent. Finally, he says, "Call it karma."

I feel the saliva pooling in my mouth. "I'm opting out."

His voice tightens. "Then you're not getting your options. We'll send your correspondence with *BusinessWeek* to the board of directors, your amorous IMs to all of FlowBid."

Another hard kick.

"You don't have to send the IMs."

"But I will."

"She's married, you know? That woman? She's married."

"Her name's been removed. God, you're an idiot."

A huge sigh of relief. "Plus, my wife knows. Cut that problem off at the knees."

"Nevertheless, titillating reading for your colleagues."

"I swear, when I find you, I'm going to beat the shit out of you."

His voice weakens. "There's still a chance. You don't have to do this."

Hard kick. The door buckles.

"I'm flushing the tape, asshole."

"No." His voice tightens. "Don't. Please."

Another kick, and the door gives. Krista pushes in a little, grunts, "Stop."

I reach into my pocket, pull out the tape. "Listen closely."

Another kick, and the door teeters and rotates on its bottom hinge.

Someone says, "Hey, cool it."

Krista reaches over the door and swipes at the cassette. My hand trembling, I drop it into the toilet and look at it a second before I wave my hand over the sensor. Water rushes in, and the cassette circles the bowl twice before rocketing down the hatch. I hold my cell over the toilet.

Krista watches, yells, "YOU . . . FUCKING . . . ASS-HOLE."

I'm sniffling.

High Rider sounds like he's about to cry. "I'll have them send out your items now."

I end the call, fall to my knees, and vomit into the toilet as Krista scrambles over the door, lands on my back, and drags her nails across my face one last time.

Twelve

The coast, somewhere between Santa Cruz and Monterey

· · · · · · · · · · · · · · · · · ·

Two months later

As we walk along the beach, following the boys as they run their toy cars along the hard-pack, the setting sun shining through the tips of the waves, it finally happens.

Kate lets me slip my hand into hers.

It's been two months. I feel like I'm about to cry, but I don't want to make a big deal about it. I glance at her, and she's got that look on her face, that look I haven't seen in a long time, that look she doesn't even know she makes—her lids a little lower, her left brow lifting, her jaw sliding in the delight of a nice moment as she realizes that, yes, I've always been in love with her, and no one else, that we're on the way back to being husband and wife.

The boys chase each other in tight circles, their laughter muffled by the surf.

Kate lets me pull her in but keeps her hands at her chest. I wrap her up in my arms, rest my forehead on hers, and fall into her eyes. The softness is returning there, and I'm the luckiest guy in the world.

"What's next for us, Dan?"

What's next?

I lost my stock options, sure. In fact, I was fired before my flight began its descent into Boise; the IT guys delivered on their promise to send out all those damaging details about me and then slipped back into the shadows. But we still cashed out, in our own way. I guess I'd never realized that we didn't really even need my stock options, or anything else; we just sold our house, paid off the home loan, and headed for the coast with a tidy sum. We didn't buy a shack on the beach, but we found a rental nearly a mile from the water, and that was okay—more than okay, really. It didn't keep me from walking barefoot around town, from riding our cruisers to the ocean, from taking my dad's old Coleman to the beach, from talking to neighbors and listening, from walking across the street every morning to check in on Eleanor the elderly shut-in, from having time to take a deep breath and let it out slowly.

Yeah, we've cashed out.

I look into her blues. "What's next is, we go get some Mexican."

"Avocados, too. Harry wants your guacamole."

"And orange soda."

"And Calhoun wants to join us."

She closes her eyes, whimpers. "Not again. Please."

"No sleepovers, this time. I promise."

She looks at my mouth. "Okay, and what about the bigger picture?"

I feign confusion. "Bigger picture?"

Tiny nod.

"The bigger picture is, Larry's just a little misunderstood."

She smiles to herself, plays along. "Dan."

"The bigger picture is, no one really knows how those guys ended up in the Alaskan wilderness. Thousands of miles away."

Closes her eyes, smiles. "Dan."

"I mean, not even David Duncan will talk."

"You know what I'm—"

"Hard for the D.A. to charge Larry with anything when the so-called victims refuse to say a word about who had them, why they were shaved bald and dressed like monks. Hard to do anything when Larry just sits there on his porch, day after day, staring into space, as the authorities still have no freaking clue how they ended up in that shed out there in the woods, all the way near the Arctic—"

She pinches my lips. "I'm not talking about this again."

I shrug, and she releases.

"What's next for us, honey?"

"What's next is, we stay here."

"Keep renting?"

"For now, sure."

"Hold on to those investments?"

"Investments? We have everything in bonds and CDs."

"No, that short-message thing."

I scrunch my face. "Twitter?"

"Yeah, those guys with the short-message rule."

"We just wrote the check out."

"Dan, c'mon. How many people are going to use a site that only lets you write a hundred and forty characters?"

I have no answer.

"And who's going to want to read that stuff?"

"They're doing okay so far."

"Dan, they don't make any money. You admitted that."

"They'll figure that out."

She looks away and laughs. "I just don't think we should go around funding start-ups based on the advice of a man who craps in upper decks."

"Honey," I say, "Do you understand about Calhoun? That he was employee number eighty at Google, that he's a millionaire many times over, that he's friends with this venture capital guy who swears by these short-message dudes?"

"These guys with no revenue."

"The point is, we wrote the check. They seemed like scary smart guys. And the twenty thousand has already crossed. They've cashed it. So I think we chill awhile, see if it turns into anything."

She smirks, looks away. "So you're gonna be a venture capitalist? That's your new job?"

"Never." I bring her in closer.

"Or you're gonna be a 'thought leader,' like that new guy you hospitalized with the laxatives? That guy they had to re-hydrate for two days?"

"Let's worry about that next week."

A moment's pause. Then Kate breaks out into this toothy smile. "Dan," she says, looking at my chest, "aren't you wondering why I keep asking about our plans?"

I wasn't, but *now* I am.

"Honey," she says, extra sweet, "I think I'm nesting."

"Nesting?"

"Got a new egg to hatch," she says in a mock-girlish voice.

I feel my body sway. "What?"

She looks up at me with tears of joy. "We're gonna have a baby." Her voice breaks. "A beautiful little beach baby."

How is that even . . . Whoa. I'm getting *really* dizzy.

"Dan?" Finger snapping near my ear. "Honey. Deep breaths."

Deep breaths? Okay, I can do that. And slowly, with oxygen returning to my brain, it all starts to make sense. Kate's slightly fuller cheeks. Her switch to virgin margaritas. The time she had me go on a 1 A.M. peperoncini and grapefruit run.

And, just like that, a half-forgotten warning echoes in my ear.

You're still packing heat the next ten times.

"Dan?"

So be careful where you point that thing.

"Heat!" I gaze out to the sea as if it holds all the secrets. "I was packing heat."

Kate says, "I've decided to look at it this way . . ."

I take a big breath and let it out slowly.

". . . we can sleep when we're fifty."

One day at a time.

Then, just as I'm beginning to feel my face again, a familiar figure appears up on the bluff. Those broad shoulders. That stance, one foot out a little, a hand in a pocket. The hard lines of a profile like no other.

Rod Stone.

What the—

He realizes that I see him.

I stand there with Kate in my arms, gazing up as he lifts a fist into the air triumphantly, then turns and walks away, his fist still skyward, as Harry and Ben attack from behind and pull us to the sand.

Acknowledgments

I would like to acknowledge early mentors who offered encouragement I never forgot; they include Dorothy Davis, Clark Brown, Robert Nowell, Sandra Cisneros, George Thurlow, and Nell Doty. For their support, wisdom, and commiseration, I thank fellow writers Al Riske, Mark Richardson, Rachel Canon, Kieran Shea, Jedidiah Ayres, Frank Bill, Steve Pipe, Matthew Budman, Keith Rawson, and Terry McKenzie. Anthony Neil Smith single-handedly advanced my cause years before publishing knew anything about rogue upper-deckers or sociopath retirees who lounge in Speedos. Generous vets like Charlie Huston, Ken Bruen, Tony Black, Marcus Sakey, and Doug Dorst didn't have to lend a hand, but did. I also am indebted to Victor Gischler, who after a long day of German sausage and beer introduced me to my future agent, the brilliant David Hale Smith, who in turn set me up with the ultimate dream team for this book: Cal Morgan and his thoughtful creatives at Harper Perennial. Mallory Farrugia has been invaluable on multiple fronts. Finally, I would like to acknowledge my people, including my late father, Mil Bardsley, with whom I shared an appreciation of "special characters," and my mother, Carmen Bardsley, whose "follow your passion" advice never wavers. My sister Jennifer Bardsley has been an amazing scout for low-functioning behavior and a relentless supporter. And finally, I couldn't have done this if it hadn't been for the love, support, and feedback of my wife, Nancy Bardsley, my toughest reader, and our sons, Jack and Dylan, whose delight in (and suggestions for) Crazy Larry set me on my way.

About the author

About the book

Read on

Insights,
Interviews
& More . . .

A Conversation with Greg Bardsley

Jedidiah Ayres and Greg Bardsley met through the interwebs after their short stories appeared together in a series of journals. Greg is the author of Cash Out *and numerous short stories. Jedidiah writes fiction, keeps the blog* Hardboiled Wonderland, *and coedited the anthology* Noir at the Bar. *They and cohort Kieran Shea edited the anthology* D*CKED: Dark Fiction Inspired by Dick Cheney, *and swear never to do anything like that again.*

Jedidiah: *Your work tends to feature straight men surrounded, frustrated, and thwarted by a collective of cultural fun-house reflections. Where does that come from?*

Greg: Good question. I *do* have an affinity for oddball characters. A number of friends and family (especially those who dabble in psychology) have tried to understand why—and failed.

What I do know is that I try to write stories I'd love to read, and I've always loved oddballs who come in and turn things upside down. I guess I like the fact that they're defiant and transgressive in their own amusing ways. In a world of rules and convention and required behavior, these characters personify defiance and individualism. They are subversive. This may have something to do with the fact that I started out as a newspaper reporter, which was a subversive job by nature: If you had a good story, no one could stop you from writing it, even if it would piss a lot of folks off.

In terms of my fiction, I *have* noticed one thing. In my longer fiction, I tend to focus on reliable narrators. But the supposed straight men in my stories (as in "Upper Deck," "Microprimus Volatitus," or "Some Kind of Rugged Genius") often turn out to be anything but normal as the stories unfold. Kind of the way life is, maybe? It's like my basketball game: I'm right-handed, but I shoot left. Can't help it.

Jedidiah: *I know you covered the crime beat in the San Francisco Bay Area for a while. Is that where you got infected? Do you mine that period for fiction?*

Greg: You know, I'm not sure about that. For a few years, I covered crime several nights a week in Hayward, a pretty tough city south of Oakland. The crimes I covered weren't really funny, and I haven't really written about them. That said, in order to cover some of these nasty stories, I sometimes had to sit through hours of arraignments or page through reams of court dockets involving smaller-time criminals who kept making really poor decisions. That could be pretty amusing, but it was usually kind of sad, too. I did develop one character based on this profile of the repeat offender, who's certainly mischievous in a penal-code kind of way but also kind of lovable. ▶

A Conversation with Greg Bardsley
(continued)

But with *Cash Out*, I just let my imagination go "off-leash."

Jedidiah: *Do your family and friends recognize you in your work?*

Greg: Not with the short stories, thank God. No one wants to be "recognized" in stories like those.

At work, most people know very little about my fiction. My friends and family do recognize parts of me in some of my protagonists, including Dan Jordan in *Cash Out*. My wife is willing to go a little further; she thinks even the kooks are a reflection of my innermost desire to be unbelievably obnoxious. Based on my childhood, my sister probably agrees with her.

Jedidiah: *When did you decide you wanted to write?*

Greg: I knew in high school that I wanted to write for a living. I'd never done anything else (besides making funny faces) that got the response my writing got, and that felt great. But I think I was reluctant to share that dream with people. I was afraid someone would think I wasn't up to the challenge.

Recently, though, I discovered that I must have had this dream, in a subconscious way, a lot longer than I'd known. This past year I was helping my mom pack up her house, and we found my first-grade report card. My teacher had noted that I was working on a "book," that I was showing a lot of interest in it, sticking with it. Reading that as an adult really blew me away. I'd completely forgotten it, and it's still only a faint memory. It's not like I spent my childhood writing books.

Jedidiah: *What will you do when your own kids want to write for a living?*

Greg: I will support my boys and their aspirations, regardless of their career goals—with the exception of "medical insurance executive" and "aggressive telemarketer."

Jedidiah: *As a satirical novelist, do you hold dear any targets in particular?*

Greg: That's interesting. I seem to write about people and issues that either amuse me or get me riled up. Lately, I've been thinking about selfishness in its various forms. That, and arrogance. Oh, and pedigree. And rich and out-of-touch people. Oh, and the pretentious.

Maybe a bigger theme for me as a writer is, In this modern world, how are we supposed to live the way we really should? How can we survive in a meaningful and deep way despite these modern challenges—despite ▶

A Conversation with Greg Bardsley
(continued)

ourselves? When it came to *Cash Out*,
I was interested in that universal impulse
to step back, examine your life, and
then make a run for it. That was one
of the ideas that drove me to write
the book. That and the fun of
putting all these characters together
at a really important moment in
someone's life.

Jedidiah: *Are there any misconceptions
you'd like to dissuade readers from
forming about you?*

Greg: Well, I wouldn't want readers to
assume that Dan Jordan is me, or that
the events in *Cash Out* are based on my
own experiences. Truth is, it's all fiction.
I've never worked with people like the
new guy, Stephen Fitzroy, or even Beth
Gavin. I've never worked at a place like
Flowbid; I work at a much older and
larger tech company where some
great folks run very large, established
businesses. And I've never had a
corporate muscleman rough me up.
For me, that was the fun of writing
this book: taking a character with
my sensibilities and background,
and putting him on a collision
course with mayhem. Do you
remember what you said when
I showed you the first seventy-five
pages of the book? You said something
like, "Pile it on, Bardsley. Pile those
problems onto Dan. Make him work."
That's exactly what I tried to do.

Jedidiah: *Any misconceptions you'd like to start?*

Greg: Sure. That I wrote *Cash Out* on a whim, during an inspired three-day weekend.

Jedidiah: *What's next for you, sir?*

Greg: Sleep, and then back to work.

∾

A Rare Bird in My Native Land

YEARS AGO, I was talking with a software engineer when he looked at me and proclaimed, "You're kind of a rare bird, aren't you?"

Rare bird?

"You know," he said, eyeing me, "you work at a tech company on the San Francisco peninsula, and you actually grew up around here."

He was right. I *was* kind of alone that way. Often I had stopped and wondered, Where were the people I grew up with? Where were the fellow souls of my Bay Area youth? Where were all those people who, like me, were thrilled to get into a public university somewhere in the state and return four or five years later to chase dreams? How could it be that, less than twenty years later, so few of my people—the locals—could be found at my tech company?

Why did I feel like an outsider?

At night, when I went home to a nearby community packed with seemingly modest homes on seemingly modest streets, I often felt the same way. Where were the people I'd grown up with, the sons and daughters of teachers, electricians, accountants, receptionists, civil servants, and utility workers?

What had happened to the middle class?

It was no different when I visited my mom and sister in nearby San Francisco. The city had changed. Gone, it seemed, were the values of socioeconomic diversity and tolerance that had made this place so special in my youth. How had we ended up with this new culture of status and affluence? Did anyone else notice how empty some neighborhoods got during the holidays, when people would return to their true hometowns?

Was I witnessing that dreaded phenomenon: gentrification?

And then later I wondered: was *I* gentrifying, too?

In about ten years, I had gone from "starving journalist" to "Silicon Valley speechwriter." From East Bay everyman to peninsula property owner. And as the years passed, I wondered if I was slowly losing my way. Was I becoming a fancy boy? Hell, no, I decided. I embraced my old Honda, my Chico State sweatshirts, my power tools and flip-flops. I built things with my hands and got dirt under my fingernails. I got back into volleyball, explored coastal towns packed with longtime Californians who seemed to smile back a little more often. Even so, back in the Valley, I couldn't relax. Had I been sucked slowly into the hyperventilating, overachieving lifestyle of the peninsula, this twenty-first-century magnet for highly educated fortune-seekers? Was I losing this battle with myself?

As I watched a new wave of people strike it rich, I thought about some of the people I was meeting along the way—good people, like a former WD-40 public relations guy who had become one of the first one hundred employees at Google. What would *I* do if I were in his shoes and could cash ▸

out? Would I chase new dreams? Would I try to put balance and moderation and human connections back into my life?

Reflecting on all of this—the changing demographics and culture of the Bay Area, the unprecedented wealth events of my surroundings—I wondered if anyone was writing about this. Sure, people were writing about the riches folks were making, and some were noting a new kind of gold rush for California, but was anyone exploring this from a more personal and cultural level? This story, which I felt so deep in my bones, hadn't been told.

In writing *Cash Out*, I decided to stick with what I knew best. In some ways, I gave my protagonist, Dan Jordan, some of my own traits and circumstances. Like me, Dan would be a speechwriter in Silicon Valley working with an array of really smart and interesting people. Like me, he'd feel tired and overworked and worried about losing himself in frothy white waters of the Valley. Like me, he'd have a wife and two boys he'd love with all his heart. And like me, he'd reexamine some of the big decisions he'd made over the years.

Unlike me, he'd be days away from cashing out a fortune. And unlike me, he'd live across the street from a spry older man who saunters about his front yard in a skin-colored Speedo.

I decided to put Dan on a collision course with some of my favorite characters, and then pile on the pressure: put his cash-out money on the line, put his family life in jeopardy. As I wrote, I found a connection to some of those larger themes (the pursuit of balance and meaning) that I think so many of us in the Valley and beyond think about. I drew from my own dreams, added new challenges wherever they would advance the story. Onto Dan's shoulders I piled motive upon motive, burden upon burden.

I wrote late at night, after my wife and kids had fallen asleep. Some days I wrote at lunch, or when the family was out for an hour. Some nights I couldn't stop, and I'd write into the very early morning. The first draft of *Cash Out* was written during a thousand stolen moments over the course of a few years.

But at last I got the story out. I took Dan Jordan right to the edge, to a place where resolution, one way or the other, would be obvious and within reach—if not in our own lives, at least for him. ∽

Author Recommendations

IF YOU ENJOYED *CASH OUT*, consider these suggestions for more good times.

Read

Boonville by Robert Mailer Anderson
When I first read Anderson's novel, I was delighted to see someone finally capture Northern California in all its diverse and off-the-wall glory. Touching, captivating, and hilarious, this book still sits on my top shelf ten years later.

Florida Roadkill by Tim Dorsey
I still remember where I was when I read Tim Dorsey's first book (on a beach), and what I said to my wife after reading the first few pages: "This guy's nuts." Dorsey is sidesplittingly funny, wonderfully ungoverned, and afraid of nothing.

Go-Go Girls of the Apocalypse by Victor Gischler
I have yet to read anything by Victor Gischler that I haven't really admired. In *Go-Go Girls of the Apocalypse*, he applies his wide range of talents to new heights. Inventive, funny, and off-balance in a wonderful way, *Go-Go Girls* seems to do whatever it wishes—without any negative consequences.

Music for Torching by A. M. Homes
This book took control of me and didn't let go. The tale of a married couple who find themselves stuck in affluent suburbia had me engrossed, titillated, and ultimately stunned.

The Financial Lives of the Poets
by Jess Walter
I hadn't read Jess Walter until my editor, Cal Morgan, mentioned *Financial Lives* during a discussion about my own book. I soon got a dose of what I'd been missing all those years: insight, compassion, humor, and depth, served up with grace.

Me Talk Pretty One Day
by David Sedaris
Among the funniest books I've read, this collection of essays is a pure joy. The highlight of the book for readers with my kind of sensibilities? Perhaps a small piece about one very "Big Boy."

The Mystic Arts of Erasing All Signs of Death by Charlie Huston
I inhale anything written by Huston, who happened to grow up a few miles from me and even attended the same college, although we never knew each other. He also happens to be one of the most talented authors, period. *Cash Out* readers also might be interested in another of Huston's California tales, *The Shotgun Rule*, which is set in 1980s Livermore. ▶

Author Recommendations *(continued)*

A Confederacy of Dunces
by John Kennedy Toole
Four hundred and five pages of comic
genius that eventually won the Pulitzer
Prize for fiction.

Frank Sinatra in a Blender
by Matthew McBride
McBride's debut novel is one of the
funniest books I've read in a long time.
I laughed hard—so hard, in fact, that
I wept, tears rolling down my cheeks,
my nose running. There's also a pretty
compelling story in there, centering on
the wonderfully drawn Nick Valentine
(think *Bad Santa* meets Hunter S.
Thompson) and his hilarious little
dog, Frank Sinatra. I couldn't put it
down.

Sabrina's Window **by Al Riske**
The debut novel by one of my favorite
authors tells the story of a woman who
dares to break out of her normal life,
and creates a town scandal along the
way. Whimsical, touching, and uniquely
unpredictable.

Green with Envy **by Shira Boss**
My lone nonfiction selection, *Green
with Envy* touches on many of the
themes I ended up exploring in
Cash Out, including America's
battle with overindulgence and
how it's preventing so many people
from living free. I could not put it
down, and I still find myself revisiting
its stories and insights.

Taste

Guacamole Gregorio
I get cocky about only one thing: my guacamole. Enjoyed with the right music and Mexican beer, great guac is more than just food; it's a reminder of what's great about California living. In the fictional world, my guac makes cameo appearances in two novels, including *Cash Out*. In real life, it has won a series of "guacamole showdowns." In 2008, in a fit of philanthropy, I finally opened up my recipe for worldwide consumption. Visit gregbardsley.com and make your own batch today!

Listen

A stash of Latin jazz for the rest of us
In *Cash Out*, Crazy Larry gets his hands on Dan Jordan's personal stash of authentic, old-school Latin jazz. This part of the story was inspired by a friend of mine who got his hands on 152 tracks of the real stuff, thanks to a Guatemalan connection. That connection is long gone, but there *is* a great resource streaming across the Web every Sunday afternoon, which is when Latin-jazz aficionado Jesse "Chuy" Varela airs his world-class radio program. Goes great with guacamole: kcsm.org/jazzprograms/latinjazz.php.

Connect

Poke me
Join me on Facebook, where I'll bring you an endless series of posts, photos, ▶

clips, stories, and two-line observations. Also, be sure to "friend" me with "full access," so I can voyeur you and your friends and check out your college spring break photos from the 1900s. God, I love the Internet. ◠

D on't miss the next book by your favorite author. Sign up now for AuthorTracker by visiting www.AuthorTracker.com.

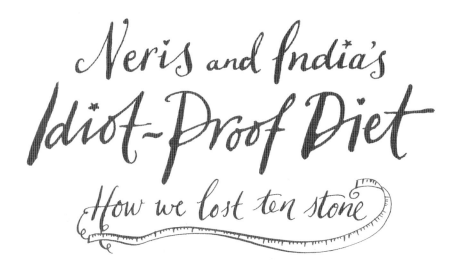

Neris and India's Idiot-Proof Diet

How we lost ten stone

India Knight and Neris Thomas

who would really like to call this book

FROM PIG TO TWIG !

Illustrations by Neris Thomas

PENGUIN
FIG TREE

AN IMPRINT OF PENGUIN BOOKS

FIG TREE

Published by the Penguin Group
Penguin Books Ltd, 80 Strand, London WC2R ORL, England
Penguin Group (USA) Inc., 375 Hudson Street, New York,
    New York 10014, USA
Penguin Group (Canada), 90 Eglinton Avenue East, Suite 700,
    Toronto, Ontario, Canada M4P 2Y3
    (a division of Pearson Penguin Canada Inc.)
Penguin Ireland, 25 St Stephen's Green, Dublin 2, Ireland
    (a division of Penguin Books Ltd)
Penguin Group (Australia), 250 Camberwell Road,
    Camberwell, Victoria 3124, Australia (a division of Pearson
    Australia Group Pty Ltd)
Penguin Books India Pvt Ltd, 11 Community Centre,
Panchsheel Park, New Delhi - 110 017, India
Penguin Group (NZ), 67 Apollo Drive, Mairangi Bay, Auckland 1310,
    New Zealand (a division of Pearson New Zealand Ltd)
Penguin Books (South Africa) (Pty) Ltd, 24 Sturdee Avenue,
    Rosebank, Johannesburg 2196, South Africa

Penguin Books Ltd, Registered Offices: 80 Strand,
    London WC2R ORL, England

www.penguin.com

First published 2007
2

Copyright © Neris Thomas and India Knight, 2007

Illustrations copyright © Neris Thomas, 2007
Photographs copyright © Shaun Webb, Neris Thomas
and India Knight, 2007
Additional photographs (pages 77, 90, 97, 108, 122, 125, 128, 134,
136, 157, 182) copyright © Lis Parsons, 2007

The moral right of the authors has been asserted

Designed and typeset by Smith & Gilmour, London
Set in Plantin and Thesis Sans
Colour reproduction by Dot Gradations Ltd, UK
Printed in Germany by Mohn media

A CIP catalogue record for this book is available from the British Library

ISBN: 978-0-670-91648-1

This diet is not suitable for pregnant or nursing women, children,
diabetics or people with kidney disease. It is not entirely impossible to
follow if you are vegetarian, but it is not by any means vegetarian-friendly.
Always consult your doctor before embarking on a new eating plan.
If you are diabetic, we very highly recommend Dr Richard K. Bernstein's
The Diabetes Diet.

Contents

Eggs on legs.

Introduction

So here we have it: yet another diet book. And none of the usual qualifications for writing one, either – we're not doctors, we're not nutritionists, we're not former soap stars on our uppers. We're not unusually obsessed by other people's poos, happily enough. We have no immediate plans for an exercise DVD.

Ho no. We can do better than that.

Between us, Neris and I have lost ten stone, give or take the odd pound. It took us a year, and we have maintained the weight loss. Ten stone is a lot of weight. It's a shedload. It's as much as a whole other person (Lordy, what a thought). And we think it's pretty damned impressive. Unusual, too. Show us a diet book written by someone who's actually lost more than a few measly pounds and we'll eat a whole bag of potatoes and a tub of lard for seconds. Other diet book writers talk the talk. We walk the walk. Well, we walk it now. We used to just waddle, thighs chafing attractively together.

That's the problem with the usual diet books. We're not going to say they don't work, because many of them do – the majority, probably – why wouldn't they? All kinds of diets work; the problem is sticking to them. That's because diet books are not written by people with a lot of weight to lose. They don't come from the minds of the formerly fat. So you get these grim, gloomy volumes of finger-wagging directions: boil a fish, steam a sprout, run for two hours. And those books are unbelievably depressing. They make you feel like you've been punished, excluded from normal life, and they make you want to give up before you've even begun. They expect you to do ridiculous things, and eat in a ridiculous way – one that, we've found, is not sustainable in the long term, and that is of itself incredibly demoralizing. Most diets are a disaster if you have families; they sit there with their delicious dinner, you sit there nibbling on a leaf, feeling leprous. It's just horrible.

We really like food - this diet was conceived and developed in a restaurant. Neris and I used to meet for lunch every week and one summer afternoon, a couple of bottles in, we got to talking about weight, for the hundredth time. Neris had just bought *The GI Diet* and could make neither head nor tail of it; India – as you will read in a minute – had had a moment of extreme sartorial crisis in a department store. We both knew we needed to lose weight and suddenly, during our conversation, the idea became a real possibility – because it occurred to us that we could do it together. Two minds are better than one, after all, and we liked (rightly, it turns out) the idea of the inbuilt support system.

We're greedy, which is how we came to be so weeble-ish in the first place. And while we understood, when we first embarked on our diet, that we would obviously have to make *some* sacrifices, we didn't want to feel like total freaks, either. We wanted to be able to go out for dinner. We wanted to eat at friends' houses without first having to email them a great, long, tiresomely anti-social list of our dietary requirements. We wanted to go to the pub, on girls' nights out, to weddings, to parties, and not feel like Fatty On a Diet sitting in the corner with a diet soda and a crudité.

We all know what to do to lose weight, in theory: eat less and move around more just about covers it. Makes sense. Sounds perfectly reasonable. Indeed, it *is* perfectly reasonable, if you want to lose five pounds. But the eat-less/move-more method is a thin person's mantra, and comes from a thin person's mindset. If you're the kind of person that weighs eight stone and occasionally 'forgets to eat', eat-less/move-more is blindingly obvious and true. But we've never forgotten to eat – in fact, we used to be starving hungry at pretty much any given time of the day. We don't have a thin person's mindset, one that assumes the self-discipline that many dieters – ourselves included – find easy to grasp in theory but rather trickier to put into practice. For us, eat-less/move-more simply isn't enough. Nice idea, but some people are just, well, *too fat* for such a vague instruction. Besides, eat-less/move-more doesn't even begin to address what goes on in your head when it comes to food, or the fact that so much overeating is emotional. And it fails to acknowledge that the gym is anathema if you're uncomfortable with the concept of crop tops, bare arms and paying for the pleasure of being in a room full of toned, trim people who are your physical opposites. If it were really as simple as eating a wee bit less and doing more sit-ups, we'd all be waifs.

What we wanted was to find a way of eating that was on the one hand very straightforward – no calorie-counting, no points, no having to think too hard – and on the other incredibly detailed. We wanted a plan to adhere to. A serious plan that went into minute detail, but that was flexible. Not a fortnight's worth, either; we wanted precise directions to stick to for as long as it took – which is why this book gives you a lifetime's worth of instructions. And we wanted recipes that we'd want to cook regardless of whether or not we were on a diet (and cheaty, easy-peasy recipes for when we didn't feel like cooking). We wanted to know what to eat and drink in any number of situations, at any given time of day – including feeling a bit peckish at midnight, or weirdly ravenous at 11am – so that we never had to pause to ask ourselves what was and what wasn't allowed. It feels very comforting, sticking to a plan in this way, and sooner or later you learn it by heart and it becomes second nature. And it absolutely, 100 per cent hand-on-heart works: check out the pictures for the rather hideously graphic evidence.

Is it easy? Kind of. We're going to start this book as we mean to go on, which means absolutely no lies (it works both ways: we don't want you to lie to yourself any more either – much more on this later). For the majority of the time, it's so easy that you completely forget you're on a diet. Sometimes it's harder. Very occasionally, you'll feel pretty majorly pissed off, to be frank. But the elation you feel as the pounds drop off and the compliments start flowing should override any difficulties, and besides, you're going to be eating delicious food – warm, hearty, rib-sticking food of the kind that is not usually associated with the word 'diet'. We're not expecting you to survive on salad. Our way of eating is not going to interfere with your life, either. It just quietly goes on in the background while you get on with the other stuff, such as selling your too-big clothes on eBay once a month. In terms of easiness, the thing we found vitally important about our diet was to understand that in order for it to work, the transformation – the moment when it all clicks into place – needs to happen before you start out, not after. That means right now. There will, obviously, be a dramatic physical transformation at the end of your diet, but we have discovered that for any diet to succeed, an emotional transformation is not only necessary but crucial. That means starting off at a place of self-love, not self-disgust. It means making the most of yourself right now – not tomorrow, not in a month, not in a year's time. We know you're beautiful now (and we're going to be showing you ways of building on that) – but we need you to believe it too. In our now considerable experience, no diet will work long term until that 'mental click'. It is a powerful and invaluable tool. If you have no idea of what we're talking about here, read on: the first part of the book is all about getting you to the point where you have faith in yourself.

We're working mothers, with four children between us. We have babies, jobs, dogs, partners, houses to clean, chores to do, homework to supervise, stuff going on. We don't have the time to cook ourselves separate meals, or to avoid the supermarket for fear of temptation, or to work out for a couple of hours a day. Life is short, and we are busy. And yet, almost miraculously, we've dropped all this horrible weight (and yes, it was horrible. Horrible, horrible, horrible[1]) without much hardship. We thought we'd tell you how we did it.

We make no spectacular claims for the diet; like we said above, all sorts of diets work. We chose to go the low-carb

[1] For more on the myth of the Happy Fatty, see page 22.

Introduction

route. There is no earth-shattering hype to the way we dieted, no magic trick, except 1: it works – and how; 2: it allows you to live a normal life; and 3: crucially, you don't feel deprived, punished, denied, or like you're sitting in the corner wearing a big Fatty hat.

Neris and I were lucky – we did the diet together, which was like having your own mini support system. This book is here to fulfil the same function: think of it not just as a manual but as your friend, there by your side through thick and thin, through success and failure, through the bad days as well as the good ones. Carry it in your handbag. Re-read it often. Scribble in it and make notes. Let the recipe pages get sticky with use. Learn to love it – and yourself. It won't let you down.

Before that, though, let's go back to the beginning. How did we get so bloody fat in the first place? Do try to read this next bit, and not skip straight to the actual diet, because we have found that understanding how and why we got fat really helped us to understand how and why to stay thin, or thinner. That's another thing: we're not body-fascists. We don't believe that everyone should be a size ten (or, God forbid, a size 00). By all means, go ahead and shrink to a ten if that's what you really want, but please understand that there's a cut-off point. If you started off being a size twenty-two, for instance, you may find yourself blissfully, deliriously happy being a size sixteen. Remember that, a: you need to set yourself realistic goals, because crazily unrealistic goals are the ones that are easiest to abandon; and b: there comes a stage in weight-loss when your face goes all wrinkly and gaunt, like a very old monkey's, and in our book it's a stage best avoided. Wrinkly and gaunt is not a good look on anyone. Also, grim things can happen to your boobs, if you go from vast to minute. More on this in the relevant chapter, but please bear it in mind. You want to look fabulous – and more often than not, that means curvy, not anorexic. This is especially true if you're anywhere upwards of forty, because if you want to keep wrinkles at bay and generally look well, rather than gaunt or slightly simian, you have to be careful not to get too skinny. There's a lot of truth in the saying that, past forty, you need to choose between your arse and your face. We say it's a no-brainer: go for the face, every time. Unless you work in the adult film industry and earn your living as somebody's arse-double, obviously.

Here's a table, in good old feet, inches and pounds, which can help you determine a healthy and foxy-looking weight for your height and build.

Height	Small Frame	Medium Frame	Large Frame
4'10"	102–111	109–121	118–131
4'11"	103–113	111–123	120–134
5'0"	104–115	113–126	122–137
5'1"	106–118	115–129	125–140
5'2"	108–121	118–132	128–143
5'3"	111–124	121–135	131–147
5'4"	114–127	124–138	134–151
5'5"	117–130	127–141	137–155
5'6"	120–133	130–144	140–159
5'7"	123–136	133–147	143–163
5'8"	126–139	136–150	146–167
5'9"	129–142	139–153	149–170
5'10"	132–145	142–156	152–173
5'11"	135–148	145–159	155–176
6'0"	138–151	148–162	158–179

So, the podge. How did it get there? How did we get to the point where we became experts at avoiding communal changing rooms, at never acknowledging a full-length mirror, at flicking past the fashion pages of magazines because not a lot of clothes came in our size, at never having sex on top (excess flesh + gravity = aargh)? It's a long story, but worth telling, we think, because chances are yours is pretty similar.

The Stakes

We found it helpful to know precisely why weight loss
was so important to us – the 'why here, why now?' question.
We also found it helpful to keep reminding ourselves of these
stakes, at various stages of the diet – it helps focus the mind.
These were our stakes as we began the diet. Please fill in
yours, and refer back to them whenever you're feeling
wobbly or doubtful.

Neris:
- ▸ I wanted to get back to pre-pregnancy weight.
- ▸ I wanted to buy clothes in a normal shop.
- ▸ I wanted to be at my sister-in-law's wedding and look
and feel good.
- ▸ I wanted to stop crying hysterically at transformation
programmes on telly.
- ▸ I wanted to feel that my husband fancied me.
- ▸ I wanted my wedding ring to fit me again.
- ▸ I wanted to wear the size fourteen jacket I bought six years ago.
- ▸ I wanted to be fit, for my daughter's sake.

India:
- ▸ I wanted to go shopping and be able to buy any clothes
from any shop.
- ▸ I wanted to wear high heels and not feel they might snap.
- ▸ I wanted to feel physically confident enough to be naked.
- ▸ I wanted my children to feel proud of the way I looked.
- ▸ I wanted to buy bracelets that fitted my wrists.
- ▸ I wanted to stop feeling foggy and lethargic.
- ▸ I wanted to look nice in photographs.
- ▸ I wanted to look hot for my fortieth birthday party.

What are your initial stakes?
Write them down here.

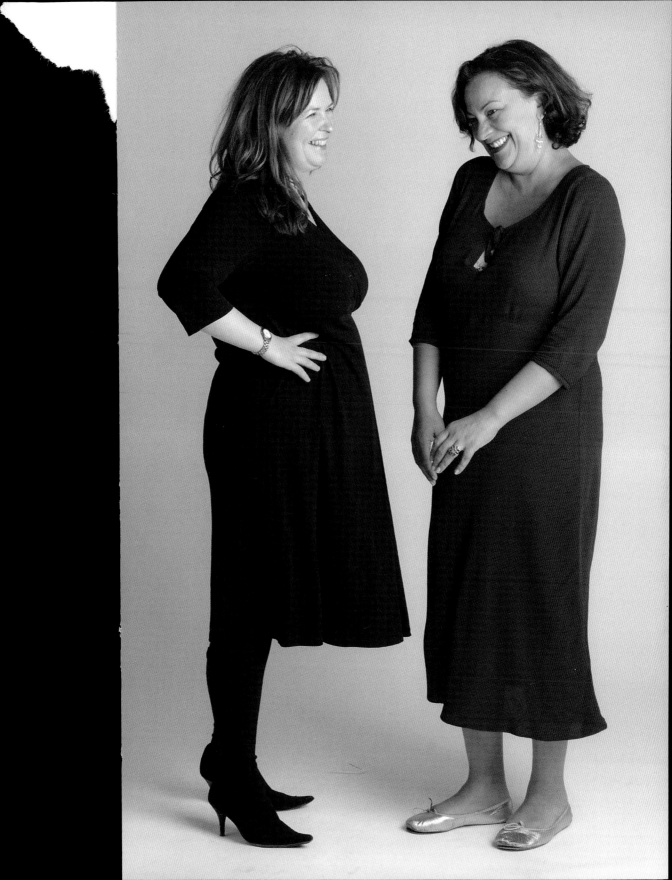

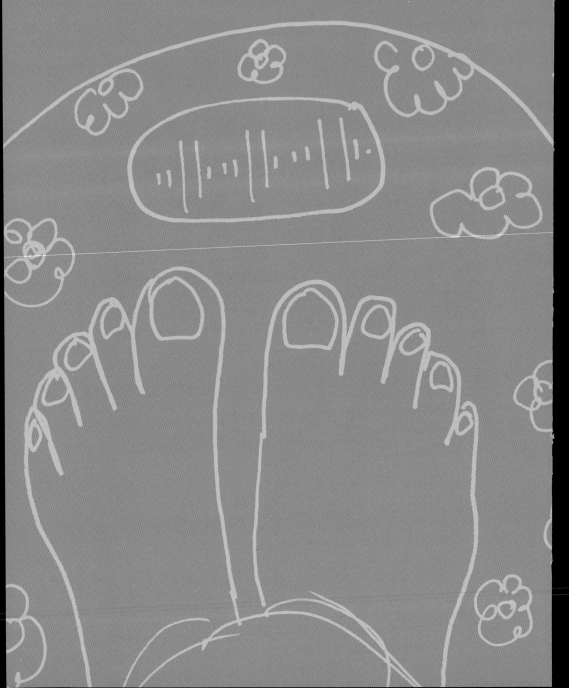

Part One
The Basics

1. Our Diet Histories

India

I was never fat. I was a tall, skinny child – flat-chested, no hips to speak of, very often mistaken for a boy. I always liked food – I come from a family that really appreciates their dinners – but I also regarded it as fuel. It appeared three times a day, I ate it, I ran off to play.

I went to boarding school at thirteen which, looking back, is where I think the problem started. The seeds of it were sown, at any rate. My mother is a fantastic cook, as were all the women in my family, and I was brought up eating really well in several different countries. My previous (day) school had been French, and its lunches were, as far as I can remember, pretty nice. Now I suddenly found myself in the depths of Buckinghamshire, faced with old-school-style meals I simply couldn't eat. It's the usual story: boiled mince, grey and worm-like, overcooked vegetables and weird, fatty, gristly bits of meat that looked and tasted like donkey. No spices, no dressings, no flavour at all, as far as I was concerned. And it all smelled vile. We were supposed to finish everything on our plates, because of the starving children in Africa. I was always having to stay behind with my housemistress, while she sat hectoring me, and I mutinously refused to eat, and she told me I had to, for hours on end. I actually threw up a couple of times, once while being forced to eat stuffed lambs' hearts. I don't want to sound too princess-and-the-peaish about this, but it really was difficult: the food we were given literally stuck in my throat. And, obviously, being at boarding school, this went on for weeks and weeks at a time – I couldn't run home and have a nice supper at the end of the day.

I eventually realized that I liked puddings. I don't have a sweet tooth, oddly enough (my downfall is salty things, like cheese and biscuits), but those very English things like steamed sponge and custard, or spotted dick, or jam roly-poly did at least taste quite nice. The breakfasts were okay, too – I ignored the congealed, lumpy porridge and filled up

on toast (plastic bread) with extra butter. We had a gas
fire in the common room, and we used to sneak out bread,
butter and Marmite and make toasties. We were allowed out
into the local town on Saturday mornings, and stocked up
on crisps and sweets and, in my case, Ritz crackers and
cheese biscuits. Parents could come and take us out to tea,
which someone or other's did most Saturdays, and I'd be
taken along as a guest and encouraged to devour the full
monty, with scones and clotted cream and tiers of little cakes
and sandwiches (The Copper Kettle in Marlow still holds
a special place in my heart). When no parents materialized,
the school provided a fairly fancy tea anyway, every day.
More bread, more cakes, more stodge.

At this point, my incredibly carb-heavy diet wasn't a
problem: we walked for miles every day and games were
compulsory. Much as I loathed them at the time, they saved
me from being completely spherical. But, a: I learned to
associate food with comfort – the toasties and cakes and
Double Deckers from the tuck shop acting as respite from
the grey weariness of school life, food generally being
something nice to turn to whenever I felt lonely or bored;
and b: I developed a life-long love of, and dependence on,
carbohydrates. Which, as we will see, are the devil when
they are totally processed, bleached and fiddled about with
until they are shorn of any goodness or nutritional value.

I left boarding school at seventeen, when I was a size
twelve to fourteen on top (I have big tits) and a ten
underneath. I'm five feet ten, so this seemed about right.
I lived at home some of the time, or in flats with girlfriends,
and food didn't really feature much – I was too busy running
about having a lovely time. I ate a lot of cereal (more carbs)
and a lot of sandwiches (ditto), usually at weird times of
the day.

At eighteen I went to university. While the food in college
was marginally better than the food at school – along the
same lines, though – I more or less dispensed with it and